Every Silent Lie

Jodi Ellen Malpas

First published in 2025 by Jodi Ellen Malpas

ISBN eBook 978-1-957597-60-7
ISBN Paperback 978-1-957597-61-4

Editing by - Marion Archer

Proofing by - Karen Lawson

Cover design by Shannon Passmore - Shanoff Designs

Praise for Jodi Ellen Malpas

“Malpas’s sexy love scenes scorch the page, and her sensitive, multilayered hero and heroine will easily capture readers’ hearts. A taut plot and a first-rate lineup of supporting characters make this a keeper.” *—Publishers Weekly on Gentleman Sinner*

“This book is JEM at her best, the secrets, lies, enemies... and tongue it cheek humour. It’s all there on every single page! I had no idea where this book was going or how the book would end. The journey was as captivating as it was enigmatic.” - *Kindle and Koffee Book Blog on Wicked Truths*

“It's just twist after dark and delicious twist; a completely, unquestionably unpredictable ride from start to finish. This is the kind of book where every page is important, because there is just SO MUCH going on, and it's an intricate dance from loathe to love for this couple.” - *Jeeves Reads Romance on The Brit*

“So it's safe to say, Jodi has once again completely smashed it with another sensation making it the best read of 2021! Hold on tight you’re about to be enthralled.” - *Booksobsessive on The Enigma*

"The characters are realistic and relatable and the tension ratchets up to an explosive conclusion. For anyone who enjoys Sleeping with the Enemy-style stories, this is a perfect choice."*—Library Journal on Leave Me Breathless*

“A brave, cutting-edge romance...This is a worthwhile read.” —*Library Journal on The Forbidden*

"Unpredictable and addictive."—*Booklist on The Forbidden*

"Super steamy and emotionally intense." –*The Library Journal on With ThisMan*

"Jodi Ellen Malpas delivers a new heart-wrenching, addicting read."— *RT Book Reviews on With This Man*

Note To Reader.

Every Silent Lie is a story of second chances, silent grief, and the kind of love that finds you when you're at your most lost. It delves into subjects that some readers might find upsetting or disturbing.

I'm not listing them here, as some are major plot spoilers and may tarnish the reader experience for some.

If you would like to see the trigger warnings, please head to

https://jodiellenmalpas.co.uk/every-silent-lie-trigger-warnings/

where you will find a comprehensive list.

Thank you.

JEM x

For the silent hearts.
And the voices that teach them to speak again.

JODI ELLEN
MALPAS

December 1st

The sound of enthusiastic chatter and cheerfulness seeps through the wood of my office door. The only closed door on the sixth floor of the building. Always.

Do not disturb.

Stay out.

Enter at your own risk.

My legs crossed under my desk, my high heel dangling from my toes, my pen drags back and forth across the pile of paperwork as I check each line. Another swig of coffee. How long until I can have something stronger? I glance at the clock. Five forty-five. Why the hell are people still here?

There's a knock at the door, a familiar sequence of taps, and I call out an okay for my boss to enter. He pokes his head around and removes his glasses. "Still here?" he asks, closing the door but remaining exactly where he is, scared to come farther into my office.

"No, I left two hours ago, Thomas." I drop my pen and work my foot back into my heel. "Why's everyone still here?"

"It's the first of December, Camryn."

"And?"

Frowning, Thomas shakes his head. "And . . . it's tradition for me to bring in a crate of champagne and let my staff knock off work an hour early to enjoy it."

"Why?"

"Jesus Christ, Camryn. Because it's December first. Because we're entering the final month of the year. Because, because, because."

"Right."

"Joining us?"

"No."

"Of course you're not. You've been working for me for two years and *never* have you joined in on any of the networking events or office drinks."

You wouldn't want to see me with alcohol in me, Thomas. "With such emphasis put on *never*." I get up and swing my coat over my shoulders. "I'm not here to network," I remind him. "I'm here to get your company in the best financial shape, ready for the team you're hiring to help make TF Shipping's debut on the market."

"Those reports are two years in the making." Thomas nods at my bag where I've just put said reports. "And you're *still* not happy with the company's financial position."

"No, I'm not." Collecting up some other files, enough to keep me busy this weekend, I slip them into my bag. "Because you keep buying ships, Thomas." *Among other things the company doesn't need.* "And your board members, aka your son and wife, seem to think a company business card seconds as a personal credit card."

"I'm a shipping company. I need ships."

It doesn't escape my notice that he swerves my comment about his son and wife. "You have plenty of ships for now. You're being competitive, trying to own the most floating towns. You need contracts to fill those ships with things to ship, Thomas. Your company's numbers need to be healthy to be taken seriously. An IPO team will need a good foundation to get TF Shipping hitting the market strong if you want any credibility to get the investment you're looking for to execute the growth plan." I tap my bag where it's hanging on my shoulder. "Any reputable IPO team would laugh at the state of these."

"God, you just sucked the joy right out of my Friday." Thomas opens the door as I pace toward him, pushing his back against it, ready to let me pass.

"Just keeping it real for you. My job's hard enough without having to nag my boss about his and the board's spending habits." I come to a startled stop, something about the corridor vastly different from this morning. Tinsel. Everywhere. Every colour. Hanging off every door, including my own. My entire office door is framed in red sparkly tinsel. I want to reach up and rip it down. And the tree that looks like it's had a bag of flour launched at it? I want to kick it. December. The month I dread most of all the months. "I see you've let Crystal loose," I murmur, spotting a family of glowing reindeers by the elevators down the hall.

"I suppose you're going to give me a hard time about increasing her budget for the holiday decorations this year, huh?"

"I'm not Scrooge, Thomas."

A brief silence tells me he might not agree. "Didn't she do a fabulous job?"

"Terrific."

"Look, Cam, I know—"

"It's Camryn."

"Camryn," he breathes. "Sorry. Look, I know you're not a fan of Christmas—"

"Not particularly."

"And I don't know why that is—religion, whatever—but I need you to be at the Inter City Reception next Friday. You'll have the answers to every question I might be asked about us floating TF Shipping."

"Where?" I ask, picking up my feet, keen to get through the grotto ahead. Thomas chases my heels as I march down the corridor through the throngs of people sipping champagne and the endless Christmas creatures—snowmen, elves, Mrs. Clause—all grinning at me. There is nothing to celebrate about December. There's nothing to celebrate about *anything*.

"The Dorchester."

"Time?"

"Seven."

"I'll come for an hour so make the most of me." I hit the call button for the elevator and step in the second the doors slide open, wrapping my cream silk scarf around my neck.

"Great." Thomas smiles, and I force one in return. I like the guy, I'll admit. He's a bit of a loose cannon, a child that needs keeping in line, but he's a good guy. His wife and son, however, I can hardly stand. And I know the feeling is mutual since I came in here and started questioning every financial decision being made and penny being spent. "Have a good weekend, Cam . . . ryn."

The doors meet, and I exhale a long breath, not quite breathing easy again, but certainly better than I was. I have to close my eyes for a moment, not only to avoid the woman I don't recognise in the mirror before me, but to concentrate on swallowing the constant ball of anxiety in my throat. It's Friday, which means I've two days ahead of no work *days*, just work in an apartment that's not a home, just a place to sleep, shower, and keep my things.

I avoid it at all costs.

Which is why I'm not going *home* now.

As soon as I hear the doors slide open, granting my freedom, I open my eyes and hurry across the foyer, pushing out through the revolving door into the frigid evening air. I look down at the bottom half of my legs. Bare. I shiver, tying the belt of my camel trench coat and glancing down the street.

Once upon a time, Christmas lights would only grace the main shopping streets and tourist areas of London. Now, they seem to be everywhere—on every corner, in every window. Flashing lights at every turn, making me squint as I walk. I'd usually avoid Regent Street like the plague, but it's my quickest route to where I need to be, and I really need to be there now.

Ducking and swerving through the crowds, I hurry across the

road, dipping between the stationary cars, then up one of the side streets, leaving the masses of people behind when I step into The Royal Constantine Hotel. It's one of my preferred hideaways.

My heels click on the lobby's marble floor as I walk through. It's all standard and familiar. A nod from the concierge, a smile from the guy behind reception, and when I make it into the bar, the barman immediately gets to making two dirty martinis.

My escape.

Peace. Anonymity. No one disturbs the woman at the end of the bar with two drinks before her and a coat draped over the next stool. In the office, I'm fair game. In a coffee house, bustling chaos assaults my ears. Yes, I could block it out, slip in my AirPods.

But I can't get a dirty martini in a coffee house.

With my coat in position over the back of the second stool from the end of the bar, I take the last stool, setting some papers from my bag on the bar and checking my phone. There are no notifications —no texts, WhatsApp messages, or missed calls. Just work emails.

I stare down at the papers. Inhale. Debate if I should read them for the tenth time. No, I should just sign them. Except the barman places the drinks in front of me, distracting me from torturing myself for that tenth time. "Thank you." I slide one glass over to the spare seat beside me and raise the other to my lips, sipping and swallowing, closing my eyes.

"Good?"

"Always." This particular barman at The Royal Constantine does the best dirty martinis of all the barmen in all the hotels that I hide in. I nod my approval and set the glass down, scissoring the stem with my fingers. "It's busy tonight," I muse, glancing around at the tables. Six people. It's a record.

The barman chuckles. "Tab?"

"Please." Another sip. "It's Friday." And I have plenty of time to kill.

"I'll leave you in peace. Just tap the bar when you need another."

"It's like you know me." I get back to the papers, to torturing myself, chewing the corner of my lip as I scan the first page. Then I push them away, not up for dealing with my personal affairs, and get my laptop, opening up my work email account. I start archiving the bullshit I've been copied in on from various staff members and Thomas, shit I don't need to know. It takes me down to a satisfying fifty emails to work through this weekend, and I'm finished my first martini by the time I've closed my laptop. I set the empty down and tap the bar, and the barman—as they all do—casts a brief look to the untouched one next to me waiting to be drank. I ignore him, and he starts working on my second drink.

"Oh, and it's busier," he muses, getting rid of my dirty empty and sliding the fresh one into my hand.

With the glass to my lips, I look over my shoulder, seeing a man in a navy trench coat heading to a table in the corner. He drops his briefcase on one of the velvet chairs and shrugs off his coat, throwing it on another chair. His tall, lean frame is carrying a beautiful mid-grey suit. His dark hair has flecks of silver on his temples, only noticeable because of the nearby spotlight shining on him briefly before he moves out of the light into the shadows and drops heavily into a seat, taking his mobile to his ear and raking a hand through his hair. Then his eyes meet mine, his head tilting. Refined, classic, a square jaw and heavy brow that makes him look as if he's permanently in deep thought. Handsome. I hum under my breath and turn back toward the bar, resuming avoiding reading the paperwork, working my way through my second martini.

By the third, the much-needed, warm sense of disconnection comes over me, and I feel my strung muscles finally loosen and stop aching.

By my fourth, I still haven't read the papers. Not that I need to —the words are imprinted on my brain, every last one of them. On a sigh, I hold up my glass and study the last inch in the bottom, wondering if I should have a fifth. Undoubtedly not. And yet I tap the bar anyway. One more before I start the slow walk home, take a long shower, and spend hours trying to get to sleep. Maybe I'll have two more martinis. It's the only thing that helps with my eternal insomnia.

Nothing else. Not sleeping pills, not therapy.

Only alcohol.

As I contemplate that, I notice the sitcom playing on the telly in the bar. *Good God.* Is that a *best of* from Fawlty Towers? I sit up straighter, focused, remembering watching the reruns with Dad. It was his absolute favourite. I watch as Basil and Manuel heave a dead guest out of a huge basket. "Oh shit. I remember this scene." And then I chuckle as they enter a room where another guest is blowing up a naked inflatable woman doll. English humour at its best.

When was the last time I laughed like that?

I smile and knock back the last of my fourth martini as something appears in my side vision, in between the stool by me and the next one. A man. The man I watched settle at the back table over an hour ago. He's removed his suit jacket, and my eyes travel up his shirt, his neck, across his dark stubble, until I'm looking straight into his eyes. Grey eyes. Lazy, grey eyes that shimmer a little under the hazy glow of the lights hanging over the bar. "Do you need a pen?" he asks.

"Excuse me?"

"You've been looking at that paperwork for over an hour, so I wondered in maybe you needed a pen."

I chuckle. God, that's twice tonight. "Cute. I haven't heard that one before." He's original too. This man has a lot going for him. But then I come to my senses. *I do not want to flirt. Not tonight.* "I don't need a pen."

His nod is slow and thoughtful as he accepts a short fat glass of clear liquid from the barman. "What about a date?"

I look at the empty seat next to me, the martini before it still waiting to be drank. Drops of condensation slide down the glass to the paper coaster beneath it. The drink is purposeless . . . just like this stranger's question. "I don't need a date."

He rests a forearm on the bar, leaning on it, and faces me. His eyes are something else. Glittery but cold, still slightly narrowed. Thinking deeply. About me? Trying to figure me out? *Please don't bother, handsome stranger. I'm not worth the effort.*

His lips are full, slightly parted. Raising his glass to them, as if he knows my focus is glued there, he sips, and my gaze follows, watching as he licks his bottom lip, waiting for me to answer.

"You're very handsome," I say out of nowhere, definitely making him pause a beat.

"Thank you." He points to the martini that's still untouched in front of the stool next me. "So whose is this if you don't need a date?"

"Mine."

His frown is quite stunning, a delicate fan of lines springing from the corners of his eyes. "Yours?"

"It's a deterrent. Stops unwanted men joining me and trying to talk me into bed." If they're wanted, I'll drink the martini. I expect a smile from him, but there's no hint of amusement.

"Is that a common problem? Random men in hotel bars trying to talk you into bed?"

I point to the martini. "It was before the deterrent. It seems you're immune to my tactics." And I'm apparently not immune to this guy's looks, which are creeping into the realms of stunning. I look down at my empty martini glass. I've had too many.

"Wondering if you've had too many?"

I'm unable to hide my surprise when my head snaps back up. "Maybe."

"You haven't." A slow sip of his drink. "I'd say you've had just enough." And with that, he pushes off the bar and wanders back to his table, and I turn on my stool to follow him, my eyes greedy. Wide shoulders. A perfect arse. Long legs. Thick thighs.

I breathe out and return to face the bar, catching the barman's raised brow before he quickly lowers it. "It's nothing," I assure him, taking the deterrent martini and knocking it back. "And now I've definitely had too much to drink." I slip down off my stool and hand my card over, letting him charge it while I get my coat on and pack my things into my bag. "Thank you." I slide a ten-pound tip across the bar and head out, stopping at the guy's table. He didn't pursue me. Didn't ask me to a room. And that strangely intrigues me. Little does, normally. "It was nice to meet you."

"We didn't really meet." He stands, every tall inch of him rising deliberately and slowly from his chair.

"Camryn." I offer my hand, and he takes it, holding it lightly as he shakes. His persona may be cool, but his touch is fire, and the heat works its way through my body, all the way to between my legs. It makes me stand up straighter, the warmth generating a pulse deep in my belly.

"Dec," he murmurs, his eyes on my mouth, surely noticing that I've had to part my lips to subtly pull in some air.

"That's a pretty lame shake for a businessman, Dec."

I can tell he's amused, though his mouth doesn't show it, only his eyes. "You want me to shake your hand like I'd shake the hand of the man I'm about to screw over?"

"Yes."

His hold tightens. "Better?"

"Much," I reply, tightening my hold too.

His head does that wonderful, thoughtful slight tilt again, his eyes twinkling. "Take a seat."

"I've had too much to drink to do that."

He nods, contemplative, and it's so fucking sexy. His broodiness. His impassiveness. His detachment. How he isn't revealing his cards. I like it. Most men I encounter in hotel bars lay it on thick. Throw some naff one-liners, chat-up lines, or a strategically placed fact about themselves hoping to impress and seal the deal. They never impress. I'm not interested in being impressed. I'm interested in escaping. Killing time. They help with that for a while. Until they don't.

It's unhealthy, even I, in my warped walk-through life, can appreciate that. Which is why I tell myself it won't happen again, usually immediately after it's happened. They never turn me on.

Never make me come, so I do that myself. And they never spike the incredible tingles like I'm feeling all over my skin now.

"Don't you trust yourself?" he asks.

I pull my hand from his, and it's instantly cold again. "Not in the least."

Lowering to his chair, Dec relaxes back, drink in hand, and kicks his ankle up onto his knee. Every perfect inch of him pushes against the material of his shirt and trousers, giving me a good idea of just how perfect he is beneath. "Well, it was nice to nearly get to know you, Camryn."

"Good evening, Dec." I slowly turn and walk away, stopping at the entrance when he calls my name. I'm forced to take a breath before I look back. He's still relaxed in his chair. Still casual. Still impassive.

"You're very beautiful," he says quietly.

I don't thank him, because he's wrong. I get out of there before I do something utterly stupid. It wouldn't be the first time, but I vowed the last time would actually be the last time.

You're very beautiful.

He wouldn't say that if he knew me. I'm a mess. No one truly wants a mess.

I push through the revolving door and break out into the cold, dark air, tying the belt of my coat, my shoulders a little hunched. The temperature has dropped, but the martinis will keep me warm on the walk home. The martinis are undoubtedly also the reason why I turn onto Regent Street and brave the pre-Christmas chaos, as well as the twinkling light displays stretching from one side of the street to the other.

Following the curve of the buildings, I walk slowly, dragging out my journey, unable to stop myself from taking in the faces of people I pass. Most smiling, either with someone or chatting on the phone.

My pace automatically slows as I approach a particularly busy stretch of the pavement, pedestrians stepping into the road to avoid the bottleneck of people trying to get into a store. A toy store. The sound of children screeching their delight invades my ears, parents laughing at the staff dressed as elves on the door blowing massive bubbles, enticing the kids into the magical wonderland full of toys and teddy bears.

I don't realise I've stopped walking completely until someone brushes my shoulder as they pass me, making me stumble a few steps forward. I right myself quickly, catching my bag as it falls off my shoulder. "Excuse me," I murmur, leaning back on my heels when a huge bubble appears before me. It hits the tip of my nose and pops, and an eruption of laughter breaks out, startling me more than the bubble. I glance around, seeing all attention pointed my way, and the six-foot elf responsible for blowing the bubble is approaching me. I can see what's about to happen a mile off. I'm going to be used as a prop. Of course he'd find the most wretched person within reach. The person who looks like a challenge. I'm certainly that. "Oh, no," I say, backing up as I lift my hand, warning him back with that too.

"Oh, yes!"

"No, no, no." I laugh, nervous and wary, as children in the line outside the store start jumping up and down, egging the elf on.

"Yes, yes, yes," he sings, putting the bubble wand at his lips.

I feel the inevitable churn of my stomach as I back up, the unbearable slice of pain through my heart. "Please, I'm really not in the mood for fun and games." My eyes dart from the elf to the kids in the line, taking in each of their smiles, their happiness, their excitement. And then the parents all delighting in the sounds of their kids' happiness.

Another bubble comes at me, and I lean back, as well as step back.

Too far.

"Fuck!" My heel slips off the edge of the curb as a collection of loud, horrified gasps fill the air. Bracing myself to hit by the ground or be taken out by a car, I clench my eyes closed, holding my breath.

"I got you."

I'm suddenly buried face first in a chest, and the smell that hits me saturates my senses. Clean. Manly. *Sexy*. I look up and meet eyes I've seen before this evening. The impact of them staring into mine so closely steals my breath and makes my heart ping. "Are you following me?" I break away, uncomfortable with the warmth rising from my toes into my belly, the same warmth I felt when he held my hand to shake it.

He steps back too. "I'm not following you."

"So you often hang around toy stores, huh?"

"No, I don't. But you do."

I flinch, stung, pulling my bag onto my shoulder again, being forced to look away, to escape the scrutiny I'm under. Kids outside the store turn to their parents, expressing their outrage as they point at me. The lady on the street who's just turned the pure, Christmassy air outside their favourite toy store blue with her foul language. My cringe has my shoulders rising and my eyes returning to Dec to escape the condemning parents' glares. "I should leave before they come at me with pitchforks." Stepping back, I take in the man before me. *Beautiful*. My silent observation jars me. I don't see beauty in this world anymore. I'm a robot going through the motions of life, limping my way through each day, constantly wondering if this unrelenting pain will fuck off. Wondering if I'll ever appreciate colour again. Hear laughing and not want to curl into a ball and cry. "Thanks for saving me."

I get nothing from him, not one hint of . . . anything, so I turn and walk away, before I'm drawn into his warm chest again.

"Where are you heading?"

I stop, staring at the street ahead. "Home."

"I'll walk you."

I turn, just as he reaches me. "That didn't sound like you were offering, more telling."

"Correct." He passes me but stops when he realises I'm not following him, looking back.

"You don't know where I'm walking to."

"I don't need to. I assume you know the way." That eyebrow lifts again.

"Camden."

"You're walking to Camden? That's a long walk."

"Maybe fifty minutes. Changed your mind?"

"No." He watches my every step as I approach him, and he falls into stride beside me as I continue past, our walk slow and silent. But it's not awkward. It's strangely comfortable. A man by my side. Just there, relaxed. Few people are relaxed around me anymore. Most avoid me.

I look up at him, taking in his profile, thinking again how lovely it is. His lashes are long, some strands of his dark hair falling across his forehead. His stubble is on the longer side of tidy, some flecks of grey peppering that too. After a few moments, he starts to slow, and I naturally drop my pace until we stop in the middle of the pavement. Then he turns his eyes onto me. In this moment, I decide they're my favourite part of all the parts of him. His eyes. They're expressive without giving anything at all away.

"Changed your mind?" he asks.

"About what?"

"If I'm very handsome."

"No."

"Good. My turn," he says, and I tilt my head in question, just as he reaches for my cheek and encourages me to face away again. The warmth of his skin on mine, even if it's just his fingertips, makes every muscle in me tense to sustain the pleasure. His gaze burns into my profile as I remain still, my breathing slowing, letting him have his time, not feeling at all uncomfortable. That in itself is odd. I hate attention on me. Will avoid it at all costs. But Dec looking at me? I like it.

I eventually turn my eyes but keep my head relatively straight. "Done?"

"No."

I chew on the corner of my lip, and I realise it's to stop a smile from breaking. Just feeling my face muscles twitch is unusual.

"Okay, I'm done." By the tiny twitch of his eyes, I can tell he saw my brief smile. But he carries on his way without another word, and I watch him, releasing my lip and taking in air as I catch up, the silence falling again. And it's comfortable again.

I hear the distant sound of Mariah Carey singing, getting progressively louder, until it's upon us, unbearably loud, and yet today I can bear it. A rickshaw drenched in multicoloured Christmas lights and dripping in tinsel passes, the two passengers singing along, arms in the air. I can feel Dec looking at me again, but I return my attention forward.

And we walk.

And walk.

No more words, no conversation, but plenty of fleeting looks.

No facial expressions.

Not until we reach Camden High Street. "So what was the document that needed signing?" he asks.

"Why do you assume it needed signing?"

"Because no one gives a document that much attention without it needing a signature."

"Are you speaking from experience?"

"Yes."

I look up at him, just as he looks down at me, and there's that flutter in my stomach again. And this time, not a ping, but an explosion in my chest. I have to look away. "What do you do?" I ask.

"For a living?"

"Yes."

"Acquiring and merging. More acquiring. You?"

"CFO."

"Of?"

"A shipping company. TF Shipping. I was brought in to get it in a healthy financial shape ready for the owner to bring in a team who'll prepare it for public debut."

"So that was the paperwork."

"No, the paperwork was my divorce papers." I don't know why

I peek up at him now, maybe to see his reaction? I should have known, though. There is no reaction.

"Struggling to sign them?"

"No." I have no idea where these words are coming from. And yet they won't stop coming. "I'm struggling to accept the reasons he's cited."

"Which are?"

"Not going to be discussed with you." I swallow down the predictable lump growing, frustrated it still exists. "And you?" I ask, moving things along.

"Me, what?"

"Are you married?"

"Yes."

My steps falter a little too much to go unnoticed. What is that inside? Disappointment? I frown to myself, my gaze dropping to my feet. And now I have no clue what to say. The silence has been comfortable. The conversation *had* been surprisingly easy, and I don't want that to change. "How long have you been married?"

"Technically, five years."

"Technically?"

"I'd have been divorced four years ago, but I don't know where to send the papers." He looks at me. Holds my eyes. Now he's searching for *my* reaction and, like him, I don't have one.

"You don't know where she is?"

He shakes his head as we turn onto my street, and naturally my mind races. What's his story? Where is she? Why did they break up? But more than my endless questions about Dec, what is happening inside me?

The heat, the flutters, the breathlessness.

"I've never met someone who also enjoys walking, despite the cold," he says, breaking the silence.

"I walk everywhere I can. It's something my mum and I used to enjoy."

"Interesting. My mum was similar. She used to say that walking in the cold staved off sickness because it built our immunity. I don't think it's true anymore, but I still equate the cold with good things."

"I like that sentiment." I like this man. This walk has stirred something inside, and it isn't just intrigue. "This is me," I say, pointing to the door into my apartment block. Dec looks up at the building as we stand at the bottom of the steps, only a few feet between our chests. "Thank you for walking me home."

"Wouldn't want you to get attacked by any killer bubbles again, would we?"

My smile is small, definitely unseen. "Want to come in?" The question jolts me. What am I saying? I don't want him to see my *home*. I find myself holding my breath as he slowly turns his eyes back onto me.

"I probably shouldn't."

"Don't you trust yourself?"

"Not in the least," he whispers, his gaze falling to my mouth. My lungs start to burn, my eyes on his mouth too.

And suddenly his lips are coming closer.

Closer.

I breathe out slowly, starting to shake, asking myself repeatedly what the hell I'm doing. What's happening? How did we arrive at this intimate, close moment?

I close my eyes.

Yes, what are you doing, Camryn? This isn't how you operate.

I come into myself and pull back, at the very moment Dec pulls away too. He glances away, his eyes squinting in silent contemplation. "I definitely don't trust myself." Two steps back puts more space between us, but I don't breathe easy again. Nowhere close. "Goodnight, Camryn."

"Goodnight, Dec," I whisper.

His tall body turns, and he walks away, his gait smooth, his strides long but not fast. And when he reaches the end of my street, he looks back to find I haven't moved a muscle. Stopping, his body slowly turns. And I'm holding my breath again, anticipating his next move, shaking where I stand. He starts coming back, and I inhale sharply, but when he gets halfway, he stops abruptly again. Then he takes a moment, thinks, watching me, while I wait, breathless.

Begging.

But he eventually backs up slowly, turns, as if fighting an unseen force, and walks away, rounding the corner. I catch a rake of his hand through his hair. Frustration? It's the most emotion he's shown since I encountered him in the hotel bar.

Exhaling, I lift my hands and watch as they tremble, clenching them into fists to try and stop it. I fail.

My legs shake as I take the steps up to the glass door, letting myself in and walking slowly down the corridor. As soon as I'm in my cold, clinical apartment, I strip and get in the shower, standing under the hot spray, letting the water pour down on me. It's soothing, and it should help me get to sleep tonight.

If I can get his handsome face out of my head.

December 2nd

It's baltic, the mixture of hot sweat and the chilly air burning my skin. My ears sting. My nose is running. My temples are pounding with a growing headache. They're all typical winter running side effects. And I'm here for them.

My lungs now burning too, I push myself to the limit, sprinting the final stretch of pathway through the park, relishing the icy air on my numbing face. Every pound of my feet sends a vibration through my body, each one booming in my head. I can no longer feel my legs.

So I run faster.

My short, sharp, hot breaths hit the frigid air, forming temporary clouds before they dissolve, disappearing, being replaced by another. A stitch comes and goes. My eyes are glued to the last tree in the line of dozens down the path, the branches naked except for a kiss of frost.

The second I reach it, I stop dead in my tracks, folding over and bracing my hands on my knees, gasping down at the concrete, watching beads of sweat drip down. I try to control the air entering and leaving my body, feeling my heart pounding in my chest and ears as I check my watch, hitting *End Run* with a very trembly fingertip, my adrenaline rampant. And then as I straighten up, the nausea kicks in and my legs start to wobble too. "Jesus," I whisper on a gasp, blowing out air and starting a steady jog out of the park, shaking my hands, trying to get some feeling back.

Once I make it to the exit onto the main road, I stop and take a moment, hands on my hips, panting up to the sky, still dripping wet, but the shakes are subsiding. I no longer feel sick. I think I'm past heart attack territory.

I shrug my way out of my running jacket and tie it around my waist, welcoming the freezing cold air on my clammy skin as I start to jog again, warming down, until I reach Pret. I grab a coffee and walk the final stretch home, slow and meandering, in no rush at all.

The old boy in the apartment next to mine is struggling to get his shopping trolley out the door when I make it back. "Here," I say, holding the door open with my hip and pulling his trolley through.

"Very kind." He holds the doorframe as he shuffles past, looking up and down my bare arms. "You'll catch a chill, dear."

"I've been running," I say, as way of an explanation for my half-dressed state.

"Running?" He chuckles, hobbling on. "I'm lucky I can walk these days." And as if to prove his point, he wobbles, making me jerk and reach for his arm. "See?"

I frown, looking out into the street, where there are endless icy patches. "Are you sure you're all right to go out there, Mr. . . ."

"Percival." He smiles at me, his old eyes glassy, his wrinkles deepening. "You've lived here for two years and we're only now introducing ourselves."

"Well, we've never bumped into each other."

"Indeed. Because you leave at the crack of dawn and come back after my bedtime. At least, you do in the week. At the weekends, you leave at the crack of dawn for a run and return just before I leave to go to the market." He pulls an old watch out of his pocket, the leather strap hanging on by a thread. "You're late today."

"I am?"

"By ten minutes."

"That's because I had to walk slower to avoid the icy patches on our street. You should be careful."

"Oh, no need to worry about me." Taking the doorframe with both hands, he lifts his foot, prompting me to look down. "Got myself some snow boots." Claiming back his trolley, he gets on his way. "Good day to you . . ."

"Camryn."

"Pretty," he chimes. "Good day, Camryn."

"Good day, Mr. Percival," I murmur, making sure he's fully through the door before I let it close. I watch him through the glass as he makes it out of the gate onto the pavement, releasing his trolley to fasten the last button on his coat and popping a flat cap on his head before ambling on his way slowly. Two years. Have I really lived here that long? It's not home, never will be, but it's better than the hotel room I lived in for a few months.

Letting myself in, I throw my keys on the empty wooden cabinet and wander into the kitchen, sipping my coffee as I go. The middle shelf of the fridge is stacked with bottles of water, and I grab one, taking the small velvet pouch from my handbag and lowering to one of the two chairs at the small table. Unzipping it, I tip out the box and pop a pill out of the foil, placing it on my tongue and swallowing it with some water. The pain that courses through me as the small tablet works its way into my system is as strong now as it was the day I started taking these pills. So I pop a few painkillers too, dragging my laptop close and scanning my emails. Sixty-two. I delete eight. Only fifty-four to work through. It'll keep me busy for the rest of the day and part of my Sunday.

Chugging down the rest of my water, I get up and toss the bottle in the recycling bin, my muscles screaming perfectly as I head for the shower. I strip down, avoid the mirror, and step in, my face pointed up at the spray.

I see him the moment I close my eyes. Feel his breath on my face as his lips came close before we retreated. I promised myself I wouldn't have mindless sex with random men again, and yet there's something about Dec that doesn't feel random. And it definitely isn't mindless because he's in my head again. "Fuck." I slap a palm into the tile and drop my head. Goddamn it for being the weekend.

December 3rd

I'm down to five emails. It's not enough when I have endless hours to kill. So I save them for later, pushing my laptop off my lap and gazing around the lounge. A sofa. A coffee table. A TV I rarely watch. Endless boxes stacked in every corner. I get up and wander over to a pile, gingerly pulling the flap of one open, wondering if today will be the day I finally brave facing the contents. My heart begins to race, and my soul's invaded by the long-lost sound of laughter from my past. Smiles I won't see again. This box, like every other one it's stacked on, and every other unpacked box in this apartment, is like Pandora's box. Many boxes that should never be opened. I'm stable enough to know I'm existing in dark places. Stumbling through this life aimlessly, my goal simply to make it through each day alive. These boxes might end me.

I quickly snap it shut again. I can't face it. Will never be able to face the boxes.

A chime sounds as I step back, pulling my attention over my shoulder to the couch where my phone is sitting on the arm. A text. My messenger inbox feels like Pandora's box too. I shake my head and walk over with purpose I don't feel, snatching it up and slamming my thumb on the screen to open the message. My heart drops into my stomach as I read the words, and then the anger rises.

> My solicitor still hasn't received the papers. Come on, Camryn. I know you're busy, but it's just a signature. Sign the papers and get your PA to post them so we can proceed.

I toss my phone on the couch, untold pain hitting me in the gut, forcing me to fold to the floor and curl up into a ball. But I don't cry. The tears don't come anymore. I experience every telltale sign of pain and loss—the ball in my throat, the tightening of my chest, the wobble of my lip from time to time—but never tears. My eyes have dried up. Empty. No more tears to give. I'm hollow. A broken, empty vessel of a woman who once smiled and celebrated life with a partner. Those happy times feel like eons ago.

I clench my eyes closed and ball my fists, wishing the day away so I can get on with my working week. "Fuck you," I yell at my phone, slamming my fist into the floor. "Fuck you, fuck you, fuck you!" I stand abruptly and march into the kitchen, swinging open cupboard door after cupboard door, searching for something that'll numb this relentless agony.

Empty.

They're all empty.

"Goddamn it!" I slam the last door shut with such force, it jumps off its hinges and hits the floor, narrowly missing the bridge of my foot. It clatters around until it settles. "Fuck," I breathe, dropping to a chair. I wedge my elbows on the table and rest my head in my hands, my fingers clawing my dark hair, pulling at my scalp.

Breathe.

Half hour later, I'm still taking in controlled breaths, still staring at the tabletop, my head hanging. I stand, holding the edge of the table, and take a few moments before reattaching the door and going to my bedroom, pulling my hair into a ponytail on my way. I tug on some baggy jeans, thick socks, a roll-neck jumper, and slip my feet into my Merry People boots—oh, the irony—wrapping a scarf around my neck and swinging my Dry Robe coat on.

Pocketing my mobile, his message unanswered, I leave my apartment and start the five-mile walk, hands in my pockets, head down.

Unable to face the world.

I have to take a few moments outside before I push my way through the glass doors, as I always do. The heat smacks me in the face, and I make quick work of stripping out of my coat and scarf, draping them over the crook of my arm before signing myself in. The lady behind the reception desk, I forget her name, doesn't greet me, just nods, before pressing the door release button to let me through. Glittery tinsel and fake snow adorn the corridor, baubles in every colour and size dangling from the ceiling on ribbons. Another gauntlet to run. Taking a deep breath, I walk on fast feet, looking straight ahead to the door at the very end of the corridor.

Another breath before I enter.

The room is dark, the curtains drawn, only a glimmer of the winter sun peeking through a small gap at the edge. I see her silhouette on the bed, hear her light snore. The second the door clicks closed, she stirs, so I hurry over to the lamp and flick it on, letting the soft light illuminate the room so she can see me when she opens her eyes. Then I pull a chair over, draping my coat and scarf over the back, take a seat, and wait.

Her head turns, her eyelids flicker, and the moment she opens her eyes, I know today is a bad day. Her frown confirms it. "It's Camryn," I say, watching as she tries to figure out who I am. If she knows me. Most of the time, she doesn't, is adamant she's never seen me before in her life. It's just another layer of pain to the endless pain.

Her grey eyebrows pinch more. "Where's Noah?"

I swallow, feeling my back pushing into the chair. "He doesn't visit anymore." I don't bother telling her who I am beyond my name. It's a waste of time and energy and only stresses her out. "Have you eaten?"

"What do you mean, he doesn't visit anymore? He was here just yesterday."

"He was?" I say, just as the door opens and a nurse enters.

"Camryn," she says, smiling mildly as she assesses my mother. "It's been a few days."

I smile tightly, not feeling the need to explain myself. "It's been crazy at work."

Her hum is borderline condescending.

"Who's Camryn? I don't know no Camryn." Mum starts struggling to sit up, her emaciated arms flailing, every vein visible through her paper-thin skin. "Get out!"

"Now, now, Celeste," the nurse coos, calm as can be. "This is your daughter."

"Where's Noah?" she yells, her voice broken, unrecognisable. "I want to see Noah."

"Excuse me." I get up, feeling the walls closing in on me, and make my hasty exit, resting my back against the wall in the corridor, looking up at the ceiling briefly before the endless baubles force my gaze to my boots.

The nurse joins me after a few moments. Her smile is drenched in sympathy I just can't take. "It's the Christmas carols service soon. It would be lovely if you could join us."

"I'm working."

"But I haven't told you when it is."

I push my back away from the wall and pull my coat on as I walk away. "She won't want me there."

"She can't help it, Camryn," she calls. "You know that."

"I know that, Deirdre," I murmur, pulling my phone out of my pocket as I reach the double doors that lead into reception. I hit the button to alert the lady on the desk I need letting out, my eyes scanning the space for her as I make a call.

"Hey," he says in answer.

"You need to come see Mum." I hit the button again, getting hotter and hotter.

"I did."

"When?"

"A few weeks ago."

"It was the end of October, before you went on a three-week holiday."

"I'm busy, Cam."

"So am I." I see the lady appear behind the reception area, but she doesn't look this way and disappears again into the office, so I hit the button repeatedly, my breathing becoming laboured.

"You're the daughter. It's your job to look after her. I'm paying for that outrageously expensive care home, Cam. I do what I can. You're local, it's easier for you."

"Easy?" I blurt, starting to pound the glass with the side of my fist. "You think it's easy coming here for her to look at me blankly? For her to ask for—"

"It's a good distraction for you."

"Fuck you."

"God, you're poisonous."

I hang up. "Will someone please let me the fuck out of here?"

The door clicks, and I push my way through, rushing across the space and practically falling out onto the street, gasping in the cold air until my lungs scream. It takes a solid ten minutes to calm myself down until my hands aren't shaking and I can type out a shitty message to my brother.

And then I start the long trek home, taking endless detours down the safe, Christmas-free side streets, hating the awful disease that stole my mum, hating my egotistical, misogynist brother. Hating my soon-to-be ex-husband.

Wondering if my life will ever hold any joy again.

December 4th

"Jesus, Thomas." I push my foot into my heel and stand, striding to the door and swinging it open. I take a moment to assess the corridor. "It's like Santa's fucking grotto," I mutter, making Debbie, my assistant, look up from her computer screen. People move out of my path as I march on, and conversations die. Which means the sound of WHAM! gets louder. It's December 4th, for Christ's sake. *Give it a rest!*

I don't bother knocking, instead barging right in, catching Thomas with his feet up, relaxed back, his desk phone held to his ear as he tosses a cricket ball up and down.

The moment he clocks me, his smile falls. "I'll call you back." He drops his feet, sets the receiver calmly in the cradle, and places the ball down, clearing his throat. "Camryn."

"Tell me I didn't just read the email I read."

His lips twist. He's thinking, really thinking, which means there could be a few different emails I could have read. "Want to help me out?"

"The bonuses." I remain standing in the open doorway, prompting Thomas to look past me. I glance over my shoulder and see a few staff loitering, feigning the scanning of files as they wander, pretending to be on calls. I slam the door closed.

"It's Christmas." he says, slightly high-pitched.

"Thomas, you have one hundred and two members of staff in this building. You have just authorised the payroll department to pay bonuses between one thousand and twenty thousand to each and every one of them."

"It's Christmas?" he says again.

"Half a million, Thomas!" I yell. "That's straight off your profit."

"I authorised twenty thousand for you," he says, smiling. It drops the second he realises I'm not impressed.

"Show me the appraisals."

"What?"

I give him grabby hands. "The performance reports. Show me the performance reviews that determined each and every bonus amount."

He scans his desk, as if looking for them. We both know there are no reports. *Does he actually know what they fucking are?*

"Profit, Thomas. To take this company to the next level, to attract the right board, you need to make a healthy *profit*. Right now, you're undoing everything I'm working toward to ensure TF Shipping gets there, Thomas."

"I'm the boss, Camryn." He picks up his pen and starts clicking the end fast and furiously. "I can do what I like."

"Do you want to take this company to the next level?"

He gives me a tired look. "I hired you, didn't I?"

"Then you need to get used to how things will be moving forward, and no new board would agree to your bonus plan, especially without concrete evidence of staff performances. If this company floats, you'll lose an element of control, Thomas. You'll be answerable to a board that *doesn't* include your wife and son. Buying ships will involve many meetings and strategic planning." I go to his desk and pick up his cricket ball, tossing it in the air. He catches it. "Stop spending money or this isn't going to work." I pivot and walk out.

"I suppose now would be a bad time to tell you I just bought hospitality tickets for Wimbledon next year."

I stop in my tracks, my teeth gritted. "Yes, now would be a *very* bad time."

"I'll rein it in."

"You've been saying that for the past two years." Truth is, I would have walked out on this job last year when I admitted to myself it was going to be next to impossible to work with Thomas's son and wife, who show zero respect for me and my purpose here. And given how expensive it is to live in London as a newly single woman, my fat salary is a basic necessity. So even though I despise many attributes of this job, they need me, and I need them.

"From now on, I promise," he calls.

"That goes for Barbara and Anthony too," I snap, exasperated. "And I don't want to see any personal spend on their business credit cards either."

As I near my office door, Debbie comes out from behind her desk, and I skid to a stop, my eyes on her legs. "What the hell are you wearing?" I ask, squinting.

"These are my advent calendar tights."

"They're hideous."

"But of course you'd love them," she sings, completely unaffected by my curtness, something I quietly appreciate. I actually like Debbie. "I can't wait for you to see my elf ones."

"You're a fifty-year-old woman."

"Forty-nine, actually."

"Oh, well then, this"—I wave a hand up and down her legs—"is perfectly acceptable." I push my way into my office and grab my coat and bag, leaving over an hour earlier than usual.

"Where are you going?" Debbie calls, alarmed.

"I have somewhere I need to be." I keep my eyes forward as I navigate the Christmas-infested corridor. "You make me need a drink, Thomas," I mutter under my breath.

Standing on the threshold of the bar at The Royal Constantine, I scan the tables. It's not something I usually do, and I hardly want to admit why I do it this evening. It's quiet. One man in the corner reading a paper. Not *him*.

Setting my coat and bag on the second stool in, I take the end one, smiling when two martinis slide toward me. "Good day?" the barman asks, making my drink pause at my lips.

"I've been coming here for two years, and I don't know your name. You don't know mine. You have *never* asked me if I've had a good day."

"I know your name."

"You do?"

"Camryn. I heard you telling the guy who was here on Friday."

"Then I suppose you should tell me yours."

"Julio."

"Nice to meet you, Julio."

"He was here."

My glass is now resting on my lips, the alcohol within licking distance. "Excuse me?"

"The man. Dec. He was here again last night." Julio starts chipping away at a block of ice.

"A coincidence?" I ask, my mind racing.

"Maybe. Maybe not."

"What's your gut telling you?"

He smirks, attention on the block of ice. "It's telling me not."

"Why?"

"Because he was looking for you."

I lower my glass, still having not taken a sip. "How do you know he was looking for me?"

"Because he asked if you'd been in since Friday."

"Oh." I inhale, picking up my martini and having a long swig before Julio here says something else that catches me off guard. Then I tap the bar, blinking when he drops a cube of ice into a glass and it chinks loudly. He was here? Looking for me? I frown down at the bar, my heart now racing with my mind.

Odd.

Don't you trust yourself?

Not in the least.

I take another sip of my drink, but for some reason tonight, the strong hit of alcohol doesn't have the usual or desired effect. I swallow and place my glass down, easing back on the stool.

The barman clears his throat, so I glance up at him. He nods past me.

And something deep inside stirs. My shoulders roll of their own volition, and I slowly swivel on the stool. My inhale is sharp and unstoppable when I find him on the threshold of the bar, his stance wide as he slowly pulls the navy scarf from around his neck. Our eyes meet, my stomach flips, and I swallow down my awe. He doesn't smile, doesn't speak. He just wanders over to me and drops his case between the stools, removes his coat, collects mine off the stool next to me, and hangs them on the nearby coat stand. Then he helps himself to the stool beside me, pulling my spare martini close by the tips of his fingers on the base.

I let my stool turn until I'm facing him, my knees nearly touching his thighs. "Hello again," I say quietly as he helps himself to a sip of my deterrent drink.

"Hello." He turns his eyes my way, and my world seems to shift as I stare into them. "Tell me why you come here," he orders softly.

"No."

He pouts, squinting thoughtfully as he sips some more. "Tell me how old you are."

"Thirty-seven."

"Tell me the reason your husband wants a divorce."

"No."

"Tell me your favourite Christmas movie."

"I don't have one."

"Tell me how long you were married."

"Nine years."

"Together?"

"Twelve."

"Your birthday."

"Tenth of March."

"Your favourite colour?"

I remain quiet. I don't see colour anymore.

"Food?"

"I eat to survive."

"You must have a favourite food."

I take a sip of my drink on a shrug, making him inhale deeply and exhale loudly. I don't have a favourite anything.

"Have you signed your divorce papers yet?"

I shake my head.

"Do you still want to be married to him?"

I pause, my drink on its way back down to the bar, and the welcome sense of lightness vanishes. I look away from him, feeling him assessing me. Trying to figure me out.

And I can't let him. I've said too much, told him too much. I place my drink down and slip off my stool. "It was nice to see you again," I say, edging out, brushing past him as I do.

His hand shoots out and grabs my arm, and the feel of his touch, even over the arm of my long-sleeved dress, makes me freeze. I look at his big fingers wrapped around me. "Don't go," he says quietly.

"And why do you want me to stay?"

"Because I like you."

I brave facing him. He likes me. I like him too. But I don't say so, my head telling me to get the hell out of here before I get myself into something I'm not ready for.

Or want.

And yet I take my stool anyway, and Dec nods to Julio for two more martinis. "I have one more question," he says, turning on his stool to face me. He reaches for my bare knees and lays his hands on them, and my heart beats its way up to my throat, making breathing hard. "Why did you come here tonight?" he asks softly, holding my eyes.

"Because I was hoping to see you." It comes out without

thought, and I close my eyes on a swallow, immediately regretting it.

"That's what I was hoping you'd say." He releases me, prompting me to open my eyes. "So why try and leave?"

"Because you ask too many questions."

"You don't want me to know you."

"You don't want to know me."

"Wrong."

"Why?"

"That I haven't figured out yet." Facing the bar, he taps the base of the glass. "So let's set some boundaries."

"Okay."

"No personal questions."

My lips purse. If he can't ask me, I can't ask him. "I've just sat through a quickfire round with you," I point out.

"You really didn't reveal much, Camryn. You're thirty-seven, a CFO, you apparently don't have any favourites, you're divorced but not, and deeply unhappy."

I recoil. *Deeply unhappy*. "It's more than I know about you," I say quietly, not refuting his analysis.

"Maybe that's best for both of us."

"Maybe," I agree. But I don't agree. Surprisingly, I want to know every tiny detail there is to know about Dec. And now I can't ask.

"Drink," he whispers, pushing my glass toward me. I blindly reach for it, lost in his silver gaze as he watches me take a sip. "Let me tell you what I know about you."

"You just did."

"Things you haven't told me." He leans in closer, and I get a stronger hit of his heady scent. "Your dark hair reflects golden strands when the light catches it," he says quietly, his eyes flicking to my hair. "You have a layer here that's a fraction too short to stay comfortably behind your ear when you tuck it there, which is usually when you're uncomfortable."

I feel my hand twitch to do exactly that—pointlessly tuck that shorter layer behind my ear. Dec's lips twitch, and he reaches for it. "Let me do that for you," he says, pushing it back. My heart booms as I study his face, unable to take my eyes off him. "You don't wear lipstick, but you don't need to." The pad of his index finger meets my cupid's bow. "Because your lips are naturally rosy." The feeling of his finger dragging across my top lip to the corner heats me between my legs. "This mole," he murmurs, moving his light touch to the top of my cheek, "I love it."

"I hate it."

"It's beautiful." His bottom lip disappears between his teeth. "And your eyes," he whispers, edging closer to the point I'm sure he's moving in for a kiss. "They speak to me more than you probably want them to."

A soft hitch of breath escapes as I stare at him, my mind telling me to retreat, but my heart begging me to explore this. "And what do they say?" *What am I doing?*

His palm opens and slides onto my cheek. "They're telling me you're wildly attracted to me," he breathes.

"That's some intuition you have, Dec."

"It's not intuition." He releases my cheek and leans back. "It's fact. And the feeling is shared."

"So this is just physical?"

"Oh, I don't think so, Camryn. You've revealed too much, so not only do I have your beauty to contend with, I also have my intrigue."

"I've revealed too much?"

"You want to get to know me." His head tilts, waiting for me to correct him. He knows I won't. "You're surprised by that. Am I close?"

It's not just physical.

He's intrigued.

Fuck.

"Maybe," I murmur. And he nods.

I should have gotten up and left the bar. I didn't. At least, not on my own.

The walk home is quiet and comfortable. Our shoulders brush a few times, and neither of us apologise for it. In fact, we seem to get closer and closer with every step. When we reach my apartment building, I slow to a stop and breathe in deep, facing him. He has some fluff from his scarf caught in his rough stubble. "What?" he asks, seeing me staring at the delicate piece of fuzz on the corner of his lip.

"You have something here." I point to my mouth.

"Then get it."

I shoot my eyes to his shimmering gaze, seeing his order there too, and slowly reach for the fluff, pulling it free. "There."

"You have something too."

I brush at my mouth.

"Not there."

"Where?"

"Just"—he leans forward, his face a fraction from mine, and my senses are immediately overwhelmed by his closeness, my nose invaded by his rich, clean cologne—"here." He breathes across my cheek, only a second before he presses his lips into my skin. I close my eyes, paralysed by the warmth that sails through my cold body from a simple kiss—just a press of his lips on my cheek.

Then he pulls away, and I mourn the loss.

Dec steps back, sucking his lip between his teeth, as if tasting me. "Goodnight, Camryn."

"Goodnight, Dec."

He turns away, strolling off down the road, and this time he doesn't stop at the corner.

But somehow I know it's okay.

Because I'll see him again.

December 5th

At bang on five, I scoop up my things and leave my office, pulling on my coat as I walk the corridor to the elevator, feeling eyes on me as I go. Debbie glances up from her desk, looks back down, then sharply back up again, her face a picture of uncertainty. She discreetly checks the time on her screen before making a few clicks, undoubtedly checking if I have any off-site meetings that's pulling me away from the office earlier than usual. "Those tights are hideous too," I call.

"I knew you'd love them."

I hit the call button and tie the belt of my coat, getting my bag onto my shoulder. I falter, feeling the weight is lighter than usual. No files. I look back to my office. I should get some files.

"Camryn?" Thomas comes out of his office, frowning toward me. Then he checks his watch. "Everything okay?"

"Everything's fine." Everything except for the grotto he's allowed Crystal to make of the offices. "I'm done for the day."

"But it's only five."

"My contracted hours are nine till five."

"But for two years, you've arrived at eight and left at six or seven."

I ignore his observation and step into the elevator when the doors slide open. "See you tomorrow." I go to the mirror and brave facing myself, combing my fingers through my loose hair, tucking the front, shorter layer over my ear. It immediately jumps back out, falling across my eye. I rub my rosy lips together then reach for the mole on my cheek and trace the circumference, stopping when I realise what I'm doing. What *am* I doing?

Dropping my hand, I step back, staring into my dark eyes, my lips infinitely straight. There was a time I wouldn't leave the house without my signature raspberry lipstick, the edges artfully lined in a matching lip pencil. Alive. Colourful. Now, they're permanently bare. *He likes them bare and rosy.* I blink, checking my lashes. Mascara. No false lashes. Just a tinted moisturiser to even out my olive skin. To look less sallow. Less . . . sad.

I sigh, leaving the cart when the doors open, wrapping my cream scarf around my neck as I walk through the lobby. I don't think about where I'm heading, I just head there, taking the quickest route, running the Christmas gauntlet, focused on getting to where I need to be.

I've never frequented the same hotel bar two nights in a row. Until now. And I've never been here this early.

I pass through the lobby of The Royal Constantine, feeling the staff's surprised eyes following me, and when I make it to the bar, I stop at the door and exhale, breathing easy when I see he's here already. Julio looks up first, a knowing smile tickling the corner of his mouth, prompting Dec to turn on his stool—the second from the end—and find me.

I slowly exhale at the sight of him and try with all my might to move. But my feet refuse to work, as if listening to my mind, which is screaming at me to stay here. Stay here and admire his impassive beauty. He finally stands from the stool, and I notice he's more casual today, no suit. Instead, he's wearing a pair of jeans and a thin Barbour quarter zip, knitted jumper. Classic.

"Are you going to stand there all evening or join me?" he asks, motioning to the stool beside him.

I swallow and move toward him, feeling a charged energy drawing me to him. "You're here," I say quietly.

"As are you." He seems to take me in from top to toe. Such scrutiny would usually have me shying away, make me feel uncomfortable, but not today. Not when it's Dec's eyes. "Here." He reaches for the strap of my bag and eases it off my shoulder, lowering it to the floor, but he pauses halfway. "Do you need anything out of your bag?"

I shake my head, so he releases it, then places his hands on my shoulders. My breathing hitches, the warmth of his big palms soaking into my skin through my dress. I look up at him, drawn to his lips.

"Turn around," he says quietly, applying a little pressure to help me. He comes in close, so close I can feel his breath on my neck as he draws my coat down my arms. My lips part, air suddenly nowhere to be found. I turn my head and open my eyes, finding his face a whisper away from mine, his eyes closed. He looks serene, and this close, I see every tiny imperfection, every line, every bristle of his stubble. His lips are parted too.

"Thank you," I murmur. He opens his eyes, and our gazes collide, something powerful coasting through my body fast, making me jolt a little.

"Welcome." He swallows and pulls away, taking my coat to the stand in the corner and hanging it with his. "I saved your favourite seat," he says as he pulls out my stool. "And ordered your favourite drink. But only one of them."

I get onto the stool, nodding my hello to Julio, as I pull my dirty martini close, noticing Dec's short glass. "What's your poison?"

He turns toward me on his stool, resting an elbow on the bar, his drink in his suspended hand, his other on his knee. "I've got a feeling it could be you."

God, you're poisonous.

My recoil is unstoppable, even if it's not justified, because the voice catches me off guard. And today, it hurts more. "And what if it is?"

"I'll find an antidote." Dec sips his drink, casual, considering me carefully.

"You want to cure me?" I ask, looking down, seeing our knees nearly touching. I discreetly put more space between them, though not discreetly enough judging by Dec's minuscule raised brow when he looks down.

"I never said that. The antidote is for me."

"When I poison you," I murmur.

"Will you?"

"Probably." I lose myself in my drink, wondering what I'm doing. Or what I'm saying. Managing his expectations? Managing mine? "So tell me why you're here early."

"Tell me why you are."

My shoulders drop a little. "Do you always answer questions with questions?"

"Why are you asking questions that you know the answer to? You know why I'm here. I know why you're here. What neither of us know is why we're here ourselves."

"You've asked yourself that?"

"Have you?"

I shake my head, smiling down at my lap. "A million times."

"Me too."

"And you don't know?"

"I know you're beautiful. That can't be missed."

"I know you're handsome." That *definitely* can't be missed.

"But I see many beautiful women. None of them have drawn me in like you, and it's really messing with my head, because there's an aura of graveness floating around you like a warning beacon." He watches for my reaction. He doesn't get one. "You won't let anyone in," he goes on. "You're a wounded animal ready to attack anyone who dares to try and get close."

"You dared."

"And I really don't want to live to regret it," he whispers, his eyes scanning every tiny bit of my face. "But I don't want to regret *not* getting too close too."

I still for a moment, soaking in his statement, before I lower my glass to the bar. Our knees have somehow got close again, the gap between them a hair's breadth. I don't make space again. It's pointless. He doesn't want to live with regrets. I have so many regrets, they've buried my soul. And yet endless questions run amok in my mind, but I can't ask any of them.

"Tell me about your day," Dec says, killing that topic of conversation.

"It was standard."

"What's standard?"

"Me buried under endless files and in endless emails trying to make what seems like the impossible, possible."

He nods, as if understanding. "Everything is possible."

That's not true. Happiness is impossible. "Tell me about yours."

"I worked from home, hence the casual attire." He motions down his jumper and jeans.

"Acquiring and merging," I murmur. "But mostly acquiring."

"That's right."

"And what did you acquire today?"

"A failing media company that's fallen on the modern-day online sword." His lips move with a slow purpose as he talks, his eye contact unwavering.

"And what will you do with it?"

"Sell it."

"You've bought it to sell it?"

"That's right."

"Where do you live?"

"Central."

"That's broad." He doesn't want me to know.

Knocking back his drink, Dec pushes his glass onto the bar, an instruction for another. "Have you signed your divorce papers yet?"

"Have you found your wife yet?"

His lips roll in, his smile suppressed, and for the first time I wonder where this is going. Whatever this is. This is taking a different direction to what I'm used to.

Small talk.

Bed.

Attempted release.

Forgotten.

And yet I've seen Dec three times now, we've not fallen into bed, and we're talking but both clearly being cautious, getting to know each other but also not.

But I feel like I know him.

The sound of my mobile ringing from my bag on the floor pulls my attention there, and I stare, in no rush to answer.

"Do you need to get that?" he asks.

"No." I redirect my attention to him. This suits me. This distraction suits me.

He suits me.

My stranger.

An hour later, we've talked more about nothing, shared many fleeting looks, and many long, lingering, heated gazes too. I know sexual chemistry when I feel it, it's different to simply being horny. I've never looked at any of the endless men I've slept with and paused a beat to admire them. Never wondered what they do, who they are, where they've come from. I need to rein in this wondering. Keep this clean. Am I a complete idiot?

Dec looks down at his watch. "I have to go," he says, sounding regretful. "I'll walk you home." He gets down from the stool and fetches our coats, while I check the time. It's not even seven. Too early for me to go home, plus I left the office without any files so there's nothing to keep me busy if I do go home now. I look around the bar instinctively, and when I realise what I'm doing, I pull myself up on it, finding Dec as he holds my coat up for me.

"You don't have to walk me home."

My coat drops a few inches, following his wide shoulders.

"Yeah, I do, Camryn," he says seriously, gazing around the bar to the few single businessmen. Just as I did. Leaning back on my stool, I suddenly understand what he's saying but not saying as he keeps my coat up.

It's beyond me why I do, but I stand and turn, feeding my arms through the sleeves, freezing when I feel his front meet my back, his arms reaching between mine for the belt of my coat. I look down at him tying it. Then he turns me and wraps my scarf around my neck, his face so close again as he concentrates on getting each end even. I stare at him. Just stare.

Mesmerised.

Confused by this. By *him*. By this whole thing that's going on.

Dec slips some cash onto the bar and swings his coat on as I get my bag, then holds his hand out to me. I hesitate. "Take it," he orders softly. I want to take it. I want to feel the warmth and strength of his hold around my hand. But, again, what is this?

Unable to answer, I tentatively accept and gulp down the endless, annoying questions. I don't have a moment to admire the sight of my hand being held before he's leading me out of the bar.

Dec doesn't let go the entire way back to my apartment, and I'm in utter awe of the strength pouring into me through our held hands. As we round the corner onto my street, he looks up to the dark sky, breathing in deeply. "Okay?" I ask.

"Yeah." He slows to a stop and directs me to in front of him, releasing my hand. I mourn the loss. Then we go through what's becoming so familiar and comforting, a dance of gazes drifting back and forth between our eyes and mouths. Does he want to kiss me as desperately as I want to kiss him? And why hasn't he? Why haven't I?

Because it might change this.

"Goodnight, Camryn," he says, reaching for my face and cupping my cheek, gently holding me.

I automatically nuzzle into it. "Goodnight."

The second he breaks contact, reversing his steps, I want to scream at him to come back. Hold me again, even if it's just my hand or my cheek. But he turns away before I have the chance.

Or can make that mistake.

I watch him until he disappears around the corner before I take myself inside. Closing the door behind me, I listen to the sound of silence for a few moments before flicking the lights on and tossing my keys on the table by the door. Wandering into the kitchen, I home in on the sound of the fridge whirring and drop my bag on the table. What the hell was I thinking letting him convince me to come home at this hour? Why the hell didn't I bring any files home? Why on earth haven't I slept with him yet?

Knock, knock, knock.

My body tenses, my gaze darting to the kitchen doorway. He's back.

Heat pounding, my mouth dry with anticipation, I walk faster than I would ever admit to the door and swing it open.

Coming face to face with someone I never want to see again.

"Camryn." My husband carries indifference so well these days. Did I ever know him? He walks past me without an invitation to enter and, as he has done on the handful of other times he's tracked me down to my apartment, stops and takes in the soulless space. But this time he doesn't pass comment on it. He pushes his jacket back and slips his hands into his pockets, facing me. Takes me in, up and down. I'd ask what he wants, but that would be a stupid question.

"You can leave," I say, keeping the door open for him.

"Not until you've signed the papers." He stalks into the kitchen, and I follow, finding him rummaging through my handbag.

"They're not in there," I say, folding my arms and resting my shoulder on the doorframe, fighting to keep the monster inside buried.

"Just sign the damn papers, Cam."

I bite down on my back teeth. "And agree to unreasonable behaviour?" No, I don't think so.

"You don't think you were unreasonable?" he asks, his surprise maddening, as he starts opening empty cupboards and drawers, searching. "I still can't believe you've not unpacked your fucking things."

"Get out," I grate.

He huffs and passes me, forcing my back to the door to avoid touching him. *Do not touch him.* I don't know how you can love someone and hate them at the same time. But I do. I love him. I love what we had, what we were. And now I hate him for destroying it all. Destroying *me*.

But I hate myself more.

He finds what he's looking for on the footstool and flicks through, looking for my signature, and exhales his exasperation when he doesn't find it, dropping them again, raking a hand through his hair. "Why are you dragging this out, Cam?"

I stare at him, out of words, but full to the brim with resentment.

Reaching into his pocket, he pulls out a pen and lays it on our divorce papers. "Please, just sign them." Then he walks out, slamming the door behind him. I roll onto my back, the silence screaming at me again, staring at the papers for an eternity.

Just sign them. Move on.

But I can never move on.

I leave the papers and head to the shower.

December 6th

I sigh and push the file away, resting my head back and looking at the ceiling. TF Shipping isn't strong enough, will never be at this rate, no matter what I do. I feel like I'm swimming against the tide, talking to a brick fucking wall. I pick up my desk phone and call Thomas's line.

"Camryn," he says, a definite wary edge to his voice.

"We need to talk."

"Why do we need to talk?"

Why do we need to talk? Yesterday, I tried to talk him out of thousands of pounds on unmerited bonuses—not that I was successful. TF Shipping needs to be attractive to an investment bank. We should have achieved the necessary profit margins within the last forty-eight months. There needs to be full business operational transparency, and I'm still finding odd transactions that have nothing to do with the business but are claimed as such. If Thomas wants to issue an initial IPO where an investment bank underwrites his process and determines share prices, then promotes stock for potential investors, he needs to have a clear reason for floating, and credible share price growth. His operating costs need to reduce, and profits need to increase. And yet . . . *We've been over this a thousand times, Thomas.* "You know what? I've nothing new to say. I'll review last month's figures." I hang up, frustrated, and email Finance for this month's numbers, answering my phone when it rings and placing it in the crook of my neck so I can keep typing. "Debbie."

"Thomas wanted me to remind you about Friday."

"I just spoke to Thomas. He never mentioned Friday. What's Friday?"

"The Dorchester at seven."

I inwardly groan. "Right, yeah. I said yes to that, didn't I?"

"And I have someone called Dec Ellis on the line for you."

My typing fingers still on the keys, my email unfinished. "Ellis?" He's not told me his surname. "Dec Ellis?"

"Shall I put him through?"

My stomach flips. "Um . . . yeah, sure, put him through." I wriggle my foot back into my heel under my desk and stand, picking up my phone and walking up and down. Nervous. *Alive.* "Hello?"

"Hey," he says, soft and low. I close my eyes and breathe through the shudder rippling down my spine. He really has the most incredible voice—deep but silky. "Lunch?"

"Lunch?"

"Are you free for lunch?"

"You want to have lunch?"

"No, I want to see you."

I stop pacing as a rush of warmth fills me. "I don't take lunches." Never. Not in the history of my employment have I taken a lunchbreak.

"Take one today."

I don't realise I'm biting down on my lip until I feel a sharp stab. Why am I doing that? Biting down on my lip, trying to stop myself smiling? Because I don't think I should smile? Am almost afraid to? For so long, I've stumbled through my days, hollow, lost, desperately sad, and now I don't know how else to be. But around Dec, the weight of my past seems to lift a little.

And that's something to smile about.

I breathe in deep, release my lip from my teeth, and allow myself the privilege of smiling, albeit small. "Okay."

An audible rush of breath travels down the line. Relief. "Where works for you?" he asks. "I'm at the top end of The Strand."

"I'm on the other side of Piccadilly Circus."

"Meet in the middle?"

"Now?"

"I'm on my way." He hangs up, and I pull my phone away, looking at the receiver. He's on his way. A surge of energy hits me, and I become a bit of a flustered—very unusual—mess, dropping my phone clumsily on my desk, getting all caught up in the cord as I do. "Fuck it," I say, trying to unravel myself. How the hell did it end up round my thighs? The door knocks. "Don't come in," I yell, just as the door opens.

Thomas stops dead in his tracks, taking me in, a state of a woman tangled in a bloody phone cord. "All right?"

"Fine." I lift a foot in turn and step out of my trap as gracefully as I can before claiming my bag and unhooking my coat off the wall. "I'm going for lunch."

"Huh?"

"Lunch. I'm going for lunch." I pass a very concerned-looking Thomas.

"You don't eat lunch. In fact, I've never seen anything but coffee pass your lips."

Thomas hasn't seen me outside these offices, where plenty of alcohol passes my lips. "See you in an hour or so." I walk with purpose to the elevator, disregarding the interested looks coming my way, and board, swinging on my coat, managing a quick check in the mirror. I pull my hair over one shoulder and lift the collar of my coat, and as soon as the doors open, I exit, walking with purpose.

Out my building.

Up Regent Street.

Across Piccadilly Circus.

Onto Leicester Square.

I'm very aware of Christmas on steroids around me, can smell the mulled wine and toasted chestnuts. But today, it's okay. I dip and weave through the endless crowds, urgent for a different reason.

Him.

I'm halfway across the square when I spot him, just one man amid masses of people.

And my heart blasts, pounding so hard, I can feel it in my throat. "God, you beautiful, unexpected man." I stop, a static form in the middle of the square, forced to take a moment and a breath at the sight of him. He stops too, seeming to take me in, his face endlessly expressionless. His suit's back, his navy, double-breasted overcoat fastened, his scarf wrapped around his neck. The way he stands, his stance wide, his body lifted from the chest, his hands in his coat pockets. *He's . . .*

Magnificent.

Strong.

I walk to him, our eyes glued, and slow to a stop a foot away. He says nothing, but he pulls a hand from one of his pockets and offers it to me.

Taking it is easy.

And without one word spoken but a million unspoken, he starts to walk us away from the chaos. Not that I'm registering the madness around me. The ball of anxiety isn't following me. I feel nothing, only awe and, I fear . . .

Something deeper.

Dec seems to know exactly where he's going. We arrive at a little deli on the corner of a back street, and he pushes his way in, making a bell above the door ding our arrival. There's room for only a handful of tables and chairs, all taken bar one at the back by the stairs. He unravels his scarf and hangs it with his coat on the back of a chair, and I follow his lead.

"Let me," he says, rounding me and easing my coat off my

shoulders. I feel his breath at my ear, his front virtually pushed into my back.

"Do you need to be so close when you help me out of my coat?" I ask, my smile hidden.

"Absolutely." His lips meet my jawbone, and the sensations are arresting. "Coffee?" he whispers.

"Please." I can hardly talk.

"How do you take it?"

"Black."

He breaks away, allowing me air, not that I want it, and hangs my coat on the back of my chair before he heads to the counter. Lowering to my seat, I watch him while he orders, the eternal impassive man not even cracking a smile for the server, just a stern nod when she says she'll bring our drinks over. Joining me back at the table, he sits in the chair, looking big and uncomfortable. His phone rings, forcing him up again to dig it out of his pocket. He rejects the call, and it immediately rings again.

"Do you need to get that?"

"Probably, but I don't want to." A fleeting moment of exasperation passes across his face.

"Bad day?"

"Had better," he replies sharply, rejecting the call again. "I had a last-minute unexpected rescue bid come in on a company I'm acquiring. I had to escape the circus for a while."

"So you called me."

One of his brows lifts, and he rests back in his seat as the server approaches, giving her room to slide the tray onto the tiny table. "Are you hungry?"

I shake my head and thank the server for my coffee and water. "Don't let me stop you."

"It's fine. I don't think we'll fit anything else on this table." He starts moving things around, a semi-scowl on his handsome face, making the lines across his forehead deepen. And his phone rings again. Every muscle in him seems to tense, his jaw twitching as if he's gathering patience. "Do you mind?"

I wave him off, taking some water as he answers.

"What?" he says, short, listening for a few moments, his eyes narrowing. He fascinates me. I could watch him for an eternity, and it's in this moment I realise he's not actually eternally impassive. I see emotion on his face, like now as he scowls his irritation. I've seen mild frustration, and I've seen relief. But no joy. No warmth, although I feel warmth from him. But does anyone else? Or do they get the stern man I'm looking at now, as he listens, obviously wound up about something? I can see why someone would be wary of him.

The formidable businessman.

Or simply a formidable man?

The person on the other end of the line's voice is clear, not because they're speaking loudly, but because it's so quiet in here. "What do you want us to do?" they ask.

"They want a bidding war, we'll give them one."

"Dec, as your adviser, I'm telling you you're already paying too much for this company."

"They're cowboys looking to make their name by chasing me out of the deal. I'm not backing down. Ten million."

"Jesus."

"Do it." He hangs up and calmly rests his phone down, taking a deep breath. "Tell me about your day."

"It sounds like it's going better than yours."

"Mine will be fine."

"You don't look like it will be."

"It will be. Tell me about your day." He picks up his cup and blows across the top, momentarily making me forget where I am and what I'm doing here. His lips . . . "Camryn?"

I blink and pull my thoughts into line. "I took this job two years ago." *It was a lifesaver.* "It was supposed to be a two-year project but I'm no closer to improving the numbers than when I first walked into TF Shipping, which is really hard for me to admit because I've done this a dozen times in my career, with success."

"My father lived by the rule that if something is draining you, walk away."

His father. The first mention of any family. "Who said I was drained?"

"Your entire aura."

I clear my throat and focus on my coffee, my hands wrapped around it. "It'll work out."

"And if it doesn't?"

"Then it doesn't," I reply simply. I've lost a lot more than my work reputation in this world. I'll live, for what living is worth. Which isn't much now. My life; it's just a crawl through a never-ending hell. "Does your father live in London?"

"He's dead."

I flinch. "I'm sorry."

"Don't be, I hated him." Dec finishes blowing his coffee and downs it. "Do you want my advice?"

"On what?"

"Your job."

"Go on."

"You can't pull a company into shape if you don't have the full commitment of the owner."

"I know that," I say, sounding bored. "I need another year."

"Why?"

"So I can get it in its best shape."

"You already wasted two years. You want to waste another?"

"I'm being paid."

"Are you enjoying it?"

"I didn't realise I was signing up for a career coaching session when I agreed to lunch."

"Are you enjoying it?" he repeats.

I sit back, wondering if he thinks my job forms part of the black cloud that's casting a shadow over my life. "No." It's a distraction, that's all. A distraction that turned into a challenge, which made it an even better distraction. "Do you enjoy what *you* do?" I fire back.

"Yes."

"What do you love so much about it?"

"Succeeding. Achieving." His lovely brow hitches a smidge. "Power."

"Are you an egomaniac?"

"No, Camryn. Are you?"

On reflection, I think I used to be. I was a ball-breaker. Top of my game. Now? Now I operate on fear. Not fear of losing respect in my field or failing, or even not being able to afford to pay my rent, but fear of not having a job, and failing could mean I lose my job. "I'm not an egomaniac." Although I'm one hundred percent certain every employee at TF Shipping, including my boss, his wife, and his son, would disagree. "I do, however, expect respect in the workplace."

"As you should." Dec's phone rings again, and he sighs, looking at me in apology.

"It's fine, you take it."

"It's my assistant," he says, taking his phone to his ear. "Tina." He listens, his eyes squinting. "Thanks." Hanging up, he turns his phone in his hold. "I have to go."

"Me too." I stand and swing on my coat. "But this was nice," I add, the words coming from nowhere. "Short but nice." I frown to myself as I collect my bag and Dec stands.

"Take your coat off."

"What?"

"Your coat, Camryn. Take it off."

"But I just put it on." I glance down my front. "Because we're leaving." Returning my eyes to Dec, I see impatience past the glittery grey of his gaze. It's beyond me why I do, but I place my bag on the table and slowly get out of my coat as Dec rounds the table and claims it. Then he moves in behind me and holds it up for me to slip my arms in. On an unsure smile, I do as I'm being silently bid, then I hold my breath when he moves into my back and reaches around me to tie the belt, virtually hugging me from behind. I savour his closeness. The feel of this man's warmth.

His stubble grazes my cheek, his smell overwhelming me.

"Now we can go," he murmurs in my ear. He must feel my shudder. "Ready?"

No. No, I'm not ready. But I nod anyway, accepting my bag when he hands it to me, and let him lead me out of the deli. When he walks in the direction of Regent Street—therefore away from The Strand where he works—I tug him to a stop. "You don't have to walk me back."

"I want to."

"But you have to go," I remind him.

"I like walking with you, so I'll walk with you." He pulls me on, and I follow, at the mercy of his hand holding mine tightly. And I'm smiling again. It's small, but it's there.

The crowds vanish, the world vanishes.

It's beautiful.

A small part of my mind is yelling at me, trying to break through this unfamiliar sense of peace, trying to remind me that getting close to anyone isn't an option for me anymore. Right now, while I'm holding his hand, it's easy to ignore it. But I know it will eventually catch up with me. Because how long can we do this without actually getting to know each other? Our histories. My pain. My demons.

This has an expiry date, and I really don't want it to.

With a few directions from me, Dec delivers me back to my office, and we stand on the pavement, face to face. "Don't go to the bar tonight," he says out of the blue, catching me off guard.

"Why?"

"Because I can't be there."

"Oh." I drop my gaze to my shoes, disappointed. "Is that why we did lunch with no lunch?"

"Yes. Tell me you won't go to the bar tonight."

"I can't do that."

"Why?"

Because now I know I won't see you, I'll need a drink. "Because I want to go to the bar tonight." Not that bar. *Any* bar.

He takes one step closer, looking down at me, our chests one inhale away from touching. "Please."

He knows. But he doesn't know. "Okay," I whisper, wondering what the hell my mouth is playing at. And my heart. What business does it have beating so fast around this man? And my head. It's thinking things it shouldn't be thinking. "I won't go." I look up at him and see his appreciation. "When will I see you again?"

"Get your phone," he orders gently, pulling his from his coat pocket and holding a hand out for mine. I unlock it and pass it to him, and he types in his number and calls himself. "I'll call you later."

"Okay." I don't have a moment to wonder if he will kiss me, because I'm suddenly completely enveloped in his body, being hugged like I never knew I needed to be hugged. My arms lift to his back and hold on, every inch of me softening into him. *I really like being held by you, Dec Ellis.*

He's pulling away too soon. "Speak later," he says, turning and leaving me on the pavement, desperate for another one of those hugs.

"Speak later," I whisper, as always, unable to rip my eyes away from him walking away. "Dec," I call. He stops and turns. "I can't have children." What the hell am I saying? Where did that come from? "I mean—" Oh God, he must think I'm completely off my rocker. We've had a few drinks. A few walks. I pull up and rewind. No. It's more than that. Because I thought I was emotionally dead, and yet he's made me start feeling again. "I can't have children," I say again, my eyes focused past him, something inside unwilling to see his reaction.

"Camryn," he calls, and I dare to look at him. "Me neither."

My entire being deflates, the rush of air that leaves me making the top half of my body fold over, too much to hide my relief. And my lip wobbles. My eyes sting. My heart bursts. "Okay."

"Okay," he mimics. "Can I go, now you've got that off your chest?"

"You don't smile much."

"Neither do you."

"I smiled earlier when you asked me to lunch."

And he smiles. It's like the sun breaking through a black, stormy cloud. And I think I fall in love with him on the spot. The thought jars me.

Fuck.

I pivot on my heels, hurrying into the building.

Smiling.

December 7th

I went straight home after work yesterday and waited for his call. It came at nine, and the rush of blood to my head made me dizzy, no matter how hard I tried to control it. I faced up to myself in the mirror—had a stern word with myself—and repeatedly stated that I'm not falling for him. I *can't* fall for him. And then I answered his call, heard his voice, and was freefalling once again.

I can't have children.

Me neither.

The question is, does he *want* them?

We talked for an hour. He walked me through the rest of his day—the ten million was accepted, the competition chased away—and I listened, his deep, smooth voice sinking past me and warming me deeply. The tug inside is getting stronger, as is my conflict. Getting close means getting *close*. Sharing.

Exposing myself, being vulnerable.

I hate it, but I also hate the constant constriction in my throat—*of having no purpose*—the dizziness, the regret, the heaviness.

The unbearable pain of self-inflicted solitude.

And the fact that his call brought light into the cold silence of my apartment. *My life*.

Don't grow dependent, Camryn.

How long can we talk, be together, and not get deeper? More personal? And will I withdraw when we do? Or is it okay to start feeling a modicum of joy? Have I done my time feeling so broken? They're all hard-hitting questions that I have no answers to. Will I ever?

Today's banal workday included waiting to hear back from Finance, which eventually happened at six o'clock. The company accountant requested a call tomorrow. I punch out a reply on my way to the elevator, slightly concerned by his request but too gripped by anticipation too see Dec to really pay much attention to it. "Camryn!"

I look back, seeing Debbie hurrying my way, today's tights a rare shade of emerald-green. She reaches up and pulls the reindeer antlers off her head, smiling awkwardly. She's obviously forgotten about the tinsel wrapped around her wrists and ankles. "You're late this evening," I say.

"I've been wrapping gifts for . . . never mind." She comes to a stop, a little out of breath, and realises she's forgot about her bracelets and anklets, quickly ripping them off. Her scraps of tinsel are the least of my problems. "The draw for Secret Santa was today." The caution in her voice is borderline pitiful. I know what's happened here. They've drawn straws over who's going to tell me who I need to buy for.

"And you excluded me from the draw, right?"

"Not right. You see, the new girl, Lacy, she wasn't told that you don't . . . well, take part, so you were included and emails have gone out to everyone. You've got me." She smiles, toothy and wide. Nervous. "But it's fine because I'll pretend I don't know who my gift is from."

"What's the budget?" The doors open, and I step inside.

"Twenty quid."

"I'll give you twenty quid. You can buy yourself something."

"Where's your Christmas spirit?"

"Dead."

"Right." She shakes her head in exasperation. "Thomas asked me to make sure you've not forgotten the event tomorrow evening."

"I haven't forgotten since the last time he asked you to remind me."

Her lips press into a straight line. "Dress code is glam."

My hand shoots up, stopping the doors from meeting in the middle. "Glam as in glamorous?"

She nods.

"Of course it is." I let the doors close and drop my head back, mentally searching through the endless unopened boxes for something I can wear. I see in my mind's eye many things I can't face, so actually searching them? No. I'll have to buy something.

My phone rings as I'm heading across the road to The Royal Constantine, and I stop just shy of the kerbside, my stomach dropping. "Hello."

"Mrs. Moore, it's D—"

"It's Ms."

"*Ms.* Moore, it's Deirdre from Long Acres."

"How can I help you?"

"It's your mother."

A horrible sick feeling rises. "What about her?"

"She's asking for you."

My spine lengthens, my eyes staring forward at nothing. "What?" She's not asked for me for months. Rarely recognises me at all anymore.

"She's getting rather distressed. Crying for you. I think you should come."

The lump in my throat is instant. I feel like I could choke when I try to swallow it down. "I'm on my way." I hang up and reroute to the Tube. No walking today, I haven't got time. I text Dec as I'm hurrying down the steps to let him know I can't make drinks, and he answers immediately, telling me to call him when I can.

She's asking for me?

I push my way through the door and dash past the receptionist. "Can you open the doors?"

"You need to sign in," she yells after me.

My teeth grit as I do an about-turn and rush back to the desk, scribbling my name, time, and who I'm visiting, throwing the pen back down. "Done." I hear the door click as I grab the handle, and I haul it open with too much force, making it smack the wall behind it. Mum's room in the last on the left, and I hurry in, out of breath but still managing to hold it. Three nurses are surrounding the bed, all bent over her. "Are you kidding?" I yell outraged, muscling my way through them. "She scarcely weighs ninety pounds, it does not need three of you to hold her down." No one should be holding her anywhere; it's not as if she can escape, she can't even fucking walk now, her strength gone. "Mum," I say, throwing my bag to the floor. "Mum, I'm here, it's okay."

Her flailing limbs still, her clenched eyes pop open, and she looks me directly in the eyes. My heart squeezes, searching for any recognition. *Please know who I am today. Please.*

"It's me, Mum. Camryn."

"They're trying to kill me!" she yells "Making me take pills so they can get my money. They've taken all of my money! The cash in the wardrobe. In a Tesco bag. They've taken it, the robbing bastards. They're stealing my money!"

"Your money is safe, Mum. I have your money." I've done this a million times and will do it a million more. "They were bringing your money to me so I can keep it safe for you."

Her frail body rolls with her laboured breathing. "Who are you?" My heart falls. "You're stealing my money too! I don't know this woman. Who is she? Get her out. Out!"

"Mum, it's me. Camryn," I say, moving in, taking her hand and holding on tightly. Desperately. *See me.*

"I don't know no Camryn."

"Your daughter. I'm your little buttercup, Mum."

Her hand comes at me so fast, I don't have a chance to dodge her slap, and my head snaps to the side, my neck cricking. The sting is instant, the afterburn brutal. "Shit," I whisper, releasing her and clenching my cheek. She's weak, yes, but that slap was far from it.

"Get her out!" she shrieks. "I want Noah. Where's my little Noah?"

I step away when the nurse moves back in, one of them armed with a needle. I can't watch, so I turn my back on my mum, thankful that she settles after they administer a sedative to calm her down.

She hit me. My mum hit me.

No, it's not your mum.

The confused, angry lady in that bed isn't the beautiful, kind woman who raised me. I'm still grieving the loss of her to Alzheimer's. "Let me check you over, Camryn," Deirdre says, coming at me, concern drenching her face.

"It's fine. I'm fine." I release my cheek, feeling a wet warmth trickling down my skin.

The nurse hisses, taking my wrist and pulling it down to get a better look. "She's caught you with her ring."

"I'm okay." I swoop up my bag and leave, the walls closing in again. I don't need to bang on the door this time, as another visitor is coming through when I get there. I make it outside and take a moment, wiping my sore cheek with a tissue from my bag, hissing and wincing. *Who is she? Get her out!*

My heart breaks a little bit more as I fumble through my bag for my phone, texting my brother.

I can't do this anymore. You have to come and help me.

My weak legs give way, and I lower to one of the steps, sliding my fingers into my hair. Clenching. *I don't know no Camryn.* What hurts most is she's right. I'm not her daughter. Not how she would have remembered her girl, if she could even remember. She doesn't know me. I don't even know myself anymore. Everything I've ever known, ever loved? It's all gone. Predictably, resentment and anger rise and start to blend with my relentless grief.

I check the time; it's just past seven.

A drink. I need a drink.

I clench the rail and drag myself up, my weary body protesting. But I don't go to the bar. I hate myself for it, but I don't go. Because today, oddly, I would hate myself more if I did.

And with that revelation bouncing around rapidly in my mind, I walk home, feeling the most alone I have since my life was torn apart.

As I turn up the path to the door of my building, I come to a startled stop, my lagging, tired mind trying to compute what I'm looking at. "Mr. Percival?" I say, tilting my head and dipping, seeing his snow boots sticking out from beneath the bottom of a Christmas tree.

That's wedged in the doorway.

"Yes, dear?" he yells, his voice muffled.

"Are you okay?" What a daft question. He's clearly not okay—the top half of his body's inside the building with the top of the tree, his lower half hanging out the door with the bottom of it.

"I seem to have got myself stuck."

"You don't say," I mumble, making my way up the path, something crunching under my heels. I look down, lifting each shoe, finding a blanket of pine needles paving the way. Did he actually drag this tree home from wherever he's bought it? How? He can hardly hold himself up. I shake my head and assess the situation. This tree is worthy of Trafalgar Square, for Christ's sake. Bending, looking through the busy branches, I try to figure out who to try and get out first—the tree or Mr. Percival. "Are you lying down?"

"I fell, dear. Or folded."

"Are you hurt?"

"Only my ego, dear."

I huff, dropping my bag and scanning up and down. "I'm going to have to push it through."

"Okay, dear."

"It might strip some of the branches."

"Okay, dear. I'm starting to get cramp in my thigh. Would you mind hurrying things along?"

"Jesus Christ." I push my hand through the foliage and take hold of the trunk, giving it a little wiggle. "Ready?"

He grunts, as do I when I push my weight into the tree, getting a face full of branches. "It's *really* stuck," I puff, leaning into it more, bracing myself for the moment it dislodges. "Okay down there?"

"I can see light."

"But it's dark."

"The hallway lights. Keep pushing!"

"Fucking hell," I grumble, kicking my heels off to get better stability. A loud crack sounds, and I'm suddenly stumbling forward. "Shit." I release the tree and grab the doorframe, saving myself, as the tree shoots forward and Mr. Percival's arms raise, fighting off the attack of branches.

"What a disaster!" He chuckles, rolling from side to side. "I might need a hand, dear."

Exasperated, I go to him, taking both his old hands and easing him up slowly, watching his worn old face for discomfort, worried he's broken something. "Are you sure you've not hurt yourself?"

"Yes, yes, very sure."

Only when I'm certain he's steady on his feet do I release him, and he brushes himself down and shuffles round to take in the damage. "Where's your walking frame?" I ask.

"In my flat."

"Well, that's a bit silly, isn't it?" I find my heels and hang on to the doorframe as I get them on. "How long have you been here?"

His watch appears from his pocket, and he holds it up close and personal to his face. "Thirty-five minutes."

"Mr. Percival." I scold him lightly, dipping to pick up his flat cap. "What are you doing dragging trees five times the size of you around? You should have called someone."

"Like whom?" He faces me as he slips his watch back into his pocket, accepting his hat and popping it on.

"I don't know. Family?"

"I don't have one of those, dear." Taking hold of the wall, he gingerly steps up the corridor over various arms of the tree. No family at all? "So you're going to have to help me."

He's all alone. Not through choice. "Help you?" I retrieve my bag and put it on the stairs. "Right, yes. Help you."

Mr. Percival places his hands on his hips and stands over the tree, and I join him, kicking my shoes back off. "Camryn, you're bleeding!" A hanky is quickly on my cheek, dabbing. "Oh no, well now I feel terrible."

Telling him the tree isn't responsible for my injury would mean telling him who is. But not telling him means he'll feel guilty, and I don't want the old boy to feel bad. "It's okay, it wasn't the tree." I scratch through my mind for something—anything—I can claim *is* responsible. "I wasn't looking where I was going in the office and got caught up in some Christmas decorations."

He withdraws and checks my cheek. "You need some alcohol on that."

"Let's get this monster of a tree in your apartment first, shall we? It's blocking the way." Turning back to the tree, I ponder how exactly I'm going to manage this. Mr. Percival is a small, frail old man. So I'm on my own.

Lunging over the tree, I bend and grasp the top with both hands, starting to drag it toward his front door. "We should go in bottom first so the branches bend the right way through the door."

"Good idea." He hobbles to his front door and opens it.

Endless needles stab my feet as I hoof the tree up and prop it against the wall, my breathing already shot. "Right." I bend and grab the trunk, backing up until I have to lean back, tugging on endless grunts to get the fattest end through. "It's going to be bald, Mr. Percival. Why on earth did you buy such a big tree?"

"For the gnomes, dear."

"What?"

"And Maureen. She likes a big tree." Maureen. Lady friend? "That's it, dear, you're nearly there."

The rustle of branches has me wincing, as they're surely scratching all the paintwork off, but it's plain sailing once the base dislodges, only sheer endurance required to drag it into his lounge. "There." I push it up against the nearest wall and blow out my cheeks, knackered, my surroundings registering as I slowly turn on the spot, taking it all in.

"What a lifesaver you are, dear." Mr. Percival shuffles through the clutter with ease, not even looking down to make sure he won't stumble over any of the endless trip hazards. And he's completely unperturbed by my obvious surprise. "Now if we could just get it in the bucket I can pour this bag of sand in." Another chuckle. "Don't tell anyone, but I pinched it off the building site at the end of the road." Facing me, he frowns. "Are you okay, dear?"

My eyes cast across his lounge again, feeling watched by the million sets of eyes staring back at me. "Mr. Percival, why is your lounge full of gnomes?"

"Oh!" He chuckles and takes one that's nestled in the corner of one of his recliner armchairs, looking at it fondly. It's Father Christmas—its face jolly, its cheeks red, a lantern held up in one hand. "I'm rather attached to them, dear."

"How many do you have?"

"Last count, nine hundred and three."

I cough and peek through a doorway to his small kitchen. More gnomes. Everywhere—on the table, the counter, the floor, the window ledge. I laugh under my breath at the fisherman on the edge of the sink with a fish dangling on the end of his line.

"I couldn't let them go, you see, when I moved from my semi in Epsom, and I have no outside space here. So they live with me indoors these days." He places Father Christmas back in the chair. "Now, about this tree."

. . .

Half an hour later, I've tripped over endless gnomes and Mr. Percival has tripped over none, but the tree is in the bucket, and I've emptied the bag of sand in too, making sure it's secure. "Maybe a smaller tree next year," I suggest, gazing up the length. The top is bent over by a foot, wedged against the ceiling. "I think we need to trim it."

"Hmmm." He stands beside me. "It didn't look this big in the garden centre."

Something kicks inside me, and suddenly all I can see is my husband staring at our newly delivered corner couch in the lounge taking up two thirds of the space, me beside him.

"I hope you weren't planning on having anything else in here." He looks at me, eyebrows raised.

"It didn't look this big in the store."

"The store is the size of a hangar, Cam. Our lounge is twenty feet by thirty."

I dance forward and fall into the corner, snuggling. "But it's super cosy."

"It's practically a bed."

I laugh, giving him grabbing hands, and he rolls his eyes, coming to me and falling onto the velvet fabric. "See," I say, rolling over into his side. "And it'll last until we're old, wrinkly, and still in love."

"I'm sure it will."

I snuggle into his chest and sigh.

"Camryn?"

I look to my left, finding Mr. Percival holding up a shoebox full of mini hanging gnomes. "You can help decorate it if you like."

"I have to go." Pivoting, I make my escape, stopping when I see one of the gnomes, his trousers pulled down over his arse, pissing up a wall.

"Make sure you clean that cheek!"

"I will." I leave, collecting my kicked-off shoes from the floor and my bag from the stairs, hurrying to my apartment and closing the door behind me.

I don't know no Camryn.

I'm sure it will.

The urge to open the door again and head to a bar overcomes me, and I push the back of my head into the wood, gritting my teeth. "No," I say to myself, gazing around the soulless space as I shrug out of my coat. I hold it up and see half of Mr. Percival's tree is littering it, and a quick feel of my hair confirms a head full of needles too. Dropping my shoes to the floor, along with my coat, I pad across the wooden floor, heading for my bathroom. I need to feel . . . I don't know. Something other than this suffocating solitude.

Dim light glows down on me as I stand in front of the mirror, stripping out of my clothes until I'm naked. I sweep my hair back over my ears, my gaze falling to my breasts. It's been a while since I've seen them. Or felt them. Many men have over the past two years, but never me. I reach for one and cup it, the flesh spilling over my hold, and I start to massage, watching as my nipple slowly hardens until it's a small bullet, the areola perfectly round and dark against my olive skin. I tilt my head as I massage the other, thinking how they're not as high as they once were. Not as pert. They're useless now. Except for pleasure. Not mine, but men's. A handful for them, just enough. Soft skin, nicely shaped nipples that point in the right direction. My gaze moves up and meets my reflection. What are these thoughts?

Toxic.

I drop my breasts, look away from myself, and step into the shower, hoping the pounding water beats away the torment in my mind. It doesn't. As I soap my body, I see my mother. When I wash my hair, I hear my soon-to-be ex-husband telling me he's leaving. Closing my eyes, I see my perfect life playing out in the darkness, a reel of snapshots flickering through my mind. My wonderful father. A mother who knows me. A husband who loved me unconditionally. Until he didn't. My fingers clench at my hair as I stand under the spray, my gaze dropped, watching the soap slide down my wet body and gather around the drain. The building tears are from the soap that has gotten into my eyes. *I don't cry anymore.*

Turning my face up, I let the water run into them, rinsing them clean. It's then I hear something in the distance and shut off the shower, listening as I reach for a towel and pat my face. It comes again, this time louder now the water isn't raining down around me. Knocking. "Shit." I make a rushed, half-baked attempt of drying myself, my thoughts going to Mr. Percival and what mess he may have got himself into now. "Coming," I call, leaving my hair sopping wet, pulling on my robe and hurrying to the door as I tie the belt. Wet strands stick to my neck, the cool hallway air hitting my damp legs. I gather up my coat and shoes and shove them on the table before I swing the door open.

My breath catches at the back of my throat.

"Dec?" I murmur, tugging my robe in. "What are you doing here?"

Standing on the threshold, dishevelled but glorious, his stormy eyes search mine. "I needed to see you." His voice is low, tinged with something I can't quite pin. Urgency? Concern? His eyes darken more as they settle on my cheek, and he steps closer, his broad frame filling the doorway. "What the hell happened to your face?"

"It's nothing." I blink, my fingers unconsciously touching the cut on my cheek. The sharp sting catches me off guard, and I pull my hand away to find a little blood.

"What happened, Camryn?"

"Just an accident. Really, it's fine."

"Camryn." His voice softens, but the intensity in his gaze doesn't waver, and I shift under his scrutiny, acutely aware of the robe wrapped around me and the water trickling down my back from my drenched hair. Dec reaches out, his fingers hovering near my cheek. "Talk to me."

I move back a pace. Talk. Sounds easy, doesn't it? "You

shouldn't have come." I don't want him to see this place. Judge me. Wonder why the hell I live in such stark solitude.

"You didn't answer my messages, and I—" He lets out a rough breath, undoing the space I've just put between us, his hand resting on my cheek. "I've been worried."

My heart thuds, my resolve cracking under his touch. It isn't fair how easily he can dismantle my walls, how just his presence filling this small, desolate apartment suddenly makes it bearable.

"I was just in the shower," I murmur, unsure why I feel the need to explain. It's quite obvious. "I haven't checked my phone."

His thumb brushes near the cut, as gentle as a feather. "You're hurt."

"It's nothing, just a scratch." My words are sure, though my voice betrays me. Yes, it's just a scratch, but how it came to be marring my cheek isn't nothing.

"You're shaking."

I hadn't realised I was. Whether from the chill of the air or his closeness, I couldn't tell you. Dec closes the door behind him, his presence wrapping around me like a warm, strong—needed—protective blanket. "Let me take a look," he says softly.

I hesitate for a moment, but the pleading in his unsettled eyes unravels my flimsy resolve. Talk. I'm going to have to talk. The closer I'm getting to him, the closer he's getting to my life.

Am I ready for that?

I'm not only letting him into my apartment if I don't ask him to leave. "Okay," I breathe, stepping back, opening up the way to him.

An odd sense of shame cloaks me as Dec passes me and casts his eyes around the space. I follow him, fixing my robe that really doesn't need fixing, my mind emptying. I don't know what to say, and for the first time when I've been with him, the silence is uncomfortable. What is he thinking? What is he making of my sparse apartment? I can't even offer him a tea or a coffee, unless, of course, he takes them black. It also occurs to me as I trail behind him that he's the first person I've invited in. My husband's never invited—he just helps himself when he wants to put pressure on me. And on that thought, my eyes fall to the footrest where my divorce papers are, the pen on top.

Unsigned.

Dec stops, reaching up to his neck, scratching it lightly under his ear. It's a classic sign of someone wondering what the fuck they're faced with. I start preparing my response to his impending interrogation, my chest tightening with a pressure I've never had to deal with before. Or cared to.

"Have you just moved in?" he asks. I can't see exactly where his eyes are directed, but I know, I just know, they're taking in the boxes that are stacked everywhere, five high and as many wide.

"Yes," I say, as simple as that, because what else can I say?

He turns to me, his face not questioning. It's not anything, really. It's just what I've come to expect—and like—from Dec. Impassive. No judgment. No pressing. "But . . ." He takes another peek around. Then he shrugs off his coat and lays it on the back of the armchair. "Never mind. Let me look at that cut." He points to the doorway across the room. "Kitchen?"

I nod, and he wastes no time heading that way, causing the tightening in my chest to squeeze further. A vision creeps into my mind, one of my pills on the counter by the sink. Following him on quick, bare feet, I overtake him and slide them off the counter, slipping them into my robe pocket before heading to the fridge. I know he's watching me. "Can I get you a water or anything?"

"What are the *anything* options?"

I still, staring at the fridge. "I've not got to the supermarket this week."

"Then I guess I'll take the water option."

I clench my eyes shut briefly and move across to the cupboard where I would keep glasses if I had more than two and they weren't on rotation—in the dishwasher or on my bedside table. And now, they're both on my bedside table. I open the cupboard and close it again.

"Out of glasses?"

"Yeah." I want the ground the swallow me whole. "Just give me a second." As I'm passing him, he takes my wrist, stopping me.

"Don't worry about the water."

A lump builds in my throat, infuriating me, and I look at him, desperate for him to see me. Understand me. But I'm terrified he could never. And then I wonder why now I care.

Again, it's a stupid question.

He's so unexpected, a relief from life I never dared wish to have. A distraction of the kind I could never consider, because the constant, consistent stench of misery lingers around me, day in, day out. He doesn't know me. He doesn't know anything, and if sharing might mean he walks away, I can't let my walls drop. On top of that, the thought of being vulnerable, of showing him who I am and why I'm so utterly broken, makes me want to curl into a tighter ball than I usually do.

"Fuck, I hate this look on you," he breathes, turning into me and completely encasing me in his arms. I melt into him, letting him hold me up, hugging me like I'd never admit I need to be hugged. It's beautiful, and the tears that haven't come for so long pinch at the backs of my eyes. I don't know why I do, it seems really fucking pointless, but I will them away with everything I have. I don't want to be pathetic to him.

A voice in my head screams, *too late!*

And yet he's still here. Hugging me.

The strength in his cuddle should crush my weak form, but I never want him to let me go. He couldn't get me any closer if he tried, our chest's compressed, his arms around my shoulders overlapping, squeezing me to him. His mouth is resting on top of my head, his breath hot against my cold, wet scalp. And he holds me. And holds me. My fingers claw into the back of his suit jacket, clinging on. So much warmth. So much strength. I feel so safe.

At least, for now. In this moment. Can it last? *Will* it last?

It's too soon—never would be too soon—but he eventually gently pulls away, just enough to look down at me buried in his chest. I tilt my head up, catching his eyes. I could drown in them.

I've thought about many ways to die, and I'd do it happily right now. "I'm here," he says gently, bringing one hand to my face and tracing the line of my jaw. So gentle. And as he showers me in his concern, I realise Dec's not the man I first pinned him as.

Cold.

He's got so much depth. So many sides.

They all intrigue me. He's so multifaceted.

"My cheek was my mother," I say, my mouth developing a mind of its own. "She's not well."

His heavy brow becomes heavier with a frown. "Is that why you couldn't meet me?"

I nod, small and reluctantly. "I got a call from the care home. It's Alzheimer's. They said she was getting herself in a pickle, was asking for me."

There's definitely a fleeting look of relief that passes across his face, and it makes me wonder what conclusions he was drawing about my injury, or about why I cancelled meeting him. "Come." He walks me to one of the two chairs and pulls it out, encouraging me to sit, before he leaves the kitchen and comes back with his coat, his hand in his inside pocket. He pulls out a pack of tissues and goes to the sink, running some water over one. He carries a pack of tissues. How charming. "This will have to do." Dragging the other chair close, he sits and leans in, dabbing at my cheek. I watch him, completely fascinated by the concentration on his face, the lines on his forehead deep. "It's not so bad." One more dab before he puts the tissue on the table and exhales, leaning back in his chair.

I reach up and feel. "It was her ring," I explain. "She was lashing out."

"How long has she been in the care home?"

"Two years. She's gotten worse these past few months. Hasn't recognised me for some time, but they called as I was leaving the office and said she was asking for me. But when I got there . . ."

I don't know no Camryn.

"I'm sorry," Dec whispers.

"You don't have to be sorry."

"But I am."

He's sorry. I don't want him to be sorry. I want him to be the medicine I need. The cure. And yet I know deep down in my gut I'm incurable. There's nothing to be done but accept things will never be the same.

"Why can't you have children?"

His question jars me, and my eyes instinctively drop, avoiding his suddenly shrewd gaze. "Women's problems," I murmur. "You?"

"Men's problems." A strong palm lands on the towelling robe covering my thigh, squeezing gently. I stare at his long, thick fingers. His nails are clean, short, and neat. The indentation on his ring finger catches my eye, and without thought or instruction, my right hand reaches for my left and feels at where my rings once sat. The rings that are now lost at the bottom of the Thames, thrown there in a moment of insanity and rage. "Let me take care of you," he murmurs, his words a silky, cruel promise that sink deep inside me. Words that should be dug out immediately. "Your hair needs drying."

I look up at him. Of course he didn't mean to actually look after me forever. Dec hadn't originally struck me as the kind of man looking for forever. Now, after seeing various sides of him, I honestly don't know what to think. But it's all moot, anyway, because even if he was, I can never have a happy, content, peaceful forever, and that's nothing to do with Dec. "Then dry it." The temperature in the room shifts significantly, his eyes smoking as he moves his palm in small, steady circles on my thigh.

"I will."

"That sounds like a threat."

His parting lips are arresting as he swallows hard, blinking repeatedly. I can't help but wonder if he's fighting the urge to take in my robe. Remove it. *Expose me.* Both of us suddenly seem acutely aware that there's merely a loose scrap of soft towelling between my naked body and his hungry eyes. "Maybe it is." His hand glides inward a few inches, getting alarmingly close to the bare flesh of my inner thigh. My naked pussy. A surge of desperation rushes south, making me throb so hard, I'm sure he can feel it. I want to kiss him. I want to kiss him so badly, to taste his tongue, feel his soft, wet lips on mine.

Fascination and anticipation swirl in my tummy as he finally allows his gaze to fall down my front. I've never felt so bared, even completely covered. He swallows hard, blinking rapidly for a few painfully long moments, before he seems to shake himself from his thoughts, retreating. My heart screams for him to come back. My head wills him out of my life.

"Where will I find your hair dryer?" He stands abruptly, so abruptly the legs of his chair scrape the tile floor, filling the kitchen with an ear-piercing screech.

I look at him towering over me. Can he see the devastation in my eyes? He's had multiple opportunities to kiss me, and he's taken none. "In my bedroom." Uncertainty weighs me down as I stand and leave him in the kitchen, cringing my way to the bedroom, wondering if I'm being ridiculous, imaging the brief moments of electricity between us. Is it hope and nothing else? For over two years, my mind has been so reliant on any form of distraction I can find, I'm scared I'm reading into things that shouldn't be read into. Take the sex. It's what I've done—given my empty vessel of a body to any man who's unknowingly offered me a respite from my wretchedness. Screamed while they've fucked me, stroked their egos, and made them feel like heroes.

No numbers are exchanged. No feelings are ever caught. There's no meaningful conversation. Not even a kiss goodbye when I dress and leave their room before they've even caught their breath. There are only suggestive smiles. Meaningless, brief pleasure.

I go to the corner of my bedroom. My dryer's in front of the mirror propped against the wall, the lead in a tangled mess. It takes me a good two minutes to unravel it, and when I turn, I find Dec in the doorway taking in this room too. The unmade bed. The closed curtains. The makeshift rail in the corner where a few work dresses hang, the rest of my clothes strewn on various pieces of furniture—the chair in the corner, the blanket box at the end of my bed, the headboard, the chest of drawers. A new dose of shame grabs me. "Life's been a bit hectic lately."

"Sorry?" Dec blinks again, his impassiveness turning my way. I can see it on him, even if he's trying so very hard not to let it show. Shock. Disgust?

"It doesn't matter." I pass him, and he's once again claiming a limb to stop me. I freeze, staring forward, scared to look at him.

"Something tells me it does matter," he says quietly, his hand sliding down into mine and holding it.

Why am I letting him in? Because this? It doesn't feel good. I cast my eyes to his, only my head moving. "It really doesn't." I gently pull my hand from his grip. "This is too much."

"What's too much, Camryn?"

"You. Here. In my . . . space." I toss my hair dryer onto my bed, and it bounces a few times, before it gets lost in the strewn covers.

"Actually," he whispers, his big body turning slowly into me. "I don't think it's enough." His exhales roll over my exposed skin like delicate licks of a cool breeze on an unbearably hot day. Relief. Our gazes collide, and a swirl of fire stares back at me. And then his lips are creeping closer. My chest swells as I suck air deep into my lungs. "Goodnight, Camryn," he breathes across my mouth, diverting his lips to my cheek and kissing it softly.

Such a small thing.

And yet the impact sends my entire world spinning so fast, everything's suddenly a blur, and all I can hear is my mind yelling at me to embrace this unexpected gift. He saturates my senses. With just a kiss on my cheek. His heady, musky but clean scent bombards my nose, his rough stubble scraping my freshly washed face. Every nerve seems to spark all at once, reminding me I'm alive. And in this moment, alive feels good.

"Goodnight," I murmur as he breaks away, so slowly, I'm sure I could lose my mind if he doesn't free me of every beautiful, intoxicating piece of him. Leaving me an inert, breathless statue in my bedroom, he walks out, and a few moments later I hear the door close quietly behind him. My hand lifts to my face where he kissed me. To the small cut.

It doesn't sting anymore.

Gazing around the bedroom, I take in the jumble sale before me. It *does* matter. *I* matter. This isn't how I want this room to be.

So I slowly start to collect up all the strewn clothes and hang them on the rail.

December 8th

A string of bunting attacks me as I step off the elevator the next morning, my sight robbed from me by a mass of swinging elves in my face, the cord they're dangling from all caught around my head. My knee-jerk reaction to rip them all off nearly gets the better of me, my hands flexing and fisting as a collection of gasps ring out and then . . . silence. My mind's eye gives me a clear vision of Crystal staring in horror, wondering why of all the people in this office who could have exited the elevator at this very moment, it was me.

Reaching up to my face, I calmly pull the elves away, finding her. She's still on the stepladder, one end of the bunting hanging limply from her grasp. "Let me help you," she blurts out, scrambling down and rushing to me as I try unsuccessfully to unravel the string.

"Jesus Christ," I mutter, now tied up around the waist. "There's not enough decorations splattered all over the place already?" The coiled string falls to my knees. If I try to walk, I'll fall flat on my bloody face. "You'll have to cut it."

"Cut it?"

"Yes, cut it."

"But then it'll be ruined," she says, crouching in front of me, frantically trying to unravel the knots. "Just give me a minute."

"I don't have a minute, Crystal, I have to dial in on a call."

"This moment?"

I look around, spotting Debbie coming this way, her face a picture of surprise and horror at the sight of me mummified by bunting. "Scissors," I bark, making her jump before she dashes into the nearest office and appears a moment later brandishing a pair.

"No, it's okay, I've nearly got it," Crystal says from the floor, her face up close to my knees as she picks at the string.

Debbie passes the scissors, and I dip, snipping my way through the bunting. It falls to the floor in various pieces. "There." A few bits dangle from my legs, and I reach down as I stride on, pulling them all off and dropping them, leaving a trail of broken elves in my wake. "Can I get an espresso?" I call back, pushing into my office. As I turn to close the door, Thomas appears, all smiles. I've worked for this guy long enough to know what I'm looking at. He's nervous. His smile twitches when he's nervous. "What is it?" I ask.

"Tonight. You haven't forgotten, have you?"

"No, Thomas, because you had Debbie remind me numerous times." Fuck, why did I agree to go, especially on a Friday? And, fuck, fuck, fuck, I have nothing to wear.

"Okay, was just checking."

"What time?"

"Seven."

"Remind me where."

"The Dorchester."

"Got it." I go to shut the door, but he puts his hand out, stepping forward, albeit apprehensively. "What now?"

"The dress code—"

"Is glam for glamorous, I know."

"And Christmassy."

And there explains the nerves. "Christmas glam," I say, wary.

"Yeah."

I laugh, slamming the door, making him jump back to avoid

being clattered in the face. "Shit." I look down at my watch. *Double shit.*

Scooting around my desk, I drop into my chair and quickly dial in, kicking my shoes off. Jeff—a poker-faced string of a man with wire hair and a bulbus nose too big for his face—is waiting, head down as he makes notes. He doesn't look up, even after the system dings my arrival to the meeting. I like Jeff. No small-talk is expected, and there's no diversion from business or annoying intervals. He gets done and gets off. "Morning, Jeff," I say, pulling my phone out of my bag and setting it on my desk.

"Morning," he says, still not looking up. I've had meetings with Jeff before when he's not looked at me the whole time. He's marvellously efficient. "You requested the accounts."

"I did."

"You're not going to like what you see."

I sigh. "Half expected."

"And they're not finalised just yet."

"Can you give me drafts?"

"Indeed."

"Thanks."

"By end of play today."

I lean forward on my forearms, my brow knitting. "You wanted a call, Jeff. Why?"

"Just wanted to say goodbye."

"You're retiring?"

His pen stops moving across the notepad, and he slowly lifts unamused eyes to mine. I know instantly I've put my foot in my mouth. "I'm fifty."

Fuck. Life has *not* been kind to him. My flinch is hard. Do I look older than my years, because life has definitely been cruel to me? A total, unrelenting, brutal bitch, actually. "Of course," I say, shrinking. "So, where are you going?"

"Nowhere."

"I'm really fucking confused, Jeff."

"I'm saying goodbye, because you're leaving TF Shipping."

"I am? Since when?"

"When you see the accounts that land in your inbox later today and you quit." Jeff disappears from my screen, just as a knock rings out. "Yes, Thomas?"

He pops his head around the door. "I have a problem."

So do I, it seems, Thomas. "What's the problem?" Fucking hell, how bad is it? Irreparable? *I need this job.*

"I need to launch an investigation and I'll be spending money."

"Why? The investigation, not the money."

"There's been a complaint made about someone."

"Who?"

"Meredith."

"Why?"

"She got a little . . . aggressive toward someone."

"Meredith from Payments?"

"Yes."

"Who was she allegedly aggressive toward?"

"Phillip."

My eyes widen and blink. "Her husband?"

"Yeah. They've separated."

"Right." I rise, marching around my desk and past Thomas.

"What are you doing?"

"Dealing with it."

"Whoa, Camryn, we have to follow protocol." He chases my heels, blabbering a load of nonsense about policies and employee rights. I make it to Meredith's office. Poor thing looks scared out of her skin faced with me. Placing my palms on her desk, I lean closer, dropping my voice. "What's going on?"

Her eyes dart, checking the vicinity before she swallows, regret contorting her pretty face. "He called me crazy."

"Well, that's not so bad." Thomas pipes up from behind me, laughing lightly but stopping the moment I turn a killer glare his way.

"I'm not crazy," she says meekly. "I'm emotional. How does he expect me to be? He's telling everyone I'm unhinged."

And now he's trying to get her fired. "Where did you supposedly get aggressive toward him?"

"In the kitchen."

"When?"

"Last Friday when we all finished early and Thomas brought in the champagne to celebrate December." Her lip wobbles. "I mean, I'd had a glass, but I wasn't drunk, Camryn."

I turn on my heels and head for the security office, entering and asking one of the tech people to pull up the kitchen CCTV from last Friday. "Sorry, I don't have it."

"What do you mean, you don't have it?" I ask, watching as he merrily goes back to his screen, not giving me a second look.

"I mean, we assess footage regularly and delete it from the server to free up disk space."

"Fuck." I turn and leave, feeling myself getting more and more worked up.

"Ms. Moore?"

I stop and find one of the juniors pulling the door to the security room closed behind him. "Can I have a quiet word?"

Thomas looks between us, frowning. "What is it, Reggie?" he asks.

I point to a spare office, and he nods, accepting my silent offer and wandering in. I follow him and watch as his hands play nervously, closing the door when Thomas is through it. "I don't want any backlash." he says.

"For what?" I ask.

"Telling you something."

"Go on."

He nods. "We keep footage for two weeks."

"But it's only been one week since last Friday," I muse.

"I came back from my lunch early yesterday and found Phillip West in the security office. He was handing over some money."

I laugh, a light puff of utter disbelief, and slam my phone down, making both Reggie and Thomas jump. "The arsehole."

"Oh no," Thomas breathes. "Before you go in all guns blaz—"

I march out, on a mission, straight to Phillip's office. He's reclined in his chair behind his desk, relaxed on the phone, unperturbed, unbothered by the fact his wife's falling apart. Just cracking on with his life, trying to eradicate her from his. Get rid of the *crazy*.

While simultaneously getting rid of the guilt he doesn't want to feel for upending her world.

"I'll call you back," he says, setting the phone in the cradle. "What can I help you with, Camryn?"

"You're fired."

He laughs, eyes moving to Thomas beside me. "What?"

I don't repeat myself, joining him on his side of the desk and pulling open drawer after drawer, scooping out the contents and dumping it on his desk.

"What the fuck are you doing?" he blurts, pushing away in his chair. Removing himself from the *crazy* woman.

"I'm helping pack your shit, Phillip, so we can get you away from all these crazy women before they cause you mental distress."

"Are you fucking joking? She slapped me."

"Really?" I ask, facing the waste of space.

"Yes, really. You can't fire me, you need to fire *her*."

"You want us to fire your wife?"

"Yes. She's lost the fucking plot."

"Why?"

He recoils, eyes darting between us. "We've separated." He looks at Thomas. "You know that. She's being unreasonable. Completely off her fucking rocker."

My blood simmers so hot, I'm sure it could burn its way through my veins and have me bleeding out. "Would you prefer a hearing? You sitting opposite Thomas, me, and the board while we talk about how you paid someone in security to wipe the footage from the system that shows your wife *not* being aggressive toward you? *Not* slapping you?" I have to steady myself on the side of his desk to stop myself staggering back with the force of my raised voice. "Would you prefer that, Phillip?"

Poor, useless fuck head looks startled. "No, I wouldn't prefer that."

"Didn't think so." I shove his stuff across his desk. He's a bully. I fucking hate bullies. *You hate everything, Camryn.* "I'll get you a box." I walk out, vaguely registering Thomas's wary eyes on me as I go. What a fucking start to my day. "I need a box," I bark at Debbie when I make it to her desk. She blinks at me. *Calm down.* "I need a box, please," I say, softer, straining a smile.

She magics one from the cupboard behind her desk. "Everything okay?" she asks, cautious.

"Just dealing with one of life's injustices." The irony that I'm about to pack today's injustice into a box and snap a lid on it doesn't escape my notice as I walk back to Phillip's office and dump the box on his desk. He still appears in a state of shock, his usually loud, tall presence shrunk. "Security will see you out." I glance at Thomas who nods at my silent request to call someone to escort Phillip off the premises, and then I go back to my office and sit quietly in my chair for half an hour, cooling off. I close my eyes and rest my head back, seeing my unsigned divorce papers. *Unreasonable behaviour*. Was it any fucking wonder?

I exhale and reach for my throat, massaging the lump away. Then I send a message that I really don't want to send.

I have a work commitment this evening.

He replies quickly.

What time will you be done?

Eight, maybe nine.

The three dots on the screen dance forever, to the point I'm obsessing about what he's saying that could take so long. And my heart sinks when I read his message.

I'll call you tomorrow.

I drop my phone on my desk heavily, breathing deeply. Calming the storm within. Tomorrow. It feels like an eternity away from relief.

At four, I pack up and leave, clocking Debbie's raised brows as I go. "Off to buy an outfit for tonight?" she asks as I breeze past.

I throw a pointed glare her way, and she does a terrible job of hiding her amusement.

There are no dangling elves when I make it to the elevator, and a mild, unfamiliar pang of guilt grabs me as I look over my shoulder toward Crystal's office. "Shit," I murmur, backing away from the doors currently sliding open, and doing the right thing. Her door is open, so there's no need to knock. Fucking hell, her office looks like Christmas threw up all over it. "Is that fake snow?" I blurt, looking at my feet as I tread on the spot, frowning at the white puffs of something sticking to the soles of my heels.

Crystal looks up and leans back in her chair, wary. "Thomas told me to fill my boots."

I laugh sardonically. "And you sure did." And now this fucking snow is filling *my* boots.

"Can I help?"

"I um . . . I . . ." Goddamn it. "I'm sorry about how I behaved this morning."

She stares at me and says absolutely nothing, quite happy to watch me squirm on the threshold of her office. She has every right to relish my unusually acquiescent state.

"Okay then." I turn.

"Camryn?"

Looking back, I see she's stood up. I'm quite sure I don't like the bravery coming back at me. Bravery mixed with curiosity. "Why do you hate Christmas so much?"

"I—"

"It's just that, well, if we knew, maybe we would understand."

"I—"

"And could be more sensitive."

"Will you let me fucking speak?" I snap, and immediately regret it. Crystal jumps, startled, then lowers to her chair like a scorned child. I push my fingertips into my temple. *Because my love of Christmas was stolen when my entire world fell apart.* "It's personal."

"Oh."

"I'm sorry for snapping."

"No problem."

"Okay. I'll be going then."

"Enjoy this evening."

"I won't." I leave before she can push, or maybe point out she's no closer to understanding my aversion to the holidays, stopping at the elevator to lift a foot in turn and brush off the white stuff. And now I have to face the shops and find something to wear to this glamorous gala thing that I'm obliged to attend.

Something Christmassy.

I don't think so.

My body refuses to take me farther into the clothes store, unwilling to expose me to the bedlam. It's organised chaos. Sequins, glitter, and sparkles litter the space, every man and his dog rummaging through the rails. Which is fine. I don't need to wrestle my way through this crowd, elbow people out of the way, or fight over the last size in any of the festive pieces on offer. I'm looking for something less . . . triggering.

Bypassing the throngs of shoppers in the party section, I make my way to the back of the store and start sifting through the rails. It takes me less than a minute to find something suitable.

A black dress. Simple, plunging, satin, long sleeves. I very nearly don't buy it because of a single gold button at the top of the back slit, but I reason with myself. If it can be worn outside of

December, it's not Christmassy. I grab some black suede sling-backs, gold hoops, and head for the pay desk.

Easy. Done.

But I'm still feeling breathless, and by the time I've paid and made it out of the store, I'm hot, bothered, and short of breath. My flustered state is a reminder that I haven't been to a social event for over three years. I haven't mingled or made conversation.

Smiled.

When I make it to the corner of Regent Street, the accounts Jeff promised me land, and reading them is the best distraction while I take the Tube home, the walk too long to fit into tonight's out-of-scope schedule. Even if, as Jeff predicted, I don't like what I read. It's worse than I thought. Terrible, in fact.

Deep breath, Camryn. I even *almost* smile thinking of Jeff's suggestion that he wanted to say goodbye to me once I saw this report. He's not fucking far off. "Jesus, Thomas," I murmur, as I hop off the train and push my way through the clueless, lost tourists with the rest of London's impatient commuters.

Dread coils up my spine like rising, thick smoke as I enter The Dorchester. I'm directed to the ballroom around the side, and I count five Christmas trees from the lobby to where the function's being held. Endless giant baubles are scattered among snow-peppered foliage hanging from every available space. It's over the top in a classy kind of way. I'd appreciate it if I didn't hate December so much.

Christmas.

The season of joy and laughter, gratitude and perpetual hope.

Until it wasn't. Until it only meant devastation.

I suddenly feel sick, my hand wrapped around my beaded clutch like it's a life jacket. A dozen waiters and waitresses loiter by the double doors, wide smiles on their faces, a tray of champagne balanced artfully on one palm, the other tucked neatly away behind their back. My eyes instinctively scan the clusters of glasses full of golden popping liquid, searching in vain for the non-alcoholic option. *Please don't make me ask for it.*

"Champagne?" a young lad asks. A student, no doubt. "Or an elderflower spritz?"

My relief is palpable. "The elderflower, please." More so when he hands me a glass that's only slightly paler in its golden appearance than the champagne. Not different enough for anyone to raise a brow and wonder why I'm not drinking. Because it's Christmas, of course. Also the season of perpetual insobriety. "Thank you." The sound of the crowds beyond the open doors, matched with the hordes of people dressed to impress, brings a mild sweat to my brow.

My feet refuse to carry me over the threshold into the room that glitters and sparkles, with fairy lights draping from one side to the other, forming a glowing crown above the Christmas kings and queens, who are all drenched in glitzy gowns and sharp tuxedos, smiles as wide as the hotel. The sight is blinding, the cheer deafening.

I need a moment.

Backing away, my hand squeezing the flute to the point I might shatter it, I divert to the ladies', pushing my way in and taking a breath. I promised Thomas an hour, but I have no idea how I'll make it through that hour. I'm struggling to even put myself in the room.

The marble vanity unit chinks when I place my beaded purse and glass down, and I take a breath. Two. Three. "Goddamn it," I whisper, in a starring deadlock with myself in the mirror, glaring at my reflection while silently screaming to not let myself down. *A drink will calm you.* "No." My voice is broken but adamant.

I puff up my already failing waves—I'm out of practice—and rub my lips together. The low neckline of my dress makes the dips above my collarbones look exaggerated too. Bony. I sigh, paying attention to my body for the first time in forever. I'm too thin. The long sleeves of the dress and the tight fit make it impossible not to notice. I can't remember the last time I ate three meals in a day. Shopping and cooking for one feels like an impossible task. And pointless. I've never been a foodie. But I ate a lot, and I ate healthily. He insisted. And I didn't object, because it was his arena, the kitchen, where he'd spend most of his evening prepping and serving, while I . . . did other things. I ate to live. He lived to eat. I was healthy without trying, and I was grateful for that. Completely. As I was grateful for the nutrition lessons with each meal.

"Fuck," I curse, snapping myself away from my memories and rummaging through my purse for my lipstick. My shaky hands don't help when I reapply, the colour falling outside the line of my lips. Or is that because I'm out of practice in this area too? I peek down at the gold Charlotte Tilbury tube, wondering if I should even be using this lipstick. I can't remember the last time I did. *When your life had colour.* Finding it was like a haphazard stumble around the landmines in my life as I blindly felt through the box marked CAMRYN - DRESSING TABLE endless inanimate objects from my past waiting to be pulled free so they could explode in my face.

I reach for my mouth and trace the tip of my finger across my bottom lip, tidying it up.

You don't wear lipstick, but you don't need to. Because your lips are naturally rosy.

Ringing from inside my purse makes it vibrate on the counter, and I snap out of my thoughts, pulling it out and answering. "Thomas." I pop the lid on my lipstick and stuff it back into my purse.

"Just checking you're still coming." I hear the caution in his voice as well as I see the stranger in the mirror before me.

"I'm just walking in." I hang up, collect my things, and drag my game face from deep down. My shoulders are back, my spine straight as I hoof the door open. Three strides in toward the ballroom, Thomas appears at the doors, his green velvet tuxedo beyond the realms of extravagant. He's walking proof that money doesn't buy you taste. He looks like an elf gone wrong.

His eyes fall down my black dress when he finds me.

"Problem?" I ask.

"Not at all."

"Good." I pass him, and he quickly catches up, falling into stride beside me. "One hour," I remind him.

"Yes, yes."

"I might hang around longer so you can explain why your accounts look like a CFO's nightmare."

He skids to a stop on his black patent dress shoes that wouldn't look out of place on the Child Catcher from *Chitty Chitty Bang Bang*. "You've seen the draft accounts?"

Realising he's fallen behind, I stop too, assessing his disposition. I can't fathom whether he's annoyed or embarrassed. Perhaps annoyed with Jeff. The embarrassment must be for me. Did he tell Jeff not to share the accounts with me? "Something tells me you're aware of the mess they're in."

"Let's chat on Monday." He makes to walk on, but halts obediently when I deliver his name on a sharp hiss, and his green velvet shoulders drop as he braves facing me. "It's in hand."

"Thomas, can I remind you of the position you gave me?"

He rolls his eyes. "You don't need to remind me, Camryn."

"I think I do, Thomas, because since you've hired me, you've persistently broken my budgets, made financial decisions behind my back, let your wife and son go off on spending tangents, and obliterated my financial forecasts, which would have had your company ready for the team to move in and get to work *well* before now."

"It's not so bad."

"You've paid yourself and your board members, aka your wife and son, over ten million this year. What do you think that looks like to potential investors? And that's before we take into consideration all of the transactions I'm finding on the business credit cards that aren't business related."

"Can we discuss this on Monday?"

"What am I doing here?"

"What?"

"Why am I here, Thomas? I'm the CFO of your company, a role your wife begrudgingly stepped away from, and I have absolutely no control of the company's finances. Am I expected to paint a glorious picture of your profitability? Lead the industry to believe you're smashing it out of the park?"

"A little support wouldn't go a miss."

"For what purpose?"

His head drops back, his mouth open. It's the most insulting display of exasperation. "Is this eating into my one hour?"

"Yes."

"Thought so. Look, I just want people to see we're making strides. I've got Camryn Moore on the payroll, for Christ's sake. Everyone knows what you do and why you do it."

"Yes, they do, and I've got a clean sheet of victories. That doesn't stop now." I can't threaten him that I'll quit, and it's not because quitting would tarnish that clean sheet. I simply can't go back to endless, long days of nothing, when I had all the time in the world for my regrets and fuck-ups to torment me. Suffocate me. Thomas's frivolousness has extended my initial contract term, which was a welcomed gift, but failing is not an option. Failing will mean no other company will be interested in hiring me in the future, and no work means no reprieve.

"All duly noted," Thomas says, stepping closer and dropping his voice. "Like I said, we'll talk on Monday." His smile is half-baked and nervous as shit.

"Fine."

"Okay, let's go mingle." He cocks his arm out for me to hook. "Let's start with Holcot."

I disregard his offer and throw myself into the den. "*The* Holcot? The Holcot from Atlantic Sea Global?"

"Who else? They're out to tender."

I raise my brows as we pass through various groups, my eyes forced into a wince to ease the glare of the sequin epidemic. "And you want me to rain glory all over TF Shipping."

"They listen to CFOs, especially ones of your calibre."

"Flattery will get you nowhere."

"Oh, I know that, Camryn. Especially with you. I'm stating facts, is all."

"I'd be lying if I told anyone you're a safe bet right now."

"I have the ships."

"You need more than ships to take on a business like Atlantic Sea Global. A company like yours would require no other business if you got Holcot's signature on the bottom line."

"Exactly."

"But that's dangerous."

"Eggs in one basket and all that?"

"Clever boy." I find Holcot at the end of the bar, a harem of women surrounding him. It's no surprise; he's famously handsome and notoriously charming. He's also a ball-breaker of a businessman. "You've got competition," I muse, nodding to all of the women.

"I've also got you."

"Excuse me?" I jerk to a stop, so abruptly, my drink spills over the side of my glass, splashing both of us. "Is that why you brought me? As a piece of arse to bat my lashes for you?"

"Fucking hell, Camryn," he mutters. "You see the best in everyone, don't you?" He licks the back of his hand, lapping up my spilled drink. "Elderflower?"

"What of it?"

Hands up, he backs off. "I've brought you because you're brilliant at what you do."

"Sure," I mutter. I should be flattered. It's been a while seen I've felt seen. *Until Dec.* "And I'm not exactly being brilliant at the moment because you're undoing everything I'm doing."

"Let's keep it casual," Thomas says, ignoring my jab. "I'll crack a few jokes, you'll laugh."

"When have you ever heard me laugh?"

"You've never heard my jokes."

I snort as Thomas leads the way. "And for the record, it's hard to see the best in everyone when humans are such wankers all the time. Phillip West case in point."

"I don't think he'll go quietly."

"He will if he knows what's good for him."

"You terrify me." Thomas slaps on an embarrassingly big smile and holds my elbow.

"What are you doing?" I ask, looking down his hold on me.

He frowns and quickly removes it. "Showing an alliance."

"Don't be ridiculous."

"God, you're in a pleasant mood." He waves a hand out in an over-the-top gesture to lead on, and I do, eyeing a tray of champagne as I pass, resisting the urge to switch to alcohol. "As always," he adds on a whisper I'm sure I'm not supposed to hear. "Holcot!" Thomas's velvet-green arms spread wide, his face lighting up like the Blackpool Illuminations, courtesy of the fairy-light-encrusted angel hanging over the bar behind Holcot.

My gaze travels the full length of it, taking in every one of the lights that look like little drops of pure melted gold ready to drip onto us mere mortals below. And I wonder . . .

Do they exist?

Angels?

Are they unsullied and serene? Do they float above us in a place where only the kind and unspoiled are welcome? Do they watch over us? Silently guide us?

"Camryn?"

I blink back the black dots in my vision, finding Thomas before me next to Holcot. He's even more handsome up close and in the flesh. And considerably younger. Mid-forties, perhaps? I had him as mid-fifties. I notice his hand is extended. "Pleasure," I say, taking it and shaking firmly. "Sorry, I was just admiring the angel."

He cranes his head back, stretching his throat to look up at it. "Stunning, isn't it?" His eyes drop. "I would say it's not the only stunning thing around here, but I fear I'm on the edge of being politically incorrect."

"You must be talking about the endless middle-aged women that look like sugar plum fairies gone wrong."

A sharp bark of laughter erupts, his hand still holding mine. I can feel Thomas's stupid grin on me. *For God's sake.* "Very good," Holcot says. "I'm Edward."

"Camryn. And for the record, it is most definitely politically incorrect."

"And such a shame too, don't you think? That a man can't tell a lady that she's beautiful."

I haven't been called beautiful in a very long time. *Until Dec.* Tonight, I'm putting it down to the dress. But when I encountered Dec in the bar at The Royal Constantine, I wasn't glammed up. So what drew him to me? "It's deemed leery these days, Edward."

"Tell me about it. I have to think before I say anything for fear of being sued to high heaven."

I smile. "I won't sue you."

"Well, that's a relief." He chinks my glass with his, and Thomas laughs loudly, in his fucking element.

We chat casually for a while, and if Thomas cracked his jokes, they went way over my head. But I'm running out of steam, my social battery draining fast after being redundant for so long. "Would you excuse me?" I say, moving away from the men, set to go and recharge in the ladies' and assess just how much longer I have to be here.

Edward Holcot smiles. "I'd say it's been an absolute, unexpected pleasure but, again . . ."

"Charming," I say, leaving after forcing one more smile, but as I lift my eyes, something across the room stops me dead in my tracks and has me forgetting where I am, why I'm here, *and* that I'm running out of steam.

And, Jesus, he looks spectacular in a tuxedo. His eyes find mine, and though there's nothing there to tell me what he's thinking—classic Dec—I know he's spotted me before now.

I tilt my head in question.

He tilts his.

And after a few moments of sizzling eye contact, he makes his way over, coming to a stop before me, a glass held lightly between his fingertips. He's such a sight for sore eyes. "Evening." The deep, husky timbre gets beneath the material of my dress and rests on my skin.

"Evening."

"Fancy seeing you here."

"Fancy seeing *you* here," I reply coolly, spotting and loving the minuscule tilt of his mouth at the corner as he takes a sip of his drink. His gorgeous grey eyes keep me rooted to the spot.

"I noticed a certain dashing Edward Holcot sniffed you out."

I look over my shoulder, seeing the harem of women are all back around him like flies around shit. "He's a charmer."

"Be careful with him, Camryn," Dec warns lightly, bringing my interested eyes back to him.

"Jealous?"

"Wildly," he answers, unabashed. "Were you going somewhere?"

"I was just escaping to the ladies'."

"Escaping?"

"He's not my cup of tea."

"What's your cup of tea?"

"I think you know the answer to that."

His heavy brow smooths out as his eyebrows lift. "Me."

I hum, taking a sip of my drink.

"Do you still want to escape?"

I shake my head, saying all the things without saying them. *No. No, I don't. Not now you're here.*

"Can I buy you a drink?"

"Maybe."

"I'm taking that as a resounding yes." Dec nods toward the bar, and we both wander through the crowds to the quieter side. "Two dirty martinis, please."

"Only champagne and beer are included in the open bar, sir."

"I'll pay." He pushes his card across and faces me, making no bones about drinking me in, up and down. "You look beautiful."

"So do you."

He nods mildly, thoughtfully as he reaches for my cheek, stopping himself before he feels at it. Checking my cut, that's got more concealer on it than I've used all year. "How's it been for you?"

"This evening?" I ask, and he nods. "I could think of better places to be." Like in a hotel bar, any hotel bar, with Dec sitting next to me talking about everything but nothing, being silent from time to time. Nearly kissing me again. "My boss roped me in. It's been challenging."

"How so?"

"I had a call with the company accountant today. It's all a bit of a mess, and in truth, I'm not sure how to handle it."

"What's the problem?"

"My boss is shit with money."

"It's your job to handle the finances."

"Tell *him* that," I quip, virtually smelling the martinis as the waiter pushes them toward us.

Dec picks one up, takes my elderflower drink, and replaces it with my favourite. "Drink up."

I reach for the other on the bar and hand it to him, and he shows his amusement as he takes it, holding his glass toward me. "What are we drinking to?" I ask.

Tapping his glass with mine, he comes close to my face, his mouth at my ear. "I'll tell you later," he whispers. It feels as if a missile could have hit me in the chest, the force of my exhale audible, as the warmth of his breath creeps across my skin. "Don't leave without me." A light squeeze of my wrist before he wanders away, leaving me a shaky wreck, my drink jumping up the side of my glass. It's not long before I lose him in the crowds, and the loss hits me deep.

Don't leave without me.

Liquor hits my fingers, trickling down to my wrist, and I dip to lick it up but stop myself. No. Placing the untouched martini on the bar and grabbing a napkin to wipe my hands, I start weaving through the room, heading for the ladies'. "Excuse me," I mutter constantly, turning from side to side to squeeze through various crowds of people. "Pardon me." I'm taking fairy steps in my heels, unable to walk with any pace. "Exc—" I stop dead in my very slow tracks when I literally bump into Thomas.

"Camryn," he says, looking all kinds of awkward.

"What?"

"You're leaving?"

"No, I need the ladies'. But I'm already over my promised time, Thomas. Is there anyone else you want me to bullshit before I leave?"

Laughter erupts from him, sending his body bending back. "Yes, yes, ha-ha-ha-ha!"

"Are you all right?"

"Yes, yes, I'm very all right." He clears his throat. "Camryn, this is Dec Ellis."

My heart feels like it grinds to a stop in my chest as I cast my eyes to the left. And I stare at him. Just stare at him, as he stares at me, a drop of his martini left in the glass. "Camryn," he says, his voice doing all its usual things to me, his hand extending. "What a pleasure."

Ha. Ha.

So we don't know each other? Right. Okay.

With slightly narrowed eyes, I put my hand in his, certain it's not a good idea. And it's not. Merely his skin on mine sets off tiny explosions across my body. It takes everything in me and more to keep myself steady and poised in front of my boss. "The pleasure is all mine." Something scarily similar to a sickly-sweet smile breaks my pursed mouth without instruction, and a cocky one definitely ghosts Dec's.

"It will be," he mouths, tightening his hold. *Fuck.* My composure is slipping. Can't have that. I tighten my hand too.

"How's the handshake?" Dec asks, pouting his lips over the rim of his glass as he finishes the last drop.

"Pretty pathetic for a businessman."

"Ha-ha-ha!" Thomas blurts, holding his belly. "I told you she's a firecracker."

"You've been talking about me?"

"Were your ears burning?" Dec raises his brows. *No, Dec. Not my ears. Just the rest of my body.*

I'm acutely aware that to these two men, I am two vastly different women. Dec's seen moments of vulnerability, a woman who's conflicted and at odds with her past and future. *He's seen the cracks.* Thomas has only ever encountered me at work, where I show no fear or hesitancy, where I command and dictate. Where I am cold and hard-nosed.

Interest is a storm in Dec's eyes. How long will he hold back the questions written all over his magnificent face? "Care to catch me up?" I ask, tearing my gaze off Dec and my hand from his before Thomas notices our . . . what? Connection? The electricity subtly sizzling between us? The fact I'm wobbling slightly on my heels? All of these reactions to Dec Ellis have taken me by surprise to say the least.

Thomas snorts, flapping a hand flippantly. "Just friendly chitchat."

"Friendly chitchat," Dec confirms quietly, almost tiredly.

"Oh look, dinner's up." Thomas points toward the ballroom as he heads that way, the crowds starting to bottleneck there. I hadn't even noticed everyone had moved from around us, giving me air. Because with Dec around, breathing is hard, whether I'm stifled or not.

"Wanna get out of here?" he asks, moving into my side.

I look up at him, this fine form of a man, and not for the first time I ask myself . . . why me? My heart's beating so hard, there's no mistaking that I'm alive. I sometimes wonder. If I'm really alive or not, I wonder that. Only the grief confirms I am.

Cruel.

"Yes," I breathe. "I do."

"Let's go." Dropping his glass on a passing waiter's tray, Dec places his hand on the small of my back and guides me toward the exit. "Do you have a coat?"

"No."

"Really? It's five degrees out there, Camryn." He stops at the cloakroom and hands over a ticket, and a moment later he's covering my shoulders with a black wool overcoat. "I have a feeling you're going to suggest walking home," he says on an unimpressed mutter.

"I like walking with you."

"I like walking with you too." He holds his hand out to me. "I don't want you to shake it this time."

I place my hand in his and let him lead me out of The Dorchester, then we start the long walk home that's going to feel much shorter than it is.

The silence is comfortable, as it is more often than not, but I hear the endless questions swirling in that mind of his. Which will he lead with, if any?

We're at Euston Road before Dec finally breaks the silence. "Your boss's description of you is contradictory to who I know."

"Maybe you don't know me."

"We both know it's your boss who doesn't know you."

I nod mildly, as if in agreement. "My boss knows the career woman I used to be. You know the woman I am now." I look up at him, relying on him to ensure I don't bump into anything or anyone, my steps now blind. And that's something else I appreciate about Dec. Feeling safe. "Tell me what we were drinking to," I order gently, feeling my body pushing closer into his side.

He smiles mildly as he looks ahead. "Our first kiss."

"We haven't had a first kiss."

At that very second, he stops us and turns into me, taking my cheeks in his palms gently and scanning my face. Hope is a vise on my sensibility, squeezing it until it finally pops and I'm mentally begging him to kiss me. His jacket falls from my shoulders to the pavement when I reach up to his wrists, clinging to them. "It's time to fix that," he murmurs, his mouth slowly falling onto mine. His tongue sweeps my bottom lip, gently encouraging me to open up to him, and my world is suddenly lighter, the black cloud that shadows me constantly lifting a fraction to allow the sun to shine on me. My tongue meets his, warm, lax, and slippery, and follows his pace without much thought at all. To not think feels like a blessing I don't deserve. My hands slip from his wrists to his strong shoulders, my body pressing closer to him. It's a slow, peaceful duel, and my entire existence is consumed in this moment.

It will take me forever to get over this kiss, which is fine because I don't want to ever get over it. Here, now, will be imprinted on my heart forevermore, no matter what happens between us. It's something I'm thinking about more and more, and to think about it is to worry about it. *What is happening between us?*

His hands move to my hair, his fingers weaving through the strands, his mouth trailing from one side of mine to the other, giving me brief moments of anticipation before he resumes his mind-spinning assault of my mouth. Feathery soft. Purposely slow. A submissive whimpers ripple through my body.

It's over too soon, despite it being the longest kiss I've shared with anyone. And the most passionate. And the most meaningful. Dec's lips leave mine and rest on my forehead, his chest pressing into mine with his deep inhale. I sense relief. Feel it in myself too.

Suddenly, I have something that could possibly save me.

My heart is begging for that . . . to be saved. My mind is telling me not to be hasty. Don't depend on anyone but myself.

Don't be vulnerable.

Because I can't take any more pain.

"To our first kiss," he whispers across my skin, pulling back to find my eyes. I'm certain he must be faced with wonder.

And without another word, Dec collects up his jacket, drapes it over my shoulders again, and curls his arm around me, tucking me closely into his side. My belly feels like a swarm of butterflies have been let loose, and my skin tingles madly. I look up at him, in absolute awe.

You made me feel like this, Dec Ellis.

And I think I love you for it.

Jarred by my thoughts and the insane sense of tranquillity inside, I bury the side of my face into his chest, and we walk the rest of the way home in silence. No words are needed, not for now. We both seem content letting the impact of that kiss sink in. Contemplate it. I only pray I'm not alone in thinking that it was the most magical moment I've had. At least since—

I swallow, fighting the pain back and the black cloud away.

Take this moment.

Because it's the first time in too long that I've felt peace.

Camden is a hive of festive activity, the normal, expected Friday night drinkers coupled with Christmas shindigs and tourists at every turn making it impossible to walk in a straight line down the pavement. Every other person sports some kind of Christmas getup —a hat, reindeer antlers, a cup of mulled wine or a cone of roasted hazelnuts.

The smell of Christmas is like a deeply rooted splinter. Nothing can get it out, you just have to wait until it fucks off. A seasoned Londoner, Dec gets progressively more impatient and resorts to stepping into the road each time the traffic is clear, pulling me along, checking over his shoulder to make sure I'm keeping up.

My eyes are on his back and his back alone. Nothing else exists.

But there comes a point when we have no choice but to cross the pavement when we're approaching the turning to my street. I clutch Dec's hand tighter as he assesses the pedestrian traffic, looking for a gap in the crowd for us to dip through. And when he sees one, he takes off, pulling me through the madness. I feel his coat slip from my shoulders and try in vain to grab it with my spare hand. "Dec," I say, not nearly loud enough for him to hear me over the Christmas tracks booming from the pub on the corner. I look back, cringing when I see his coat on the damp ground being trampled by the stampede. "Dec!" I tug my hand from his and turn to rescue his beautiful wool coat, but immediately get swarmed, people bumping into me, knocking me, happy faces turning grumpy when I get in the way. "Shit." I circle, losing my bearings, feeling a sweat sprinkling my forehead. My eyes on the ground, I try to overcome the panic attack threatening, the old familiar sense of suffocation getting me. My heart beats too fast, my palms clam up, my neck burns, no doubt turning bright red.

Oh God.

"There you are."

My feet disappear from beneath me, and I'm suddenly bobbing up and down, draped across a pair of hard, strong arms. I swiftly remember to breath and take in air urgently, clinging to his neck as he fights his way through.

We break free of the hustle, being spat out of the chaos onto the bottom of my street, and Dec sets me on my heels, checking me over, as if making sure I'm still in one piece. I would never have taken that route without him. I would have diverted around everything busy and Christmassy. "Your coat," I breathe, reaching for my shoulders as if to demonstrate it's not there.

"I don't care about the coat." Picking up my hands off my shoulders, he holds them between us. "I care about you."

"You do?" I ask on a breathy whisper, my panic wilting under the force of my hope.

"Are you that numb you haven't felt it yet?"

He's not particularly emotional, doesn't give much away, but I can read him. I hear him. Feel him. Sense him when he's close.

"No," I admit. "Because I don't feel numb around you."

He shudders with his exhale, nodding as if in understanding, though I know he couldn't possibly. Dec is together. Stable. He's everything I want to be but can't.

Silently, he tucks me into his side and walks me slowly down the street, and my heart sinks with every step in the knowledge that my time with him is coming to an end again. I'm no longer anticipating a martini at my lips and a stranger as my distraction. My vice has changed. Now, it's becoming a matter of surviving in between the interludes of Dec.

Outside my building, he turns me to face him and takes his time conjuring up whatever it is he wants to say. So when his simply lifts my hand and kisses the back before wandering off, I'm more than confused.

The rumble of the unspoken is starting to get too loud.

I sigh, caught between elation and despair, as I stand on the pavement watching him getting farther and farther away. The despair's winning. I should be full of hope, clinging to it. But the moment he walks away like that, the loneliness returns. And that frightens me. Because I can't control Dec. I can't rely on something I'm not in control of.

I'm in control of the martinis. They're solid, dependable. I'm in control of my career. I huff a little, correcting myself. I *thought* I was in control of my career. Thomas is squashing that notion more each day. But I can pull it back. I can drag Thomas into line.

Dec, though?

Does this have a shelf life? Should I depend on something that I can't depend on?

I can't afford to lose again. My heart won't take it.

"Are you that numb you haven't felt it yet?"

Detachment.

It's safer.

Nothing can hurt you if you don't let it close enough.

Problem is, Dec's already close. Closer than I'm comfortable with. It's easy to forget that when he's saturating my senses with his beauty and cold gentleness.

Except . . . he keeps walking away from me.

December 9th

My legs work like pistons as I run through the park, the cold, gusting wind coming at me making me work harder.

Don't get close.

Easier said than done when what you're trying to avoid is the positive to your negative. The most powerful magnet. Except he walked away after kissing me. Will he call?

Don't get close.

I growl under my breath, pumping my legs harder, faster, wanting to pound the conflict away. I don't stop sprinting at the end of the park pathway. Not even when I approach Pret. Or when I make it back to Camden.

I keep running until I make it to my apartment, my lungs burning, my body dripping.

"Camryn, are you trying to run yourself to death?" Mr. Percival asks as I hang on to the railings that flank the path to our building, my breathing loud and strained. "My God, girl, you're as red as a beetroot."

I can't even talk, unable to draw in air to get any words out. So I flap a hand, reassuring him I'm fine. That's debatable. My heart's booming in my ears, blood whooshing, making my hearing crackle.

My hands squeezing the icy, black iron spear tips of the bars, my arms braced, I lift my head, my face hot with the blood in my cheeks. "Morning," I puff, my chest tight. Christ, am I going to have a heart attack? "I'm okay."

He shakes his head, the wiry hair of both his eyebrows meeting in the middle when they pinch together. "You young folk," he mutters, hobbling along with the help of his walking frame. "Obsessing about the extra pounds you're going to put on over the holidays with all the mince pies and eggnog. We didn't worry about that in my day."

"Mr. Percival, please be careful." I'm not operating on full steam at the moment, so there will be no dramatic dive to catch him if he tips over.

"Steady as a rock, me, dear." He stops and lifts his walking frame off the ground, performing what I think are supposed to be chest presses.

"Except when you're put on your arse by a Christmas tree."

"Mitigating circumstances." Slapping his gloved hands together, he rubs them and blows into them at the same time. "It's chilly today."

"Freezing." I turn and lean against the railings, my legs like jelly, and reach up to pull my hair tie out. "Where are you off to?"

"To order the turkey. Ahead of the game, me, dear. You can't be too careful. Last year, I was laid up with the flu and couldn't get to the butchers until December sixteenth. I had to make do with a crown. There were no turkey sandwiches on Boxing Day, turkey curry on the twenty-seventh, or stew on the twenty-eighth for me, dear. I'm not making that mistake again."

"That's a lot of turkey. Who are you having over for Christmas, Mr. Percival?"

"Maureen," he declares. "It's her favourite."

"Right," I muse, still not sure who Maureen is. There's no wife, no family. "Have a good day, Mr. Percival."

His gloved hand comes up in goodbye, he slips his flat cap on, and I trudge up to the door, swinging it open, hearing the tree pines crunching under my trainers as I walk down the corridor, slowing when I spot something on the floor outside my door. A round cake tin. I crouch and pick it up, removing the lid, and a waft of something rich and indulgent hits my nose. Brandy and fruit. “Christmas cake.” I take in the uneven icing encasing it as I push through my legs to rise again. “Jesus,” I groan, my muscles screaming, each one feeling like it’s being stretched to capacity and could ping at any moment.

I’d have a bath, soak in some Radox.

If I had a bath.

Throwing my keys on the side, I go to the kitchen and slide my cake onto the counter, drilling holes into it. There aren’t many suspects. Only one, in fact. Sighing, I get a blunt dinner knife, not a sharp chef’s knife—don’t have one of those—and push it into the icing with some weight behind me, cutting a small slice. My conscience is the only thing making me try a piece—and the fact I could do with a sugar hit.

I wrap my lips around it and lower to the chair. The fruit drenched in brandy hits my taste buds like a torpedo, exploding in my mouth. “Wow,” I mumble around my chews. Mr. Percival knows how to make good Christmas cake. Five bites are all it takes to finish the slice, and I want more. So I cut another piece, catching a crumb on the edge of my lip and sucking it off the tip of my finger. My chewing slows when my phone beeps. Not a message, not a call, not an email.

A weather warning. I stare down at that one fatal word.

Snow.

“No,” I whisper, opening BBC News, scanning the report detailing the impending cold snap moving in later, the snow, the ice, the disruption.

No transport.

No running.

No work?

I jump up and go to the window, looking up to the sky, as if that might tell me the weather reporter is wrong. A white, dense blanket greets me. "Shit," I sigh, slipping the last of my second slice into my mouth and chewing as I go back to the kitchen.

I put the cake in the fridge.

It's a splash of colour in the pallid space.

Grit lorries are out in force when I leave a couple of hours later, chugging up and down the main roads spitting out stones. And the temperature feels like it's dropped even more, making the walk to see Mum feel so much longer.

My fingers are like freeze pops by the time I arrive, my nose certainly glowing, my lips blue. I need a hat. Some gloves. I wouldn't know which box to search for those, and I wouldn't want to even if I did. I'll grab some from a shop when I'm passing.

I nod my hello to the lady on the desk as I sign in, the urge to ask how Mum is nearly getting the better of me. Her health isn't a marker on whether she'll recognise me today.

The double doors click as I'm approaching, allowing me through, and one of Mum's nurses, Deirdre, spots me and makes her way over, falling into side beside me. "How's your cheek, Camryn?"

"It's nothing."

"Did you have it checked out?"

My hand instinctively reaches for it as snapshots of Thursday evening parade through my mind—all Dec. His worry when I opened the door. His hand on my cheek. How his presence provided unexplainable healing powers. And then, inevitably, the kiss we shared last night. I lay awake for hours agonising over what happens next, and the fact I simply do not know only makes the voice in my head louder. The voice that's telling me to protect what's left of my devastated heart at all costs. "Yes," I say. Why hasn't he been in touch? A text, a call. Anything. After that kiss, I feel like I need *something* from him.

No, you don't.

Yes, you do.

"About the carols service."

"What about it?" I ask, reaching up and rubbing my achy head.

"It's December twenty-first, in case you're not working."

"I am."

I hear Deirdre sigh. I'm not sure if I was meant to. "She's been better today."

Again, better doesn't mean she'll recognise me. "That's good to hear." I reach Mum's door and push my way in, completely taken aback when I find my brother's wife, Mindy, by Mum's bed. I haven't seen her for months.

"Camryn," she says, almost embarrassed, standing.

"Camryn?" Mum says, her wishy-washy eyes turning my way. "Who's Camryn?"

Mindy visibly flinches as I stand here, broken again, wondering if Mum recognises Mindy. I have a feeling she must, judging by the fact she's calm and Mindy is close by the bed. Plus, my sister-in-law's reaction. "This is Camryn," Mindy virtually shouts. "You know Camryn."

"She's not deaf, Mindy, she's senile." I unzip my coat and wriggle out of it, popping it on the radiator to warm it up for when I leave. "So where's my dear brother?" Mindy and I have always got along. She's been around for as long as I remember, which makes the fact that she's been absent all the more painful too.

"Working."

"A lot to catch up after your three-week holiday, I suppose." I can hear myself, sounding twisted and full of resentment. How is it fair Mum recognises my brother's wife and not her own daughter? Mindy's here as a token gesture, a way to appease me, the whiny sister who sees nothing but injustice in the world. How is it fair Dad passed away when I needed him the most? How is it fair Mum fell ill and forgot who I was? How is it fair my marriage failed? How is it fair I lost my friends and my family? How is it fair . . .?

I quickly pull myself into line before I spiral into a full-blown meltdown in the care home.

Mindy lowers to the chair, shrinking. "How have you been?" she asks and immediately flinches.

I look out the corner of my eye at her as I take Mum's water jug and rinse it in the sink in the corner. "Dandy."

"Right." She sighs, going back to my mother, giving up on me. Like everyone else in my world. I can hardly blame them, given I gave up on myself long ago. Water gushes from the tap into the jug, muffling whatever Mindy is saying to Mum, and I proceed to faff around the bed, making myself useful while they have a conversation—something I so desperately want with my mother.

See me!

I miss her wise words. I miss her reason and the way she could clutch at my hand and tell me I've got this. It doesn't matter that now, if she were to do that, tell me I've got this, it would be a lie. Just her belief in me, her way of being strong for me when I couldn't be strong myself, is what I need. What I miss. And her hugs. The best hugs. Hugs that made even the worst times feel like they could be okay. *I need my mum.*

I place her vase back on the cabinet, letting my eyes find her on the bed. Mindy's holding her hand. The hand that struck me.

"Where's Noah?" Mum asks out of the blue, jarring me.

"He's not coming, Mum," I say, my voice brittle, the weight of Mindy's gaze heavy on me. I turn my welling eyes onto her. "He's never coming." I dip and kiss Mum's cheek before grabbing my coat from the radiator and leaving, resentment and hurt twisting my stomach to the point I might vomit.

"Camryn, wait," Mindy calls, coming after me as I swing on my coat, my strides purposeful, the predictable suffocation sneaking up on me. "Camryn, please."

I stop abruptly, staring at the doors ahead.

"I can't pretend to understand what you've been through," she says, her words like sandpaper across my skin. What I've been through? It's what I'm *still* going through. "I mean, your entire world imploded."

I face her, my expression detached and cold. "No, you couldn't pretend to understand because your life is fucking perfect, Mindy. Your marriage is perfect. Your home is perfect. Your kids are fucking perfect. And I'm just here picking up the pieces, trying to figure out what my purpose is now. Send my brother my love." I stuff my hands in my pockets and walk away from her, choking on the lump in my throat I'm desperately trying to swallow down.

"He stopped round yesterday," she calls, freezing me at the doors, my hand hovering over the button to call reception. Of course, they're still chummy. How can my brother and Mindy even tolerate being around him? How is that fair? "He said you're refusing to sign the papers."

"You know why. He wants me to accept that I've behaved unreasonably."

"What does it matter, Cam? All this is just delaying things. The sale of the house, the settlement, everything. You both need the money, and you've got to get out of that poky flat, find yourself a new place, and make a new start."

To what end? I've lost every fucking thing that counts as good in my life. And he wants money so he can keep *moving on.*

Fuck.

Him.

And he now has my sister-in-law doing his grovelling?

Fuck that hurts.

I hit the button and wait for the sound of the click that'll free me, then turn to Mindy. I hate how perfectly together she is, her bags always matching her shoes and her lipstick, her blowout as perfect in the evening as it is in the morning, freshly washed and styled. Always perfect. "You think money and a new home makes everything better?"

Her mouth opens and closes like a fish for a few awkward moments. Awkward for her, not me. "Your house is empty," she says. "You should be there. He left so you didn't have to."

"How honourable of him." The door clicks, and I leave. I could never be there, surrounded by the memories of my previous life. Everything that I lost. Everything that he stole from me. Fuck him. Fuck everything.

If it's possible, it's even colder when I make it outside, the white sky so low I'm sure I could reach up and touch the snow waiting to fall. I lower to the top step by a potted tree, needing to take the weight off my feet for a few moments. How I wish I could take the weight off my shoulders too.

I sigh and reach for a branch, pulling a closed bud off but faltering when something glistens at me, catching the low winter sun and making me blink back the sharp flash of light.

A spear of ice.

It's cascading from a branch, a perfect white feather fossilised inside. Crystal clear. Beautiful. I trail my fingertip down, studying it, strangely rapt.

Trapped.

Like me.

December 10th

Icing cakes my lips, my chews slow, and my arse is numb from my place sitting in the window, feet up, my T-shirt pulled over my bent knees. It's a perfect white blanket out there, London a blank canvas. Pure, clean, untarnished. It should stay that way until it melts away. But no. Humans will spoil it, traffic and feet ruining the perfection, turning it into a sludgy, dirty mess that'll become a man-made eyesore rather than remaining a natural beauty. *Where were you, Snow, when I wished for you four years ago?* "You're late," I whisper, taking another mouthful of my breakfast, watching the world go by, the white stuff bringing people out in force, all of them celebrating the arrival, dragging sledges, rolling snowballs. Dogs create trails with their snouts, leap like lambs, collapse into downward dog and yell at the weird-looking, soft, wet powder. Idiots crawl along in cars until the wheels give up and start spinning on the spot, leaving the drivers revving the engines, adding another layer of noise to the yells of excitement and joy. *Excitement and joy*. Maybe now, yes. People are dashing out into the white winter wonderland to enjoy it. But by the end of the day, they'll be wishing the snow away, their lives disrupted.

They have no idea.

Their disruption is temporary.

I pop the last piece of my cake into my mouth and chew, licking my fingers, deciding that Mr. Percival's Christmas cake is the only thing Christmassy I actually like. My phone rings from the kitchen. It's the fifth time he's tried to call me since I saw Mindy yesterday. And it'll be the fifth time I haven't answered. He thinks a little extra pressure from my family will solve this? Make me less . . . . unreasonable? I rest my head back on the wall and go back to watching the world go by.

Persistent.

He was always that.

It's how we ended up dating in the first place. I had a friend who had a friend who had a friend who had a brother. The brother came alone to a cricket match. It was a hot day, we had a basket full of beers and tinned cocktails, and we got tipsy on sunshine and alcohol. He tried to kiss me; I turned away. He didn't give up, got my number from the friend of a friend of a friend, called me, texted me, until I finally relented and had dinner with him. I made it clear I wasn't looking for anything serious—I was on a career trajectory.

He just smiled.

And I went out with him again the next night.

I don't see any of those friends anymore either. And I wonder where I'd be now if I hadn't gone to that cricket match all those years ago.

And would I be happy?

I pull my knees in closer, shaking my head clear, but that only leaves space for Dec. He hasn't called. Hasn't texted. And I still don't know if I want him to.

I get up and find my laptop, dropping to the couch and opening my inbox. I try to focus on the emails I saved to work on this weekend.

To our first kiss.

I snap the lid of my computer closed and toss it aside on a yell.

Wrapped up warm in endless layers—no gloves or hat—I slip my feet into my boots and brace myself for the cold as I open my front door into the corridor. Mr. Percival is standing at the exit doors, looking out onto the street, his walking frame holding him up. "Thank you for the cake," I say as I near him, his flat-capped head turning to find me. "It's really very good."

"Where's your hat and gloves, girl? It's brass monkeys out there."

"Where's yours?" I retort with as much scold. "That hat is hardly keeping your ears warm."

"Have you seen the size of my ears, dear? Ain't no hat covering these things."

A little snort escapes, surprising me. "So it's true what they say?"

"About what?"

"Ears. They don't stop growing."

"Oh no, mine have been this big since I was knee-high to a grasshopper."

"Really?"

"Really. My ma always said I'd grow into them." He steps back with the help of his walking frame. "I never did. Where are you off to? Your tree? A turkey? Or Christmas shopping?"

"None of the above."

"Oh, I bet you're one of those modern types, aren't you? Everything ordered online. Such a shame for the High Street."

Tightness forms in my lips without instruction, my compassionate side trying to smile but my damaged side not allowing it. "As you've noticed, I need some gloves and a hat," I say, holding up my bare hands. "It looks like this weather isn't going anywhere anytime soon."

"I hope it stays for the big day," he chirps. I hope it doesn't. It would make it a perfect Christmas, and that would be excruciating. "You need to get yourself some snow boots like mine."

I peek down at the monstrosities gracing Mr. Percival's feet on a frown. "Maybe I will."

"Here, let me get out of your way." He shuffles to the side.

"You're not venturing out?"

"With all those flying snowballs? No, thank you. I'll watch from behind the screen. I'm not as young and fit as you, dear, therefore I can't dodge them."

I'm blasted by the cold when I heave the door open, and quickly put myself on the other side, letting it close to save Mr. Percival freezing. "Christ," I breathe.

He gives me an excited wave. "Be careful out there," he calls through the glass.

"I will." I face the white world outside and zip up my coat to my chin, gauging the depth I'm dealing with. A few inches, at least. My boots sink, and the crunches create a beat as I trudge down the path to the street. This is going to be a workout. I stuff my hands in my pockets and lift my chin, looking up.

And then I see it in slow motion.

Sailing directly toward me.

"Fuck," I murmur, clenching my eyes closed a second before the giant snowball smashes me straight in my face, exploding and sprinkling my entire front with snow. "Are you fucking kidding me?" I yell, wiping my face with my cuffs, the sound of young boys in hysterics hitting my ears, loud at first, but then fading away. The little fuckers. They're running away? I frantically scan the street for them, ready to . . . what? Chase them down? Teach them a lesson?

My shoulders drop, and I look over my shoulder. Why am I not surprised to find Mr. Percival doubled over, clenching his belly as he howls his amusement?

"Yes, very funny," I mumble, brushing off my coat with rough hands.

"Little bleeders, ain't they?" he yells. "Takes me back!"

I shake my head and scan the street again, seeing the boys disappear down by the canal. This is heaven for them. A limitless supply of missiles, endless bystanders for targets. Maybe this wasn't such a good idea. But I'm committed now and, well, we don't want Mr. Percival thinking I'm a wimp.

So shoulders back, I get on my way, vigilant, eyes peeled, watching out for the little beasts as I go. It's takes double the time to get to where I'm heading, and I'm almost sorry I don't appreciate the beauty of London under snow.

Almost.

Mostly, I'm just getting to where I need to be.

Heat blasts out from the vent above the shop doors as they slide open, thawing my frozen cheeks. Puddles of defrosted snow scatter the huge mat, and I stamp my boots to knock off the remnants before venturing into the quiet store, focused on my route and shutting my ears off to Slade screaming at me through the speakers.

"Hat," I say, grabbing a black beanie and a matching pair of thick gloves. "Done." I head for the checkout and join the small line, only one woman in front of me. Her free arm clutches a bunch of kids' clothes to her body as she chats on the phone, laughing, engrossed. Therefore she hasn't noticed one of the girls on the checkouts calling her to be served.

"Excuse me," I say, but she doesn't hear me. "Excuse me," I repeat, louder. Still nothing. So I tap her on the shoulder. "That checkout is free."

She turns toward me, phone still at her ear, a smile in place, and when her face comes into view, my heart feels like it jumps out of my chest and splatters all over the store floor.

No.

Air leaves my lungs on a sound laced with pain as I step back.

No.

Her smile drops, as does her phone from her ear. And we stare at each other, neither of us knowing what to do or say.

I'm paralysed.

I can't breathe.

The gloves and hat fall from my hands.

"Camryn," she breathes.

Run.

I turn and hurry out of the store, hearing her calling me as I go. My rushed steps turn into a jog. "Camryn, please!" My jog turns into a run.

And I don't stop.

Not until I make it back to my apartment.

Kicking my boots off and letting my coat drop to the floor, I rush to my bedroom and crawl under the covers, letting the darkness swallow me whole.

Hiding.

But the problem with being in darkness? There's nothing else to focus on, leaving only the face of the woman who destroyed my life.

December 11th

The office is sparse of employees, all having used the snow as an excuse not to come in to work. Flakes. I left home half hour earlier than usual this morning, sporting a sophisticated pencil dress and my Merry People wellington boots, my heels in my bag, but I still made it to the office. I look over to the radiator that's buried under my coat and boots. I was soaked through, my lips blue, but I made it.

Trying to find warmth has been a waste of time, the tips of my fingers still slightly numb come four o'clock. I've been lost in the draft accounts for most of the day, silently seething. Not just because of what I'm reading, but because Thomas isn't here, and the snow is a perfect excuse for him to avoid me. I'm also wondering why I've not heard from Dec. I've typed out endless messages to him when I've taken breaks from the carnage that is the draft accounts for TF Shipping, but I didn't send any of them. My heart is willing me on, demanding I reach out to him. It's screaming, "Heal me, save me." My head wants nothing to do with the madness.

Debbie enters after knocking and gives me an apologetic smile, having me immediately worried about what's happened. "What is it?" I ask.

"It's my husband."

"What about your husband?"

"Well, you see, the schools are closed, and my husband's day was cancelled, but he's had an emergency crop up and needs to go into work. Do you mind if I shoot off? I'm up to date, and I've cleared my in tray."

"Your husband's job is more important than yours?"

"He's a surgeon."

"Oh."

"All his ops were cancelled, given the weather, but there's been an RTA on the M25."

I flinch, nodding. "Sure, get yourself home."

"Thanks, Camryn. Just give me a call if you need anything."

I nod, the door closes, and I blink rapidly, fighting back the flashbacks that come at me without mercy. "Fuck off," I murmur, dipping and reaching into my bag, dragging out my divorce papers and slamming them on my desk. My pen is a weight in my hand as I flick through to the final page, finding the empty signature line and staring at it.

Unreasonable behaviour.

They're the only words I see.

Unreasonable. Behaviour.

We're getting divorced because I was behaving unreasonably.

I toss down the pen and scrub my palms down my face. My phone ringing makes me jump and drop my hands, and his name on the screen throws me into an infuriating conflict of hope and hate. It's been three days since he kissed me and walked away. He's left me hanging, waiting for contact, and he chooses *now* to call me? At gone four o'clock on Monday? Is he checking if I'm going to the bar? Will he tell me not to if he can't make it? I breathe in, not liking the direction of my thoughts. Why else would he call now? Why wouldn't he just head to the bar and see me there?

Where was he on Saturday and Sunday? With not even a message—anything after that kiss to tell me . . . I don't know. *Something.*

It could be my low mood after such a shitty weekend—seeing *her* in the store, seeing Mindy at Mum's care home, the extra pressure my ex is putting on me through my family, and his persistent calls. It could be my disappointment that Dec kissed me like he was breathing life into me again and then left me to survive all weekend alone. It could be the battle my heart and head are having. *Get close. Don't.* I don't know, but I reject his call, dropping my mobile into my bag, then I knock my divorce papers away with an angry sweep of my hand, and yell at thin air.

Not surprisingly, the bar is dead, only one guy in the corner on his phone, and Julio is slicing lemons. I don't miss his surprise when he clocks me, but he doesn't say a word as he prepares my drinks. "Just one," I say as I dump my things on the second to last stool. Another inevitable fleeting look of surprise comes my way, but, again, he doesn't say a word, making me just one dirty martini instead of my usual two.

My eyes follow his working hands as he prepares my drink, waiting for him to speak up. Ask me what I'm doing here. Ask me where Dec is. He doesn't. "One martini," he says, sliding it across the bar and wiping his hands on the towel hanging from one of the belt loops on his trousers. "Enjoying the weather?"

"Do I look like I'm enjoying the weather?" I ask, on autopilot, reaching down to my boots and pulling them off, replacing them with my heels.

"I can't tell." He gets back to his lemons, pulling his chopping board closer to us so he can keep his voice low in the quiet bar. "You're hard to read." One quick flick of his curious eyes up to me. "Your friend not joining you?"

"What friend?" I ask, picking up the cocktail stick and pulling the olive off with my teeth.

"So it's like that, huh?"

"Like what?"

His knife lowers, his hands bracing on the bar as he takes an inhale. "Forgive me if I'm speaking out of turn but, Christ, lady, you're cooler than the sub-zero temperature out there."

Whether it's warranted or not, I bristle. I can't help it. "You're definitely speaking out of turn."

"Then I don't suppose I'm getting a tip today."

I laugh on the inside—it's sardonic—and take my first glorious sip of the martini. "You know, you make the best ones."

"Is that why you come here most?" I tilt my head, and Julio smiles out the corner of his mouth as he gets back to slicing, this time limes. "My brother works at The Regent."

"Ah," I breathe. "Short guy, receding hairline, charming twinkle in his eyes?"

"That's him. Ren."

"And how did you two come to make the connection with me, The Regent, and here?"

His smile stretches, the kind of smile that's somewhere between cheeky and embarrassed. "He mentioned a lady in her thirties, dark, mid-length hair, an attractive mole on her cheek, on the slimmer side of slender, stoic, always orders two dirty martinis, one of which remains on the bar while she drinks a further three, four, five, sometimes six, before she finally drinks that initial second martini."

What he hasn't finished with is, *and then leaves with a man.* "I guess that second martini gave the game away, huh?"

He chuckles as I sip, and he loads his sliced fruits into a tub. "Do you know what I'm wondering?"

"I don't know, and I'm not sure I want to."

The lid clicks onto the pot with a few loud pops, and he leans across the bar, making me recline back on my stool. "You're right. You probably don't." He nods past me, and I peek back to see the guy in the corner looking this way. "Someone's got his eye on you."

"Hasn't he just," I muse, turning slightly on my stool. "How do I look?"

"Cold. But he looks like he wants to warm you up."

"Ha ha," I drone, maintaining eye contact with the man. He's handsome, in a Hugh Grant kind of way. A bit preppy. A lot floppy. He's too far away to see if there's a ring. *No married men.*

I inhale and face the bar again, having a little argument with myself. Dec's married. *I'm* married. *Take the distraction.* Irritatingly, it's not just my past I need distracting from.

Dec.

I growl under my breath and neck the rest of my drink. *Leave.* I should go home before I find out if that man behind me has a ring on his finger. Before I succumb to brief, mindless pleasure. Before I return to old habits. "One more, please," I say, pushing my glass to Julio. He gets to work, as my phone vibrates on the bar, the screen lighting up.

> Camryn, the next step is for me to apply to the court so we can move forward. That's a lengthy and expensive process for both of us. Please, can you just sign the acknowledgment form and hire legal counsel so we can start to get the financial settlement agreed and both of us can move on?

My phone hits the marble bar with a thud when I drop it, and Julio delivers my second martini at the perfect time. I throw it back and gasp after swallowing hard. Move on? So we can *both* move on? I will never move on.

"Want some company?"

I turn toward the voice, looking him up and down. There's no ring. "Yes," I say without much thought, indicating the stool. "Why not." There are a dozen reasons, all of which, in this moment, I'm prepared to ignore. "What are you drinking?"

"Negroni," he says to Julio as he perches on the stool, resting his forearms on the bar so the overhead bar lights shine down on his hands. I've seen this move endless times before. A subtle demonstration that there's no ring. He doesn't know that I already spotted that, except I didn't have the benefit of light on his hands then. And I do now.

"When did you remove it?" I ask, tapping the base of my glass with my fingertip.

"Excuse me?"

"Your ring. Was it off before you saw me, or did you take it off before you decided to come over?"

Laughing under his breath, he starts doing the motions, spinning the wedding band that isn't there. "Caught red-handed."

"American?" I ask.

"New York."

"Here on business?"

"And now stranded."

"How inconvenient," I murmur, crossing one leg over the other and turning slightly toward him.

"I thought so too until a few minutes ago." His eyes drop down my seated body as he extends a hand. "Hugh."

I laugh on the inside at the irony. "Camryn," I say, accepting and shaking. "That's a strong shake."

"Touché." He narrows his eyes, my hand still in his, his unspoken intentions clear.

"You're staying here?" I ask.

Julio clears his throat and places two fresh drinks on the bar. "Would you like me to charge these to your room, Mr. Colton?"

"Yes, good man." Huge takes a cool sip of his drink. "Six-one-eight."

"Subtle," I say quietly, laughing to myself. "What do you do?"

"Financial technology. You?"

"CFO."

He can't hide his surprise, or his delight. "Really?"

"That doesn't make us kindred spirits."

He lets out a bark of laughter, caressing the rim of his short, fat glass with his fingertip in slow circles. "You're very intriguing."

"Don't be intrigued, Hugh. It's dangerous."

His smile slowly drops as he casts his eyes my way. "How many men have been intrigued by you, Camryn?"

"Enough for me to know what I'm doing." Not enough for me to be cured.

Two small leather folders are placed before us, courtesy of Julio, and I watch, expressionless, as Hugh scribbles his signature in his first, before helping himself to mine. Flicking me a look annoyingly on the edge of self-assuredness, he stands. "Excuse me while I use the men's." I watch him stride away, my top lip sucked between my teeth, and I rest back on my stool, contemplating. Questioning.

Hesitating.

He's married.

It grates on me. Do I want to sleep with Hugh? No. Should I? No.

Will I?

"Don't look at me like that," I say, catching Julio's mild look of disapproval. "I don't touch married men." He's observed me many times in recent years. He knows this.

His eyebrows lift. "So you're just leading him on?"

"He deserves it." I give him a sardonic smile. "You can watch him wilt when he realises I'm not going to follow him up to room six-one-eight. You can make me another martini now. Maybe a single guy will show up soon."

Julio shakes his head and pulls the vodka off the glass shelf. "I have a feeling the disappointment will be real."

"Really?" I ask. "Why? Because I dazzled him with my charm? Swooned all over him? Made hi—"

"Indirectly promised him a night of sex with no strings attached."

I pause for thought and then nod mildly in agreement. "Every sex-deprived, married man's dream."

"But what about the single men?"

"They're usually emotionally unavailable." *Except Dec.* I flinch and check the progress of my next drink.

"You're a stunning woman, Camryn," Julio says, surprising me. "I'm just being honest here, okay?"

"Okay," I say slowly, quite sure I'm not going to want to hear this.

"You're obviously smart, confident, successful, and very intriguing."

And utterly fucking broken. None of them see that part. *Except Dec.* Julio starts shaking my drink, and it can't come soon enough. The moment the sound of ice crashing against the metal stops, he pushes a clean glass toward me and pours, eyes on his task. "Men love those qualities, but many don't want to marry them."

"They just want to fuck them," I murmur, just as he looks past me.

"There's sometimes the odd exception who wants to go deeper." His eyes come back to me. "I'll leave you to your third martini." And he goes to the sink and washes the shaker as I stare at my drink for a few moments, my spine tingling.

I eventually bring myself to look over my shoulder.

Dec's at the entrance, slap bang in the middle of the open double doors, eyes like spears aimed my way. "I had a feeling." His voice is deep and grainy, as if his vocal cords are straining, a certain edge of darkness dripping from his tone I'm sure I should be wary of.

And I am.

He looks somewhere between anger and disappointment, like a parent who's dealing with an errant child. My hackles rise. *He had a feeling?* Endless retorts run amok in my mind, not one of them willing to come forward. The collar of his navy coat is turned up, flakes of snow dusting his shoulders and hair.

Indignance and sheer stubbornness demands me to turn away, give him the cold shoulder, but my eyes have other ideas, continuing with their appreciative jaunt down his tall frame to his feet. His brown leather dress shoes are dark around the toes, stained by the snow. *Why did you leave me hanging all weekend? Why did you leave me alone?*

No. "You had a feeling," I murmur.

His astute gaze scans the empty bar as he approaches, his gait smooth, his posture tall and intimidating. "What's going on, Camryn?" He flicks a small nod to Julio, his lips straight.

"I'm having a drink."

Julio disappears to the other end of the bar, pulling open the glass washer. Steam billows out, misting the space between the bar and the ceiling, making the hazy lighting even hazier. My eyes drop to the half-drunk Negroni next to my martini, and I just know that's what Dec's gaze is set on too. A cautious peek out the corner of my eyes confirms it. If the tumbler shattered under the weight of his concentrated glare, I wouldn't be surprised. He's livid. And yet still unbelievably handsome. His lips should be thinner given how stretched they are, but they remain plump. Kissable. "Whose is it?" he asks, his question brittle. "Answer me, Camryn."

"You didn't give me a chance to."

"I'm giving you the chance now." His towering body turns into me, coming closer, forcing my neck back to look up at him. A familiar wave of panic starts to rise from the pit of my stomach, my thoughts scrambling in a hundred directions. Fight? Flee?

"You're talking like I owe you an explanation."

"You do. Tell me."

Because I have no idea how to handle this situation, or Dec's hostility, I swivel away from him. Hiding. *Coward*. My reprieve from his foul mood is short-lived, and he turns me straight back toward him, taking my glass from my hand and placing it on the bar before taking Hugh's stool and pulling it as close as he can, invading my personal space.

"Whose glass is it, Camryn?"

I stare straight into his darkening eyes. "A man's."

I'm sure I hear the sound of his teeth grinding. "Get your coat on, we're leaving."

"What?"

He stands abruptly and dips into his pocket, throwing a pile of notes on the bar. "Get up."

I stare at the money as Julio dares to venture back to this end of the bar, his lips straight too. "The tab's been settled," he says, almost with regret, throwing me an apologetic look.

"By whom?" Dec asks shortly.

Julio peeks at me.

"I'm asking you," he grates. "Not Camryn."

"Dec, stop it," I warn.

He wraps his big hand around my upper arm, trying to stand me up with a gentle but firm force.

"Stop it," I snap, wriggling free of his hold. "What are you doing?"

It's the worst timing, and yet I expected it. Hugh strolls out of the men's, his hands on his zipper still fastening himself. *Fuck.* His broad smile wavers, and I sigh, reaching for my nose and pinching the bridge as I squeeze my eyes closed. And yet I can't really play a victim. I knew what I was doing when I came here. The vulnerable, broken woman was hoping to find Dec. The acrimonious, twisted wench whose mother doesn't recognise her wanted to prove she's not worthy of his acceptance. Of *anyone's* acceptance. I'm a lost cause. Dec can't save me, and he'd be a fool to believe he can.

"That's my seat," Hugh says, his chest puffing out.

"It is not your seat." Dec swipes up the Negroni and shoves it into Hugh's chest, spilling the orange liquid down his crisp white shirt. "Take your drink *and* yourself back to wherever you were sitting before you moved in on the beautiful, intriguing woman at the bar."

Hugh laughs lightly, looking down his stained shirt. "She never mentioned a boyfriend."

"Because she doesn't have one."

"Then who the fuck are you?"

Something switches in Dec, a red mist of rage dropping and veiling his handsome face, contorting it. He moves closer, his voice dropping to a menacing whisper. "I'm the man who'll fuck you up if you don't get the fuck away from her now."

"Dec," I breathe, shocked.

"Gentlemen," Julio calls sternly, ready to fly over the bar and drag Dec off Hugh.

"Leave," Dec grits out. "She won't be opening her legs for you."

I balk, my lax mouth falling open. How dare he? "You can stay," I snap.

Hugh looks absolutely bewildered, his head batting back and forth between us. "The lady would like me to stay."

"I strongly advise against it," Dec says quietly, one shoulder leaning forward. His fist could be mistaken for giant snowballs, all the blood squeezed out of his hands. It takes Hugh only a couple more seconds of deliberation before he backs off, collecting his things and leaving the bar. And I don't blame him. Dec looks as if he could explode at any moment.

And I stand still and quiet, ashamed, embarrassed, the ache in my chest bringing my hand up to try and massage it away. *Humiliated.*

Shaking, Dec lowers to the stool. I don't, remaining on my feet, waiting for him to cool off. "I'll ask you again," he says, calm but definitely not. "What's going on?"

I don't know what to say as I frantically try to keep the bricks of my wall in place. An impossible task when Dec just keeps smashing through them. We kissed, it was amazing, but he left me in limbo all weekend to fend off the blasts of my past coming at me mercifully. He left me to talk myself round in circles over that kiss. He left me to convince myself he can't handle me.

Don't get close.

He cares about you.

But he doesn't *know* me.

"I kissed you, Camryn."

Oh, Dec, you certainly did. I look away when his gaze drops to my mouth, as if he's considering reminding me of how magical that kiss was. He doesn't need to. It's etched in my mind, carved deeply, never to be forgotten.

"I thought that's what you wanted."

I did, I did, I did. Admittedly, initially, I wanted him to kiss the life out of me and fuck me hard to take me away from this godforsaken world even just for a little while, but it was quickly and suddenly more than that. I didn't want him to kiss me because it would lead to sex and escape, but because I so desperately wanted to be that close to him. Taste him. Feel him. The hunger in the desperation was suddenly different, and so much more than I'm used to dealing with. And then it happened, and it was so incredibly wonderful. The kiss, his words, the way he looked at me. It was so *so* much more.

But then I pined for him. Got mad with him. Got mad with *myself*.

And now I'm sabotaging whatever this is.

You can't let someone close without letting them *in*. And after that kiss, after this weekend, after tonight, I know this man could break me even more than I'm already broken.

"You shouldn't have come here," I say, trying to sound sure and strong, wondering if I could be anymore broken.

He drags tired, empty eyes my way. "Right." He rises from his stool lethargically, as if it's an effort. As if he's had all the fight knocked out of him. "I shouldn't have come." His sneer cuts deep, as I know he intended it to. And I deserve it. "Goodbye, Camryn."

"Your money, sir." Julio scoops up the notes and holds them out, and Dec considers the handful of cash for a few long moments before he takes it and drops it at my feet. "For the kiss."

He stalks off, and I'm once again rendered useless. And unreasonably hurt. The pain in my chest is excruciating—but I deserve that too.

It takes me a few too many seconds to gather my scattered thoughts, for my sensibility to wade through the perpetual bog of grief, and surface. I look at Julio like he might be able to help me out. Guide me. I get nothing. "I deserved that, didn't I?"

His hands come up, and he backs off. It's a resounding yes without speaking up.

Sabotage.

He *had a feeling* I'd be here. He *knew*. *Because he wants to know you.* He cares. "Shit." I scoop up my things and go after Dec, hurrying through the lobby and breaking out into a blizzard. "Oh my God," I breathe, the baltic air nearly taking me off my feet. I hurry into my coat, scanning up and down the street for him, squinting to see past the fast-falling flurry of snow. He's crossing the road at the end of the road. "Dec," I yell, hurrying after him, my heels getting lost in the snow. "Dec, wait. Shit!" My foot slips from under me, forcing me to grab a nearby railing. "Dec!" He becomes blurrier. "God damn me." I take off my shoes and, like a mad woman, brave the snow barefoot, jogging down the street. "Oh my God," I gasp, my feet frozen.

He opens the back door of a grey Defender.

"Dec!"

Looking up, his hand still clenching the handle, he finds me on the pavement through the snow, and an eternity passes, him staring at me, me waiting, rolling around the words I need to make this right. "I'm sorry," I whisper, not nearly loud enough to be heard.

He shakes his head and slips into the back of the car, and my heart sinks as the door closes and it pulls away, handling the conditions with smooth grace and ease, eventually disappearing around the corner.

And I stand, a stupid, wet, cold, barefoot mess on the pavement in the snow watching him go.

Because I pushed him away.

The best thing that's happened to me in so long.

Gone.

December 12th

"Don't forget Christmas Jumper Day tomorrow," Crystal sings to anyone and everyone as I trudge down the corridor, weighed down with layers, my boots heavy with compacted snow on the soles. "Damn, I'm going to have to send an email," she mutters. "Snow should pull people out, not keep them in." She wilts when she spots me. "Oh, hi, Camryn."

"Hi." I step into my office and drop my bags to the floor, stripping out of my coat, scarf, and hoodie, hanging everything on the radiator before I pull my heels out and get them on.

When I land at my desk, I chew my lip, staring down at my phone as I revisit last night for the thousandth time, picking it all to pieces. His anger. The hurt he couldn't hide. How he walked away when I went after him. I wanted to call him and blurt my truths, try to make him understand me.

But I bottled it.

Because I'm a coward.

Just burying my head in the sand again.

When will I stop doing that?

Now? And is it too late? Will Dec even answer if I call?

I grab my mobile and dial him, pacing up and down, trying to conjure up some words. None come to me. So I cut the call before it rings and hang my head in exasperation as I drop to my chair and a knock sounds. "Come in, Thomas." His head pops around the door as I'm fixing my fluffy hair in a low knot, his smile big and cheesy. I'm surprised he's shown his face. "Let's talk about the draft accounts," I say, stern.

"I have a better idea."

"What?"

He moves aside, opening the door wide, revealing Crystal. Not that I can see her, because she's concealed. "Let's talk about who could have sent you these beautiful flowers."

I stare at the extravagant spray of winter blooms, my heart bucking. "You can leave them on the table," I murmur, eyes fixed on them as Crystal makes her way across my office and sets them on the coffee table by the chair.

"So pretty," she says, petting the petal of a rose. "Would you like me to get a vase?"

"What?"

"A vase. To put your flowers in."

"No." I get up and usher them out of my office, slamming the door and resting my back against it. He sent me flowers? He saw me on the pavement, cold, wet, barefoot, he drove away leaving me there, but he's sent me flowers?

I approach my desk like a nervous dog, almost cowering, unsure about the gift before me that's enticing me with promises of hope and affection.

The card is lost amid the foliage, a small white fleck among the abundance of bright colours. Lowering to the chair, I pluck it out and hold my breath as I open the envelope. Is this his way of confirming that what we could've had is gone? That I'm too broken, too cold, too spineless, and too weak for him to bother anymore? They're all fair assessments. But, no. Why would he send flowers to mark the end?

Sliding the card out, I exhale when I read the words.

. . .

I don't fuck for the sake of fucking, Camryn. And I don't kiss for the sake of kissing. I want that to be clear. The ball is in your court. Dec.

There are so many unwritten words on this card, so many words left unsaid, but I hear them all. The ball is in my court. He won't pursue me. And he's not interested in doing *anything* for the sake of it. So he expects the same from me.

I sink into the chair, regret and shame sweeping in and eating me alive from the inside out. They're the brightest flowers he could have found. An explosion of colour on the blank canvas of my life.

Symbolic.

I remain in my office for the rest of the day, distracted, obsessing over his words, pacing up and down, dialling him endless times and not following through with the call, because what would I say to him? Thank you? Sorry? Can we start again? Or do I let all of my demons pour out of me? Tell him the truth. Not that I've lied.

At least, not vocally. More . . . silently.

At four thirty, I'm going out of my mind, searching for the courage I need to move forward. It's not so much calling Dec or even talking to him, but it's what I've finally accepted it's leading to.

I read the card for the millionth time, slipping it into my bag when Debbie wanders in. She eyes my flowers but doesn't pass comment. "These need your signature, and I've been asked to remind you about Christmas Jumper Day tomorrow and Secret Santa on Thursday." Her face is a picture of awkwardness, her pink lips rolling inward and disappearing.

"I don't own any Christmas jumpers."

"Of course you don't, Camryn. Why would you?" She pivots and leaves. "Just delivering the message."

"Hey, Debbie." She stops at the door and looks back. "Your husband."

"What about him?"

"Did he . . . you know . . . after what you said yesterday. About the accident on the M25."

"Did he save her? No, he didn't. Two weeks before Christmas." Her gaze drops to the floor, but I still see her frown as well as I feel the ache in my stomach. "Life's cruel, huh?"

I swallow around my nod as Debbie leaves and proceed to stare at the flowers, considering her words. Life can be exceedingly cruel.

For many, Camryn, not just you.

The moment I open my office door, I feel all eyes on me, and they follow me all the way to the elevator. Once I push the button, I look back. "What?" I ask no one in particular but everyone at the same time.

"Nothing," they sing.

"Sure." I roll my eyes and step into the cart, hoping no one joins me on the way down because there isn't a square inch of spare space, the flowers touching each side of the cart. And now my face is so close, I can appreciate the scent. I inhale and close my eyes, letting it sink into me, which only makes me crave Dec more than usual. His warmth.

Halfway across the lobby, I juggle the bouquet into one arm and pull my scarf up to my chin, bracing for the shock of cold. "Good Lord," I breathe when it hits me, speeding up, hoping my faster pace will warm me up a bit. It doesn't.

I'm a fucking icicle by the time I make it to where I want to be, and as I stare up at the impressive building, I wonder . . . what now? Do I go in? Wait outside?

I decide to wait. I don't want people to ask questions he might not be comfortable with. *No, that's just how you'd feel if he showed up at your office.* I'm rolling my eyes again, exasperated by myself, as I scan the vicinity, finding a post to perch on.

And I wait.

And wait.

And with each minute that passes, I lose feeling in one more finger until my hands are like blocks of ice. *I must get some gloves.* Surely I can find a store where I won't bump into my devastating past so I can get myself a pair of gloves. My eyes narrow as the unstoppable force of her smiling face infiltrates my mind. How blissfully happy she'd sounded talking on the phone. How at peace she looked in her life.

How just seeing her sent me down a rabbit hole of agony and desolation.

Mildly shaking my head, I close my eyes and hear her apologies. I see the sheen of tears in her eyes when she had the nerve to come to our home and say sorry. My husband's anger when I slapped her face.

No.

I jerk, my eyes snapping open, and find my flowers.

Colour.

Focus on the colour.

The door to the building opens endless times, various people coming and going, but none of them are Dec. I'm about all out of hope, sure he's left early, or maybe not come to his office at all today, when a grey Defender pulls up at the curb, the hazards flashing. My deep inhale lifts me to my feet as I watch a man hop out. Not Dec. He's short and stocky in build, with a mop of dark curly hair. Jogging across the pavement to the gold doors of the building, he disappears through them, appearing moments later with a few boxes stacked in his arms.

Dec's following him, fastening the buttons of his coat.

My heart stops at the mere sight of him. How his tall body moves so sinuously, how his silver gaze seems infinitely lazy, how his lips maintain that constant slight parting. He adjusts the scarf around his neck with leather-gloved hands, getting the collar of his coat flat under the wool wrapped around his neck. I can't convince my legs to walk me over to him. I can't convince my mouth to call his name.

But I don't need to, because he looks up and sees me. Whether because he's sensed me nearby or by chance, I don't know. He freezes for a moment, taking me in, while I continue refreshing my mind of every magnificent bit of him. I'm so nervous. Ready to expose myself but not.

Somehow, I finally convince by legs to move and walk over to him, setting the flowers on the ground by my feet.

The man from the Defender appears next to us. "Dec?"

"Just give me a moment," Dec says quietly, his gaze remaining on me.

"Of course."

My mind's empty.

"How long have you been out here?" he asks.

"Not long."

"Your blue lips don't agree."

"I needed to tell you something."

"What?"

I throw caution to the wind and step into his body, sliding my hand onto his neck and pulling his face close to mine, my breath shaky as I exhale, our noses so close, if I were to blink, our lashes would brush.

"Your hand's really fucking cold," he whispers, looking so deeply into my eyes, I'm sure he must see to the very depths of my soul. "So whatever you need to tell me, get on with it."

I swoop in and catch his mouth, and he's holding me in his arms a second later, completely encasing me in his warm body, right in the middle of The Strand. People are certainly dodging us —staring—but I don't care.

My lips thaw immediately, warmth sailing through my frozen body and lighting up my insides. Lighting up my life.

Colour and light.

Because of him.

Sparks sizzle and bang around us, a kaleidoscope of colour erupting in my darkness, his hot tongue lapping around mine with a gentle ease. The pressure is perfect. I could kiss him forever and never come up for air. Never relent to the scratch of his bristle across my skin. Never get tired of hearing his quiet hums of pleasure.

I know I'll be devasted if he slows this kiss to a stop first, so I find the strength I need to slow it myself until our lips are resting together. Not moving but just touching.

I open my eyes. His are still closed . . . until they're not.

His lashes flutter, his grey eyes opening and sending my world into a further spin, the sparkle making me as dizzy as his kiss. Moving back out of his body takes everything in me and more. But the warmth is bone deep. I can't feel the cold now.

Dec tilts his head in question as I collect my flowers, then I turn and walk away, a small, rare smile tugging the corner of my mouth. My steps are light, and the cold can't touch me. I reach up and feel at my lips, spellbound, hoping he heard every word I spoke in that kiss.

Someone has shovelled the snow from the pathway up to my building—an admiral and good service to all residents.

Except now in its place is a sheet of ice, which is something I only discover when I take my first step off the street. "Fuck!" My body goes rigid, my spine bending back, and my feet must be blurry they're spinning so fast, trying to keep me upright. "Fucking weather."

"Stay where you are!"

I grab the railing, juggling my flowers, trying to save us both. Mr. Percival is in the doorway with his walking frame in one hand, a bucket in the other. "What are you doing?" I call, clinging on with one hand, the frozen metal burning my palm.

"Salt, dear," he says, starting to grab handfuls and throw it toward me.

"Did you shovel all that snow?"

"Who else?"

"Someone who's not ancient or incapacitated, preferably."

"Oh, I see someone woke up with some sass today. Nice flowers. Anyway, what else am I going to do with my time?"

"Play with your gnomes?" I mutter under my breath, regaining some balance and tentatively releasing the railing to reposition the flowers. "Mr. Percival," I say with a voice full of authority, wrapping a palm around the next railing, moving up the path in slow, cautious steps. "A man of your age shouldn't be shovelling snow."

"So who bought you the flowers?"

"Someone."

"Maybe a tall, dapper, handsome *someone* with greying, longish hair and rather sparkly silvery grey eyes?"

I stop, narrowing one eye. That's quite specific. "Maybe," I confirm, dragging the word out, sounding as cagey as I am. "Are you spying on me?"

He snorts, chucking more salt around my feet. "I was being a good neighbour. What's his name?"

Grit sprinkles my boots as I make my way up the path. "Mr. Percival, your aim is terrible. Dec. His name's Dec."

"Dec? And how old is Dec?"

I frown. "I don't know."

He laughs. "You don't know? He's bought you those beautiful flowers and you don't even know how old he is?"

"I don't know how old *you* are," I point out.

"I didn't buy you flowers."

"No, but you made me a cake."

His grin is epic, and impossible not to return. "I did, didn't I? Was it good?"

"Delicious," I admit.

He drops the bucket by his walking frame. "There. It should be safe now."

"Thank you."

"Wel—" Mr. Percival stands up straight, his old eyes suddenly as alert as his posture.

"What is it?" I ask, looking over my shoulder. "Oh no." Two kids, the same little shits that pelted me with a snowball to the face, are at the end of the path, each with a perfectly formed, fucking *massive* snowballs in their gloved hands. "Don't you dare," I warn.

They smirk, draw back.

"No!"

And fire.

One gets me square in the face, the other in my chest. The power behind their missiles would be impressive if I wasn't the target. "God damn!" My curse comes out on a garbled snort, diluted by a mouthful of snow. I can't see, can't talk, and dare not move, but I can hear a mixture of old chuckles and young, boisterous laughs.

I spit out the snow and wipe my face with my spare hand, my flowers safe in the crook of my arm. "This is victimisation."

"Come on, dear. It's safe in here."

I risk releasing the railing and dusting myself off, seeing the two little shits running off down the road. "Little fuckers." I move slowly and carefully toward the door as Mr. Percival titters, moving aside to let me through. "Now, I'm no detective, Camryn, as you well know, so I'm working on intuition and nothing else."

"And what's your intuition say?"

"It says this Dec bloke is fond of you. What do you think?"

"I think you might be onto something."

"Me too."

We walk down the corridor side by side. "He's a very lovely man," I say quietly, my mind returning to our second kiss, my smile discreet, my lips still warm from his mouth on mine.

We make it to Mr. Percival's flat first, and I hold back to make sure he makes it inside safely. "Christmas," he says, wistful, hovering on the threshold. "What a wonderful time to fall in love."

"Who said anything about love?"

"You did."

"I did no such thing."

He hums, his chin lifting. "Maybe not with words. Goodnight, dear." The door closes in my face abruptly but then swings back open just as fast. "And get yourself a hat and some gloves, for the love of God."

Slam.

I recoil, just as the door opens once again. "That smile suits you."

"Are you done?"

"For now."

Slam.

"Strange old man," I muse, carrying on up the hallway.

"I heard that!"

"Then stop spying on me," I say over a laugh, worrying my key into the lock and letting myself in. The usual cold space greets me, the smell nothingy, no washing, no room scents, or cooking. It's just . . . nothingy.

The flowers might change that. And luckily, they're in a bag of water so I set them straight on the table in the lounge—no vase required—bringing a little colour into my domain. Into my life. I stand back, nodding my own approval. Then shiver, feeling a bit of ice slip past my neck onto my back. "Jesus." I bow my back, trying to avoid the chill, and make my way to my bedroom.

After I change out of my wet clothes, I get another slice of Mr. P's cake and sit on the couch in front of the coffee table, admiring the flowers, and when a message comes through, my heart skips a few too many beats.

I loved what you told me.

I inhale, falling back against the couch.

And next time, get in the fucking car instead of walking home in the cold.

I smile, reading his message over and over again, keeping the warmth inside alive.

And the colour.

And the hope.

December 13th

I woke up late. I don't know how that happened.

Yes, you do.

My run was abandoned, and in a total flap, I raced around my apartment getting ready, all while marvelling at just how good my sleep was—I didn't wake up once—at the same time relishing the gorgeous scent of my flowers.

I'm halfway to the office, an hour later than usual, when I remember something.

Christmas Jumper Day.

"Fuck." I stop at the corner of the street, nibbling on the inside of my cheek as I glance down my black wool trench coat, seeing in my mind's eye the black dress beneath. I would never usually subscribe to festive activities, would never give two shits what my colleagues think when I show up in my usual black wardrobe casting my eternal doom across the merriment, but today, for some unbeknown reason to me, I'm feeling a little acquiescent.

And I need a hat and gloves, anyway.

Diverting up Oxford Street, I find the nearest open store that'll give me what I need and grab the first jumper I can lay my hands on. A black—bonus—chunky knitted oversized, cropped affair with an understated Christmas hat on the right breast. Perfect. I grab my size and find myself a bobble hat and gloves—both black—and head for the checkout.

But stop halfway, thinking, looking at the matching hat and gloves. Before I know what I'm doing, I'm reversing my steps and swapping my obligatory black for the cream set.

I don't read too much into it. I'm here buying a Christmas jumper, for fuck's sake.

"Do you need a bag?"

"No thanks," I say, tapping my card and wriggling out of my coat. "Can you cut the tags off for me, please?"

She laughs. "Sure."

"Thanks." I get into the jumper, blowing my hair out of my face, pull the hat and gloves on, and get back into my coat.

Done.

The bling, sparkle, and glitz that hits me when the elevator doors open nearly catapult me into the back wall. It seems everyone's made it into the office for Christmas Jumper Day, despite the snow still being ankle deep. And they're all currently in the corridor checking out each other's efforts. It's no surprise that the chatter dies down when they spot me. It's no surprise that every set of eyebrows shoot up in shock when they see I'm wearing a Christmas jumper.

"Let's not make a big deal of it," I say, laying my coat over my arm and stepping off the elevator. "It's just a jumper."

"And what a wonderful jumper it is," Thomas says, serious.

I look back over my shoulder when I hear a collection of suppressed sniggers, rolling my eyes at the culprits. All of them. "Oh, do grow up."

My office door hits the frame with more force than I intended, and the sniggers turn into full-blown belly laughs. I frown and look down my front, wondering what the fuck is so funny. As far as Christmas jumpers go, this one's on the classier side of god-awful, unlike the garish horrors adorning every one of my colleagues. It's me. They're laughing at me trying to make an effort.

Indignant, I hang my coat and put my hat and gloves on the radiator, leaving my boots on—heels really won't work with the jumper—taking a seat at my desk, irritated by the buzz outside my office. So I rootle through my bag for my AirPods and drown it out with some RIOPY, settling down to work through my emails and bracing myself to go over the company credit card statement that's landed.

Six hours later, I'm bursting for a wee and have redlined a dozen transactions on the statements that I have questions about. This has got to the busiest statement to date. And the largest. My God, Anthony and Barbara have absolutely no respect for my job, Thomas, or this company. It's a fucking free-for-all.

My Christmas jumper and I can no longer hide. I send the statement to the printer and take a breath, pulling my AirPods out and leaving my office. Debbie peeks up, the corner of her lip quirking. "What?" I ask, knowing I sound hostile. "Jesus, if I'd known my partaking in the dumb Christmas Jumper Day was going to cause such a drama, I wouldn't have bothered."

Her shoulders drop on a small sigh. "Camryn, you terrify most of the people at this company."

"I don't talk to half the people at this company, so how can I terrify them?"

Her expression is something that could only be interpreted as *really*?

I shrug. "I don't like Christmas."

"What's your excuse for the other eleven months of the year?"

"Ouch."

"You know, it would be helpful if people had some context," she says, quietly, almost reluctantly.

As she should. "Not gonna happen, Debbie," I motion to the printer. "There should be a credit card statement for me."

She kicks off with her feet, rolling herself to the printer, and pulls off the sheets. "What about the flowers?"

"What about them?"

"Oh my God, Camryn, crack a smile, for the love of God." She slaps the papers down, a wave of annoyance I've not seen on Debbie before twisting her round face.

"Are you done?" I ask, swiping the papers up, my jaw a little tense, making Deb remember herself and wilt.

"Yes."

"Good. I have a job to do." I march onward, armed, and pass Crystal's desk, my attention on Thomas's office.

"Oh, oh, he's in a private meeting," she calls out urgently as I burst through his door.

"We need to talk."

"Camryn," he says, rising from his chair as I wave the papers in my hand at him. "What's that?"

"The latest business card statement."

"Can it wait?" He motions to the corner of his office, where Barbara and Anthony are reclined on the black leather couch, sipping coffees.

Ah, the wife and son. The *Board*. Perfect. "Actually, this concerns you two as well," I say, helping myself to a seat.

"Oh." Thomas retakes his chair, showing the ceiling his palms when his wife gives him a sharp look. Of course, Barbara is bejewelled in red sequins. She looks like an angry zit, and Anthony looks like he wants to launch me into outer space, as usual.

"There are a few things on here I need more information on." I flick to the second page. "Like this transaction for ten thousand five hundred pounds on November first to Royal Caribbean."

"How much?" Thomas blurts, as Anthony starts squirming in his seat, diverting his eyes from mine.

"Ten thousand five hundred," I confirm, my pen poised and ready, my expectant look pointed at Thomas, making him look across to his son and wife.

"Any offers?" he asks.

Anthony clears his throat. "That was me," he says quietly.

"Pardon?" I turn my ear toward them.

"It was me," he says, louder this time, doing a terrible job of hiding his scowl. "I have a meeting in Miami in January."

"Yes, I can see the return flights here," I say, pointing down at my lap where the statement covers my knees. "Fifteen thousand to British Airways. Oh, and of course the seven and a half thousand for four nights at a beach front villa in Miami."

Thomas's eyes look they're about to pop out of his head, the glutaral sound that rises sounding scarily like he's choking. "How much?"

"That's for two people first class," I say, wondering if I need to get him a drink of water.

"*Two* people?" He looks back to Anthony, as do I, waiting.

Poor guy looks like he could sink into the creases on the leather couch. "Me and Leah."

"You paid for Leah's ticket on your company card?"

"And for their accommodation and cruise," I remind him. "All in all, give or take a few quid, twenty-five thousand."

"Jesus Christ."

I dump the papers on the desk, acutely aware that Thomas's wife is remaining very still and exceedingly quiet where she is. I won't hit Thomas with the transaction mid-November for a doctor on Harley Street. "Thomas, I've said it before, and I'll say it again. I cannot make your company accounts pretty if money is being spent with zero regard. No investor will gloss over the fact that the business cards are being abused and used for personal gain, not to mention the fact that Inland Revenue will deem this tax evasion."

"So fucking dramatic," Anthony mumbles.

"Thomas, there's over eighty-five thousand that shouldn't be claimed as business expenses on these statements." Anthony has the gall to roll his eyes. *Arsehole.* "I can't work with this," I say straight, not biting to Anthony, or he'll likely have no head. I really don't feel like I can be taken seriously when I'm sitting here in a fucking Christmas jumper, but here I am. In a Christmas jumper. It's bad enough dealing with my boss's desire to reward subpar performances with bonuses, but at least his intentions are admirable—even if he shouldn't be so frivolous at such a crucial time.

Thomas shakes his head, as my phone vibrates on my lap. I look down and see a preview of a message from Dec, and my skin becomes all tingly. "I'll leave it with you," I say, handing over the statements with all the highlighted transactions, making my escape before any more bombs go off.

"Nice jumper," Anthony calls with spite as I close the door behind me.

"Oh fuck off," I mutter.

Crystal looks up, eyes wide.

"Not you." I force a smile, breathe out, and open Dec's message.

My world shows some semblance of rightness once again.

Bar. Half hour.

My teeth sink into my lip, restricting my smile, as I send a thumbs up.

"Nice jumper," Crystal says as I pass her desk.

"Thanks." I stop dead in my tracks when I hear Thomas's voice rise, followed by Anthony's. Crystal immediately loses all interest in my jumper, her eyes darting to Thomas's door. "Family politics," I say. "I'd go get yourself a coffee."

She's up like a shot, joining me on my walk back to my end of the floor. Crystal dips into the kitchen as Meredith comes out, cupping her mug with both hands. "Camryn," she says, stopping. "I just wanted to—"

"Please don't mention the jumper."

She smiles. "I wanted to thank you for stepping in."

"You shouldn't have to thank me, it should never have come to that." I carry on, Meredith flanking me, our pace leisurely. "Have you heard from him?"

"I've filed for a divorce."

I wince. "Good luck."

"Thanks."

"Nice jumper, Camryn," Joshua says, holding up his Christmas mug in cheers.

I roll my eyes as we reach Debbie's desk, and Meredith sets her coffee down. "I just have a few things to run over with Debbie," she says.

"Then I'll leave you to it." I take the handle of my door.

"Where did you get it?" Meredith calls.

I turn my frown back to the two women. "What?"

"The jumper."

I look down my front. "Some tat store around the corner. Why?" Both women claim their mugs and take sips, and it's so fucking obvious that they're doing it to restrain their smiles. "Okay," I breathe, facing them. "What's going on?" I feel like I'm the butt of everyone's jokes today.

"It's a cool jumper."

"It's a black fucking jumper with a Christmas hat on the front. It hardly justifies the airtime it's getting."

Debbie and Meredith cast looks to each other.

"What?" I snap, throwing my arms up.

"I wasn't referring to the front of the jumper." Debbie cocks a questioning look. "It's the back that's getting the airtime."

"The back?"

"You didn't see the back?"

"No, I didn't see the back," I say, looking over my shoulder, trying to see the back. "Is there something on the back?" I find myself turning a full circle as I crane my neck, eventually giving up and taking it off. And I die a million deaths when I see the words, big, fat red letters knitted into the design across the entire back.

"Oh. My. God," I whisper, fucking horrified.

I turn my wide eyes and open mouth to Debbie and Meredith, who proceed to fall apart all over Debbie's desk, cackling like witches.

"Why didn't anyone tell me?" I ask.

They can't answer, because both of them are incapable of

speech right now. So I go back to the words, as if I need it reaffirmed, as if the words might morph into other words, and I haven't been walking around with SANTA'S FAVORITE HO emblazoned across my back all day.

Mortified, I bunch the jumper up in my fists, huffing out my indignation, but seeing Debbie and Meredith in a full-blown laughing fit takes the edge off my irritation. Both women needed a laugh, and for that reason alone, I'm surprisingly happy to provide it, even if I'm rolling my eyes. Besides, perhaps it serves me right for being so unapproachable, I reluctantly concede. "I'll be here same time tomorrow," I quip, leaving them to pull themselves together, shutting my office door on their laughter.

I look at the jumper screwed up in my hand and shake my head to myself, stuffing it in my bag and calling the care home to check on Mum. "Hi, Deirdre, it's Camryn."

"Oh, Camryn, how are you?"

I frown. "Good." I frown harder. "How are you?"

There's a slight pause, and I wince, knowing Deirdre will be looking somewhat surprised. Have I ever asked her that? How she is? "I'm well."

"Any visitors?" I ask, wondering if my brother's finally shown his face.

"No visitors, Camryn."

I shouldn't be disappointed, but I am. "I'll be there tomorrow." As I go to hang up, I hear Deirdre call me, so I return my phone to my ear. "Yes?"

"The carols service."

"What about it?"

"I wondered if perhaps you'd reconsidered."

I press my lips together, my instinct yelling at me to shut this down, but I'm clearly behaving extremely out of character today, and I find some very unexpected words falling past my lips. "Let me see if I can move some things around."

"Oh," she sounds shocked. "That's wonderful."

Is it? I'm not so sure. I hang up and take a moment to process what I've just agreed to. Honestly, I can't; I'm doing things and saying things I'm not sure are wise, and yet I can't stop myself doing them and saying them.

I loved what you told me.

Dec.

A man of few words, and yet each one he speaks packs such a powerful and invigorating punch.

I've practiced my apology all the way here. Not to Dec, I hope he heard my sorry amid all the other things I told him when I kissed him outside his office. I'm yet to analyse what that was, it just feels so fucking huge. My apology is for Julio.

He clocks me the moment I step into the bar, and my face bunches. "I'm surprised to see you here," he says, polishing a glass as I approach. "Or maybe I'm not."

"I owe you an apology."

"Sit down," he says, dismissing me, flicking his head to my usual stool. "Two?"

I nod and do as I'm bid, perching and lowering my bag to the floor, rather than dropping it to the seat beside me, before making a quick scan of the bar.

"Who are you looking for?"

I throw Julio a tired look. "No one." I reach down and pull my boots off, swapping them for my heels.

"The American checked out this morning, in case you were looking for him."

"I wasn't." But I'm eternally relieved.

"Still snowing out there?" he asks.

"Relentlessly."

"They're predicting we've got weeks of it."

I smile mildly, setting my phone on the bar. "Is this what we're resorting to now? Mindless chitchat about the weather?"

"Do you want to talk about something else?"

I shrug, watching him go through the motions of making my

dirty martinis. "I suppose it makes me just like any other patron you encounter daily."

He laughs under his breath. "You are unlike *any* of my other patrons."

"I'm not taking that as a compliment."

"You should. You're fascinating."

I let out a light, low breath of laughter. "Stop talking, Julio, and get me my drinks."

"Yes, ma'am," he says around a smile, pouring and setting the olives atop, then sliding them simultaneously across the bar to me. I push one in front of the stool next to me. Then I inhale, long and deep, glancing down at my phone to check the time, mentally working back to how long ago he messaged me to be here in half an hour. It was thirty-five minutes ago. Butterflies are fluttering like crazy in my tummy, and I reach down, rubbing circles to try and calm them. It's no good. God, I'm so nervous.

What did I say in that kiss? I accept you? I accept what this is? And what is *this*?

Growling my frustration under my breath, I reach for my glass and pull it forward, placing the olive aside—my mouth too dry to eat it—and take a sip, fidgeting terribly. I check the time again. Check my messages.

"Waiting for someone?" Julio asks.

"He's late." I smile timidly. "How rude."

"He wasn't late."

"Sorry?"

Julio nods past me. "He's been there for ten minutes watching you."

I look over my shoulder, the butterflies flapping harder when I see Dec standing in the doorway, fully suited, his coat lying over the crook of his arm with his scarf. Have I ever set eyes on such a beautiful man? "Watching me," I murmur as he slowly strides over. "What a creep."

Julio laughs when I face him, the sound fading as he wanders out from behind the bar to serve a young couple who've settled in the far corner.

"Hello," Dec says on an intentional whisper when he makes it to me, his eyes shining, sparkling so madly, like champagne bubbles popping in a glass.

"Hello," I breathe, enamoured. So completely enamoured. I can do this. I can be vulnerable. I can allow the bricks to tumble and let him in.

A hardly-seen smile lifts one corner of his mouth, and he dips, slipping one hand onto my nape. The closeness, the contact, sets off a bomb in my chest, as he drops a featherlike kiss on my cheek. It's light, it's chaste, but God help me, it's earthmoving. I close my eyes and soak up every wonderful bit of him. He smells outrageously wonderful. His bristles pressed against my cheek force me to concentrate on taking in air. I'm rendered breathless when he pulls away.

"Two martinis?" he asks, turning the stool toward me and sitting.

I slide one closer to him. "This one's for you."

He can't hide his small, satisfied smile. "Tell me about your day."

"My day?"

He sips, eyes on me. "Yes, your day."

"Okay," I say, unsure. "Well, I ratted out the boss's son."

"Oh?"

The corners of his eyes crease as he squints in interest, silently encouraging me to go on. To talk. "He paid for first-class flights and a luxury cruise on his business card and was going to try and pass it off as a business expense."

"Risky," Dec muses. "And very, *very* stupid."

"Agreed."

"So how did you snitching on him go down?"

"Like a cup of puke."

He huffs an amused puff of laughter. These smiles I'm not used to, the light bouts of laughter, they're like preludes to the main event, a breathtaking buildup to something that could rob me of the ability to breathe completely. To hear him laugh. I want that, and it's an odd desire for me. To want distraction by someone's aura, their beautiful glow, rather than physical, mindless distraction. I want that too. God, I want that too. But I'm also really fucking terrified it will seal the deal on my feelings for Dec. The chemistry is potent, a constant sizzle between our bodies. Our kisses have been like nothing I've experienced before. *Healing*.

"Sounds like you've had a day," he says.

And now you're here to take me away. "That's not the half of it," I go on, and Dec's head tilts in question. "It was Christmas Jumper Day."

He looks down my front, to my requisite black dress. "I can see you didn't take part."

"I did, actually. But wish I hadn't."

"Why?"

"It was all a bit of a rush," I explain. "I dipped into a store this morning and grabbed the first jumper I found." I lean down and pull the offending object from my bag, then place it on Dec's lap. He puts his drink down and lifts it, and the words on the back glow, an encore of mortification creeping back up on me.

"What's wrong with it?" he asks.

"The back."

His face appears as he lowers the jumper, the most beautiful frown creasing his brow. He turns it around, and a few seconds silence linger. I cringe as Dec lowers the stupid jumper. "You're the CFO of TF Shipping, and you wore *this* jumper to work?"

"Yes," I breathe. "Yes, I did that."

"You didn't realise?"

I give him a tired look, like *do I look like the kind of woman who would wear a jumper insinuating I'm a whore, whether playful or not*? I wince to myself.

"All day?" he asks.

"Until my assistant kindly informed me why everyone had been laughing at me since I stepped off the elevator this morning."

And my wish comes true.

He laughs, the sound so rich and natural, and the sight is quite possibly one of the most incredible things I've ever seen. And I know in this moment, without question . . .

Fucking hell, I'm falling.

"My God, Camryn." Dec dumps the jumper on the bar and drops to his feet, gathering me up from my stool and pulling me into his chest, hugging me so hard, his body jerking from his persistent chuckles.

I'm a big girl. I don't need him to hug me to ease my embarrassment, but I'll take it. Every day, I'll take one of these hugs. Every bit of me melts into his chest, my arms circling his back, clinging to him. The warmth inside intensifies. I've missed hugs. Deep, enfolding, and warm. Like my mum's.

Like . . .

"A woman of your stature should be far more organised in order to avoid such fuck-ups."

I smile as Dec pulls back, looking down at me, those eyes of his hypnotising. I know my gaze is begging him to kiss me again, whisk me away, drown me in something special and unforgettable.

Make me want him more.

Recognition stares back at me. He knows what I want, but does Dec know how much I need it?

He does. I know he does.

But he doesn't kiss me.

Because there's more between us than anything sexual.

Moving his hands to my hips, he lifts me with ease and sits me back on the stool. "How's your mum?" he asks, taking his seat, reclaiming his drink.

How I'd like to say she's okay. I scramble for the courage to talk about Mum, to open up and show him—and myself—that I can do this. Baby steps. And Mum is the first baby step. "It was too long before we put the small things together and realised there was a problem." He's looking at me so closely, silently assessing my state of mind.

"We?"

"My dad, brother, and I."

He nods.

"It started with irritation—she'd get worked up about the silliest of things. Dad thought she was menopausal." I smile on the inside, seeing him shaking his head to himself when Mum would start a conversation that they'd had just a few hours before. Brain fog, he thought. "She lost interest in tennis, and she was the queen of the tennis club, she'd forget our birthdays then try to convince us we were wrong, our birthdays were in fact on entirely different days, and then a huge argument would erupt because we didn't know what we were dealing with." His face is pained, his hand coming to rest on mine and squeezing. Again, I don't need the comfort. I've not accepted what's happened to my vivacious, bright mother, but I've long stopped crying about it. There were too many other things thrown into the equation of my grief. "And then one day she called me to say she was lost."

"Where was she?"

"In Carlisle."

"Scotland?"

"She doesn't remember how she got there, why she was there. We found a train ticket in her coat pocket, London to Northampton."

Another frown.

"Her sister lives in Northampton. Dad said she was visiting her sister. We figured she didn't get off the train."

"Wow," he murmurs.

"And that was that. It felt like the moment she was diagnosed, she rapidly went downhill. Dad was struggling to cope, she got aggressive, didn't trust anyone." I subtly clear my throat and try to swallow that permanent ball of desolation that's wedged there. But I'm on a roll. *Get it all out.* "Then Dad died suddenly. Heart attack." Dec's shoulders drop in silent disbelief. My God, he's not even heard me verbally paint the whole, horrid picture. "His doctor said he'd visited months earlier with chest pains and was sent for an ECG, but he didn't go." And I know it's because we were all so lost amid the mess of Mum's aggressive illness and her fast decline. He was too worried about her, and he didn't want to worry us even more. And perhaps because he's my father, and I know how stubborn he was, he was in denial. "She's just a shell now with nothing behind her eyes. The odd flicker of hope comes, but it goes even faster. I just have to wait for her to die, although, really, *my* mum died a few years ago." I breathe out through my nose, my lips pressed tight, my ironic smile light. "Glad you asked?"

"Don't do that," he murmurs. "Don't try to lighten your grief, Camryn. It bleeds out of you like blood from a deep cut."

"I'm so tired of hating the world," I say without thinking, for so many more reasons that Dec can ever know. This, just this one monumental devastation, broke me. Add the rest of my shitty life?

"I want to make you love it again." He holds my hand and squeezes. "Is that possible?"

"Maybe," I murmur, moving my hand in his, feeling him, screaming yes in my head but being too frightened to voice it. Because I'm not sure I could ever love a world that's been so cruel to me.

"You mentioned your brother."

I laugh a little. "My busy brother," I breathe, with all the cynicism I intended. "He's good at burying his head in the sand." I've often wondered if that's a man thing. Do they feel the need to put on a brave face, box things up and shove them away so they don't have to face their vulnerabilities? It's not fair for me to think that. I know I've done it to an extent, and I know Dec's worked that out. It's why I went to a bar every evening rather than going home and confronting the emptiness. It's why I got myself a high-profile, high-pressure job, so I could allow myself, to some extent, to be consumed.

The mask in place. The ice queen throwing out standoffish vibes, making sure no one got close.

I look down at our joined hands. Dec dared to get close. Will he regret that? I desperately hope he doesn't. "I'm done talking about me," I say, letting go of his hand to claim my drink, finishing the last drop. Julio looks a little thrown when I look up at him. I haven't tapped my glass. I was too busy spilling a part of my miserable story.

"She'll have a water," Dec says, pushing his empty to join mine. "We'll both have water."

I look at Dec in interest, not that he pays much attention to it.

"Water," he reiterates.

Poor Julio doesn't know what to do. "Looks like I'm having water," I murmur, unable to stop myself reading into what Dec wants me to make of that. No more escape? I don't need to drink now?

"And your marriage?" Dec says.

I fail spectacularly in my attempt not to go rigid. "This conversation feels a little one-sided."

"Have you acknowledged the papers?"

"No," I say shortly, silently willing him not to ruin the evening. "Have you found your wife?"

"No."

"So we're both still married."

"True. The difference is, I don't want to be."

I withdraw, stung, and my eyes drop to my lap, the sudden urge to bolt overcoming me. *Ouch*. I try to fight it, I really do. But I'm wasting time. I'll never win. "Excuse me," I say, dropping from the stool and fleeing. But I didn't grab my bag or coat in my haste, limiting where I can run to.

So the ladies' it is.

I push both palms into the door and rush through, flinching when I hear the wood smack the wall behind it. Two more doors get the brunt of my urgency before I'm safely in the ladies', braced over the sink, my loose hair veiling my face, my eyes on my shoes. Why? Why would he say that? Think it, but don't fucking say it. *Never* say it. The butterflies are swiftly burned to a cinder by the inferno of anger raging in my belly.

Every brick he's just carefully deconstructed from my wall—

the bricks I allowed him to remove—is flying back into place. I breathe in through my nose, my fists balling, my chest expanding, as I try to cool down. Try to reason with myself.

Before I react and ruin this.

It's not unreasonable for him to ask that question. To make that statement. He's every right to draw his conclusions, to test the water by voicing them, but I still resent him for it.

How do I come back from this? How do I make it clear that any talk about that part of my life isn't going to happen?

I don't have time to figure that out. The door opens and Dec appears, stoic but so obviously bracing himself for a backlash. "I'm done talking about me," I say with grit. "Don't make me want to leave."

"You don't already?"

"No." My answer is quick and very wobbly, not through doubt, but through emotion. "I don't want to leave."

"Then don't," he murmurs, but there's one thing he doesn't say, the same thing I'm thinking.

We can't avoid it forever.

How long is forever? And am I thinking that far ahead in this moment?

My gaze drops from his to the floor, uncertainty back with a vengeance.

"Stop overthinking it, Camryn," he warns with gentle scorn, his voice getting louder as he closes in on me. My spine clicks one vertebra at a time until it's poker straight, my shoulder blades pinching. He puts himself behind me, eyes on mine in the mirror, and slowly sweeps my hair aside, exposing my neck. I'm rapt, tingling all over, as he lowers his mouth to the column of my throat, gently pressing his lips into my skin. My exhale is a quiet, quivering sound, as my blood throbs in my veins. The way he's looking at me, not touching me anywhere with his hands, only his lips, watching my unstoppable reaction. I'm not overthinking anything now, because my brain has short-circuited.

And I'm done for when he drags his lips to the small, sensitive hollow beneath my lobe, his hot breath close to my ear, sending a wildfire of desire racing through me. I lean into his body, my head falling onto his shoulder, my eyes closing. The burning, wet sensation of his tongue licking up the shell of my ear is my undoing, and my moan's lost in the back of my throat.

"Turn around," he whispers, looping an arm around my waist and turning me. My hands land on his shoulders, and I wait with agonising anticipation for him to kiss me. "I'm sorry I pushed your boundaries." His fingertip traces the fading nick on my cheek, his other palm cupping my arse, forcing me closer.

"It's okay."

He gently kisses the corner of my mouth. "Something tells me you'd say anything in this moment. It wasn't okay." Kissing the other side of my mouth, he withdraws. "I just want to get to know the woman I'm falling for before I take her to bed."

If a cannon ball hit me in the stomach right now, I wouldn't feel it. Because the weight of that statement feels like it's knocked me out.

He's falling for me?

I don't have the capacity to unpack that in this moment, but I vow to myself to revisit it as soon as cognitive thinking is mine again.

He's smouldering so fiercely as he holds me tight to his body, our breathing ragged, mixing between our close mouths. "I'm not going to be a man you fuck and forget, Camryn," he whispers, his fingertip tracing back down my cheek to my bottom lip. "There won't be any walks of shame, you won't be slipping out in the dead of night and disappearing into the darkness. When I make love to you, we're moving on to the next stage, and I want you to accept that before I take you home, not because you desperately need me inside you right now, but because you're falling for me too."

He sees me. He sees my pain.

No.

He wants to *understand* my pain. Understand so he can help me overcome it.

I'm so tired of hating the world.

I want to make you love it again. Is that possible?

Is it?

Can he?

My mind feels as if it could explode under the pressure of thoughts pouring in, quickly filling my head to capacity. I haven't got it in me to unravel this now. It's too . . . charged. But I do know one thing beyond all the things I'm sure I *don't* know.

I am falling for him too.

I want him to make love to me, not fuck me. I want him to hug me, kiss me, talk to me, listen, give me those smiles on repeat. It's lightened up my world, offered a reprieve in my tragedy-filled existence.

I can't hope for him to be my cure, I know I will never be completely cured, but I can hope he eases my heartache and gives me something to live for.

I swallow, what I'm about to say feeling so monumental.

Because it is.

"I'm falling for you too," I say. "I've been falling for you since the moment you caught me on the pavement and walked me home."

His answer is a suppressed, satisfied groan, as he lifts me and seals our lips.

Seals the deal.

We're falling.

Together.

I get utterly lost in his worshipful kiss. "Do you trust yourself?" he murmurs around my mouth, sweeping his tongue through, delaying my answer.

"No," I admit, halting our kiss in its tracks. "But I trust you."

He nods, setting me on my feet and framing my face with both hands, pushing his mouth onto my forehead. "Time to go."

I'm led out of the ladies' back into the bar. Dec finds my coat and holds it open, helping me into it before getting his own on as I switch my heels for my boots. He grabs my bag, then the jumper off the bar and chucks it to Julio. "Merry Christmas." Two twenties follow the jumper. "It was nice knowing you."

Translated: you won't see us again.

I look back over my shoulder as I'm being pulled from the bar, hearing Julio laughing behind the jumper. "Nice knowing you," I say quietly, throwing him a smile when his face appears.

He mouths something to me, tapping his chest as he does.

Be brave.

My God, am I that transparent?

I nod, repeating the mantra over and over as Dec walks us through the lobby and past reception. "Where are we going?"

"You think I'm taking you to a hotel room, Camryn?" he says, not stopping.

"Wait, we're going to your house?"

"Yes, we're going to my house." He looks back as he pushes round the revolving door, making sure I get in the same section as him. "Problem?"

"This suddenly feels very serious," I murmur, and Dec laughs, the same, soulful laugh he laughed earlier over the jumper. I smile at the back of his head.

"In you get." He pulls open the back door of the grey Defender, and I take a deep breath, getting in.

"Evening," the driver says, the same guy I saw outside Dec's office.

"Evening." I settle in my seat, Dec climbing in after me, and watch as he taps at the screen of his phone.

"Home, please, Ron."

"Sure thing, boss." He flicks his eyes to me in the rearview mirror, and though I can't see his face, I know he's smiling. I look away, down to my hand when Dec takes it, still focused on his phone. It's an unconscious move. Natural.

"I've just got to take care of a few things before I turn off my notifications."

"Okay."

"Done."

"That was quick."

"It's amazing how fast I work when there's something special waiting for my attention."

"I'm not waiting for your attention."

"No, you're not. You have it."

His phone rings in his hand, *Dad* lighting the screen. Dec rejects the call. "I thought you said your father's dead," I say, confused.

"He is." He kind of shrugs, kind of sneers. "To me."

"Wow," I blurt, withdrawing. "There's something we need to unpack."

"There's not much to unpack. Bank it and ask me another time."

I mentally file my questions away for a more appropriate time, turning my attention to our joined hands. His fingers are weaving languidly through mine, easy and slow. "Is it far to your home?"

"Fifteen minutes, depending on traffic."

"Twenty-four," Ron says from up front. "Can I offer any ambient music?"

"No," Dec says slowly, seriously, his eyes narrowed Ron's way. "Just get me home as quick as you can."

"Right, boss."

Exactly twenty-four minutes later, Ron slows down outside a line of Georgian houses and eventually stops, and I lean forward in my seat. I can't exactly see the top of the low box hedging lining the front garden, but if there wasn't a sheet of snow hiding it, I know I'd see it's impossible pristine, not one leaf out of place. Two snow-topped bay trees, cut into perfect spheres, flank the central stone steps that lead to the front door. "You live on Ilchester Place?" I ask, trying not to sound intimidated.

"I believe that's where home is, yes." Dec steps out, and I shuffle along the seat, taking his offered hand. "It's slippery, be careful."

My neck cranes to look up the face of the house. "Jesus, Dec," I breathe, losing my battle. "You live here?"

"That's what I just said." He dips when Ron lowers the driver's window. "You can knock off now, unless Lynette needs to be anywhere."

"She's good, I checked in with her an hour ago."

"Good man." Dec slaps the side of the Defender. "See you in the morning." I'm still taking in Dec's home, a beautiful Georgian double-fronted townhouse, every detail in keeping with its era—the symmetrical sash windows, the cast stone door surround, the pediment, the hipped roof with three dormers. *Iconic*. And right now, under a thick blanket of snow, it's also magical.

"This is so gorgeous," I muse, feeling a bit foolish. And wholly inadequate.

"I'm glad you like it." He pulls me on, leading the way, which is good because my eyes are still up, not looking where I'm going.

"How long have you lived here?"

"Ten years. Watch your step."

I peek down and get my bearings, taking the first of seven steps up, feeling grit under the soles of my boots. There's a short expanse of flat area before three more steps to the front door. Light shines out from the downstairs windows, the black cast iron lanterns, mounted either side of the door, lighting the way too. Dec slips a key into the lock and opens the door, and I step in, rendered mute, taking in the endless, exquisite detail. A crystal chandelier hangs proudly from an ornate ceiling rose, and elaborate cornicing frames the high ceilings.

"Dec," someone says, a woman, snapping me from my admiring.

"Lynette." Dec throws his keys into a gold-leaf bowl on a white console table that has a huge dumpy glass vase rammed full of clipped white roses, then kicks his shoes off, prompting me to do the same. "This is Camryn. Camryn, Lynette."

Lynette smiles, and it's such a warm smile, her brown eyes

shining. "Hi, Camryn." She tucks her mobile into the back pocket of her jeans.

"Hi."

"I just texted you," Lynette says to Dec, just as his phone dings.

He opens the message. Nods. "Got it.

"I'll leave you in peace. See you in the morning."

"Thanks, Lynette."

"Nice to meet you, Camryn," She gives me another one of those genuine, warm smiles, and I expect her to collect her coat, maybe a bag, and leave via the front door, but she gathers nothing and disappears up the sweeping staircase to the left.

"You too," I murmur.

"Housekeeper. In case you were wondering."

"You know I was wondering."

"And she lives here." He removes his coat and hangs it on a nearby coat stand. "In case you were wondering."

"She lives here?"

"She has the top floor." Dec tucks his fingers into the collar of my coat, brushing my skin, and eases it off my shoulders. "I'll give you a tour later," he whispers across my nape. My mind empties, my eyes close in bliss, and my bones turn to jelly, making me collapse against his chest as he drags his lips up to my ear. "Walk." His palm spreads across my stomach as he encourages me forward, forcing me to open my eyes. The whole staircase comes into view, circling up, a chandelier suspending from the very top of the house, cascading down the middle of the wide spiralling stairs. I fleetingly admire it as I take the steps, one unsteady foot at a time, Dec pressed into my back. My heart's beating so hard, not in anticipation, but with nerves. I can't seem to regulate my breathing, can't control my shakes. What the hell is wrong with me?

I don't fuck for the sake of fucking.

It means something.

Oh God.

We reach the top and Dec steers me to the left toward some

double doors, leaning past me to turn the gold knob. "Okay?" he asks, flicking a light on as soon as the doors open.

"Fine." The bedroom comes into view, *his* bedroom, and my soles sink into the super-soft carpet. I have only a second to take in the cosy space before Dec turns me to face him.

"Then why are you shaking?"

My exhale is long, and he nods, telling me he understands. I screw men. That's it. Take what I want and leave, not giving them a second thought again, moving on to the next man that offers a brief, woeful repose from my heartbreak. "If I kiss you here," he murmurs, dipping and resting his lips on my neck, "are you less nervous?"

I suppress my broken moan, my head rolling, as he kisses up to my jaw.

"That sounds like a yes."

I nod, speech evading me.

"And here?" he asks quietly, pressing his lips onto the side of my mouth.

Another nod, my insides aching for more.

"What about here?" I don't feel his lips anywhere, so I open my eyes, and the moment I do, I'm looking into his shining gaze. He slides a hand onto my arse and tugs me close, then drops a kiss on my lips. My hands fly up to his hair and fist handfuls, opening up to him, meeting his tongue in the middle.

"That's a definite yes." He starts walking me backward, owning my mouth, truly kissing me like I've never been kissed before. It's soft, it's slow, it's measured and purposeful. My nerves disappear as if they were never there, every part of me drowning in him. I feel his hands reach round my back for the zip of my dress, and he smoothly draws it down my spine, our kiss never faltering. My shoulder blades pull in, my arms unhooking from around his neck to allow him to get my dress off. I inhale when I feel it hit the floor around my feet. "Okay?" he murmurs again, constantly checking in, grazing a palm down my side to my hip. He just needs to keep kissing me. Never stop kissing me. "Tell me you're okay."

"I'm okay." I swallow and take my fingers to his shirt buttons, starting at the top, slowly exposing his chest as he watches me. I keep my eyes on my task, and as soon as I undo the last one, I take a moment to admire the sliver of skin before slipping my palms onto his shoulders to push it off.

His hands fly up and grab my wrists, bringing my eyes to his. "Let me," he says, stepping back, effectively giving me the best view. And him of me. It's too bright in here—I'm used to a hazy darkness, just enough light to see what I'm doing.

My eyes naturally go to the table lamps, feeling uncomfortable in my semi-nakedness. "The lights stay on," Dec says, his voice gruff with lust. "You don't get to hide from me, Camryn."

I shoot my eyes to his and hold my breath as he rolls his shoulders and shrugs out of his white shirt, teasingly slowly, and yet his face remains serious, eyes full of promises I hope he can keep. His chest makes me blink hard. The ravines between each muscle are dark, well-trimmed dark hair dusting his pecs. My mouth waters, my eyes following the trail from his belly button until it disappears past the waist of his trousers.

Dec drops his shirt with my dress and unfastens his belt. "Take your bra off," he whispers, nodding to my chest. I keep my eyes on his face as I unhook my bra and let the straps fall into the crooks of my arms, freeing my aching breasts. My nipples tingle, and Dec's eyes smoke, his hands faltering on his fly. Leaving his trousers hanging open, he dips and pulls his socks off. Then he pushes his trousers down, revealing thick thighs coated in dark hair, his boxers hugging them.

The bulge of his erection.

I bite my lip and peek up at him. This prime, virile man.

"Still nervous?" he asks quietly, as we stand opposite each other, both naked except for his boxers and my knickers.

I shake my head, unable to keep my distance a moment longer. I walk into his chest and pull his mouth down to mine, swallowing his groan. His fingers slip into the side of my knickers and shove them down my thighs, and I return the favour, slipping both hands past the material of his boxers and easing them over his arse. In just a few seconds, we're both completely naked and Dec's palms rest on my hips, lifting me to his body. My arms loop his neck, my legs curl around his waist, my lips not leaving his for even a moment. I don't need to see when I'm feeling so much.

With his head craned back to accommodate me, he circles my tongue lightly as he walks a few paces and bends, taking me down to the bed. He brushes against my entrance, and I whimper, feeling a need so powerful pounding between my thighs, feeling his too, his hard length throbbing. "I'm really fucking hoping you tell me I don't need to cover up," he says urgently, every inch of his body rubbing against me as he rips his mouth off mine, leaving me gasping, and kisses between my breasts, gently circling his floating palm above my boob, just close enough for it to graze the tip of my nipple.

We've both said we can't have kids, so we're not talking about worries of an accidental pregnancy. We're talking about my promiscuous lifestyle. "You don't need to." I writhe across the sheets, blissing out further when I feel the scratch of his bristles on the inside of my thighs. My head spins. Do I need to ask him the same? What a fool I am. "And you?" I ask, breathless.

He nips at my inside thigh and looks up my body. "What about me?"

Confusion gets me, and it gets me good. "Are you . . ." Fuck, how do I word this?

"I haven't slept with anyone in nearly five years, Camryn."

My mouth drops open as he gazes at me, unapologetic and unashamed. "Five years?"

"I haven't had the time or the desire." He turns his face into my thigh and nips again. "Now I really have the desire."

Five years? How? This gorgeous, successful brooding, sexy man. How is that even possible?

"Are we done?" he asks.

"We're done." And I'm in shock. Five years? He said his wife left four years ago.

"Good." His tongue meets my heat.

"Oh my God!" I jack up off the bed, a million bolts of pleasure shooting through me. "Dec!"

"Shh," he whispers, sucking my clit into his mouth gently. "Spread your legs more."

I'm dizzy, floating, which seems to erase the heaviness I carry around with me daily. My legs fall open, my hand slipping into his hair, as he seduces my pussy with a lax tongue, looking up at me to watch as I absorb every stroke. As much as I'd love to keep my neck craned to see him, I'm becoming boneless with pleasure. So I rest my head back on the bed, staring up at the ceiling, circling my hips onto his mouth.

Floating.

I close my eyes and sink into the sheets, stroking through his hair as he keeps the fire burning, blood rushing to my head. All thoughts of his abstinence for *five fucking years* disappears, and my feelings for him accelerate.

When his hand rests on my boob and squeezes, I reach and hold it in place, massaging with him.

I'm not going to be a man you fuck and forget, Camryn.

If Dec never laid a finger on me ever, never kissed me, never held me, was never intimate with me, I still could never forget him. There's a gentle authority about him that had me from the second he appeared next to me at the bar. A strength I'm not familiar with.

Falling.

I was falling before this moment. I was falling before he even kissed me. Now I feel like I'm past the point of return, and as he worships me, I don't care what that means.

I open my eyes as my inner walls constrict, the pressure fast approaching bursting point. My hand tightens in his hair, my other over his hold of my breast, my gaze dropping down my chest. Drowsy eyes meet mine, and I gasp, flexing my hips. His free hand slides under my thigh and pushes my leg back, opening me wider, and he comes up for air briefly, panting, his mouth glistening as he stares at my swollen pussy.

Damp strands of hair tumble across his forehead, the grey flecks glistening, and then his eyes find me again as he slowly lowers and licks up my centre, from front to back. "Dec." His name is a warning, my nerves twitching. He relieves me of his mouth, and I move his hand from my boob and push it into the centre of my chest so he can feel my heart thundering. "I think I might die of pleasure," I whisper, drunk on him. Sated without even being sated.

He crawls up my body slowly, almost prowling, and settles atop of me, from feet to head, his arousal wedged between us, hot and wet with leaking precum. He cages my head in his bent arms. "And what a way to go," he murmurs, reaching for my face and gently pushing back a piece of hair. "You taste so good."

I drag my thumb across his bottom lip, wiping myself away from his mouth, and as he stares down at me, I swallow, alarmed by the thoughts running rampant in my mind.

I love him.

It shouldn't make any sense, and yet it makes perfect sense. He's patient. He's strong without being forceful. He's sensitive without being soft. The fact he's insanely handsome just feels like a bonus. The fact I know he's about to set my world alight when he makes love to me is another bonus. Add the small matter of him not sleeping with anyone for five years makes him all the more special to me, and I truly hate myself in this moment for using sex as my escape for so long.

I love him because he didn't give up on me, which means he's found me.

But most of all, I love him because he's so fucking incredible and has shown me that I am capable of loving again.

But only if it's him.

Dec's eyes narrow a little, as if he's reading my mind and not liking my thoughts. It makes me blink and look away, suddenly aware that my thought process is outlandish. My conclusions are all irrelevant if it's unrequited, because then Dec becomes just another something that destroys me.

"Hey." He props himself up on one elbow and takes my jaw, forcing my face to his. "What's wrong?"

I shake my head, unable to speak with his hand clenching my face, and Dec studies me, the whole situation suddenly serious, lust and passion making way for something else, and I'm not sure what.

His hold relaxes, his face coming closer to mine, eyes darting across my face. "Can you breathe when we're close?" he asks quietly, his voice low and thick, as if he's got his own lump going on in his throat. "Because I can't."

I inhale, pushing my hands over his shoulders, shaking my head mildly. "I haven't been able to breathe properly since I met you," I say, feeling brave. Jumping in feet first. "And it's for the best reasons."

He swoops in and kisses me deeply, rolling us, kissing me harder, hands all over my face, my head, my back as I straddle him, until he's rolling us again, back into the middle of the bed, trapping me beneath him. My lips burn from the friction of our mouths, my tongue beginning to ache.

And yet I know I could never stop this, not if my life depended on it. So when Dec tears his mouth away, gasping for air, my instinct to reach for his neck and yank him back down can't be held back. He obliges, palms buried in the mattress either side on my head, his thick thighs straddling my waist, his dick spilling more precum all over my belly.

"Come here," he murmurs, his arms swelling beautifully as he pushes into his hands, resting back on his heels, making his thick thighs double in width. Taking my hands, he pulls and helps me onto his lap. My muscles tense to hold me up as I gaze down between us to his hand fisting himself at the root. Air catches at the back of my throat, my mouth watering. I've got to kiss him again. Kiss him while he works himself. I home in on his neck, forcing his head back on a broken moan. His throat taut, my lips brush across the tight expanse of spiky skin as he holds me close with one big palm splayed across my lower back. "Lift" he orders, turning his face into mine and pulling back so he can see me do as I'm told.

My thigh muscles scream as I rise, my buttocks pulling. Dec's gaze runs loops around my body, my hands resting lightly on his shoulders.

He bites down on his lip as the wet tip of his arousal nudges against my entrance, and I pull in air sharply, my clit tingling, begging for friction. I need to feel every hard, wet, hot inch of him sliding into me to the hilt and watch his face as I take it all.

I release my muscles and lower a fraction, watching in fascination as the veins in his neck bulge, his nostrils flaring. The fire inside rages, begging to be quenched by penetration.

Down a little farther.

I hold my breath, hold his eyes. He starts to quiver. "More, Camryn," he grates, bringing his hand to my shoulder and massaging firmly, his hand on my back slipping down to my arse.

I drop a little more and cry out.

"God damn," he barks, his chin dropping to his chest.

No, no, no. I slip my finger under and ease his face up to mine. "Can you breathe when we're close?" I whisper, slowly shaking my head from side to side, in so much awe. "Because I can't."

"Fuck," he groans, securing my neck in his palm and taking control, kissing me on a desperate murmur of my name. I ease down the rest of the way, choking on the fullness and the pleasure, my spine going ramrod straight and my torso forcing itself closer to his.

"My God, you feel so deep." I work hard to adjust to him, being forced to take deep breaths and hold still for a few moments before I brave moving.

"I don't want this to end," he breathes across my skin.

"Me neither." I start rocking into him, trying to maintain the pace of our kiss but struggling when my senses are being overloaded.

"Lean back."

I reluctantly leave his mouth and recline, and his chest rolls as he flexes into me, his grey gaze hooded and lazy. Our hips move in perfect circles, my body naturally following his unspoken instructions. His cheeks blow out, his hands taking my hips, mine grabbing his shoulders. And he watches me.

Pumps harder.

Breathes faster.

The veins in his neck throb, his eyes darken. All of the signs of Dec coasting toward detonation only encourages my own climax to steam forward. "I'm coming," I blurt in a panic.

"Fucking hell." He shoots up onto his knees, bringing me with him, both his hands cupping my arse. I feel the swell and kick of him inside me a second before I feel the buildup of pressure inside me sizzle and bang.

My boobs crush against his chest, my back arching as I yell my release to the ceiling, both my arms wrapped around his neck to keep me grounded. A wave of heat ripples through me, from my toes to my head, leaving behind the most beautiful warm feeling inside. Breathless. For so many more reasons than being replete.

The pleasure rolls through me, making sure there's not an inch of my body it doesn't touch, my skin tingling everywhere, as Dec thrusts on, smooth and concise, our chests compressed, my arms and legs wrapped around him like ivy. My head drops, I feel so dazed, and my forehead falls onto his. Strain creases his face, his concentration showing in the beautiful crinkles around his eyes.

I cup his cheek, holding him, letting him control everything, lift me, sink me, roll me, as he chases the end and my orgasm fades away slowly. This right here, watching him, is just as pleasurable.

More pleasurable.

I press my mouth to his and gently kiss him, and he stills, his chest expanding from his deep inhale. "Fuck," he breathes, his body deflating as he swells inside me and jerks, collapsing back on his heels and twitching with me held tightly in his arms. He hugs me. So closely.

Dec is warmth.

He steals my breath.

He throws light on my shade.

"That was beautiful," I murmur into the dip above his collarbone as our bodies roll and heave.

His fingers comb into my hair on my scalp and clenches, pulling ever so slightly, and he manoeuvres with ease and dexterity, falling to his back and somehow taking me with him without even slipping out of me. I settle front down on his chest, feeling him softening inside me, and bury my face under his neck, inhaling his usual smell mixed with a bit of clean sweat and sex.

With his hands tracing constant circles across my back, his breathing close, my lips stuck to his throat, and his warmth still inside me, I can't think of anywhere I'd rather be right now.

Except back in time three years ago before my life crashed down around me.

December 14th

It's the feeling of him slipping out of me that brings me round, and I blink my eyes open. The sheets are pulled over us, but I haven't moved. Neither has Dec—his arms exactly where they were when I dosed off, one holding me to his chest, the other resting on my bum. I can hear his light breathing close to my ear, and it's the only welcome noise that's invaded my waking moments for three years. No screams of my past. No everyday life happening beyond my windows. Just . . . breathing.

Gently lifting my head, I peek at him, and despite the poor light, I see him so clearly. And I smile a little, turning my head carefully toward the nightstand. Toward the glow of the digital clock shining. It's gone midnight, and I'm thirsty. But he looks so peaceful and serene, and it would be an absolute crime to disturb him.

My face bunched up, I gently ease myself off him, feeling the coolness of the bedroom meeting my skin. It's almost enough to make me want to dive back under the covers and never emerge, but now I've moved, I also need to pee.

I'm holding my breath as I hold my weight with my arms, my hands pressed into the mattress as I get my feet on the carpet. It's a miracle, but he doesn't even stir, totally out for the count.

I find a T-shirt and shimmy it on, spotting a door across the room that I pray is a bathroom, but as I head that way, I remember something.

Lynette.

I look down at my bare legs and think about the fact I have no knickers on. I don't know Lynette, have no idea how it works having a live-in housekeeper, but I do know I'd hate to bump into her half naked. I cringe and look back over my shoulder, rolling my eyes as I spot my dress on the floor. I pull the T-shirt off and get my dress on, not bothering to search for my knickers now I'm mostly decent. I pad across to the door and quietly open it, revealing an en-suite. "Oh, thank God," I whisper. The moment I step over the threshold, low-level spotlights ping on, giving me just enough light but not so much it's blinding. I go straight to the loo and lower, using the time I'm peeing—which is forever, it seems—to take in the space. It's all spectacular, all white porcelain and brushed brass fittings, but it's the claw-foot tub in front of an arched stained-glass window that gives it the true wow factor.

I'm still peeing.

The mirrors above the twin pedestal sinks are suspended on gold rods from the ceiling, the floor is a chessboard of black and white tiles, the shower enclosed by a white half-height brick-tiled wall topped with a glass screen, and a bunch of candles line the windowsill—all of them gold.

I'm still bloody peeing.

There's a tray spanning the tub, like one of those bath caddies you put things on if you're a tub dweller—a book, a glass of wine, a candle, your lotions and potions, everything within reach. Does Dec Ellis soak in a bubble bath?

I smile, picturing him relaxed back, bubbles up to his neck. Does he sing in the tub? Read?

Or was that his wife's?

My smile falls. He's lived here for ten years. He told me he'd be divorced four years ago if he could find her. She lived here.

I'm done peeing.

I wipe myself, my face bunching when I feel the remnants of his release too, and tug my dress back down. I don't flush—I don't want to wake him—but lower the seat instead and wash my hands.

He's not moved an inch when I leave the bathroom. Creeping to the door, I pull it open and peek out, listening for a minute before venturing onto the landing. I reach the stairs, the beautiful, wide spiral staircase, and take the balustrade, gazing around in awe as I take the steps down, paying more attention to the things I didn't before because I was in a state of high anticipation and complete anxiety. The chandelier spilling from the top of the house finishes just shy of a baby grand piano. A mirror hanging on the wall makes the entrance hall look even bigger than it is, and it's pretty bloody spacious. There are endless closed doors, all of which I avoid—I don't want to snoop—but there are numerous open doors too. I pass a room on the right. It's dark, but I definitely see a desk and bookcases—his home office?—and one of the closed doors is a bathroom, identifiable by the sign on the door. I approach another open door farther in, with the distinct purr of a refrigerator coming from that direction, and emerge into a beautiful kitchen, the space lit by under-counter spotlights. It's modern, contradicting the exterior original architecture and what I've seen of Dec's bathroom and the hallway. The walnut cupboards are handleless, the countertops polished cream stone. The long island running down the centre of the room is bare but for a glass vase stuffed with white roses with long stems in a tall vase as opposed to short stems in a dumpy glass like on the table in the hallway.

I take the three steps that lead down to a dining area, where a round table is edged with eight chairs. There's a snug area leading off that. A curved stone-coloured velvet couch has been placed before a wall-mounted TV that hangs above the grandiose cream-stone fireplace. It's large but cosy, traditional but modern.

Beautiful.

I go to the floor-to-ceiling doors that span the entire back and look out into the garden. Spotlights line a brick pathway through the middle that's been shovelled clear of snow.

I smile and face the room again, something past the gorgeousness of Dec's home niggling at the corner of my mind.

There are no Christmas decorations.

Not one thing.

I would wonder if maybe it's too early. Some people go full-on into Christmas mode on December 1st. Other more conservative types might wait until the first or second weekend. And then there's the ones who don't bother with decorations at all. The damaged souls who resent Christmas. *Hate* Christmas. The souls who wish they could hibernate throughout December and emerge on the safe, less glittery and joyous side of January.

Souls like me.

My teeth sink into my lip, searching for even a Christmas card. Anything to suggest Dec isn't like me. Doesn't despise Christmas like me. There are none.

"Were you leaving?"

I jump and spin round, my hand on my chest. "You frightened me." But that fright quickly transforms into something else, and I'm suddenly a puddle of mush on the dining room floor. Dec. In his boxers. I exhale my awe, taking in every glorious piece of the wonder that is Dec Ellis, and store it to memory.

In case you lose him.

I flinch that thought away, my fingers twiddling nervously together. "I was getting a glass of water," I say, motioning to the endless cupboards, where I expect there are more than just two glasses.

"So you weren't leaving?" he asks, his eyebrows arching in interest as he strolls over.

"Nooo." I stretch the word out, my lips pulling at the edges into something scarily similar to a smirk. "I wasn't running out on you."

"Good." He loops a strong arm around my waist and hauls me into his body, forcing my hands up to his chest, my spine bending back to keep him in my sights. The dark hairs beneath my palms feels soft as I skate them up to his shoulders and hold on. His lips pout in contemplation as he studies me, and I wait, breathless. "You're thirsty."

I nod, and he lifts me and sits me on the island before going to a cupboard and fetching a glass, filling it and drinking half as he comes back to me. He puts it in my hand and watches me as I drink the rest.

"Done?" he asks, taking the glass once it's empty and setting it aside.

"Done."

"So I can take you back to bed?"

I nod as his lips land on mine, and I close my eyes, opening up to him the moment our mouths brush, falling deeply into his sweet affection. He helps me down and finds the bottom of my dress, pulling it up to my waist with one swift tug. The backs of my thighs heat under his palms as they slide across my skin briefly before he lifts me, my legs finding their place around his waist, my arms around his neck.

And he kisses me all the way out of the kitchen, up the stairs, along the corridor, and into his bedroom, laying me down and swathing me in his body, taking my mouth and once again kissing me into oblivion.

"Can I ask one question?" I murmur, losing my rhythm for a second as I speak.

"Hmmm." He doesn't lose his rhythm at all.

"Do you celebrate Christmas?"

He rolls us and bites the edge of my lip, pushing me up to straddle his waist. My eyebrows jump up when his growing arousal pushes into my backside.

"I wouldn't have asked if I'd known you were going to stop kissing me."

His muscles ripple as he sits up and takes my nape, pushing his lips hard onto mine. "I have a love/hate relationship with Christmas."

Interesting. "Is that why you have no decorations or a tree?"

His brow becomes heavy as he regards me, obviously not knowing what to say.

"I wouldn't mind if you didn't have a tree or decorations." I press my lips together the moment I've uttered the words. Or, more like, uttered the subtle hint.

The scrutiny I'm suddenly under is painful, which begs the question why I opened my big mouth. "Care to enlighten me?" he asks.

"Not right now. Five years?"

"I'm a busy man."

So the last woman he slept with was his wife. "You're not very busy right now," I whisper, my eyes dropping to his mouth as I take his hands and guide them to the zip on the back of my dress.

"Then I guess I better fix that." He pulls my dress up and tosses it aside before rolling me to my back. "I think you're beautiful." he says quietly, scanning my eyes. "And it feels fucking incredible to be inside you."

I can't take it. How utterly amazing this man is, I just can't take it. I nod, agreeing, and he exhales, the sound a groan mixed with heavy breathing, and rolls his mouth onto mine as he flexes his hips and plunges deeply into me.

I've been awake since five, and despite only drifting off past one, therefore only having four hours' sleep, I feel rested. Wide awake. I should have left at six to walk home so I could dress and make it to work on time. But I couldn't bring myself to leave the warmth of Dec's bed, where I'm tucked under his arm, my cheek on his pec, my fingers brushing through the trail of hair that drifts from his belly button down to his lower stomach. Listening to his breathing. Feeling his heart beating under my cheek.

Lost in my thoughts.

Daring to hope.

Calm is a cosy blanket around my usually frantic, lonely heart.

I told myself I'd brave the Tube or get a cab, just to stay here for a while longer. And I've stretched my time in bed to the absolute limit. It's seven. I have to be at work in an hour. Not contractually—my working hours are nine to five—but for the sake of predictability. I'm always in the office for eight.

I peel myself away from Dec, pouting my sullenness as I do, and creep around his bedroom, collecting my things. I'm halfway down the stairs when Lynette appears, a basket of washing resting on her hip. I stop, clutching the balustrade, feeling all kinds of awkward. "Morning." I smile, that's awkward too, and shift on the spot.

"Morning, Camryn." Her smile isn't awkward at all. It's as genuine as a smile can be. She's not surprised I'm here. "Can I get you a coffee or anything?"

I descend the rest of the stairs and slip my heels on, unable to stop my thoughts from locking down on that. *She's not surprised I'm here.* "No, thank you, I really have to get myself home or I'll be late for work."

"You weren't expecting to stay?" she asks, carrying on to the kitchen, talking over her shoulder as she goes.

"I definitely wasn't expecting to stay," I say quietly, following her. And had I known it had been five years, I would have been more doubtful to be having a sleepover. Five years. I just can't wrap my head around that. I wouldn't be able to with any man, but Dec? He's the full package. Was he being honest? I cock my head. Why would he lie about that? "Does Dec have overnight guests often?" I blink my surprise, recoiling at my own question. "Oh God, I'm so sorry, I was only supposed to ask that in my head."

Lynette chuckles, dumping the basket on the island. "If I were in your shoes, I'd probably be asking that question too."

My nose wrinkles. "It was inappropriate."

"I've worked for Dec for four years."

"Definitely inappropriate."

"And I've never known him to have a guest overnight."

My stomach flutters. "But he's had *guests*?" Why the hell am I digging?

"Never."

"No one?"

"I assume you're talking about the female variety." She flicks on the coffee machine.

"I need to learn to control my mouth, clearly." I point behind me, guilt getting me good. Of course he wouldn't lie. I know he's a good man, and now, frankly, I feel utterly ashamed of myself for doubting that. But, in my defence, he did not have sex like it was the first time in nearly five years. "I'll just get my coat. Dec's asleep, I didn't want to disturb him."

"Should I give him a message?"

I pause for thought at the door. She thinks I'm running out too. "Do you have a pen and paper?"

She smiles, and something tells me she's pleased as she opens a drawer and pulls out a pad and pencil, pushing it toward me before giving me some privacy and disappearing through a door at the end of the kitchen—the laundry room, I assume. Picking up the pen and bending over the counter, not overthinking, I just writing what my heart tells me to write.

I'M NOT RUNNING. THANK YOU FOR BEING WONDERFULLY YOU. CAMRYN X

I set the pen down and find my bag in the hallway, throwing it on my shoulder and letting myself out. "Oh my God," I breathe, stepping into a flurry of snowflakes. A blanket of white hides the steps down to the street again, ready to be shovelled away. My gaze drops to my heels, the toes kissing the blanket of snow, my shoes safe in the sliver of ground by the front door that the snow hasn't reached. "Damn." I drop my bag, wedging my hand in the doorframe to prop myself up, and change into my boots. Crunching my way down the steps, I look back at Dec's house in the dim light of an early December morning.

It's picture-perfect.

Like the man who lives here.

My eyes peek left and right to the other houses on the street. All have fairy lights on the box hedging and trees flanking the front doors. Uniform. As if the residents have consulted each other on the theme for this year and understated and classy won the vote. No colour. No fuss.

Just pretty fairy lights, the tone a warm yellow glow, decorate each house.

Except Dec's.

I have a love/hate relationship with Christmas.

I hum, hugging myself, and start ploughing through the snow to the nearest Tube, feeling the aftereffects of Dec Ellis, the flesh of my inner thighs tender and my insides aching deeply.

Can you breathe when we're close? Because I can't.

And it truly is for the best reasons.

I smile, accepting and appreciating the true happiness that courses through me. And it's okay.

I'm okay feeling happy.

I should have anticipated it. The Tubes weren't running. All cancelled, the snow now surpassing a few inches, which takes it from disruptive to disastrous. So I trudged my way through the snow, constantly checking my Uber app for a car close by. They were thin on the ground, only drivers with vehicles built to handle the snow working.

Which wasn't many.

Which meant I walked for a solid forty minutes until one close by popped up and I nabbed it.

My toes are brittle by the time I make it home, and I have exactly ten minutes to shower, change, and get to the office. I've already accepted I'm going to be late; I'd work from home if I could bear it.

I open the gate with a few firm thrusts, pushing the snow back, and take careful steps to the door, heaving it open. My teeth chatter, my skin burns it's so cold. Why didn't I stay in bed with Dec?

My key is halfway in the lock when Mr. Percival's door swings open. He looks me up and down. I'm sure I don't like the slight drop of his mouth. "Good morning, Mr. Percival."

"And what time do you call this?"

"Huh?"

He pulls out his old watch, dangling it at me. "Seven fifty!"

"I know what the time is, Mr. Percival."

"I've been worried."

"You have?"

"Yes, I have. You leave in the morning—Monday to Friday—at five thirty to run and return at six thirty. Then you leave at seven, for work, I assume, and return at ten p.m. earliest. On Saturdays, you run a little later and then leave again at noon and return at eleven p.m. earliest. Sometimes as late as midnight. On Sundays—"

"I get it, Mr. Percival."

"So where did you stay?"

I laugh and turn the key. "That's private."

He recoils, injured.

"Mr. Percival, I appreciate your concern, but it's not needed."

He huffs, coming at me on his walking frame. "You are a very beautiful young woman, Camryn."

I smile fondly. "Thank you."

"You're single and live alone. You run here, walk there, and stay out much later than you should." He waggles a finger at me. He actually waggles a finger. "And from what I know about you since you moved into this building, there's no one to worry about you, except me."

Ouch.

"Well, there's . . ." Dec. There's Dec. Mr. Percival has seen Dec, because he spies on me.

"I'd feel much better if we exchange numbers." He whips out a phone the size of a house and thrusts it toward me. "If you don't mind."

"You want my number?"

"Just so you can let me know if your regular routine changes to save my worry."

I laugh, pulling the key out of the lock. I could refuse. But, of course, I don't. Sighing, I go to Mr. Percival, to save him the effort and trouble of hobbling to me, and take the brick from his hand. He's just looking out for me, maybe more so now he's seen Dec walk me home. "How do you work this monstrous thing?" I grumble, punching in my number, a loud beep sounding with each button I press.

"Looks like you've got the hang of it."

My number on the screen looks like it's on a calculator. I swear, you could read the digits from the fucking moon. "There." I press dial and raise my brows when my phone starts singing in my pocket. "I'll save your number, Mr. Percival, so I know it's you harassing me."

"Marvellous." He claims his mobile—if you can call it that, the thing needs its own bloody walking frame—and shuffles round, going back into his apartment.

"Ever thought about a smartphone, Mr. Percival?"

"You must be joking. It's taken me twenty years to figure out how to use this one."

"I was at Dec's, by the way."

"I thought as much." The door slams.

"So there is someone else to worry about me," I add quietly to myself, smiling.

I enter my apartment and go straight to the kitchen, pulling out Mr. Percival's cake from the fridge and cutting off a slice, feeling unusually peckish for this time of day. I wrap my lips around a piece and hum, catching a crumb as I turn.

"Fuck!" Something leaps off the kitchen table, screaming in shock as it flies through the air, landing on the counter and scurrying away.

I jump out of my fucking skin, inhaling so hard, the cake shoots to the back of my throat, and I cough, dropping my breakfast and grabbing the counter, wheezing. "Jesus Christ." It appears at the doorway again, a big fat ginger thing, sitting smack bang in the middle, staring straight at me as its tail wafts back and forth. "Shoo," I snap, flapping a hand at it. "Go away." I stamp my foot forward, but it doesn't deter the brazen moggy. "Get out of here." Its eyes are suspicious slits, its purr loud. I'm wary. It looks like it could swipe at me. "Shoo!"

Almost aloof, it stands and struts toward the front door, and I follow, finding it looking back at me, as if it's impatiently waiting for me to open it. "How did you get in here?" I ask, leaning over it and flipping the catch.

"Maureen!" Mr. Percival yells. "Where have you been?"

"Maureen?" I ask. "This is Maureen?"

"That's what I said, dear." Maureen pads on light paws past Mr. Percival, her nose high, and disappears among the sea of gnomes.

"So you're sending your cat to spy on me now, huh?"

"She can't spy on you if you're not home." He tilts his head. "Can she?"

"Have a nice day, Mr. Percival," I call, rolling my eyes and going to take a shower.

It's gone nine by the time I make it to the office, but at least I made it, unlike eighty percent of the staff. So it's quiet to say the least, and I can crack on undisturbed. At least, undisturbed by TF Shipping employees. I'm very much disturbed by Dec throughout the day, and I fall down a rabbit hole of texts, smiling each time my phone pings, waiting impatiently for each message, my stomach doing endless cartwheels.

I'm glad you didn't run. You should have woken me, I would have taken you to work. It's fucking freezing out there, Camryn. Tell me you didn't walk.

I got an Uber halfway. The Tubes were all cancelled.

No shit. Might be something to do with the two foot more of snow that fell during the night.

I like walking.

Don't do it again.

I smile, getting momentarily distracted by a company memo that lands in my inbox. I scan it quickly and get back to Dec.

What are you doing tonight?

I place my phone down and press my lips together. It's a long, painful ten minutes before he answers.

I wish I could say seeing you. Unfortunately, I have a corporate function I have to show my face at. I'll call you.

I deflate in disappointment, worried I'm forming an unhealthy attachment. But isn't that what falling in love is? Almost an obsession? Being consumed? And I'm certainly that.

Completely.

I spend the last hour of my day obsessing about obsessing, while trying to break down an email from Thomas. It's an essay, a long, detailed waffle about nothing in particular, but ends with a show of appreciation for bringing his wife's and son's recent spending splurges to his attention. "That's it?" I say to my screen.

I fire back a quick reply, asking if Barbara and Anthony will be paying back the non-business-related spends. Something tells me I'm hoping. "Oh Thomas, how you stress me out," I murmur, hitting send. His reply is immediate and short. "Seriously?" I blurt at my screen incredulously. "No, it's doesn't need to be handled delicately, Thomas," I say as I reply. They're taking the absolute piss out of you, your company, *and* me. Anyone else would be fired for gross misconduct. *Oh, Thomas, grow some fucking balls.* I continue hammering away at the keys, my teeth gritting as I do. "And I'm sure you appreciate the impact this could have on my reputation as a CFO," I mutter as I type. "You'll make me a laughingstock, Thomas, and I can't have that."

I push my keyboard away and lean back in my chair on an exasperated exhale, running my hand through my hair. No one will hire me if I'm associated with a financial shitshow, and that's what this is heading for. I growl to myself and stand, gathering all my things, wondering what on earth I'm going to do with my night after I've been to see Mum. I can't go to the bar. Don't *want* to go to the bar.

Leaving the deserted building, I brace myself for my visit, wishing I'll get more from her today but knowing deep down I won't. It's been a long time since I've looked forward to seeing her, because I no longer see my mum. Telling Dec about my parents was the first time I'd really talked to anyone about them. I dreaded it but felt an incredible release with every word I shared. I may not have physically lost Mum like I did so suddenly with Dad, but I lost the essence of her when Alzheimer's was diagnosed. She just went downhill so unfathomably fast, not really giving me time to get my head around it. And then Dad went so suddenly, too, and my world felt like it wasn't crumbling, but crashing down. And there was nothing I could do about it. I miss them. *So much.* And even though it's always the same when I visit Mum, I know Dad would want me to try and find even just a glimmer of the woman she was past the shell of a woman that lies in that bed wilting away. And yet, somehow, devastatingly, my existence in her life has been completely blocked from her memory.

Mum won't get better, and Dad will never come back. I didn't think it could get any worse.

I swallow down the lump growing and trudge through the snow, pulling on my gloves and hat. It's eerily quiet for six o'clock in central London, the darkness illuminated by the endless sheet of white. It's also eerily beautiful. I slip down a side street—feeling bad for spoiling the perfect blanket with my boots, the crunch of my soles and the rustle of my bag on my shoulder the only noise.

Until I hear something behind me.

I look over my shoulder, scanning the space, but I'm the only living soul around, my steps the only ones in the snow. I peek up at the lamppost, seeing more snow falling. My footprints will soon be a perfectly even sheet of snow again.

Dropping my eyes, I reach into my bag for my phone when I hear it beep, looking back over my shoulder again, certain I can hear crunching footsteps behind me. But . . . nothing.

I turn right at the end of the street and pick up my pace, an odd shudder reverberating down my spine as I open the message from the unknown number.

Should I expect you home this evening?

I frown, my brain on the lag, but then click, laughing. "Silly old man," I murmur. "Unfortunately, yes, you can expect me home." I type out a reply and save his number before I pocket my phone.

A collection of dull thuds sound behind me, and I look back over my shoulder once more, slowing to a stop when I find the street empty again. I don't like the ice that glides down my spine. "Hello?" My eyes scan the deserted street, my shoulders naturally bunching up around my ears as I back up, slowly turning around and increasing my pace.

It comes again, thudding, as if someone's jogging in the snow. I swing around.

I don't see the hand sailing toward my face until it's too late.

The force jerks my head violently, and I stumble into the road, my landing soft, cushioned by the snow.

"Hey, you! Attack!" someone yells, a woman.

"Fuck," I curse, blinking the black dots from my vision, my cheek exploding into angry flames. Realisation hits me as hard as the back of whosever hand that was, and I frantically scan around me, my heart catching up and commencing a panicked banging in my chest. The street's empty, no one in sight. I spot my bag a few feet away, buried in the snow, and my phone buried a few feet the other side of me. "What the hell?" I whisper, struggling to my feet, my legs like jelly. "Shit." I wince, feeling at my cheek, my cold hand freshly unburied from the snow actually soothing it.

"Hey, are you all right?" A woman appears in a cardigan and leggings, her feet in UGG slippers.

"I'm fine." I circle on the spot, searching, shaken. Nothing. No one. But when I look closely, I see a second set of footsteps heading around another corner. And on even closer inspection, I figure whoever was following me was walking in my footprints—the bigger feet swallowing up the imprint of my smaller feet. "Thank you for scaring them off." I smile, and it's strained.

"I was hanging out of my window smoking." She comes closer, and I catch a waft of nicotine mixed with the cold, fresh air. "Oh, that looks like a stinger."

"It's not so bad." I cover my cheek and gather my things. "Thanks again." I head the opposite way, my eyes darting constantly.

"You should call the police!"

And tell them what? That some random person—I've no clue who—attacked me on a public street. And I have no clue *why* either?

I hold a hand up, waving her off, and pick up my pace.

Home. I need to get home.

I don't hang around for Mr. Percival to find me, letting myself in and bolting the door—something I have never done. An inspection in the mirror tells me I'll be sporting an impressive, bruised cheek in the morning. "Great," I breathe, my face bunching as I gently pad at it with a cold press. It just seems to get redder by the minute, probably now I have some blood circulating in my face. I sigh, wedging my palms into the edge of the sink, done with trying to stop it bruising. The whack was too hard—connecting perfectly. I suck in air past my teeth as I feel at it. My poor cheek has been abused, the nick from Mum's swiping hand only just faded. Were they opportunists? *But they didn't take my bag or mobile.* Because they were disturbed?

I make my way back to the kitchen and call Mum's care home to let them know I won't be in this evening, then toss my compress in the bin and go to my bed, dropping to the mattress. Dec doesn't call me, and despite being disappointed, I'm also relieved.

I don't want to tell him about this evening.

It would just be another silent lie.

December 15th

The snow has melted a bit. We shouldn't get too caught up in our freedom again, according to the weather reporter. He predicts a couple days of higher temperatures over the weekend before they plummet on Sunday evening, and a second wave of snow hits the UK. It's a record. There will be more snow this December than in ten years put together. It's unprecedented. And really fucking inconvenient. The kids, however, are loving the endless ammunition and school closures.

I swallow and take one more peek in the elevator mirror, cringing at my cheek. I underestimated the damage. During a night's sleep, my cheek has gone from red to *raging* red. It's already shining through the bomb-proof concealer I've slapped on. "Shit." I pull out the tube and apply yet another layer, dabbing gently at my stinging cheek. I've walked the streets of London for years, at every hour of the day and night. I've never felt unsafe. Vulnerable. But there were always people around; it's standard London.

When it's not two feet under snow.

I was a fool. I should have considered that. I reach up to my cheek and breathe out my exasperation with myself, thinking Dec is not going to be impressed. Neither will Mr. Percival.

Dangling elves greet me as the doors slide open, and I sigh as I dip beneath them. "Those things are a health and safety hazard," I mutter as Debbie gets up from her desk and joins me on the walk to my office. "Nice to see the office thriving once again."

"Liar," she retorts, handing me a file. I know when her face falls she's clocked my injury. "Oh my God, Camryn, what happened?"

"Nothing." I whip the file out of her hand. "What's this?"

Her lips purse, but she doesn't press. "Comparisons for the market you asked for."

"That *I* asked for?"

"Yes, yesterday. By email."

I cast my mind back, but for the life of me, I can't find the moment I emailed Debbie and asked for any comparisons. I do, however, know why I would have asked for them. "Is Thomas here yet?"

"Yes, in his office. And so is Barbara."

"I'm not in her good books."

"Did she really pay for her injectable fillers on the company card?"

"So it was fillers?" I hardly want to admit I was wondering what exactly she'd tweaked. "How do you know it was fillers?"

"Crystal heard Thomas on the phone to her. Not a happy bunny. And Anthony is off around the Caribbean on the company too, huh?"

"I can neither confirm nor deny." I push my way into my office. "So the office jungle drums are pounding?"

"I'd stay out of Barbara's way."

"She doesn't scare me."

"Of course she doesn't." Debbie rolls her eyes. "Don't forget Secret Santa on Monday." Her eyebrows hitch. "I'm open to giving you ideas, just say the word."

"I don't need ideas, because I'm not included in Secret Santa."

"You joined in for the Christmas jumpers," she counters, shrill.

"Yes, and look where that got me." Although, it was the first time I heard Dec laugh, so that made it almost worth it. I dump my bag on my desk. "What does a girl have to do to get a coffee around here?"

"Ask."

I grit my teeth around my smile. "Can I get a coffee, *please*?"

"Sure." Debbie curtsies. "I'd ask if you want sugar, but the whole building knows you need ten."

"Do you want this job?"

She backs out the room on a bow and closes the door, and I shrug out of my coat and hang it on the hook. Before I've even opened my inbox, a text message lands, and my heart skips a beat as I scramble to find my phone.

I don't know whether to be relieved or sad that it's not Dec. But I certainly know I feel unspeakable fire in my belly that it *is* my husband.

> I'm moving back into the house. We can't afford for it to sit empty while you bury your head in the sand, and I can't sustain a mortgage and rent forever. I'm sure you can't either.

The only thing I've wondered if I can sustain is the unbearable pain. I don't care about money. I don't care about the house. I could never step foot in that place again, and it riles me to no end that he can, let alone live there with memories in every room, around every corner. The evenings in the kitchen cooking. The lazy days on the enormous couch vegging. The summers in the garden trying to figure out what were weeds and what were plants.

"Fuck you," I mutter, going to my inbox and scrolling through the emails. Work. I need to focus on work. Not bastard exes. Not who would try to mug me on a deserted London street. Work.

I open an email from the accountant detailing the directors personal tax bills. One for the end of January and one for the end of July. "Jesus Christ." I pick up my phone and call him. "I got the personal tax predictions. Do you have a rough idea on the corporation tax bill due in October?" I ask, getting up and walking circles around my desk.

"It isn't pretty."

"They never are."

"Give or take a few million."

"I'd like to take off a few million, Jeff. Thomas's wife and son need a crash course in how tax works. They look at big fat bank accounts and rub their hands together. It doesn't enter their heads that much of it is earmarked for company and personal taxes."

"I'm not going to bullshit you, Camryn. The coughers have depleted drastically these past few months. It might come as a shock to you—"

"Nothing comes as a shock to me anymore, Jeff."

"The directors have been drawing dividends like they're going out of fashion these past few weeks."

Past few weeks? "By directors, I'm assuming you mean Barbara and Anthony specifically."

"Yes. Have you seen the bank statements?"

"For the holding account? No. I run my eye over the current running accounts daily, but the holding accounts statements land the thirtieth of the month, since the activity is minimal."

"Not so minimal at the moment. The ship is going to sink if you don't repair the leaks."

I rest my arse on the edge of the desk. "I feel like I'm fighting a losing battle."

"Why are you still there, Camryn?"

I blink, frowning. "What?"

"A woman of your calibre. Why haven't you walked?"

Because I need this job. "I like the challenge," I quip, and he laughs. "Look, Jeff, the important question is, can TF Shipping afford these tax bills?"

"Yes, but it'll wipe them out."

"No more filler on the business for Barbara," I singsong quietly.

"What?"

"Nothing." I sigh. "Thanks for shining your Friday rays of sunshine on me." I hang up and tap the desk by my butt with my phone, seriously wondering if I'm up for another battle today. I feel like I'm trying to wrangle wild horses.

And where the hell is my coffee? I swing the door open and find Debbie on the phone. I scowl at her as I pass. "I'll get my own, or I'll die of caffeine deficiency."

She looks about as impressed as a cow seeing a McDonald's truck pull up on the farm. "Sorry," she says, her hand over the receiver.

"No sweat," I mutter to myself. "I wanted to stretch my legs anyway." And duck and dive through the grotto. I frown at a twinkling snowman as I pass. Is she still adding shit to the already jammed corridor? "My God," I murmur, passing a wooden shed that's been sprayed with artificial snow.

The smell of caffeine hits me when I push the door to the kitchen open, and see Crystal pouring eggnog into cups. "Making up for the few days you couldn't make it into the office, are you?"

She flashes me a tight smile as I pull a cup down, but it falters when she clocks my cheek. She doesn't ask, though. It's a small mercy. No one will ask, except Debbie, of course. "Want some?"

"Eggnog? No." I take the percolator and pour. "You shouldn't be gossiping about Thomas and what you hear him saying on his private calls." Looking out the corner of my eye, I see her still mid-pour, her mind obviously racing.

"Sure you don't want any?" She grabs a cup and thrusts it my way with a cheesy—guilty—smile.

I take my coffee and hold it up, seeing a Panettone and some cute little Father Christmas cupcakes. "Sure," I say, slowly lifting my coffee to my lips. I blink, getting a snapshot of me in the kitchen of my old home, icing sugar everywhere. Slade yelling from the Alexa. Mulled wine simmering on the stove.

"Sure you do, or sure you don't?"

I retreat from the flashback and frown at Crystal. "What?" My eyes drop to the cup hovering between us. "I said no." Someone breezes into the kitchen, spots me, and performs a quick about-turn, heading straight back out. "Thomas," I call, going after him.

"Sorry, just remembered I'm late for a call."

It's quite an achievement in these heels, but I somehow manage to overtake him and block his path. Thomas recoils and peeks above my head, and I follow his line of sight and see a bunch of mistletoe dangling from the ceiling above us. "Why would you even allow that?" I ask, reaching up and yanking it down. "You're begging for a sexual harassment lawsuit."

"Hey, wait a minute, I wasn't suggesting—"

"I'm talking in general, Thomas." He's wary of me, like most people around here, so I'm safe from being caught under the mistletoe unexpectedly.

"What the hell's happened to your face?"

"I fell over walking home." I resist my natural instinct to reach up and cover it from his questioning eyes. "I just got off the phone with Jeff. We need—"

"Grandpa!" The screech hits my eardrums and rattles them, and Thomas is quickly gone from in front of me, being tackled by a young girl, maybe fourteen.

"Marcy," he sings, catching her in his arms and hugging her.

"Hey, Dad," a lady says, pulling off her gloves, her pink lips stretched wide.

"Gail." Thomas sighs, as if he's relieved to see her, keeping Marcy to his chest, all bundled up in her fleece, scarf, and hat, while opening his other arm for his daughter. She walks straight into it. "Where's Curtis?"

"Just parking the rental car. I thought we were leaving the snow behind in Colorado!"

"Camryn, this is my daughter, Gail, and my gorgeous granddaughter Marcy. Girls, this is Camryn. I've told you about Camryn, remember, Gail?"

Oh, is that so? I imagine it was all kinds of complimentary. I toss Thomas a knowing look as I offer my hand to Gail. "Nice to meet you." *Are you as big of an arsehole as your brother?*

Gail breaks away from her father's embrace, laughing. If she notices my face, she doesn't say anything. "I'm a hugger." Then she hauls me into her chest, squeezing me, and I have to lift my coffee over my head to avoid tipping it over both of us. Thomas grins at me as I tense from head to toe, my eyes narrowing on him. "You sure are," I say quietly, gently breaking away. "Well, it was a pleasure." I face Thomas. "I'll catch up with you later." It's a threat, and he knows it.

I leave Thomas and his family, going back to my office, holding up my coffee to Debbie as I pass. She flat out ignores my sarcasm. When I land at my desk, I re-read my husband's text, as if I need to lower my mood more. Then I delete it, like I have every other text I've gotten from him. "I don't give a fuck if you can't pay the rent and mortgage," I growl. "I'm paying my half." *Take out "unreasonable behaviour" and I'll sign the fucking papers.*

I rest back in my chair, my cheek throbbing, and pull out my compact mirror to check the situation, mentally estimating how many days it's going to take to fade enough to get a good coverage—enough to hide it completely. Three. Maybe four. If I'm lucky. I snap my mirror shut on a defeated exhalation. Right now, three or four days not seeing Dec feels like a lifetime. So when my phone starts dancing across my desk, I'm thrown into a horrible dilemma. I want to see him. Let him calm my storm. But I'm quite sure I don't want to be forced into explaining the tidy cuff on my cheek. And I definitely don't want to lie. It's burning my brain, anticipating explaining the unseen scars when he inevitably unearths them. I haven't the capacity to tackle Dec when he inevitably scolds me for being so monumentally dumb for walking home in the dark alone when the streets are deserted. And, well, my cheek is a mess. So I let my phone ring off and wince when a message pings through.

Sorry I didn't call you last night. Things ran over.
Late lunch?

I chomp on my lip and tap out a reply.

I've got a mad few days ahead. I'll call you
Monday.

I'm cringing so hard, I shrink down the chair, and I stay there for a whole fifteen minutes until Dec replies.

Okay.

It's one word. But it took fifteen minutes to send that one word, and that one word says so much more than okay. It says: Weird. It says: No, that's not okay. It says: What's going on? It says: I'm suspicious but I'm just going to say *okay* because I don't know what else to say. And it says: You're too much work after all and I'm bowing out.

God, my head!

I slam my phone down and call Debbie. "Get me the holding account statements." I hang up before she can tell me I'm two weeks early and get back to my inbox.

Three hours later, my brain is fried. Jeff wasn't wrong. The holding accounts have been hit hard, but it's Barbara who's been the most active. I email Thomas all the details of his wife's drawings, my mind racing, considering various scenarios, but always coming back to the same conclusion.

She's taking him to the cleaners.

I obviously don't say that, it would be a step too far, but I can plant the seed. He can't possibly look at this and brush it aside. I feel like they're trying to sabotage Thomas's plans. Actually, more than that, they're trying to sabotage Thomas's business, and that doesn't make sense at all. Why rob your own source of wealth that you love to flaunt? I've suspected—been certain—that Barbara and Anthony aren't all too keen on Thomas's plans to float TF Shipping. And I suspect it's because they don't like the idea of answering to a wider board. No more frivolous spending on company cards for personal luxuries.

I hit send and look up at my door when I hear something odd seeping through the wood. "Surely not?" I murmur, standing, torn between going to the door and checking I'm not going mad, or staying here, not risking it, and hiding under my desk. The latter is more appealing, and yet my legs carry me to the door and swing it open.

"Ho-ho-ho!"

I step back, trying to take everything in before me. I can't. There's too much. And then there are suddenly squeals too. Dozens of them.

Kids.

Everywhere.

Running wild, nipping at Father's Christmas's ankles as he stands, large as life, in the middle, surrounded by his believers.

A boulder hits me so hard in the stomach, I'm knocked back a few steps into my office. The noise. *It's unbearable.* I see Debbie look up at me, her smile fading. Her palms are on the shoulders of a small boy as he looks at Santa in wonder. "What's going on?" I ask, not nearly loud enough for her to hear me. "What's going on?" I yell.

She comes at me with the child, and I back away. "It's Bring Your Kid to Work Day," she says, almost in apology.

"Since when?"

"Since the memo that went out yesterday."

"I didn't see any memo." *Fuck, I did see a memo.* I just didn't read the memo properly. "I can't work in this," I say, on the cusp of outrage. "For fuck's sake."

Debbie's palms rest on the boy's ears as his eyes bug up at me. I have to get out of here.

I grab my bags and hurry through the chaos, smacking my finger on the elevator call button urgently. The doors open, and a swarm of more kids come at me, yelling at the sight of Santa Claus. My whole body tightens, pulling in my limbs, making myself as small as possible, as they dart past me on both sides.

Stepping in, I tuck myself in the corner and only breathe easy when the doors close and the elevator carries me away from the never-ending triggers. *I fucking hate Christmas.* The noise. The screaming children. The happiness everyone else experiences when it's the time of year that my life fell apart. And yet, *he*, of course, can simply move on. Because he thinks I am unreasonable. He left. He simply fucking left. I look down at my watch. Specifically, the date. The nineteenth is only four days away. How the fuck has three years passed?

The elevator is suddenly suffocating, and I will it to move faster. The moment the doors are open wide enough, I slip through the gap and hurry across the lobby, taking in precious air. I step outside and look down at my heels in the slushy snow. "Shit." Dropping my bag onto a nearby post, I pull out my boots and socks and get them on, before following my feet mindlessly.

I end up at Mum's care home. It's all standard—a tight smile to the receptionist, a slow trudge up the corridor, my stomach turning with dread, a cautious peek around the door, my heart falling when I see her.

Her lunch is untouched by the bedside, the room basked in a hazy light, and she's asleep. I push my way in and start my obligatory chores, changing the water in her jug, getting rid of the wilting flowers, cleaning the vase and trimming the stems of the new carnations, arranging them just so. Then I sit down. "You've not eaten," I say, reaching for the fork in her pasta and poking it around the bowl. "Not hungry?"

Her eyes open, and she looks at me, vacant. Nothing behind her eyes. "I could manage a few mouthfuls, Nurse," she says, straight-faced, nothing in her voice either. Just emotionless words.

I swallow and pull my chair closer, forking a piece of penne and offering it. Her mouth drops open, her head still sunk into the pillow, and I pop it in, watching her chew slowly, her empty gaze never wavering from mine. I don't tell her I love her. I don't call her *Mum*. I say nothing that'll spike a violent reaction. I just sit here, feeding her, happy to be simply *Nurse*. It's almost . . .

peaceful. The quiet. I take a deep breath, and for a moment, I can let the desperate blanket of sadness go. It's momentary, but I take it.

She surprisingly manages a quarter of her bowl before she doesn't open her mouth for me anymore. "Water?" I ask, offering her the straw. She wraps her lips around it, lips that used to never be without a red tint that would last all day long. Now, they're thin and colourless. Lifeless. They don't smile, they don't purse coyly, they don't smirk when she teases me. And they don't speak the words I so long to hear.

Mum's here, my little buttercup. It's all going to be all right.

Because she's not here anymore. And I'm scared all can never be alright again because there's no longer a soul in my life who loves me unconditionally.

I swallow down the grief and wait until she's dozed off again before I clear away the dishes and get my coat back on. I dip and kiss her forehead gently so I don't wake and alarm her. "Love you, Mum."

"Love you too, buttercup."

I smile as she squeezes me to her chest, stroking circles across my back with her palm as she breathes into my neck. "Don't you think I'm too old at thirty to be called buttercup, Mum?"

She snorts. "Never. Whether you're four or forty, you'll always be my little buttercup."

"Okay," I concede, feeling her hands move up to my hair and start combing through the strands.

"My buttercup," she murmurs.

I close my eyes, thankful that my mum never breaks her promises . . . and always gives the best, most healing hugs.

Mr. Percival's door is wide open when I let myself in the building, a racket coming from inside. I knock the wood and call out to him, but get no answer, which isn't such a surprise given the noise. "Mr.

Percival?" I call louder, treading through the gnomes flanking the hallway. "Mr. Percival, it's Camryn."

"Camryn?"

"Your door's open."

"I know, dear. Maureen opened it."

I round the corner into the kitchen, the noise deafening, and find Mr. Percival at the table with a food blender whizzing around. I shudder. Fucking hell, it's baltic in here. He sees me and smiles, flicking the switch so it drones to a gradual stop. "Making my stuffing, dear. Chopped nuts."

Woolly gloves cover his hands, a scarf is wrapped a few times around his neck, and every button on his tweed coat is fastened, his cap on his head. I'm not Mr. Percival's only spectator, either. The gnomes are all crowded round, watching. "Mr. Percival, it's freezing in here."

"The heating's broken down, dear."

"Have you called someone?"

"Yes, dear. An engineer will be here within six hours." He fumbles around in his pocket and pulls out his watch. "It's been three."

"Right." I wrap my arms around my body.

"It's only the circuit board that serves the heaters, though, so we still have power."

"Would you like to use my kitchen?"

"Why would I want to do that?"

"Because it doesn't feel like Siberia."

"You young folk." He dusts off his gloves and pours his chopped nuts into a bowl. "Try camping out in the trenches for weeks on end, dear."

"What?" I recoil. "Like, in the war?"

"World War Two, dear."

"How old are you, Mr. Percival?"

"Ninety-nine, dear."

"Fuck." I balk at him. "You're nearly one hundred."

"Holding out to get my birthday card from the King, dear." He grins at me.

"When's your birthday?"

"January." He shoves a wooden spoon in the bowl and starts mixing, and for the first time today, I smile. *You incredible man.*

"You look remarkable for a man who's nearly a century old, Mr. Percival."

"I know." His shining eyes dim when he squints. "What's happened to your cheek?"

"I had a run-in with a door at work," I say, off the cuff. "It's one of those flappy doors. I wasn't looking where I was going and someone walked through before me and it sprung back and caught my cheek." I approach the small table he's working from. "It's a bit early to be making stuffing, isn't it?"

"You can't be too prepared for Christmas, Camryn. I'll pop it in the freezer with my turkey and ham joint."

"Anything I can do?"

"You want to help?"

"Why not?" I've got nothing better to do. "You can tell me about all one hundred years of your life."

"We might be here all weekend," he says over a chuckle as I dump my bag on the floor.

"Hopefully," I reply, waiting for instruction.

"We'll put some carols on, shall we?"

"I'd rather just listen to you talk."

"Oh, well. Have it your way."

Four hours later, I've made mincemeat for his mince pies, a whole nut roast, squeezed sausage meat out of the skins, wrapped bacon around some chipolatas, and a whole lot more. And the entire time, I'm wondering who on earth Mr. Percival is cooking for and where the hell he's going to sit them. I distinctly recall him mentioning he has no family, but I haven't asked because I've been too busy listening to him talk non-stop about his time in the war—only one year, mind you, but a lifetime when you're stuck in the trenches—

as well as his marriage to Edith who passed in 1999, and their son, Miles, who Mr. Percival tragically outlived.

I continue to stir the double cream with the whisk, waiting eternally for it to thicken, while he chatters with such fond memories, and I wonder how. How can he have lost love, lost his son, and still be here smiling?

Living.

"I think there's something wrong with this cream," I say, my backside becoming dead on the stool, my arm feeling like it's about to fall off because I've been here whisking it so long. Am I sweating?

He hobbles around the table without his frame, holding the edge. It makes me twitchy, my hands bracing to catch him if he falls. "We need some intervention." Picking up the electric whisk, he raises his brows.

"You mean I've been beating it until my arm feels like it's going to fall off and you had that the whole time?"

He shrugs, a little impish. "Slipped my mind."

"Sure it did," I grumble, snatching it from his hand. I know his game. He's keeping me here for as long as he can. I don't mind. It's been a surprisingly lovely afternoon making and baking with him. I've not thought about what exactly I'm baking, I've just done as I'm told and listened to Mr. Percival chatter.

"Is that why you were home early?" he asks, pointing his spoon at my cheek.

I nod, because that's easiest, and turn on the whisk, except it doesn't come on. I scowl at it, flicking the switch a few more times. "It's broken."

He frowns and goes to the fridge, swinging it open. "Oh shoot, that's the other circuit board gone down too."

I lower the whisk on a sigh. "Great."

"Brandy!" he yells at me, flashing a hipflask and opening the cap, having a swig before he pours some into the cream and offers me the flask.

I tsk him teasingly. "Are you trying to get me drunk?"

"A flask a day keeps the lurgies away. How do you think I made it to the ripe old age of one hundred?"

"You're not there yet," I say, accepting. "So this is your secret? Brandy?"

"Bottoms up," he sings, as I tip the flask to my lips and swallow. "Jesus Christ." I gasp, blinking back the burn as it slides down my throat. It hits my belly with a bang and more burn. "This kept you alive?" I wheeze.

"Sailor's strength, dear." He winks and screws the little silver cap back on, tucking it into his coat. "How's that cream coming along?"

"Slowly." I grab the hand whisk and get back to work, switching hands constantly to split the strain, until it finally thickens. I tip the bowl upside down over my head to demonstrate, making Mr. Percival laugh loudly.

"Oh, who's this then?" he says, looking past me.

I turn, still smiling, the bowl still over my head, and see Dec in the kitchen doorway.

"The door was open," he says, eyes on me. "I called a few times, but you obviously couldn't hear me."

"Obviously," Mr. Percival says on a hum.

My smile falls with the bowl to the table. "Dec."

He steps forward, his hands in his coat pockets. "What happened to your face?"

"She did it at work," Mr. Percival says, almost proud he has the information to share.

"I did it at work," I repeat quietly. I'd say it's so lovely to see him, but he doesn't look happy.

"How?"

"A door sprung back in her face," Mr. Percival goes on.

My lips straighten as I watch Dec's eyes narrow. He's doubtful. "I was going to call you Monday."

"I know. I didn't want to wait until Monday." He goes to Mr. Percival and offers his hand. "Dec Ellis."

Mr. Percival flashes me an impressed look. "Nice to meet you,

Dec Ellis." Mr. Percival slaps his gloved hand in Dec's. "Percy Percival."

"Your name's Percy?" I ask on a light laugh. "Percy Percival?"

The old man's back straightens, making him a whole inch taller, and his shoulders push back. "That's right."

"And a great name it is, too," Dec says, catching my amusement. "Right, Camryn?"

"Right."

"Now, Percy, would you mind if I steal your sous chef?"

"Not at all!"

"Thank you." Dec pries my fingers off the bowl and claims my hand. "Let's go."

I smile my goodbye and thanks to Mr. Percival as I look back over my shoulder, and he nods his understanding. "I feel like I'm about to be scolded," I say.

"Why's it so fucking cold in there?" Dec asks, grumpy.

"His heating's broken down."

"Is it being fixed?"

"Yes."

"Good."

"The power just went out too," I add.

Dec stops at my door and points. "Open."

I get the feeling I'd be dumb to refuse, so I dig my key out and slip it into the lock, pushing the door open. I look at Dec. He nods toward the doorway in silent order, so I walk in, a little apprehensive. I'm about to be grilled about my cheek. About my brush-off text message earlier. About why I'm at home far earlier than I should be.

I hear the door close and turn around, and Dec is on me immediately, taking my mouth greedily, walking me to the nearest wall and pushing me up against it.

The misery of my day fades.

I'm kissed into oblivion, his hand cupping my neck, his thumb gently stroking my injured cheek as he blitzes my mind and assaults my mouth with gentle authority. The hairs on the back of my neck rise, every nerve ending stirring. When Dec kisses me, there is nothing else.

He eventually breaks away, his eyes glossy and soft, as I pant shallowly, my mouth open, my lips swollen and wet. "Are we clear?"

"Yes," I whisper, feeling through his hair on his nape.

"Why are you avoiding me?"

"I didn't want you to see this."

He half frowns, half scowls. "A door sprung back in your face?" he asks, wincing as he checks it.

I nod, shame and guilt getting me hard in my stomach. "I'm clumsy."

He sighs, and I see he hasn't got it in him to challenge me. "Have I got to start wrapping you in cotton wool when I'm not with you?"

Wouldn't that be wonderful? To be protected from damage. From hurt. "I wouldn't mind." I loop my arms around his neck and nuzzle under his chin. "I'm sorry."

He groans and lifts me, carrying me to my bedroom and laying me down, crowding me completely. He kisses me gently again. "You taste like brandy."

"Mr. Percival was trying to get me drunk," I say around our swirling tongues, my eyes widening when he firms against my thigh.

"Fuck it." He rips his mouth off mine, wedges his palms into the mattress, and lifts his torso. "I need to take a rain check."

"Why?"

"Ron's waiting outside and he's got somewhere he needs to be after he's dropped us off."

"Where are we going?"

"For dinner." He stands and pulls me up to my feet.

"But Dec, my face is—"

"Beautiful. Do you want to change?"

I sigh and look down my front, wondering if he's seeing what I'm seeing. "I should think so."

"I'll wait"—he gestures over his shoulder, backing away—"out here." He grimaces and adjusts himself as he turns, and I bite my lip to stop my smile. Which is crazy. Why would I stop it? So I let my happiness loose. Why would I ever deprive myself of something that seems to make everything in this godforsaken world easier to bear?

We pass an electrical engineer as we leave, which makes me feel a whole lot better about Mr. Percival and his ice box. Not that he seemed bothered. I'm still waiting for the feeling to come back in my fingers and toes.

Dec halts abruptly on the steps, and I stagger to a stop next to him, following his line of sight. I smile. Dec hums under his breath, the sound full of puzzlement. "Why is there a turkey in the snow?" he asks, pointing at the frozen bird plonked outside the doors, some wire netting laying over it, assumedly to protect it from Maureen and any other neighbourhood cats.

"Mr. Percival," I say. "His freezer will have stopped working with the electricity cut."

Dec looks at me in alarm. "You said that like it's perfectly normal for people to leave turkeys in the snow outside their house."

"It is for Mr. Percival. He's ninety-nine, Dec. Ninety-nine! Can you imagine being that old?"

He huffs. "No. I feel pretty ancient now."

I laugh. And stop. "I don't know how old you are."

"Thirty-nine. It's been a long day at work."

He looks like a healthy thirty-nine-year-old. Mature. Worn in. Perfect. "What were you merging or acquiring today?"

"I'm acquiring you." He allows a smile to break, letting his eyes fall down my front. "I like this."

"The coat?"

"No," he says, the word stretched, as he takes the sides of my long black coat and pulls it open. "This."

"It's a black dress." One I've been known to wear to work on occasions. Nothing special. Hence, I wear it to work. Truth be told, I have no differentiation in my wardrobe. No work clothes section, casual section, evening section. It's a mash-up of workout clothes and workwear. The odd pair of jeans. A few jumpers and sweaters.

All of it black.

"I like it," he declares again, pulling me on and opening the door of the Defender. "In."

I slide across the seat and smile my hello to the driver in the rearview mirror.

"Langans, thanks, Ron." Dec shuts the door and goes to his phone, his face down. The glow of his screen shines up onto his face, making his lashes seem especially long. I leave him to whatever he's doing on his mobile, despite being able to watch him all evening, and look out of the window. A rainbow of colours shoots like darts through the windscreen into the back as Ron turns onto the main road, the Christmas lights making a disco in the car.

Dec's phone rings, he sighs, and my eyes naturally turn to the screen. "Dad," I say, assessing his strung form. "Ready to unpack that?"

His head turns slowly toward me. "Nothing to unpack. My mum died, he remarried a woman half his age a year later, had two entitled brats with her, and he can't seem to figure out why I don't like him."

I blink, quite alarmed by how he reeled that off with such little emotion. "I'm sorry. About your mother."

"Me too. She was a wonderful woman."

"So why's your dad calling if you don't speak?"

"One of the brats got engaged." The look he turns onto me is quite amusing, especially since it's coming from Dec, Mr. Indiscernibly Thoughtful. There's a smidge of irony that I don't understand but perhaps will one day. There's mostly incredulity, though.

"Have you told him how you feel?" I ask.

"Should I need to?"

"Yes, if he's insular."

"Insular," he echoes, amused. "That's a nicer way of putting it. I've always called him a self-important wanker."

"To his face?"

"Once or twice." He smirks. It's a terrible attempt to convince me that his father is of no consequence.

"Dec Ellis, do you have daddy issues?" I ask, surprised by my playfulness and thrilled more when he laughs lightly, making those gorgeous eyes of his twinkle under the sporadic glow of London by night through the window. And yet, whether it delights me or not, it's another bad execution of indifference.

"Camryn Moore, I definitely do not have daddy issues."

"Hmmm."

Dec reaches for my knee and squeezes in playful warning, and I yelp, bucking up in my seat.

"He definitely has daddy issues," Ron pipes in from up front, his eyebrows disappearing above the reflection of his eyes in mirror they're so high.

"You're not included in this conversation, Ron," Dec mutters.

"Noted."

"What does your father do?" I ask, hungry for more about Dec.

"Acquisitions and mergers."

"You work together?"

"Jesus, no."

I gasp. "You're rivals?"

"You got it."

I'm building the picture. Dec's punishing his father. Punishing the entitled brats. "And you don't have daddy issues?"

"No."

"Hmmm."

He grabs me round my waist and pulls me onto his lap. "You're asking for it."

"You make love to me, Casanova." I touch my nose with his. "You're not going to be a man I fuck and forget, remember?"

"Doesn't mean I can't be a man who you fuck and remember."

"I like you making love to me."

"You romantic, you."

"Shut up." I roll my mouth onto his, forcing his head to rest back on the seat, kissing him with hungry lips and an exorable tongue. "Sorry, Ron," I mumble, and he laughs from the front.

"Don't mind me. This is a refreshing Dec."

There are few things in the world that could make me stop kissing Dec. Dec himself, obviously. And that statement. He's rolling his eyes, knowing very well my interest is piqued. I keep my gaze on Dec but speak to Ron. "Refreshing?"

"Don't read into that statement too deeply," Dec warns.

"Okay, not too deeply." I look over my shoulder. "What does that mean, Ron?"

"Nothing at all," he breathes, more awkward than Dec. "Langhans, you said?"

"Langhans," Dec confirms, putting me on the seat next to him, his hand back on my knee.

"Tell me what he meant," I push, lightly.

Dec turns serious eyes onto me. No lightness in sight. "Tell me why you're getting divorced."

I retreat, literally and metaphorically, darkness swamping the lightness I was feeling a moment ago. "I've hit a nerve, clearly," I say, turning my attention to London by night, at Christmas whizzing past. "I'm sorry." There was no need for him to fire that bullet.

"Fuck, I'm sorry." He reaches for my arm, holding it, but not tugging me closer. "Hey, come here."

I inhale deeply as I turn. "Can we rewind two minutes?"

He pulls me onto his lap and holds my face. "Doesn't mean I can't be a man who you fuck and remember," he says quietly, his eyes falling to my mouth in anticipation. I don't have a chance to instigate the kiss, as Dec takes care of it, slipping his hand onto my nape and pulling me to his lips. And now I'd like to skip dinner, go home with him, and let him take me to the stars before I fall asleep in his arms.

I push my chest into his, and he groans, his body stiffening against me. "I'm sorry," he murmurs.

"Me too."

His phone ringing brings our moment to an untimely halt, and he crinkles his nose. "My sister," he murmurs, helping me off his lap.

His sister? "The brat?"

"Not the brat."

So not a half-sister, but an actual sister? "You never mentioned you had a sister."

"I have a sister," he says, deadpan, looking down at his screen.

"Are you going to take it?"

"I'll call her back." He nods toward the windscreen. "We're here."

Ron pulls up outside the restaurant, and Dec hops out, rounding the car and opening the door for me. "Older sister, younger sister?" I ask, my curiosity raging.

"Older." His hand on the small of my back guides me to the entrance of the restaurant as he looks back at the car and waves his thanks to Ron.

"How much older?"

"Four years."

"Her name?"

He smiles down at me. "April."

"Was she born in April?"

"Yes. Our mother was very original." He heaves the door open and gets us inside, and the heater above the door blasts us with hot air.

I gaze around, seeing paper hats on every head in sight. Christmas parties. People celebrating at every turn, the pops of crackers piercing the air as people laugh and talk loudly to be heard over the background noise of everyone else talking. I haven't been in a restaurant in years, least of all at Christmas. A mild wave of panic ripples through me, but I stamp it down, looking at Dec. He appears as unenthusiastic as me.

"It's busy, huh?" I murmur as he slips his hands beneath the shoulders of my coat and eases it off.

He frowns, but as I look closer, I see it's more of a scowl. "Do you want to go somewhere else?" he asks.

"So you hate Christmas more than you love it?"

"And you just hate it, right?" he fires back coolly, and I roll my eyes, rather than freeze in terror at the potential of unearthing my demons. I know it's got to happen eventually, but not now. Tonight we're having dinner like a normal . . . couple? Is that what we are?

"Answering a question with a question isn't answering a question," I say, taking in the madness again. "We should stay." I can do this. I *should* do this.

He passes our coats to the cloakroom attendant and gives his name to the maître d, who guides us through the tables to the very back. It's no quieter, but at least it's no louder. Dec pulls my chair out and orders water. "Give me two minutes," he says, dipping and kissing my hair, before strolling away, presumably to find somewhere quieter and call his sister back. A waiter introduces himself and hands me a wine and Christmas menu.

"Thank you." I put the wine menu at Dec's place and cast my eye down the Christmas menu. "Excuse me," I call as he's walking away. "I don't suppose you have the normal menu?"

He recoils like he's been shot. "The normal menu?"

"Yes, the normal menu. The one that doesn't have everything Christmas on it."

"I'm afraid not, ma'am. We only serve the Christmas menu from December tenth through to January." And then he wanders away, passing Dec as he goes.

"What's up?" Dec asks as he lowers.

I wave the menu at him. "I hope you like Christmas food, even if you hate Christmas."

"I don't really hate it," he says, picking up the wine menu. "I just don't love it. I'm indifferent." I remain quiet as he peruses the choices, eventually peeking up at me. He sighs and lowers the menu. "Christmas doesn't hold fond memories for me."

"Oh." I have no idea what to say.

"Like I said, my father's an arsehole."

"You called him a self-important wanker, actually."

He laughs as the waiter pours us some water. "No wine, but we'll take two dirty martinis."

"Do you actually like dirty martinis?" I ask.

"I hadn't tried one until recently."

I smile. "They're not my favourite," I admit.

"Then why do you drink them?"

"Because they're strong." I shrug. That *and* my words are very revealing. The sharp hit of alcohol was like taking a pill, instantly numbing me. Then it became habit. A habit for a dark, bleak moment of time that stretched into years.

Dec's eyes squint as he sips his water, his arm raising in the air. "Excuse me, sir," he calls, getting the waiter back. "Scrap the martinis. We'll take a bottle of champagne."

My lips twitch with my smile. "What are we celebrating?"

"Mr. Percival's saved turkey."

A sharp shot of laughter rises and flies out of my mouth, and Dec rests back in his chair looking very satisfied with himself.

"Laugh often, Camryn." He puts his hand on the table palm up, his smile small but telling. I rest my hand in his and relish the feel of his fingers wrapping around mine. "I want you to feel like you can talk to me," he says. "About anything. Nothing will change. I'll still feel the same way about you."

The promise of acceptance and understanding hits me hard in my chest. It makes me fall that little bit more. How open he is. How he communicates, both with words and actions. I should be crawling into my shell, retreating. The walls should be flying up, but I'm trying to digest what's happening. What he's saying. I've thought about it, of course—this has been happening for a few weeks—but I don't think I truly appreciated what this could mean for me. And as I sit here now, looking at this man across the table, his eyes molten on me, for the first time, I do. I'm sitting in this absurdly busy restaurant at a time of year I absolutely abhor, and today it's not so bad. I'm coping.

Dec is peace in a world I don't recognise anymore. He's a second chance I never considered or expected. "December isn't a good month for me," I say, digging deep, my eyes dropping to the table. I feel Dec squeeze my hand, and I look up to see him rising from his chair.

He comes to my side of the table and crouches beside me. "Let's not do this now," he says softly. "I can't hear myself think. Let's eat, go home, let me hold you, and if you feel like it, you can talk, and I will listen. Like I said, nothing changes for me." He rises to half height and kisses my cheek, and the threat of tears gets me good. "Okay?"

"Okay," I agree, soaking up the feel of his lips on my cheek. "Thank you."

"Shut up." He takes the bottle of champagne from the waiter and pours me a glass, putting it in my hand. "I have everything we need for a martini at home if you need something a little stronger."

Something stronger for when I talk. "I don't want another martini ever again."

"Then I'll make you something else." He sits and rests his elbows on the table. "Back to Percy Percival. Ninety-fucking-nine?"

And just like that, he brings the conversation round. "Incredible, isn't he?"

"Sharp as a pin, too."

"Oh, he is." I laugh, the unusual sound becoming more familiar again.

"And what's with the hundreds of gnomes?"

"They were in his garden at his previous home." I pout, taking a sip of the champagne and humming, the cold, sparkly liquid waking up my taste buds. "I think he's lonely."

"Old and lonely," he muses. "You know that's how I'll end up one day."

"Old and lonely? A good-looking, successful man like you?"

Women must be lining up to bag him. Which begs the question . . . Why me?

He shrugs. "I'm not very good at letting go of grudges."

"Your father," I say, speaking my conclusion, leaning back in my chair as Dec fingers the stem of his glass, so obviously uncomfortable. "Tell me why you're indifferent about Christmas."

"It was always a bit of a farce. Dad disappearing, Mum pretending she hadn't noticed."

Ohhhh. "Your mum knew?"

"She knew. I think she would have left, but then she fell ill. The treatment she needed was insanely expensive, not that it mattered in the end. She died when I was thirteen, and I was shipped off to boarding school while Dad cracked on with his bit of stuff like my mother never existed. Had the Christmases that I never had with his new kids. I stopped going home in the holidays, and Dad didn't seem too bothered by that."

"And your sister?"

"She was traveling the world."

I sink into my chair, disturbed, and feeling horrible guilt. Especially when Dec peeks at me and gives a small smile that doesn't quite reach his eyes. There's so much resentment in his gaze. So much anger. It's what drives him. The anger for his father. It's why he's so successful, almost a *fuck you* to his dad. "How successful have you been at ruining him in business?" I ask.

"Enormously."

"And does that make you feel better?"

He shifts in his chair, his discomfort getting worse . . . as is my guilt. He's just given me a pass to spill, and here I am grilling him. And yet I sense he wants to share. As do I, except unlike Dec, I'm struggling to figure out where I'd start, and I know the words won't come as easily. "Well, it worked better than therapy," he says flatly, raising his glass. "And I have April who makes sure Christmas remains a thing, even if it's hard work."

I sigh, standing, and round the table, crouching next to him. I smile when he frowns down at me. "Let's not do this now," I say, mimicking his words.

He laughs lightly. "We just did, Camryn."

"Humour me."

"Okay."

I lean up and kiss him gently. "Let's eat and go home." It's my way of telling him I'm ready to share too. Because . . .

Shit.

Because I love him. I love him deeply, and to love someone, you have to expose the ugliest parts of yourself. You have to be sure the person you hope they can love back is the real you. This darkness isn't the real me, and yet there's still a niggling fear that I'll never cleanse myself of it, even with Dec in my life. But I'll never know unless I take that leap. He saw something me I didn't see in myself. Hope. Softness. And for that, I love him more.

Understanding is powerful in his gaze. "Let's order."

I nod and rise to full height, but my backside doesn't make it to the seat, my body freezing halfway when I see someone enter the restaurant.

All the blood drains from my head and runs cold through my body.

"Camryn?"

I drop to the seat, numb, dizzy, short of breath, and reach for my water, my mouth suddenly parched, but my shaking hand fails me. I knock the glass over, sending water spilling across the table.

"Camryn, what the fuck?" Dec flies up from his seat to avoid the waterfall landing in his lap, and the table is suddenly surrounded by waiters rushing to help, flapping around us, causing a scene.

I can't move, can't breathe, but I can see, and all the commotion around us means he's just spotted me too. His face falls as I cast my eyes to the woman with him. She's smiling. Oblivious.

Happy.

"Camryn?" Dec's voice is close to my ear, and I turn my eyes onto him. He withdraws, shocked as he scans my blank face. "Baby, what's going on?"

I need to leave! Get me away!

I shoot up from my chair, clumsy and chaotic, knocking things over as I do. "Camryn?" Endless waiters block my escape, forcing me to push my way through them. "Camryn!"

I can't feel my legs as I walk, my heart pumping wildly, my throat thick with anger and angst. He sees me heading for the doors and moves to the side, pulling her with him, avoiding me. She looks up at him in question.

"Camryn," Dec says, his fingers wrapping around my wrist and tugging me to a stop.

I wrench it out. "Leave me," I snap, losing my footing and grabbing a nearby chair to steady myself.

When I've found my balance, although still terribly wobbly, I turn back around. She's seen me too, and her face falling tells me she knows who I am. Whether from a picture or because I'm staring at them like I hate them, I don't know. My ability to walk has left me again, and I stand here in the middle of the restaurant a blank, shaking mess of a woman wanting to scream.

But I can't scream. I'm not "unreasonable." I laugh on the inside, a sick, dark howl. I need to get out of here before I start throwing plates.

"Camryn," Dec says, appearing in front of me, hands on my shoulders, hunkered down to get my eyes.

"My husband," I say without thinking. It sounds wrong on my tongue. A nasty word spat out to be rid of it.

Dec pulls back, his face a map of lines, and looks over his shoulder. His shoulders lift from an inhale of realisation. "Okay, let's get out of here." Wrapping an arm around me, he puts me on the side farthest away from them and starts to walk me out, but we make it only two steps before I'm a statue again, Dec's efforts to keep me moving futile.

"Camryn, come on, let's go."

My husband rakes a hand through his hair, looking up at the ceiling. "Cam, I didn't want you to find out like this."

My eyes won't leave the woman with him.

And her swollen, pregnant stomach.

"Fuck," Dec breathes, his hold of me loosening, his focus on getting me out lost momentarily as he takes in what I'm looking at. Piecing it together. Getting a clearer picture.

She's pregnant. Heavily pregnant. He's moved on, and she's *pregnant*. They're going to have a child. Be a family.

I can't have children.

"Dominic?" she says quietly, moving closer to him, her arm curling around her belly, as if she's afraid I might try to harm their unborn child. How crazy do I look right now? How unhinged?

The lump in my throat wins, choking me, as my eyes burn with tears. I look at him. Hate the guilt and shame and sadness I see in eyes that aren't familiar to me anymore. I shake my head ever so mildly, showing him my disbelief. My desolation. Suddenly, his urgency for the divorce makes complete and utter sense.

He needs me to help him hurriedly *move on*.

"Cam," Dominic says softly.

"I don't think you should be talking right now," Dec says, his voice on the dangerous side of cool. "In fact, never speak to her again." His arm lifts, a barrier between me and them. I push it down and walk out of the restaurant into the frigid air. I try to breathe but can't seem to get air into my lungs.

Walk.

I need to walk.

I don't know where to. Just away.

Far away.

Far away is a hotel bar. It's not familiar to me. Not one where I've drank myself into false peace before. I walk in, aware of the looks I must be getting in a dress, no coat, my face a busy canvas of pain and anguish, my skin probably blue from the cold. I can't feel it, if I'm cold. I can't feel anything except the constant stabs to my heart. "Two dirty martinis," I say to the bartender, sitting on the end stool. I look at the empty one next to me. I don't have a coat to put there, no bag.

She's pregnant.

I close my eyes and resist touching my stomach where I know the small scars to be. Two small incisions each side, just big enough to slip in the scissors that would cut my useless womb away so they could suck it out of me. I swallow hard, sniffing and roughly wiping my eyes with the back of my hand.

My drinks appear before me, and I slide the spare to the place next to me, ridding mine of the olive and knocking it back. "Another." I place the glass down and tap the bar impatiently while she frowns at the untouched martini next to me. "Another," I repeat, and she quickly gets to work, sliding it across. "I'll do another," I say, throwing my second back, waiting for the inevitable numbness to take hold. It doesn't come. So I take a third. And a fourth.

"Enough."

I still at the sound of Dec's voice and turn to find him in a chair across the bar, sitting quietly, our coats draped across his lap, watching me trying to drink myself into a coma.

"Enough now, Camryn."

I feel my lip wobble as he places our coats on a chair and stands, approaching like someone might approach a rabid wild animal. "She's pregnant," I murmur, and he inhales, nodding. "Not even a little bit pregnant." She's *very* pregnant. Must be seven or eight months. He's kept me in the dark and now I'm a fool. A broken, hopeless fool.

"Let me take you home," Dec says gently. Pacifyingly.

I shake my head, looking at the bartender. She's wiping the shelves, keeping a close eye on me. I nod, silently telling her to get me another and make it sharpish. She looks past me and then goes back to her task.

"Don't tell her no," I grate.

"I want to take you home."

"I don't have a home." It's a dull, lifeless apartment I can't bear to be in. I hold my empty glass up in order, but it's taken by Dec and placed down. My stool is turned toward him, and he makes sure he fills my vision, a big man with a big presence, his face soft but stern.

"I can be your home, Camryn," he says tightly, struggling to maintain his cool. "I can be your everything." He cups my face with both hands, holding me tightly, and puts his nose on mine. "You've just got to let me."

My choked sob jerks my shoulders. "You don't want me." I'm certain of it, and he'll soon figure that out. Why he hasn't already is beyond me. I can't comprehend a world where a man could want me, because everything's so distorted. I don't see the world with the same, bright, hungry eyes. I see doom and gloom. My mind is warped, my anxiety ruling me. Keeping the mask in place is wearing me down—I don't know how much longer I can do it.

It's slipped with Dec.

I need to refix it. Since I met him, the mask has been on and off. On for work, off for Dec. It doesn't work. I need it on all the time, need to protect myself *all* the time.

Starting now.

I yank his hands from my face and thrust them back to him. Hurt doesn't overcome his expression. Anger does. "Don't do that, Camryn," he warns. "Don't think you can fool me with your deceptive bravado and pitiable insincerity. I've seen too much, and if you think for one moment I'm walking out of here without you, you better have another think, and make it fucking fast because it's not beyond me to pick you up off this stool and carry you out. You are *not* having another drink. You are *not* staying here. You are *not* going to try and turn the tables. You are *not* going to fucking reject me now." He thrusts his face up close to mine again, his eyes wild, a storm of emotion and anger tumbling through their depths. I blink, and it releases the collected tears, rolling down my cold cheeks.

He exhales as he backs off and holds out his hand. All I need to do is accept it.

"Take my hand, Camryn," he orders softly.

I look up at him, and he nods. I don't have the strength to stand or even move at all. So Dec collects me from the stool, and I don't protest. I don't fight him. He throws some notes on the bar before getting my coat from where it's draped over the chair with his, and he lays it across my shoulders before leading me out to a car by the curb.

Ron.

As soon as we're in and Dec closes the door, he pulls me close and I collapse into his side, drained. "Here," he says, encouraging my head down to his lap. I stare forward at the rear of the driver's seat. "I want you to be over him," he whispers as he strokes my hair.

Be over him?

I squeeze my eyes closed, and I see what I had. The happiness that was my daily.

So how can I ever be over him?

Never.

I wake up to Dec getting me out of the car, Ron holding the door open. Draped across his arms, he carries me up the steps. "I can walk," I say, my head a little foggy.

"You don't need to."

Ron opens the door for us and nods his goodbye, and I just catch his grave expression before I lose sight of him. "You're freezing," Dec says as he sets me gently on my feet. It hits me now, my skin bumpy, every hair standing on end. I rub my arms as Dec hangs my coat on the coat stand, then drops my bag to the floor and slowly takes his off. I can hear his mind running a mile a minute, feel mine spinning too.

Exhaling loudly, he slips his hands into his pockets and faces me. Looks directly at me, no shying away. Am I supposed to talk now? And if so, what on earth do I say? Should I try—

The silence is shattered by the muffled sound of my phone ringing from my bag. Both of us look down at it, but it's Dec who dips and helps himself, pulling it out and looking at the screen. A short, sharp huff of unamused laughter rumbles at the back of his throat, and he reaches for the bridge of his nose, pinching it, the crinkles around his eyes springing out.

I don't know what to do with that. Impatience and frustration dominate every fibre of his being. And for the first time, now I've taken a moment past my shock and hurt, I consider exactly what he's thinking.

I hate my conclusion.

I want you to be over him.

I need to be brave. I have to show him.

I walk to him, albeit tentatively, and reach for my mobile, but his hand is a vise around it. "Please," I whisper, dipping to fall into his downcast gaze. His fingers peel away, and I drop my mobile onto my bag, leaving it ringing, my husband's name lighting up the screen.

Dec takes a moment, reaching for both my hands and squeezing them as he closes his eyes. I let him have his time, because I need it too.

It's a long few minutes, the silence oddly comforting, his thumbs working slow circles over the tops of my hands, before he eventually draws air and looks at me. "Do you want to be here?" he asks.

"More than anything," I whisper.

He nods, drops one of my hands, and gently pulls me toward the stairs.

I follow a few steps behind him, our arms stretched between us, all the way to his bathroom, where he releases my hand and goes to the tub, flipping on the tap and running his hand beneath it before adding some bath soak. Then he starts to strip slowly, dropping his clothes into a pile until he's naked. I take in his body, trembling, as he moves toward me, and then study his face under the dimmed light as he begins to undress me, silent and focused. I slip my shoes off and hold his shoulders as he bends, peeling my dress down, pushing it aside when I step out of it.

Everything is slow. *Silent*. Everything is measured. Everything is calm.

Even me. I'm calm. Accepting. Suddenly so very clear-headed. I made him believe I didn't want him, and that hurts. How could I not want this man?

Walking us to the bath, Dec steps in, the water still running, and helps me, holding my hands as I lower between his thighs and settle, resting against his chest. The water feels hot on my cold skin, but the atmosphere is thick with the unspoken, but by no means uncomfortable. We're both just waiting, taking our time, letting this play out naturally.

Dec eventually slices through the quiet with some soft but unbearably loud words. "I can't make you love me."

I stare forward at his bent knees framing mine, swallowing hard, unable to distinguish if the lump there represents what I've already lost or what I *could* lose. Both? And yet I accept in my heart that to lose something, you must have it in the first place. And I'm so scared of losing again. Amid the trauma of this evening, I've misplaced the magic of what Dec's brought into my life. Let his unorthodox light be shadowed by my murky past. I hate that he believes I can't love him because I love someone else. So I fill my lungs and let the words out. "You don't need to make me love you," I whisper, the words sounding tattered and torn. "I already do." His inhale lifts me with him, and I know he's holding his breath because my wet skin chills from being out of the water for a few moments until his exhale sinks me back beneath.

He reaches past me and turns off the running water, and then he turns me over so I'm lying on his front, my face level with his throat. "But you still love him."

"I don't love him. I don't need to get over him, because I *am* over him," I say with grit, fighting back the muscles in my throat from tightening. *I can do this*. If there's going to be any chance of saving myself, I *have* to do this. And I want to. For Dec. I want to show him.

I have to say it.

"But I will never be over my little boy," I murmur, my heart turning in my chest at the sound of those words out loud.

Dec jolts so hard, the water splashes, his eyes wide and haunted when I sneak a look up. "What?"

"He was four," I go on, not wanting to stop for fear of not being able to start again. To finish. To give Dec the complete picture, to erase any doubt he has about how I feel about Dominic and how I feel about him.

I want you to be over him.

Never.

"He was run down." I sound robotic. It's the only way. "By a drunk driver. It was three fifteen on a Friday. December nineteenth." He's a statue. Frozen. Disturbed. "The driver, a woman, had been for a boozy Christmas lunch with her work colleagues. She was late picking up her kid, driving too fast." I don't know how I keep our eye contact, but I do. *Resolute.* Somehow taking strength from him. Dec's holding my eyes too, and yet I know it's because of pure shock and nothing else. This isn't sinking in. "She was sentenced to two years." For the first time, I allow my eyes to leave his, frowning. "I saw her the other day. In a clothes store. She was buying kids clothes. Christmas presents, I suppose. She was smiling. Carrying on with her life after a small blip. She was released after a year. Just a year lost with her children." Looking back at Dec, I see nothing's changed in his blank face. His eyes are fixed, unblinking. It's okay. I don't want him to faff and fuss, hug me or wipe my eyes. I just need him to listen and understand. "I was supposed to pick Noah up that day, but I was called into a meeting last minute, so Dominic got him. He was on a work call. Not paying attention, not holding his hand. Everyone knows you check both ways and wait for the cars to stop before you cross a zebra crossing, and she was driving too fast to stop." I breathe out, realising I've been spitting out the words without drawing breath, desperate to just get it out there. He's still motionless, still quiet, still vacant. "Dec?"

One blink. A swallow. His chin pulls in, a slight shake of his head, as if he's shaking off a daze. The creases around his eyes are so deep, his frown heavy. Everything suggests he doesn't understand. Doesn't comprehend.

Because he could never have anticipated this, and he doesn't need to tell me that.

Slipping his hands under my armpits, he pushes me back so I'm kneeling between his legs, his gaze now avoiding mine. He rises, the water pouring from his naked body, and he steps out of the tub. He doesn't grab a towel, doesn't dry himself. Long strides take him out of the bathroom soaking wet, leaving me alone in his tub, wondering what the hell just happened.

My eyes dart across the water lapping gently around my kneeling form. Should I go after him? Should I dry myself, get dressed, and leave? A tidal wave of uncertainties circles my twisted mind, tangling it more. Don't tell me that on top of everything, seeing Dominic with a woman who's pregnant, knowing he's moving on, replacing our little boy, building a new family, I'm going to have to mourn the peace I found with Dec?

Mourn the loss of him too?

I just told him I love him. How could I have gotten it so wrong? He said nothing would change for him.

Biting down on my lip, I wince away the fresh bout of pain stabbing at my heart, reaching for the sides of the tub to lift myself out, but the sound of a loud bang, followed by a crash that echoes through the house, stops me. I stare at the doorway, hearing him curse loudly.

Then . . . silence.

And then I'm shutting down. I can feel it happening, the iron walls coming up, my mind blocking every ugly thought coming at me, trying not to let it attach and stick. Deflecting. He can't handle the truth. He can't handle me. *As I always feared.*

Every muscle in me hardens in preparation to stand up and get out of here.

And then loosens again when Dec appears in the doorway.

Still naked.

His expression now not blank but pained.

He has a short, fat crystal glass in each hand, both half full of clear liquid. Something tells me it isn't water. Dec takes a swig of one. "Is your hand bleeding?" I ask, catching the scuffs on his knuckles.

"It's nothing." He comes to me and puts the drink in my hand. "Drink it."

"All of it?"

He doesn't answer, instead necking his own and hissing. Putting his glass on the vanity unit, he shakes the bite of the strong alcohol away and steps back into the tub, kneeling opposite me. "Are you going to drink that?"

I look at the glass, just as Dec takes it and leans out of the bath, putting it on the floor. "I'm sorry I left."

My strung muscles loosen. "I understand."

He shakes his head. "I just needed a moment to process what you just told me. I didn't want to say the wrong thing."

"There's no wrong thing to say."

His face falls, his palms clamping my cheeks between them. "I love you."

The tables have turned. It's now me motionless and stunned. Staring. Watching him as he watches me trying to wrap my mind around it.

"Deeply, Camryn." His smile could make me burst into tears on the spot. "I'm so deeply in love with you, I don't know my fucking arse from my elbow."

I think I'm supposed to laugh at that.

"I love you so much, my heart aches for you. I love the ballsy career woman, but I hate why you need to be her now. I love the smile you rarely give out, which makes it all the more special when you smile for me. I love the way you close one eye when you're thinking hard. I love the way you can be in perfect silence, and I can be in it with you. I love the way you hate Christmas, but it breaks me to now know why. I love your passion. I love the mole on your cheek. I love the way you scissor your cocktail glass with your fingers, and the way you chew your lip when you're nervous." He takes in air, his shoulders slumping. "How you laughed at Fawlty Towers and quickly corrected yourself. I love how you kiss me, but more than all of that," he says, releasing my face and resting back on his heels. "More than *anything*, I love the way you look at me. And I want you to look at me like that every day for the rest of my life."

Stunned, I drop back onto my arse, the pessimistic part of my brain telling me I've misheard him. Dreamed the last few minutes. This isn't real, he can't possibly love me. Who could?

But Dec . . . does?

I want to get to know the woman I'm falling for.

And now he truly does. And . . . he loves me.

I cup my hands over my face, bringing my knees up to my chin. The tears can't be kept at bay, and I don't have it in me to even try. Seeing Dominic today, the girlfriend I didn't know he had blooming, felt like the worst day of my life since I watched the surgeon walk out of the theatre, his face grave, and I knew. I just . . . knew.

Now?

I feel like a safety net has been cast beneath me. Something to cushion the constant blows I feel each and every day I fall, when I'm doing something and then I remember . . .

My little boy died.

In a few days it will be three years since I last held his little hand. Kissed his little forehead. Saw his little smile. Heard his little voice.

"I love you, Mummy. Thiiiiiis much," he says around a cheese puff, his little arms wide.

The pain hits hard, never easing off, as strong today as it was the day I lost him. My shoulders lift and fall, my heart squeezes, my lungs burn as I try to get air into them.

I feel Dec's hands wrap around my wrists and pull firmly, revealing my tear-streaked, blotchy face. And seeing Dec's pained expression now, it just makes me cry harder. But he doesn't let me hide. He doesn't pull me close for a hug. It's as if he wants to see my emotion. Wants to see me fall apart. But I know Dec, and this, what he's doing now, leaving me wide open, exposed, crying, is because he knows I've suppressed it for years.

I've suppressed it so much I could burst.

Burst and cause irrevocable damage.

And I did.

To myself, to my husband, to my family, and to my job.

I lost them all.

Pushed them away. I harnessed the hatred inside me and made them all hate *me*. I didn't want any of them if I couldn't have Noah. Life was just so empty, to the point I wondered how I lived before him. What was my purpose? Who was I if I wasn't *Mummy*? And now I'm sitting here in a bathtub with a man who's telling me he loves me despite all of that, and I'm thrown by my feelings toward him. Have been since the day I met him, because I'm not supposed to feel anything but sadness, guilt, and grief.

Desire, amusement, peace? None of them should be in my life. How could they be?

And still, he watches me, watches it all pour out, tears, snot, chokes, snivels, and horrid, wretched sobs. I can't even wipe my face because he's still holding my wrists. It just won't stop coming, the dam open, not closing until it's drained dry. At least for today. This is three years' worth of emotion gushing out of me, and with each painful, messy, loud minute, my body becomes that little bit looser. My muscles relax. My chest doesn't squeeze so hard.

Because he loves me.

Spreading his bent legs, Dec slides me into them and cocoons me, my body bunched, his arms circling my back. He holds me until my body stops jerking and my snivels fade to light, sporadic catches of breath. "I love you," he whispers into my hair.

And I nod.

December 16th

Something's different inside me. It's like the storm that's been gusting through me for the past few years, ripping me apart, has suddenly settled. Everything's still. Calm. And the mess that it's left behind, the broken pieces of my life, are patiently being gathered up.

By Dec.

I love you so much, my heart aches for you. I love the way you can be in perfect silence, and I can be in it with you. I love the way you hate Christmas, but it breaks me to now know why.

He's saving fragments I never thought could ever be saved, gathering splitters of my life and putting them back together to make less jagged, damaging parts.

He's a lifeline.

My face is tight, my eyes sore, but I open them, squinting at the low light. My cheek is pressed into his chest, my hand on his pec, my thigh thrown over his. His hand's resting lightly on my knee.

Warm.

I feel so warm.

I gingerly peel my face from his chest and peek at him.

And lose my breath.

This beautiful man somehow loves me. He's seen something

worth saving. Seen what I could never. That makes me love him more than he could ever understand, but I hope I get to show him. Pray I do.

Slowly and carefully, I move up his body until my mouth is level with his, my boobs crushed into his naked chest. I scan his face, every beautiful bit of it, dipping and pressing a light kiss on the corner of his mouth. He smells like sleep and man.

A lazy throb starts to dully thump against my thigh, and I freeze and hold my breath when I feel him stirring. My body responds, a heaviness falling between my legs. The air suddenly feels thick, and I pull back just a fraction so I can get him in my sights. His eyelids flicker, his lips part. Waiting for him to open them feels like an eternity.

"Open," I whisper, reaching for his hair and combing my fingers through.

His eyes pop open on a small hitch of breath, his sleepy gaze meeting mine immediately. How those grey eyes shine. The throbbing against my leg becomes more intense, and in answer my insides start to pulse. It's a long few moments of gazing, and when I realise Dec's not going to make the first move—because . . . Dec—I take the lead, lowering my lips to his. He keeps his eyes open, as do I, and when our tongues brush, he exhales heavily, cupping the back of my head and rolling me onto my back. My thighs cradle him, his hips shift, my legs spread, and he pushes into me painstakingly slowly, his exhale ragged, my inhale long and deep. The moment he's filling me to the hilt, he stills, giving us both a moment to adjust, deepening his kiss. My hands are on a feeling frenzy across his back as he drags his lips up my cheek and rests them on my forehead. Connected physically as closely as two humans can be connected. But this is more than that. I don't look at Dec and see escape in the pleasure of his body. I look at him and want to walk into his chest and be held. I look at him and see hope. I look at him and feel my heart burst with love and appreciation.

He withdraws and advances slowly, and I graze my fingertips down his spine as he kisses his way back to my mouth and sweeps his tongue through. His body stills, as does his lips, and he pulls his shoulder blades in on a soft hiss into my mouth. "Tickles," he murmurs, as he kicks inside of me. My fingers pause. "Don't stop." Pushing into his forearms, he lifts his torso a tiny bit, his chest peeling away from my boobs, and he slowly inches out and works his way back inside me. "I like it." Grey eyes glisten down at me as I try to remember to breathe while he takes me to the clouds. His usually well-groomed stubble is scruffier, his mussed hair mussier.

I work my fingertips farther down, circling over his backside, and back up again, going extra slow, applying the faintest of pressure, watching with fascination as his eyes become heavier and his chest expands. A suppressed groan vibrates at the back of his throat, his rhythm faltering. "Jesus." He swoops down and claims my mouth again, finding his pace again, slow, meticulous, bloody beautiful. I moan my pleasure, my back bowing, my head shaking. He finds my throat and licks up the column to my ear, biting down on my lobe.

"Dec," I breathe, slipping my hands into his hair and clenching fistfuls. *Oh God.*

"Tell me how it feels," he whispers, his low, grainy voice in my ear shoving me closer to the edge.

I can't find the words. Couldn't speak them if I did. Dropping my head, I pull his face from my neck and look at him. I look at him closer than I've ever looked at a man before. And the way he looks at me?

It's restorative.

I swallow, the words coming to me, but I can't get them past the lump in my throat. This isn't a lump caused by grief. It's a lump triggered by hope. That I could have even some semblance of consistent happiness again has been past my comprehension. "I love you."

He shakes his head mildly, and plunges his tongue into my mouth, upping the ante, kissing me hard but briefly before tearing his mouth away and gasping down at me. Every drive goes deeper, our bodies rolling together like waves, the pressure building to the point I feel like I'm losing my mind. Sweat starts to dot my skin, my moans become breathy gasps, my light stroking of his back becoming scratches.

The veins in his neck bulge. "I'm coming," he murmurs. "Camryn, I'm coming."

His words propel me over the edge, and I whimper, my stomach muscles contracting, and I bury my face in his neck as I come, electricity cutting through me. "Oh God," I breathe, trembling from the force, as Dec jerks, stills, and groans, pushing deeper, his big body soaking up my shakes.

"Fuck." He collapses, swathing me, one forearm keeping his body from squishing me. "Okay?" he pants.

I throw my arms out to my sides, breathless, as his heavy head lifts with effort, his brow hitching too. "Camryn?"

"I can't lose again," I blurt out, feeling overcome.

Dec's one raised brow turns into two, interest becoming worry. "You won't," he counters softly.

It's okay for him to say that. Maybe he won't have a choice. Maybe he'll be taken. I shake my head, trying to evacuate the morbid thoughts after such a perfect moment with a perfect man. "I didn't think I could ever smile again," I whisper. "I didn't think I could exist in a world that could be so fucking cruel."

"Camryn, stop."

"No." I hold his face, pulling it down so he's nose to nose with me. "This is perfect. *You* are perfect. But I'm not perfect, Dec. And this moment is perfect, but there are ugly moments. If you be with me, there will be times when it will be so fucking ugly." Because Dec doesn't cure me. He might heal me, but nothing could possibly cure me.

"I can handle the ugly," he says, no hesitation. "What I can't handle is my world without you in it."

"Your world seems quite perfect." He shouldn't want me polluting it with my pain and hatred.

He puffs out amused air, his eyes dropping. "Why are you trying to sabotage this?"

"I'm not. I just—"

"What?" he asks, lifting his gaze back to mine. "Want me to be prepared?" He laughs a little. It's irony, not humour. "Don't you think I saw the hollowness the first time I saw you in that bar? Don't you think I felt the pain you couldn't hide? Felt your hopelessness past the smile you didn't think I saw. My eyes are wide open, Camryn. Wide fucking open, and they're looking right at you."

I bite down on my lip.

"And you spilled your heart out to me last night," he goes on. "Trusted me. Was vulnerable. That made me know beyond all doubt—and there wasn't much doubt—that I want you in my heart, my life, and my daily thoughts, and I really fucking want you to want all of that with me too."

Pain stabs at my lip when I increase the pressure. "Are you sure?" I ask, still holding back the full force of my relief.

"I've never been so sure about anything in my life." He holds my face, his expression pained, as if he's worried I won't believe it. "I've never felt so connected to someone, Camryn. I've never felt so at ease and at peace with someone. So are we done?"

I nod, taken aback by the fierceness in his voice. "Has it really been five years?"

"It's been worth the wait. *Now* are we done?"

My eyes widen, feeling him expand inside me. "Apparently not."

His cheeks puff out, and I grin as he releases the tension in his face and gives me a small hint of a dashing smile. My God, he's adorable when he loosens up. This big, serious man. He drifts down, his mouth open, and sucks my neck, kissing his way down to my chest.

My exhale is as peaceful as I feel, my body sinking into his soft bed, my eyes closing. "Hmmm," I exhale, as he divides his attention between my boobs. "Can we stay in bed all day?" The moment I utter my question, I hear what sounds like a doorbell in the distance, and I lift my head, looking down at Dec in question. His frown is all the answer I need. "Expecting someone?"

He shakes his head and resumes worshipping my skin. But then his phone starts ringing. "Fuck it all to hell." He slams his fists into the mattress and lifts his hips, a scowl and a wince blending as he eases out of me. I pull my legs together, and Dec plants a peck on my chin before dragging himself off the bed to go find his phone. The pull of my muscles makes me suck back a breath as I scoot up the bed and rest against the headboard. He goes through the pocket of his trousers and the second he looks at the screen, he curses under his breath and looks at the ceiling. For strength? What is that?

"Is everything okay?" I ask, unsure if I should. Because clearly it's not.

He shows me his screen, as if I could see it from the other side of the room. "My father."

"Your dad?" I ask, sitting up straight and pulling the sheet over me. The phone stops ringing, but the knocking on the door starts again. "Wait, is he here?"

"Sounds like it." Dec pulls some sweatpants off a nearby chair and starts tugging them on.

"What does he want?"

"Is that panic in your voice?" he asks, amused.

I shrink back into the bed. "I thought you hated him."

"I do."

"Then care to explain why he's here?" *Early on a Saturday morning when I'm here, naked in your bed?*

Dec's mobile starts ringing again, and this time he answers. "Hi," he says flatly, visibly taking in air. Patience. "Yes, I can hear you hammering on my door." He picks up my dress and throws it toward me. It lands on my lap, and I look at it like, what? "On my way." Hanging up, he points at my dress. "This is happening much sooner than I anticipated."

"What? Wait, what's happening, Dec?" *Please don't say what I think you're going to say.*

"You're going to meet my wonderful father." He doesn't give me anything other than those bombshell words. "See you downstairs." And then he turns and walks out, leaving me with a mouth like a goldfish on the bed.

"Oh my God," I breathe, disappearing beneath the sheets.

"You can't hide," he calls.

"I *am* hiding," I yell back.

"You can't hide from me, Camryn." The sound of his voice fades as he gets farther away. Closer to the front door. Where his father is.

"Shit." I dive out of his bed and grab my dress, rushing into his bathroom and falling in front of the mirror, feeling flustered. And I look it—a complete, agitated mess. "Oh my God," I murmur, prodding and pulling at my wild hair, trying to coax it into something reasonably acceptable. Something that doesn't look like I've just crawled out of bed. "Urgh." I flick my hair from side to side, sending water spraying onto the mirror. I give up, accepting the disastrous, untamable waves, and splash my face with cold water, slapping at my cheeks to try and get a bit of colour. "Fuck," I hiss, my glowing cheek stinging.

What am I doing?

I don't need to impress Dec's father—he hates him. "Huh." I reach for a towel, pat my face dry, pull my dress on, and leave the bathroom. Despite my head telling my hands not to, they still pull at my dress as I go. They still faff with my hair, flicking it this way and that. They still feel at my blemished cheek. I should have tried to cover it, but I don't expect Dec to have any makeup lying around. Unless, of course, he's still not cleared out his wife's things. I cringe at that thought, the squishy carpet sinking under my feet as I pad to the stairs, and the moment I take the rail, I hear the telltale signs of a coffee machine grinding beans, as well as smell it. "Meeting his bloody father," I mumble, following the curve of the staircase down to the hallway.

A mirror on the wall entices me over, and my eyes widen when I see myself in the cold, harsh, unforgiving natural light. *Oh my*

Christ, I look like I've been dug up. My eyes are puffy, my skin's blotchy, the evidence of a hard, uncontrollable crying fit written all over my face. That's it. I'm retreating upstairs, hiding. It shouldn't be a problem, since Dec hates his father.

I hurry to the stairs, but my foot doesn't even make it onto the first step. "It's malicious and you know it!" a man's voice booms from the kitchen.

"Coffee?" Dec asks calmly, unperturbed.

"No, I don't want no damn coffee. I want you to face me and tell me it's you."

"I'm going to have coffee. Mind?"

"You're a grown man, Dec. Do as you damn well please."

"I am and I will." A few plates clang on the stone worktop. "Pastry?"

"Shove your bleeding pastries."

Curiosity races like a steam train through me, pulling me toward the kitchen. A tall man in a brown suit is standing with his back to me, a matching Trilby on his grey-haired head, a polished wooden cane in his grasp. When he walks a few paces around the island without using it, I conclude it's a fashion accessory.

Dec's eyes glimmer when he sees me in the doorway. I give him a look that I hope tells him I'm feeling *more* than awkward. "Dick, this is Camryn. Camryn, Dick."

Dick?

The old man whirls around, a scowl of epic proportions contorting his face. "Who?" he barks, looking me up and down.

"Camryn," Dec repeats, licking the sugar off his fingers, a small, sick smile hiding behind his hand.

"Hi," I say, stepping forward, holding my hand out, praying to God that Dec's father doesn't go all continental on me and move in for a kiss, because it's just occurred to me that I haven't brushed my teeth. "Nice to meet you, Mr. Ellis."

I shouldn't have worried. He turns away, pointing his fancy cane back at me. "What's this then?" he asks. "Another one?"

I recoil, dropping my hand, since it's dangling uselessly in front of me.

"Are we done?" Dec asks tiredly, not at all bothered by his father's disrespect.

"No, we are far from done, my boy."

"I am not your boy," Dec grates, a flash of anger sparking from his eyes.

"Like it or not, I'm your father."

"You're the man who contributed to the biological side of my making. Nothing more."

Jesus, are we really doing this in front of me? "I'm just going to make a call," I say, thumbing over my shoulder, dying on the inside. Dec wasn't kidding when he said he hates him.

"No need." Dec comes to collect me and walks me to a stool, sitting me down. "He's leaving."

"Tell me it was you," his father demands, smacking his stick on the floor as Dec goes to the coffee machine and pulls a cup of coffee off the stand.

"It was me. Happy?" Then he sips, oh so casual, as his father starts to visibly shake, his face going an alarming shade of red.

"What the hell are you going to do with a failing whiskey empire?" he yells. "You hate whiskey."

"What am I going to do with it?" Dec asks. "Oh, Dick. From a man of your stature, that's a really dumb fucking question." Dec sets his coffee down. "I'm going to break down the company and sell off the distilleries, factories, land, and stores, bit by bit."

"You vengeful bastard."

"*Now* are we done?" Dec asks, taking a sip of his coffee.

Dick looks like steam could start gushing out of his ears. "Your mother would turn in her grave."

I jump out of my skin when Dec's cup hits the stone counter with a thwack hard enough to shatter it. It's a miracle it's still intact. "Never talk about my mother," he warns with a lethal edge. "Do you understand me? Now get out of my house."

"I assume this means you won't be at Paisley's engagement party."

"You mean to fly the flag for the Ellises? Show a united front in the face of adversary? No, Dick. You don't get my compliance so your new wife and your brats get to keep up appearances." He points past him. "The door's that way."

Dick huffs, but I see surrender. He walks to the door and looks back at me. "Don't get too cosy. Dec Ellis gets very bored *very* quickly."

I laugh, insulted, and give my attention to Dec, waiting and expecting an explanation.

"He's being spiteful. I was very active *many* years ago." He slides a pastry across the island to me. "And when he says bored, he means in business. Coffee?"

"Please." And that's that? My lips twist, uncertainty kicking me in the gut as Dec, moody, makes more coffee. *He was very active many years ago.* Before his wife? Is she why he's been celibate for nearly five years? Did she burn him that badly?

I groan to myself, suddenly more curious about her than I want to be. "How many women have you dated?" I try to sound casual. *Fail.*

Dec looks over his shoulder. "You want to have the conversation where you ask me how many women I've slept with, and I tell you it's much lower than it actually is?"

"How many?"

"Fifteen. And that's the truth. What about you?"

Oh God, I didn't think this through. My gaze drops to the stone counter. "A few," I murmur pathetically. A coffee appears in my downcast vision, and I peek up at Dec. "So what was that all about?"

"Oh, no." He laughs. "You started this. You can finish it. How many?"

"Truth?"

"Yes, the truth."

"I've lost count."

He dunks his finger in the cream on my plate and wipes it on the end of my nose. "I still love you."

And that's the end of that? I know I can't hide my surprise.

"I'm not interested in how many men you've slept with, Camryn. All I'm interested in is that you will only sleep with one man from this moment forward."

Fuck. *Could I love you more?* "You bought a whiskey brand your father wanted, then?" I ask, taking Dec's lead and moving forward rather than back. Although I'm still super curious about his father, which I appreciate is moving back a little, but still. I've gone back in time too. For the benefit of my future.

"Correct."

"Why?"

"Because it was a good deal."

I raise my brows and take a bite of my pastry.

"Don't raise your brows at me." He leans across, wiping my face with a towel.

"No daddy issues, though?" I mumble around my mouthful, restraining my smile.

"None at all."

"Okay."

"Okay," he parrots.

I shrug. "Okay."

He narrows one eye, dumping the towel and collecting his coffee, drumming his fingers on the counter. My lips purse, watching him trying to figure out what he can say that might convince me he doesn't give two shits about his father. "Okay," he murmurs, tipping his cup to his lips, circling around the island to my side, taking slow, casual paces.

I keep my body forward, my eyes following him until they can follow him no more. He's behind me. Flakes of pastry dust my fingers, floating down to the plate as Dec pushes his back up against me, leaning past me to place his coffee down. Hot breath hits my ear, and my spine rolls one vertebra at a time until it's ramrod straight. "I think it's too early to be up on a Saturday." He turns me on the stool to face him, my pastry hanging in my limp hand.

"Me too." Taking a bite out of my pastry, I chew, anticipation back with a vengeance, while Dec studies me thoughtfully. "What?" I ask, mumbling around my mouthful.

"Did you see the first aider?"

"Huh?"

He reaches for my cheek, turning my face a little.

"Oh, yes, of course."

"Does it hurt?"

"Not so much." He hums his doubt and pops a kiss on my nose, turning me back. "Does that mean we're not going back to bed?" I ask.

"Sounds like I need some energy." Reaching for the plate, Dec plucks an almond croissant off and rips off a piece like an animal.

"You better have two of those," I say, slipping the last of my breakfast past my lips. "Maybe three."

Dec laughs, and the sight is nothing less than incredible. I swallow around my smile, suitably full, and dust off my hands. "I like this Camryn," he says, taking his elbows down to the island, leaning on them, making his biceps bulge and his stomach crease.

"I like her too," I admit.

"Good." He smirks. I smirk. He raises his brows, I raise mine. He cocks his head, I cock mine.

He's teasing me. Making me wait. I'm about to go to him and physically drag him back to bed when the distant ringing of my phone reaches the kitchen. It jars me, if only because I have absolutely no idea who'd call me at this time on a Saturday morning. Dread is quick on the heels of that bewilderment. *Mum.* It must be the care home about Mum. Urgency powers my muscles as I hop off the stool and hurry out of the kitchen, following the sound of my ringing phone to the hallway. My bag is hanging on the coat stand with my coat. A number greets me. Not the care home.

"Are you okay?" Dec asks from behind me.

"I don't know who it is," I reply, staring down at the screen.

"Want to answer it and find out?"

I turn and see his naked shoulder resting on the doorframe. "Dec Ellis has a sense of humour today, huh?"

"My dry wit and comic genius weren't what attracted you to me in the first place?"

"No, it was your heartbreakingly good looks."

"I'm not going to break your heart, darling," He comes to me and drops an easy, casual kiss on my cheek. "I'm going to mend it." Said with equal casualness, and yet so much confidence, as he wanders off and climbs the stairs. "Take the call, and then take me to bed, baby."

"Or lose you forever?"

"Nothing will make you lose me."

My heart. "I love this Dec Ellis," I say, my smile unstoppably wide.

"He only makes an appearance for you."

Satisfaction so warm glides through me like melted, velvety chocolate. Smooth and rich. *Addictive.* Playful Dec. He's sweet. And very unexpected. Yes, it was his good looks. But that aside, it was his depth that got me. How I could read him without him giving me a word or even any emotion. The stoic, serious businessman everyone in his orbit gets. It makes me wonder how he was with his ex-wife. I pout and rewind. She's not his ex-wife yet. But neither is Dominic my ex-husband.

I can fix that.

Dec can't, because he can't find her. And the questions roll. Who is she, where did she go, and, most of all . . . why?

By the time I've finished pondering things that I can't possibly answer myself, my phone has stopped ringing. So I call the number back, going to the stairs and lowering to the bottom step.

Someone picks up but doesn't speak. "Hello?" I say, sounding noticeably wary.

"Hello," they reply.

I frown. "Mr. Percival?"

"Indeed it is. Thank God you're okay."

"I saved your number."

"My mobile number, dear. This is my landline."

"Do people still have landlines?"

"I used up all of my free minutes on my mobile."

"The brick."

"Huh?"

"Never mind. What do you want?"

"You didn't come home last night. I was worried."

"I stayed at a . . ..friend's."

"Ohhh, I see. A friend's, eh? Is that what we're calling him?"

Rolling my eyes, I stand. "Did your electric get fixed?"

"Yes, toasty warm now, dear. This friend . . . I'm trusting he's trustworthy?"

I smile and frown all at once. "So the turkey's not in the front garden now?"

"I'm sorry my turkey's offending you. Now, back to the *friend*. Is he—"

"I have to go. I'll be home later." I pull up. "Maybe." Hanging up, I abandon my phone and hurry up the stairs, slowing when I hear Dec talking.

"Well, he wasn't here to wish me a happy birthday, April." He sees me in the doorway, and I give him a look of utter disbelief. *It's his birthday?* Dec shrugs and lowers to the edge of his bed. "Your steadfast optimism is commendable and a waste of fucking time. The man's a fully-fledged, self-centred narcissist." My eyes widen, and Dec frowns down the line. "That's below the belt. I'm nothing like him." Feeling like a spare part and an intruder, I turn on my bare feet to head downstairs, but I make it only a few paces before an arm loops round my waist and lifts me from my feet, carrying me back into the bedroom. Dec laughs, the sound cool and sharp. "He doesn't have a fucking heart, April, so it can't be dodgy." He places me on my feet at the end of the bed. "I'll see you soon. And thanks," he adds, his genuine show of gratitude softer. "You know I appreciate you guys." His phone is tossed on the bed, and he tackles me down to the mattress, smothering me and sinking his face into my neck.

I don't know where to start. His dad's supposed dodgy heart or his birthday. "You didn't say it was your birthday." I smack his bare back, annoyed that he neglected to give me such vital information.

"It's just another day."

"No, it's not. It's your birthday."

Groaning, Dec crawls off me and lays front down on the bed, and I clamber to straddle his arse, having to shimmy my dress up to do so. He places his arms under his head and rests his cheek there so I can see his profile as I start tickling his back, grazing my fingers up and down his spine, smiling when his muscles tense and his shoulder blades pinch in the middle. "That's nice," he whispers, closing his eyes.

I lean down and get my mouth close to his ear. "Happy birthday."

He smiles, pushing his face into mine. "Thank you." Then he shuffles over. "Who was on the phone?"

"Mr. Percival. He was worried about me."

"That's sweet."

"He also asked if you're trustworthy."

"Cheeky bastard."

Falling to his chest, I frame his face with my hands and exhale as I press my mouth to his, feeling his hands sliding up my back, his mouth opening, his tongue meeting mine. "It's your fortieth."

"I know."

"Are you feeling forty?"

"No." He cups my backside with both palms. "I'm feeling thirty-seven."

I grin and nibble at his jawline, and he groans and rolls us, trapping me beneath him, taking my mouth.

"It fucking pains me to say this," he murmurs, taking moments between our kiss to speak. "But I've got to go."

"Nooooo," I groan, locking my legs around his waist and my arms around his shoulders.

"April's done lunch. She's making a fuss, and I have to pretend I'm grateful. I'd ask you to come, but—"

What? "No, no, I get it." I shake my head vehemently. I wouldn't have met his father if I'd had a choice—pleasant man. His sister? That requires preparation. Women don't exactly warm to me anymore, and I'm not entirely sure how to fix that. "Besides, it's a bit early."

"Is it?"

I recoil, my mind emptying as Dec gazes down at me. "You don't think it is?"

"Well, I think that things got quite serious last night."

I don't know if he's talking about the pile of confessions I dumped on him of the *love* thing. "I'm not sure I'm ready for that kind of scrutiny," I admit, thinking honesty is the best policy.

"Why would you feel scrutinised?"

"She's your older sister. That's what they do. Like if I had an older brother."

"Ummm, you *do* have an older brother, Camryn."

"Not one that likes me."

"Oh my God," he breathes, exasperated. "Look, I'm not asking you to come today. It would send April into a tailspin, anyway. She's one of these women who has to have everything perfect. An extra guest would throw out her ratios on food per person." He rolls his eyes when I laugh. "But I want you to meet the people I love."

"You have more siblings?"

"No, just April. And her husband, Blaine."

"Oh."

He slams a kiss on my mouth and stands. "I'll take you home."

"You or Ron?"

"Me. Ron doesn't work weekends. Neither does Lynette."

I watch him strut away, pulling his sweatpants down as he goes. Disappointment slides through me, and I pout, just getting a peek of his yummy backside before I lose him to the bathroom.

Snowflakes gently float down around us as we stand side by side outside my building looking at Mr. Percival's turkey. "I suppose I could put it in my freezer," I say, as Dec crouches and pokes at the tarpaulin now covering the wire netting, the rocks pinning it down perfectly in place. "If it'll fit." I tilt my head, mentally measuring it. "I mean, it's a monster, and I saw his freezer. It's rammed full of various Christmas treats he's been preparing. He must be feeding five thousand."

Dec rises, stuffing his hands into his pockets. "Weird old man."

"He's nearly one hundred, so he can be anything he wants to be." I push the door open slowly and gently and creep over the threshold.

"What are you doing?" Dec asks from behind me.

"Trying to get into my apartment without being accosted."

"By the weird old man?"

"He's taken it upon himself to be my guardian angel. I think he's lonely. Or bored." I hold the door open, looking over my shoulder. "You don't need to walk me to my door."

"I want to." Dec pushes the door open with brute force, and I wince when it ricochets off the wall behind it.

"Shhh," I hiss. And two seconds later, Mr. Percival's door swings open. "Shit."

"Ah, the walk of shame," he sings, chuckling to himself.

"It's not the walk of shame, Mr. Percival, if I'm not ashamed."

He hobbles out of his flat, popping his flat cap on, eyeing Dec. "What are your intentions?"

Dec balks at him. "Excuse me?"

"With the lovely Camryn. What are your intentions, son?"

"My intentions?"

"Yes, your intentions."

"I . . ." Dec looks at me, and I shrug, at a loss. "What are yours?" he fires back.

"Mine?"

"Yes, yours." Dec stands up taller, frowning to himself.

"I'm not the one who's kept her out all night, son." Mr. Percival comes closer on his walking frame, looking Dec up and down. "So come on then. Speak up."

"Mr. Percival," I say, moving in front of Dec, giving the old boy a tight smile. "Do you want me to store your turkey in my freezer?"

He sighs dramatically. "My turkey is perfectly fine where it is." He reaches for my arm and eases me aside, giving him access to Dec again. "Well?"

I've never seen a man look so uncomfortable in my life. "I'd like to date her," he replies, the words coming out sounding tired and inconvenienced.

"You mean court?"

"Call it whatever you like, Mr. Percival." Dec motions past him to my door. "Mind if we get on with our day?"

"You'll respect her?"

Dec flicks his eyes to me, and I shrug. Another sigh. "Yes."

"You'll be honest with her?"

"Yes," he grates.

"You won't take advantage of her?"

"Too late," he mutters, and I snort with the effort to keep my laugh in.

"What was that, son?"

"Sure thing, mate," Dec says, louder. "Are we done?"

"One more thing." Mr. Percival shuffles his way closer to Dec and leans forward on the tippy toes of his snow boots, and Dec crouches to listen, his brows drawing closer together. Something is whispered. Dec nods. "That'll be all." And with that, Mr. Percival turns on his walking frame and hobbles back to his flat, closing the door behind him.

"Huh," Dec murmurs, shaking his head, then chuckling.

"What did he say?"

He points to the door, prompting me to open it. "A flimsy threat on my life, a promise of retaliation, nothing too drastic."

"I don't know where this misplaced duty has come from."

"I can handle the old man. Anyway, it's sweet he's looking out for you."

I drop my bag by the front door and watch as Dec goes to the kitchen. I follow him, finding him opening the fridge door. I cringe. "What's that?" he asks.

It doesn't take me much thinking to figure out what he's talking about, since it's the only thing in the fridge. "That's Mr. Percival's cake." I nudge him aside and pull out the plate, uncovering it and cutting myself a slice. "You should try it, it's quite special."

"Fruit cake for breakfast?"

And for lunch and dinner. Sugar hits my taste buds like a torpedo as I wrap my lips around the wedge, humming. I actually can't remember the last time I ate. "It's not just any fruit cake, Dec. This is Mr. Percival's fruit cake."

He rolls his eyes and comes to me, plucking the cake from my hand and popping it on the plate, crowding me. *I don't want him to go.* I gaze up at him, screaming it over and over. When his lips straighten, discontented, I wonder if he's heard me. I swallow my cake, my lips parting, as he slips a hand into my hair and pulls my face toward his, kissing me gently. Every bone disintegrates, my body becoming heavy, my hands reaching for the lapels of his coat and clinging on. His kiss is molten. Forceful without being hard, and I have no choice but to follow the flow of his tongue.

When he breaks away, way too soon, I'm unsteady and disorientated. "I love you," he says softly, holding my gaze while cupping my face. "Okay?"

I nod, and he pushes his lips to my forehead, breathing steadily as he reinforces his words. No, I don't want him to go, but those words? I needed to hear them, and I can feel his reluctance to leave me. "Go," I order softly, as he kisses his way down my nose to my mouth again.

"Okay." He groans and tears himself away, and I smile as he backs out.

Light. I feel so light. And yet bereft.

By six o'clock, Dec hasn't called. Mr. Percival, however, has. Numerous times. A small part of me is grateful for his incessant drop-ins, another part feels downhearted that I'm depending on my ninety-nine-year-old neighbour to take my mind off things.

Why hasn't he called?

By the umpteenth time Mr. Percival knocks on my door, for one thing or another—Have I seen Maureen? Can I smell gas? What did I do last night with my new *friend*?—I'm past the point of being exasperated and instead invite the old boy in for a coffee.

"Oh, if you're not too busy," he says, wandering in on his frame.

"Wait."

"What, dear?"

"Do you like milk in your coffee?"

"Milk and two sugars, dear."

"Do you have milk and sugar?"

He's utterly thrilled I need something from him and ambles off again while I put the kettle on, trying not to constantly check my phone. He's back a few minutes later with a container of sugar and a pint of milk. "Go sit down," I say, ushering him into the lounge and finishing our coffees.

"Oh, your flowers still look beautiful."

"They do," I say on a smile, stirring some sugar into his coffee. "It's Dec's birthday today."

"Oh, are you going out for dinner? Am I keeping you?"

I wander in, forcing a smile. "He had pre-arranged plans with his sister." I shrug, lowering to the couch. "It's a bit soon to meet her."

He snorts. "It's never too soon for anything. Look at me. I'm a hundred years old next month, Camryn. One bleeding hundred! I was twenty-one what feels like yesterday."

I smile and settle back. "You've still got lots of years to fill me in on."

He beams at me, inhaling ready to launch, and I sit on my couch for the longest stretch of time since I moved in and listen to tales of years gone by, when foods were rationed, and he could walk to the end of his street and find everything he could possibly need. A butcher, a baker, Mrs. Smith's grocery store, which also, conveniently, had a post office counter in there too. A hardware store, a chemist. He lived in the East End. Drank in the same "boozer" as the Krays. Used to fix their cars too. Following his service in the war, he had a garage in the East End. "Those were the days," he says with a fond smile on his face. "Only the wealthy had cars. Now, every bleeder and their dog whizzes around London."

"I don't," I point out, pulling my feet up onto the couch. "Have you ever driven, Mr. Percival?"

He grins. "I had a Ford Capri in the eighties. It was bright green." And he goes on.

I come to with the sound of my mobile ringing from the coffee table. I frown, disorientated, trying to gather my bearings. I have a pillow from my bed under my head and my duvet draped over me.

Bleary-eyed, I reach for my phone and squint at the screen. "Hello?" I murmur sleepily.

"I woke you," Dec breathes. "I'm sorry."

He shouldn't be sorry. I'm glad he's called, no matter the time. Speaking of which . . . "What time is it?"

"Just gone ten. I just got done with some work stuff and needed to hear your voice before I go to bed."

"Swoon," I murmur sleepily, falling back to my pillow, smiling when he chuckles. "Why are you working on your birthday?"

"I had a few contracts to check. What did you do today?"

"Miss you."

"Swoon," he murmurs.

My smile widens. "Another man tucked me into bed tonight."

"Oh? Do I need to deploy my alpha streak and mark my territory?"

"Maybe. He's seriously wooing me."

"I'll be having a word." There's laughter in his voice.

"Did you have a nice time with your sister?"

"I did. She's very excited to meet you."

I'm suddenly more awake. And nervous. "You've told her about me?"

He laughs. "Are you freaking out?"

"Not at all."

"Sure," he chuckles. "Listen, get back to sleep. I'll call you tomorrow, okay?"

I pout. "Okay." And brace myself for the words that'll send me back to sleep peacefully.

"I love you."

I can't contain my smile. "I love you," I reply, a fuzzy warmth radiating through me. "Goodnight."

"Goodnight."

I hang up and snuggle down, content.

Smiling.

Not scared to go asleep alone.

December 17th

As I stand in my kitchen, munching my way through the last bit of Mr. Percival's cake, replaying Dec saying those three words over and over, I hear the intercom chime. I make my way to the door, and there's a knock as I answer the phone. "Hello?" I say as I open the door.

"Delivery for Camryn," Mr. Percival declares.

Just as someone down the line says, "Tesco delivery for number five."

I frown and poke my head out the door as I hang up and see a man with a few stacked crates wedged up against the glass door. "Tesco?"

"See!" Mr. Percival sings. "And now everything is delivered to your door. No need to even step foot outside the house!" He makes his way to the door on his walking frame. "It's a wonder he made it in the snow."

More snow. Loads of it. I follow and hover behind Mr. Percival as he hauls the door open, knocking his walking frame. "This way," he says, making way for the Tesco delivery driver. "I'll show you where you can put it."

"Thanks, geezer," he rumbles, struggling down the corridor with the crates.

"For Camryn Moore?" I ask, following him.

"That's right. There are two substitutes, and I recommend eating the strawberries today as there's a short shelf life on them." He finds his way to my kitchen, courtesy of Mr. Percival, and dumps the crates on the table, pulling out the paperwork. "No apple and ginger shots, so they've substituted with cloudy apple juice. Seems a bit stupid to me." He laughs. "This ain't no shot." A litre bottle of apple juice is held up in his hand. "And the bananas are to be ripened at home, so they're a little green. Sign here, please." He thrusts his little digital device toward me.

"I didn't order a Tesco delivery," I say, signing anyway.

"You're Camryn Moore?"

"Yes."

"This is flat five Park Way Crescent."

"Yes."

"Then it's yours, sweetheart." He starts unpacking and leaving it on the table, stacking his crates to the side. "Sorry about the boots."

I glance down his high-vis clad body to his snow-covered boots. "No worries," I murmur, at a loss.

"I'm surprised they've got you working in this weather," Mr. Percival says, helping him unpack the crates, keen to chatter with anyone and everyone.

"Ah, some of them are snowflakes." A loud eruption of laughter bursts out of him, making me jump. "Get it? Snowflakes?"

"I get it." Mr. Percival laughs. "Because it's snowing."

"Indeed it is, my friend, and it's only getting worse so I'll be going before Mother Nature buggers up my schedule. Merry Christmas to you both." He nods to me. "Your granddaughter okay? She looks a bit vacant."

"She's fine," Mr. Percival says. "Not a lot going on up here." He taps the side of his head, and the delivery man nods his understanding.

"Excuse me?" I splutter.

Mr. Percival titters to himself. "Merry Christmas to you too, sir." He dips into his pocket and pulls something out, handing it over on a wink.

I smile at the pound coin that's been placed in the delivery driver's hand. "Very kind, of you, mister." If he had a hat, he'd be tipping it right now. My heart warms, watching the interaction. I don't have the heart to tell Mr. Percival that a pound won't even get the driver a sniff of a pint at his local *boozer*. "Hope to see you again soon." Off he goes, his boots leaving lumps of snow on the wooden floor behind him, joining the other melting lumps he's left on his way in.

"Be careful, Mr. Percival," I say, grabbing a towel off the counter. "It'll be slippery."

"Fine, me, dear." He goes to the piles of groceries while I crouch and wipe up the endless puddles. "Got me snow boots on. What have we here then?"

"Your guess is as good as mine."

"Mr. Ellis," he says.

"What?" I jump up and go to Mr. Percival, who's flapping the paperwork left on top of the pile of food I haven't bought. "Dec ordered this?" The billing address confirms it, as does my recollection from yesterday when he stood in front of my empty fridge appearing alarmed. I drop the paperwork and gaze at the groceries—all healthy, it should be noted.

"Shame it didn't arrive yesterday. Would have saved you borrowing my milk and sugar."

"Well, I can give it back to you now. Thank you for tucking me up last night."

"Welcome, dear. Now, I've got to go prepare my pastry for the mince pies. The Royal British Legion are picking me up later to take them to the club. Just call if you need me, dear."

If I need him. Funny. I think we both need each other.

I gaze at the groceries on the table and sigh. Is this Dec's way of telling me to look after myself? I honestly don't know what to make of it. Grabbing my phone off the side, I tap out a message.

Thank you x

I don't add, *I miss you. When can I see you again?* Instead, I start packing away the food, most of which goes in the fridge, bar the essentials—tea, coffee, sugar, bread. There are no ready meals, just fresh produce. Ingredients. I wouldn't be surprised if I found a cookbook at the bottom of this pile.

My heart leaps when my phone dings, and I race across the kitchen to retrieve it.

You're welcome. It's not completely selfless—
you're cooking for me tomorrow night x

My grin is so wide, it could break my face.

You're chaining me to the stove?

Then the bed.

I lower to the chair, absolutely giddy, my tummy fluttering, my head whirling. December was the end of one life. Now, it feels like it could be the beginning of another. I send a simple heart emoji and inhale, exhaling my contentment, and a wave of purpose crashes through me.

I get up and finish packing away the food, while having a quick mental assessment of what I could cook for Dec tomorrow night. Maybe coq au vin, if I can remember how. It's been a while.

Then I do something I've not been able to bring myself to do for months since they arrived. I go to the lounge and find the divorce papers. I don't read them again, not this time. I flick to the back page, take the pen Dominic left me, and scribble my name across the bottom line.

Done.

I stuff them back in the envelope and put them in my bag to post tomorrow from work. No more hiding. I don't think I can accept he's having another child, can't even contemplate forgiving him for that. She looked like she was due very soon, which means

Dominic didn't hang around for long after he walked out on me, but I haven't the capacity to break that down.

It's done. The memories tarnished. At least, my memories with him.

I will keep Noah's memory alive.

And on that note, I go to the boxes in the corner and heave the one off the top of the stack, lowering it to the floor and kneeling. Lifting the flaps, I take the air I'm going to need and reach in, pulling out a framed picture.

And I look at his face for the first time in three years since I lost him. His beautiful, innocent, young face. Eyes that haven't seen nearly enough of the world. A smile that didn't bless enough people. "I miss you," I whisper, my chest tightening. "I miss you so much it hurts." I don't take my eyes off him.

And I don't hold back my tears. They hit like a tsunami, until they weaken every muscle and I fold to the floor on my side, holding his picture.

And I sob my heart out.

For my loss.

And for a future that frightens me.

I cried for an hour straight, even though I didn't think there were any tears left in me. I was wrong. I drowned in them. And it was somehow cathartic. A different version of release than I experienced with Dec's strength holding me. I didn't know I needed to do this for myself and on my own. And not feel utterly destroyed by the tears. I will always, always love my little boy, and now I know I can breathe again, I will be okay.

After I dragged myself up off the floor and set the photo of Noah on the cabinet, I wiped the glass and cleaned and polished the silver frame. My mind naturally shifted to the date. *In two days' time, it will be three years since I've held you.* A few extra tears slipped down my face.

Then I unpacked a few boxes, showered, dressed, and left to visit Mum.

I stop off at a store on my way, pulling off my hat as I walk under the heaters hanging above the door. I take a moment to scope the space before me. It's not busy, hardly surprising given the weather. Snowing. Again.

Spotting a store guide at the bottom of the escalators, I tug off my gloves too, as I make my way over and scan the floors and list of departments. Lingerie. Second floor. I hop on the elevator and tuck myself to the right, remaining on the same step all the way to the top, resisting the urge to hurry up to get to where I need to be as quickly as possible. Three people pass my stationary form. All in a hurry. *I'm not in a hurry.* Not today.

Wandering around the displays, I take my time, looking at things I don't need. Perusing. Browsing. I haven't browsed in a store for years. Only one time does the familiar bile rise from my stomach, but it doesn't make it past my chest. I push it down and focus on what I'm here for.

"Can I help you?" A smiley, middle-aged lady appears, a tape measure hanging around her neck.

"Yes, thank you. I need some tights."

"Oh, lovely. Stockings? A special Christmas treat for the man in your life?" She quickly places a palm over her mouth. "Or woman! Darn it, I'm always being told off for assuming."

I smile at her awkwardness. "Something less sexy. It's a Secret Santa gift. She loves tights. All kinds of weird and wonderful prints."

"Oh!" She chuckles. "Okay, maybe something from our novelty section."

"Sounds great."

She leads me to a table where five miniature Christmas trees twinkle atop of it, packets of tights hanging like baubles from the arms. "Something like this?" She plucks off a very familiar pair.

"She had those ones on last week," I say. "Christ, I bet she's got all of these." I finger through a few more packets and see the candy canes, the elves, the tinsel fringed monstrosities. "Oh my God, she has. She's got them all." I have no idea what else I could possibly buy for her.

"Wait, I might have something." She scurries off to the changing rooms, and I follow, my panic brewing, except today it's for a very different reason. I don't want to turn up for Secret Santa Day empty-handed, especially given I'm buying for Debbie. "These haven't been put out on the display yet," she says, rootling through a basket. "No room, you see, and we decided these ones would probably be the least popular."

"Why?"

"Well, because they're a bit snazzy."

"She loves snazzy."

The lady whips out a packet. "This snazzy?"

I take in the model sporting a full-on Lapland scene on her legs. Every possible thing you could pin on Christmas is there. Reindeers, elves, Mother Christmas, Father Christmas, gifts, stockings, snow, a sleigh, trees, reindeers, decorations. "Oh my God, she'll love them." I take them from the woman's hand. "How the hell did they fit the whole of Christmas on this woman's skinny legs?"

"Quite an achievement, isn't it?"

"I'll take them."

"Size?"

"Oh shit, they're different sizes? Don't they just stretch? One size fits all?"

"Well, they could, but Lapland might be a little faded from the stretch on the bigger lady, if you know what I mean."

"She's average, I suppose. Maybe a UK fourteen?"

"I suggest medium."

"Perfect."

"Let's take you to the checkout."

"Thank you . . ."

"Hilda."

"Thanks, Hilda."

"Very welcome . . . ?"

"Camryn. My name's Camryn." And it's in this moment I realise that I haven't cared for anyone's name or cared to offer mine in years.

It's like I'm being seen again.

Or, I *want* to be seen.

A gust of wind carries me into the reception of the care home, along with a flurry of snow. My cheeks balloon, my shoulders hunching. "Camryn, you're blue!" The receptionist, alarmed, whips a towel off the radiator behind her chair and comes at me with it. "What on earth are you doing venturing out in this weather?"

"It's not so bad," I say, pulling off my hat and gloves, my teeth chattering. "Thank you." I take the towel and pat at my frozen cheeks, feeling only mild warmth. "Mind if I keep this while I'm here?"

"Take it." She returns to behind her desk. "You're the only visitor today, and we're short-staffed, what with the weather and all."

"Snowflakes," I murmur as I sign in.

"Pardon me?"

"Nothing." I smile and pull the door open, noticing a distinct difference in the noise level, as well as foot traffic. The corridor's empty, except for the endless decorations hanging from the ceiling and every wall. Nothing on the floor though—trip hazard. Shrugging my coat off as I walk, I peek into each room as I pass. It's like a ghost town.

When I reach Mum's room, I find Deirdre checking her blood pressure. She's awake, and that stirs the dormant anxiety inside.

"Ah, look who's here," Deirdre says, tapping buttons on the machine as it whirs.

I laugh under my breath at such a stupid thing to say. Look

who's here? Like my mum might know. I dump my bags on the chair and drape my coat on the back. "How is she?"

"*She* is in the room," Mum grumbles.

My eyes must look like saucers. "Sorry," I blurt, taken aback, looking at Deirdre who's smiling. "How are you, Mum?"

She squints at me, and my heart clatters, waiting for the inevitable question.

Who are you?

I don't know no Camryn.

"What happened to your cheek?"

I raise my hand to it, drawing a blank. She noticed? *I got mugged. Wait, no, I was attacked. Jumped?* Some random believed I looked like the perfect person to rob? "I had an argument with a filing cabinet."

She frowns, confused. "Why would you have an argument with a filing cabinet?"

"I didn't mean to." I look at Deirdre, as if for encouragement or reassurance. Am I doing this right? I've completely forgotten amid the endless distress of her rejections how to handle this. "Oh, shepherd's pie," I chime, distracting her. That's it. Distraction.

"Too many carrots," she says. "They know I don't like carrots. They're taking my money too." Suspicion is rife on her face, her expression cutting on Deirdre.

"I have your money, Mum," I say, lowering to the chair and taking her hand as Deirdre removes the blood pressure band from around her arm. "I put it all in the bank for you." There is no money. This place soon swallowed it up, hence my brother paying the eight-thousand-pound monthly fee. And he doesn't let me forget it.

Mum moves her glassy eyes back onto me. They're not completely empty today, and although she's not refuted it when I've called her *Mum*, she also hasn't acknowledged I'm right. She's my mum. I feel a bit needy wanting her to see me. Call me by my name. *Please see me.*

Then her cutting look drops like a rock. "Your face," she

murmurs, lifting her arm. No name. But this? I inch forward, allowing her to reach my cheek. "What happened?"

"I walked into a door, Mum."

"Well, that was silly, wasn't it? Why'd you do that for?"

"I wasn't looking where I was going."

She huffs. "Too busy, aren't you? Always in a rush, darting here and there, getting Noah to school, yourself to work, back to school, to whatever playdate or after-school club he has to go to. All these clubs! Guitar, gymnastics, football, drama, dance. He should pick one and focus on that."

I stare at her. Just stare at her. She used to say this to me often, because she cared about our well-being. *Never judgy*. Just kind. Supportive. "Yes, he should do that."

She smiles, happy I'm agreeing. "Where is he today then? Football?"

Sundays are for football. *She knows it's Sunday*. She knows it's me. "Yeah, Mum," I say, taking her hand from my face and squeezing. "He's at football."

"Oh, yes. It must be Sunday." Her eyes narrow, as if contemplating that. "Tell me what's going on in your world. I can't keep up."

I sit forward, relishing the rare interaction. "I think I've found someone really special, Mum."

"It's about time. You need to settle down, buttercup. Have a family. You're not getting any younger."

I swallow. "I know. You tell me all the time." Until about twelve years ago when I met Dominic, got engaged within a year, married the following year, and had Noah the year after that. But that's okay. She knows who I am.

Even if she doesn't.

I have to take a breath when I step outside her room. For the first time in as long as I can remember, it's not because I'm hurting. Suffocating. Today was a good day. Deirdre follows me out, closing the door lightly so not to wake her. "The carols concert is on Thursday," she says, casually. "Weather depending, of course."

I cast her a knowing smile. She knows what she's doing—catching me on a better day.

"Did you manage to move things around?"

I drop my bags to between my feet and pull on my coat. "I did," I say, seeing her trying hard not to grin her delight. "You'll cancel if it's too bad?"

"No, not cancel. It'll just be a bit thin on the ground with relatives. I know you're not shy of a bit of snow."

I nod, but say no more, slipping my hat and gloves on. "I'll see you," I say, collecting up my bags, taking a leisurely walk down the corridor rather than scurrying along as fast as I can. The walls aren't closing in.

I hear the door click to release as I approach and laugh to myself at the irony. The one day I don't need to escape, the door is opened before I make it there. I hurry my pace and push my weight into it and nearly fall through it when someone on the other side pulls it open.

I stagger forward a few paces into a man. "Shit, I'm sorry." I look up. Realise who it is. Step back. "Graham."

"Good to see you too, sis."

"Finally found time in your schedule then?"

"I didn't come here to get earache." He looks past me through the open door. "Is she with it today?"

"With it?"

"Talking sense?"

"She never talks sense. She's got Alzheimer's."

He looks down at his watch, and I know it's because he's mentally calculating how little time he can get away with being here. To be honest, I'm even more surprised than I usually would be that he's here. The weather is the perfect excuse. "I'm picking up Mindy's present, and I'm a bit early."

Right. He's not gone out of his way. Not made a special trip. Mum's just fitting into a slot that happens to have cropped up. "I'm going." I can't be in my brother's orbit for longer than a minute without wanting to smash his ignorant face in.

"Hey, Cam," he calls.

"What?" I don't look back.

"Sign the papers, yeah?"

I stop, staring forward, trying not to let my simmering blood escalate into a full-blown boil. I did not want to do this with my brother. I truly didn't want anyone, especially him, to take away my momentary bubble of joy. Although, I do need to know one thing. "Did you know he's moved on?" I ask, facing him, watching his face. I might not like him, but I know him well, and the sudden thinning of his lips is a massive red flag. It means he's about to lie. "You knew."

"You should do the same."

"Oh yes. Move on. Easy as that. Just forget I was a mum. Just forget my son was run down and killed. My four-year-old son."

His wince gives me hope that he's not a complete inconsiderate bastard. His shoulders drop. "I'm not saying forget, Cam. Moving on isn't forgetting."

"She's pregnant." I spit the words out like they're stones choking me.

"I know."

"She's going to give Dominic a baby, and he'll love that child like we loved Noah. I can't do that, Graham. I can't have more children. I can't try to fill the void Noah left behind. All I can do is move forward and hope someday the pain becomes bearable."

"It will. You should see a doctor, Cam. You're not looking too great."

"God, you're a cock." I walk out and welcome the cold blast of air that cools my temper down. "Ugh." If brothers got medals for being dumb, mine would get the gold.

My phone ringing is the only thing that stops me from fulfilling my desire to punch my older brother, and the sight of Dec's name lights up my world as much as it lights up my screen. "Morning."

"Afternoon."

I pull my phone away and check. He's right, which means I spent much more time with Mum than I usually would. That alone is reason to smile, and now Dec's calling. I'm ignoring the interlude of my brother. "Afternoon," I say. "Sorry, time ran away with me unpacking a vanload of groceries from Tesco."

"You need a Lynette."

"Wait, did she order it?"

"Of course. I wouldn't know where to start."

"You just completely burst my bubble."

"I'll reinflate it tomorrow night when you cook for me."

"At my place?"

"Yes."

"Not your place?"

"No."

I cringe at the snow before me. His place is cosier. Nicer. Bigger. Better equipped.

"Are you out?" he asks.

"Just visited my mum."

"In this weather, Camryn?" Then he huffs. "Never mind. How is she?"

How is she?

Such a simple question, but Dec has just provided another life raft. His question makes me feel that I'm not carrying this burden alone. He cares about her because he cares about me. "She's good today." I brace myself to tell Dec I've signed the papers but decide to wait until tomorrow. At our dinner. At my place.

"That's great. And you? How's your cheek?"

"Less sore."

He hums. "Are you going to ask me what I'd like to eat tomorrow night?"

"Well, since your housekeeper ordered it all, I'm going with my gut and assuming she's catered for your tastes too, in which case I'll pull something together from the ingredients she ordered."

"What did she order?"

"You want me to list it all?"

"Yes."

"I'm not listing it all," I say around a laugh. "What are you doing today?" God, I want to see him.

He groans. "Catching up on work."

I pout to myself. It's going to be a long twenty-four hours. "Well, have fun with that," I say lightly, hiding my disappointment. "I'll see you tomorrow."

"Looking forward to it."

I smile. "Bye." Tapping the edge of my mobile on my chin, I ponder something for a few moments before I take a deep breath of bravery and head the opposite way.

Toward Selfridges.

I'm frazzled by the time I make it home, weighed down with bags, having braved Tesco too. I head straight for Mr. Percival's door and swing a bag at it, because the handles are cutting off the blood supply to my fingers. "Come on," I mutter, hearing the squeak of his walking frame getting louder. The moment he opens the door, a handle on one of my bulging bags gives and the contents crash to the floor. I leave it and face Mr. Percival. "I need you to help me make a birthday cake."

December 18th

After making Dec's birthday cake and wrapping Debbie's gift, I spent last night preparing for this evening. Cleaning, tidying, unpacking more boxes, changing my bed, then preparations for dinner. I got up early, ran, checked on Mr. Percival, who checked on the cake, and then I trudged to work in yet more snow later than usual. It's got to the point people have no choice but to get on with life, since the white stuff is here to stay for the foreseeable future. The first white Christmas in twenty-five years. I remember the last one so vividly. Dad leaving wet, muddy footprints around the house, Mum fighting her urge to whip out the mop. The absolute magic of waking up on Christmas morning to a winter wonderland. I so desperately wanted that for Noah. He didn't even get to see it snow in his short life. I fall back against the elevator wall, seeing him in my mind's eye sitting in the window on Christmas Eve, searching the sky for Santa's reindeers. I see him setting out carrots and mince pies. That one Christmas when he was just old enough to start to understand. Magical. My lip wobbles, and I quickly get it under control as the doors to the elevator open and whoops of joy and delight snap me out of my daze. Everyone's here as early as me? Just because it's Secret Santa day? *My God.*

I pull my shoulders back and head down the corridor armed

with my divorce papers. Wrapping paper's being tossed aside, and bodies are doubling over to cope with the power of their belly laughter as they reveal their gifts and showcase them.

"Can you put these though the postage machine?" I ask Meredith when I arrive at her desk, sliding the envelope across to her. "First class." I turn around, pause, then turn back. "Actually, send them Recorded Delivery." I want to know that Dominic has received and signed his much-loved divorce papers.

"Sure."

Something catches my eye by her keyboard, and I frown. "Meredith, why is there a bottle of lube and a packet of condoms on your desk?"

Her lips press into a straight line as she reaches for them and slips them into her top drawer. "Secret Santa was trying to be funny."

"Or massively insensitive."

"It's fine. I still have a sense of humour. What happened to your face?"

"I wasn't paying attention."

"To what?"

"The door."

Meredith sits back in her chair, and I'm quite sure I don't like the way she's considering me.

"What?"

"The door?"

"Yes, the door."

Nodding mildly, she picks up her pen. "The door. I may have used that a few times myself."

I recoil so much, it takes me back a few steps. "He was physical with you?" I murmur, moving in closer and checking the vicinity.

"He had anger issues. I blamed myself for a long time." She laughs, low and without humour. "You know, I used to beg him not to leave me. It only happened a few times, but each time it did, somehow I concluded it was my fault."

"Oh, Meredith."

She waves a hand flippantly, and it's wholly inappropriate. "I just hope you're not in the same situation."

Compelled to ease her mind, I lean forward on her desk. "The truth is, I got mugged."

"What?"

"Well, they didn't take anything, as someone scared them off, so I guess it was more of an attack."

"Camryn!"

"It's fine, I'm fine. But if anyone asks, a door did it."

"Did you report it to the police?"

"No." It's now my hand flapping flippantly, dismissing her. "It would be a waste of time. There was no one around, and it was dark."

"You said someone scared them off."

"She was yelling from a window, and I doubt she saw anything useful. I've learned my lesson."

"Have you?" she asks, tilting her head, her face all kinds of stern.

"I have." But have I? Because, really, it was only the snow that made the street so deserted. I've never walked the streets of central London and felt vulnerable. Could I give up walking everywhere? Do I want to? I shake my head and bring myself back to the present. "Now, then," I muse, lifting my chin, my eyes on Meredith's top drawer. "Any suspects?"

The fleeting blush that creeps onto her cheeks tells me she's wondered. And, perhaps, has a few ideas. "Maybe."

I waggle my eyebrows and leave Meredith to continue pondering that. "I'd like updates."

"Camryn," she calls. I stop and look back. "Phillip's really pissed off."

"Is he causing you problems?"

"It's fine, I've moved out. Staying with my parents, but I just thought I should warn you."

I don't tell her I can handle scumbags like Phillip, as it would be demeaning. So instead, I smile and nod, making my way back to my office.

But I don't make it anywhere near because a crowd has built up, the noise horrendous. Still no Thomas. "Is he in?" I ask Crystal.

"Not yet," she replies, distracted, as Debbie emerges from the pack, a stupid grin on her face.

She does a little twirl. "They're fabulous!" she sings. "Where on earth did you find them?"

"Find what?" I ask, passing her and pushing my way through the mob.

"Oh come on, I told you who you were buying for." She follows me, shutting the door behind us.

"Secret Santa got them for you, Debbie."

"Fine." She holds up a gift bag. "You've not claimed your present from under the tree."

"I don't do gifts."

"You bought mine," she points out.

"I didn't have much choice, Debbie. You fixed it so I had to buy for you, and you're one of the only people around here that I wouldn't want to upset."

Her ample bosom swells. "That's the sweetest thing you've ever said to me."

"Shut up and hand me the bag."

She chuckles and slides it open, then helps herself to a chair, getting comfortable.

"What are you doing?"

"Watching you open your gift."

"Oh no." I stand and round my desk, helping Debbie up. "I draw the line there."

"God, you're such a Scrooge," she mutters, shrugging me off and continuing to the door without my assistance. "I'm going to show off my fancy tights."

"You might need to hand out some sunglasses," I call as the wood comes between us. Sighing, I eye the bag dangling from my fingers and take the plunge, pulling out something heavy wrapped in tissue paper.

My first gift of any kind in three years. How pitiful.

I unwrap it and stare down at the jar in my hand. And I don't feel anything. Not amusement, not insult. Nothing. Swinging the door open, I call Debbie, stopping her muscling her way through the crowd still blocking the corridor. I hold up the jar of Humbugs, and she pouts. "The budget was twenty quid, right?"

"Right."

"I want to file a complaint."

"To be fair, they're quite fancy Humbugs."

"Who drew me?"

"Thomas." She doesn't hesitate, and I laugh. What a joke. I spend my working life trying to control his spending habits, and he couldn't even meet the poxy twenty-pound budget? "Next year, please spare me the inevitable dig." I slam my door and glance at the clock. Not at the time, but the date.

December eighteenth. I take a breath and swallow hard. For the first time, I know I won't spend *the* day in desolate loneliness, where no one else around me feels the same agony and grief. Dec's the only thing that might get me through tomorrow.

By lunchtime, the noise has finally died down outside my office. I've watched my phone between emails, waiting for it to ring, beep, vibrate. Give me anything from Dec.

Nothing.

A knock sounds, Thomas's signature knock, and I look up in surprise. He's sought me out voluntarily? "Come in."

He pokes his head around the door, obviously nervous. I don't know whether it's the Humbugs or the fact we still have things to discuss. "Where did you disappear to in such a hurry on Friday?"

"Humbugs?" I ask, holding up the jar.

His smile is more of a grimace. "Can you carve out an hour for me this afternoon?"

I've never seen my boss look so serious. "I can do now."

"I've got a one o'clock with the lawyers."

The lawyers? "Anything I should kn—" My phone rings, and I forget where I am and what I'm doing for a few moments.

"You take that," Thomas says, backing out. "Say two?" He doesn't give me a chance to answer, shutting the door as I scoop up my phone and answer Dec's call.

"Lunch?" he says.

"Lunch *and* dinner?"

"I miss you."

My heart soars as I rise, kicking my heels off and stuffing my feet into my boots. "Normal place?"

"On my way."

I can't walk fast enough across Leicester Square, every inch of me buzzing to see him. Dec rounds the corner as I'm approaching, his shoulders hunched, his hands in his coat pockets and his scarf circled a few times around his neck. The moment he spots me, his face lights up, his eyes sparkling with flecks of silver. It sends my knees weak and my heart fluttering so madly I'm sure I could take flight. Opening his arms, I walk straight into them and snuggle into the shelter and heat of his chest. "You're freezing," he mumbles into my hair, his hot breath burning my scalp.

"I don't feel it." Anticipation's kept me warm, and now Dec is. He cups the back of my head and pulls it back, his eyes falling to my lips.

"Will you feel it if I kiss you?"

"Always."

His lips are on mine in one hitch of my breath, his hot tongue exploring my mouth so softly. I hum, huddled close to him, swallowing his moans and absorbing his body pushed against mine. I would happily stand here in the snow and spend all of my lunch break kissing him. Catching up. He sucks my tongue gently and releases, keeping me close but pulling his head back to look at me. "Hello."

"Hello," I reply, smiling.

His eyes fall onto my cheek, checking the mark. "Still sore?" I shake my head and let him tuck me into his side and walk us on. "Tell me about your day," he says, guiding us across the road toward St. Martin's Lane.

"I opened my Secret Santa gift," I tell him, smiling up at him when he peeks down at me in interest. "Humbugs."

"Charming."

"I thought so too."

He points to a small café over the road. "Coffee and a sandwich?"

"Perfect."

He pushes the door open for me and immediately helps me out of my coat, pulling a chair out for me. "Take a look." He hands me a menu and goes to hang our coats up, rubbing his hands as he wanders back.

"Tea and the chicken and avocado." I pass him the menu, but he doesn't look, instead going to the counter and ordering, returning with the teas and a wooden spoon that has the number nine on it. "This is cute," I say, taking one of the mini polka dot teapots.

"The wife of a guy who works for me owns it." Dec offloads the tray onto the table and slips it onto another chair before sitting. "Best sandwiches in town." He helps himself and pours for both of us. "So what are you cooking for me tonight?"

"It's a surprise."

"What time do you want me?"

"*All* the time," I say, making him smile down at the table.

"I feel the same, in case that needs clarifying." He pushes my teacup and saucer over and rests back. "I was thinking about tomorrow."

My cup pauses at my lips. Tomorrow. I don't know how it's been three years. I'm both horrified that the time has flown past but also dragged agonisingly slowly, and thankful that this darling man has remembered the date I mentioned to him only once. "And what were you thinking?"

"I was thinking we should do something."

"After work?"

"No. Take the day off. You don't need to work to keep busy if I'm keeping you busy."

Take the day off. I'd never entertain such a crazy suggestion, not on any normal day. But on December nineteenth? "What will we do?"

"Be together," he says simply.

Be together so that I'm not alone. That lifts the heaviness of my heart a tiny bit. "I signed the acknowledgment letter with the divorce papers," I declare out of nowhere.

Dec's eyes fly up, his cup lowering, and he nods, thoughtful for a few moments. "I've asked my lawyer to widen the search for my wife."

I inhale my surprise. "Why did you marry her?" I ask, finally plucking up the courage.

He looks away, scowling at thin air. "Momentary lapse in judgment."

"And she just left?" Dec didn't leave her, she left him?

"Yes."

He's bitter, and that doesn't sit well, which is ironic coming from me, I know. But, again, *she* left *him*. "What will happen if she comes back?"

"Then I get my divorce quicker."

"So you want that. A divorce?"

He frowns. "Yes, I want a divorce." Irritation slips into his tone. "She's dead to me."

Dead. Like his father is to him. And yet I know as well as the next person that there's a fine line between love and hate. He doesn't truly hate his father. And I suspect he doesn't truly hate his wife.

I wonder again, with annoying curiosity, what happened

between them and why he's so bitter. Maybe it was simply because she left him. But, again, why would she? He's handsome, successful.

Cold.

Could that have been why? Mr. Serious was too serious? And yet I've seen Dec's many sides. He's serious, yes, but he's also light, sensitive, funny, warm, and a whole load of other things. "What's her name?"

"Chelsea."

Just a one-word answer, which is fine because it was a closed question, but something tells me I wouldn't get more out of him if I tried. I hate the fierce curiosity in me. I also hate the idea that someone could come along—his *wife*—and burst my bubble. Like I said, there's a very fine line between love and hate, and I'm worried I'm looking at it.

"I need to talk to you about something," Dec pushes his tea away, his persona not as light and easy as it was before we touched on his wife.

A man walks in, bringing a gust of cold air with him, and I shiver in my chair. Or could that be Dec's declaration that he wants to talk about something? Because everyone knows when someone says that, the chances are you're not going to like the topic. "What?" I ask, obviously cautious.

"Your face."

"My face is fine," I try not to sound tired, and I know I've failed when Dec flashes me a look somewhere between warning and disbelief.

"You didn't do it at work, Camryn."

"What?"

"I ran into Thomas."

I withdraw. "You ran into my boss, and one of the things you talked to him about, taking into consideration the gala was the first time you met him, was my face?" I inhale, something coming to me. "The gala wasn't the first time you met Thomas, was it?"

"No, it wasn't. How did you injure your face?"

"I was mugged, attacked, whatever you want to call it." I grit the words out, and Dec shifts in his chair, his neck tilting mildly, as if he's subtly cricking it. "I didn't say because I knew I was stupid for walking home late when the streets were quiet, and I didn't want you to fuss."

"Fuss?"

"Be mad with me."

"I am mad."

"I'm okay. It's done, I won't do it again, and now we need to talk about how you know Thomas."

"I'm buying his company."

I sit back sharply, like an arrow through my stomach has pinned me to the back of my chair. "What?"

"It's not a done deal yet."

"Yet?"

"We're still in negotiations."

I stare at Dec across the table, my mind blank, as a waitress appears beside us, smiling, two plates in her hands as she looks between us. "The Prawn and Marie Rose?"

I rise from my chair abruptly and pace across the café, pulling my coat off the hook. "Camryn," Dec calls, the sound of his chair legs scrapping the wooden floor screaming. "Wait."

I hurry out, swinging on my coat. He's buying the company? He's buying the fucking company I work for, and he chose to hide it from me?

"Camryn, come on."

I throw my bag onto my shoulder and walk with purpose up the street.

"Camryn." His feet crunching into the snow get louder as he gains on me, and I stop and swing around, finding him struggling to get his coat on as he jogs. "Do *not* follow me," I snap, and he halts and backs up immediately, surrendering, shaking his head on a loud exhale.

"Cam—"

"I don't want to hear it."

"Let me exp—"

"Sir, your bill!"

I look past Dec, seeing the young girl from the café waving a piece of paper. "Fuck it," he snaps, reversing his steps. "Wait there."

As soon as he disappears into the café, I walk on, and I don't stop until I make it back to my office, turning right out of the elevator and making a beeline for Thomas's office, not bothering knocking, barging in, still in my coat and boots. "You're selling the company?"

With his phone at his ear, he stills in his seat, pure dread engulfing him. "I'll call you back," he says, hanging up.

"What's going on, Thomas?"

"How long have you been seeing Dec Ellis?"

"That's none of your business."

"When you're feeding him information that's driving down the value of my company, it's my business, Camryn."

"What? I've not told Dec a damn thing about your company." Now is apparently a good time for my mind to remind me otherwise. Oh my God, have I been used to get inside information on TF Shipping?

"He's slashed his offer, and then I found out he's seeing you. Coincidence?"

Good question. "How long has this been going on?" I ask.

"A few months."

All the pieces start to click into place, and I seriously do not like the picture it's building. I've known Dec for a few weeks. *Fell in love with him in a few weeks.* "Did you plan on selling up all along?"

"No, not all along. Just until some bazillionaire came along and made me an offer I couldn't refuse."

"So what's the fucking point in me being here now?"

"There is no point."

"Then why am I?"

"Because I was too scared to fire you."

I recoil, and Thomas smiles awkwardly. "Are you firing me now?"

"Well, that's debatable. If Ellis keeps driving his price down, I'll continue with the original plan to float the company and tell him to go fuck himself. But I don't know if I can trust you, Camryn."

"Did he tell you he was seeing me?"

"No, but it was pretty bloody obvious when he asked how you were after injuring yourself at work. So how did you injure your face, because you told him you did it here, and you told me you fell over on your way home from work."

"Do I have a job?" My voice is so tight, and my throat aches.

"It'll have to go to the board."

I laugh coldly. "You mean your wife and son?" That's a no, then. *Jesus Christ*. Reality's playing a cruel fucking game with me. I need this job. Especially now my newfound source of distraction has been taken away. And that's the only reason I don't fly off the handle and tell Thomas where to shove his job and instead walk out calmly. Dec fucking lied to me. Used me. I've allowed myself to be vulnerable, and now I just look like a fool.

Problem is, I didn't allow it. Dec somehow drew out the old me, and then he gave me hope to cling to.

And now he's taken it away.

Hope. What a fucking joke. It's just a burden on one's destiny.

Just when I don't think my day can get any worse, I make it home and find Dominic loitering outside my building. As much as I tell it not to, my stomach drops, my steps faltering. "The papers are in the post," I say, passing him, armed with my keys.

"That's not why I'm here, Cam," he replies, making me still. "Can I come in?"

"Why?" I face him. "Has guilt kicked in?"

"I don't feel good about this."

"You don't feel good?" I ask. "If you're going to own your shit, Dominic, own it. Say you feel awful. Horrendous. How about you feel really fucking shit? How long have you been together?" I ask, like I need more blows today. "She must be what? Eight months?"

"Thirty-eight weeks." *Due any day*. I suck back the impact of that hit. The hit I absolutely asked for. "Look, can I come in? I don't want to do this out here."

"Do what?" I've known this man a long time. I know that when he reaches for the corner of his right eye and rubs, he's about to tell me something I'm not going to like. And he's rubbing the corner of his eye now, squinting as he does.

"We're not going inside?" he asks on a breathy sigh.

"No, I don't think I want that." Because I have a feeling I'm going to be asking him to leave immediately. I frown and look past him when I see a couple of police officers coming up the path, both of them looking at the building. Dominic glances over his shoulder to see what's got my attention as they approach, and I push my back into the glass door to allow them past.

"Thanks," one says, as the other officer follows, splitting her attention between her pad and the numbers on the doors. She stops at mine. Knocks.

"Can I help you?" I ask, prompting them both to look my way.

"We're looking for Ms. Moore."

"That's me." Feeling uneasy, I release the door I'm holding open with my back and join them outside my apartment. "Is everything okay?"

"I'm PC Jones, this is PC Hyde. We're here about a reported assault."

"On whom?"

"You."

I recoil, noting her eyes falling to my cheek. "But I haven't filed a report."

"No." She goes back to her notepad. "Mr. Ellis did."

Another recoil, this time sharper, and I'm suddenly very aware of Dominic hovering behind me. "It was nothing."

"Assaulted?" Dominic blurts. "When? Where?" The officer looks at Dominic in question. "Husband," he announces, joining my side. "Dominic Moore."

"So who's Mr. Ellis?"

Dominic turns his eyes on to me. "The guy I saw you with in the restaurant?"

I'm not derailed enough to appreciate what this must look like to the officers. "Dominic and I separated years ago. Divorce pending," I explain. "Dec Ellis is the guy I'm seeing."

"*Dec* Ellis?" Dominic blurts, his voice high-pitched.

"Are you just going to repeat everything being said?" I ask, irritated, unlocking my door. "Please, come in." I open the way for the police officers, stepping in Dominic's way when he tries to follow them inside. He doesn't take the hint, swerving my static form and putting himself in the thick of things. "This really isn't necessary," I say.

"An unprovoked assault isn't nothing." PC Jones says, lowering to the couch while Hyde remains standing. "Would you mind walking us through what happened?" she asks. I sigh, not seeing the bloody point, but I lower to the chair anyway, eyeballing Dominic, who has perched himself on the arm next to me.

I start from the beginning, clarifying the date and time as Hyde makes notes, and walk them all through step by step. "I didn't think anything of it because there were no other footprints behind me. Well, not until I looked closer."

"What do you mean?"

"He was stepping in my prints."

She nods slowly, thoughtfully. "And the woman who came down, she was at the window of her flat?"

"Smoking. She yelled before she came down."

"Do you know which flat?"

"No, sorry."

Looks of disapproval come at me from Dominic constantly.

"Okay, I think we have everything we need." Hyde stands, and my head cranes back to look up at her as she hands me a card with her details. "If you think of anything else."

"Thank you," I murmur.

"Thanks," Dominic says.

"We'll be in touch. We'll see ourselves out."

They leave, and I drop the card on the coffee table, standing and getting out of my coat.

"What are you doing walking the empty streets in the dark on your own, Camryn?"

"You didn't come here to lecture me, so why are you here, Dominic?"

"Dec Ellis?"

"Yes, Dec Ellis." Although I'm not talking to him right now.

"Dec Ellis of DEA&M?"

I frown, my mind unravelling the abbreviation. *Dec Ellis Acquisitions and Mergers.* "So you know him?"

"Not personally. DEA&M just bought Cloisters."

If I recoil anymore today, I'm going to find myself with a debilitating bout of whiplash. "He's what?" Dec's bought the company Dominic works for? *What the hell?*

"Swooped in at the eleventh hour and gazumped the firm favourite."

"Oh." What the fuck is he playing at? TF Shipping, and now my ex-husband's company?

"You're seeing him?"

I tilt my head, my jaw tight. "We're not going there, Dominic. Why are you here?"

"Right." He takes in air. Lots of it. I want to yell at him to spit it out, but I also don't want to hear whatever he's got to say. "Fuck," he breathes, reaching for his eye, rubbing. "I work with Kiera." He's unable to look at me. I don't need to ask who he's talking about. That's her name. *Kiera*. He works with her.

"You were fucking her when we were together." The words tumble out of my mouth intuitively, and just the way Dominic keeps his eyes on my feet tells me my intuition is bang on. "You were having an affair." I'm stating facts, not asking questions, my words robotic. As if I'm shutting down, once again protecting myself.

All I get from him is a small, ashamed nod. He deemed it necessary to come here and tell me this the day before the anniversary of our little boy's death? He thought that would be appropriate? For what fucking purpose? To hurt me even more?

But then something comes to me.

I inhale, scared to voice what's ping-ponging around in my head. "The work call you were on when you were picking Noah up from school that day."

His eyes shoot up to mine, wide and worried.

"It was her, wasn't it?"

"We were drifting, Cam."

Oh my God, no. "So you started fucking a tart from work?"

"It wasn't like that."

"What was it like?"

"I didn't plan for it to happen. It just . . . did."

"And then you got so wrapped up in it, you failed to stop our boy from running out into the road."

"The car was supposed to stop, Camryn. It didn't stop. She was twice over the limit, for fuck's sake."

"All attention on Noah," I grate. "That's what we agreed. Always. When we had Noah, it was all about him when we weren't at work. It's the very fucking reason I asked you to get him that day, because I didn't want to be on a call when I picked him up."

"I know, Cam. I know." His head hangs.

"Why the fuck are you telling me this now?"

There's a brief, uncomfortable silence. Another long inhale. "We had dinner with Graham and Mindy."

"How cosy." Isn't that just lovely? My brother probably always liked this shithead more than he loved his own sister. Even if he's a cheating bastard . . . and the reason Noah wasn't safe.

The reason Noah was killed.

Fucking hell.

I hate them both.

"Kiera mentioned something about work, how we met, when, and—"

"Get to the fucking point, Dominic."

"Mindy put two and two together and deduced we'd had an affair. She's given me the chance to tell you before she tells you herself."

"Right." I'm waiting for the unbridled rage to send me into a spin, or even the lump in my throat to appear. But all I feel is . . . numb. He knows what tomorrow is. Or is he too wrapped up in his happy little family now to remember? "Is that all?"

"What?"

"I said, is that all?" I walk to the door and swing it open. Mr. Percival is in the corridor, holding his walking frame with one hand and a bulging shopping bag with the other. I quietly scorn the old boy, taking the bag. "Anyone would think you want to injure yourself," I say, starting to walk him to his door. Dominic emerges from my apartment, his face blank and yet riddled with perplexity, as he quietly leaves.

Mr. Percival cranes his neck. "Who's that, dear?"

"A ghost," I murmur, and he laughs, elbowing me in my arm. "Stop playing games with me."

I turn a mild smile onto him. "I don't know who that is, Mr. Percival."

"You don't?"

I shake my head. "What on earth have you got in this bag?"

"Oh, the Christmas market's on," he says, casting one last look over his shoulder, but he doesn't push. "I got us gifts."

I get him inside his apartment and turn to shut the door. Dominic is motionless by the glass door that leads to the street. "What did you get me?" I ask, turning away, knowing that will be the last time I see my husband.

"Here, let me show you." Mr. Percival claims the bag back and pulls out a bottle of wine. "Orange wine. It's all the rage, apparently. I thought you might like to try it."

I accept the bottle, grateful, not only because I need a drink, but because maybe I can get so drunk, I don't wake up for the whole of tomorrow. "Want to share it?" I ask, encouraging him on.

"Are you asking me on a date?"

"I don't date, Mr. Percival."

"Then how do explain Dec Ellis?"

"Him?" I laugh, and the absent lump starts growing. "I haven't dated him." I'm struggling to get my words out. "I skipped dating and just fell in love with him instead."

"I thought as much."

"You did?"

"Go big or go home, dear." He chuckles. "And of course, he's coming for dinner and birthday cake tonight!"

Not happening. I will not celebrate a man who possibly used me and is feeling fucked that his gig is up. "He's not coming now."

"Oh. That's a shame."

"It's okay. I'll eat the cake myself."

Mr. Percival takes a moment, obviously reaching the right conclusion. "About that drink," he says softly.

"You know, do you mind if we defer until tomorrow? I don't think I'll be much company." The mention of Dec has apparently kick-started all the feels.

"A problem shared is a problem halved, dear."

"I won't burden you with my tragedies." I dip and drop a kiss on his wrinkly old cheek. "Thank you for the wine."

"Welcome, dear," he says, thoughtful, as I let myself out. "You know where I am."

I get inside my apartment and close the door, taking in the newly spruced-up space, before wandering to the kitchen. The table is laid for two. Ingredients I need to make a coq au vin are on the counter, the chicken in the fridge with wine. Wine that I carefully selected to match the meal I was making, rather than wine for the sake of getting mindlessly drunk.

Which is what it will be used for now.

He was having an affair. My baby is dead because he was having a fucking affair.

I didn't plan for it to happen. It just . . . did.

Such utter fucking bollocks. When will the blows stop coming? I thought Dec was healing me. I never dreamed he could be using me.

He's slashed his offer, and then I found out he's seeing you. Coincidence?

No. Probably not.

"God damn it," I yell, slapping the counter. *Why now? Why this month? This week? This fucking day?*

I set the orange wine on the counter and pull out the chilled white from the fridge, retrieving my newly bought corkscrew to remove the cork. No screw caps in sight. I pour a large glass and sip it as I put away the ingredients, then head into the lounge to the cabinet by the window. The framed picture of my boy sits there alone, tilted ever so slightly so he can see the snow.

It comes over me like a tidal wave, my muscles giving way, folding me down to the floor.

And I sob.

Silently.

I sob my fucking heart out. "I don't want tomorrow to come," I say to him. "Mummy doesn't want to do this anymore." Wake up each morning and have that brief moment where everything's okay before reality swoops in and reminds me of what I've lost. And the agony starts all over again. A never-ending cycle of pain, momentary relief, and realisation, setting off the pain again. Dec provided respite. My job was a distraction. The pain was dulled. Not gone—it will never be gone—but it was manageable. *Just.* Neither Dec nor my job can help me anymore.

I look at my glass. But wine can.

I need to feel that familiar numbness.

I sniff, wiping my eyes, and get to my feet with effort, heading for the kitchen as I neck it, but a light thump on my front door pulls me to a stop on the threshold, and I look at the ceiling, taking in air.

Finding strength.

I go to the door and push my forehead into the wood. "I can't take anymore today," I say quietly through the wood.

"And I can't leave knowing what tomorrow is," Dec replies softly. "Open the door, Camryn."

My lip wobbles, and I bite down on it viciously to stop it. *Tomorrow*. The nineteenth of December. Three years since Noah died. "Go away," I murmur, squeezing my eyes closed, rolling my head on the wood.

"No."

"Leave me alone."

"No." His soft thud on the door vibrates through my head. "I will *never* leave you alone, Camryn." Another thud. "Do you hear what I'm saying to you?"

I'm hearing. And I don't want to believe it. It would be dangerous to believe it. He lied to me. I push my palm into the wood and lift my head with effort, taking the knob and pulling the door open, finding Dec standing on the other side, tall and impassive.

And painfully beautiful.

"Can I come in?" he asks quietly.

"You lied to me."

"No, Camryn, I didn't lie. I just didn't give you the full picture." The sincerity in his eyes is hard to ignore. "I didn't need you to tell me Thomas's son and wife were spending money like it might melt if they didn't. I didn't need you to tell me money burns a hole in Thomas Fryer's pocket. I'm buying his company. I'm a businessman. I have forensic accountants looking into every company I'm interested in, so I know what's going on. I know if there are holes, if accounts are manipulated, if I'm being given a pile of bullshit to elevate the price. When I saw you in that bar the night we met, I didn't know who you were." He wedges his hands into the doorframe either side and leans into it, coming closer but keeping a respectable distance. "When I realised, I was in too deep already."

"I told you on our first walk the night I met you."

"I was in too deep already," he repeats softly, shrugging.

My stupid lip wobbles. "You should have told me."

"I know." The veins in his neck bulge. "I know I should have told you. But I didn't. That's on me. I fucked up, Camryn."

"You've bought the company my ex-husband works for too."

He definitely withdraws in surprise. "What company?"

"Cloisters."

"There's nothing in that except good business sense. How do you know that?"

"Because he was here when the police showed up earlier. They told me you'd filed a report."

"You were assaulted, Camryn. It needs to be on record."

"That was for me to decide."

"I disagree." He releases the door and takes one step over the threshold.

Everything inside me turns heavy. Or heavier. I don't have the bandwidth to deal with this. I don't have the energy to challenge him.

"Because when you love someone," he goes on, "you do everything in your power to keep them safe." He holds his hands out, asking me to accept him, and I let out a ragged sob. Hope is teasing me again. But is Dec my destiny? Does that make my hope less of a burden? "And I love you bone fucking deep, woman. Every broken, beautiful piece of you."

Emotion makes my hand shake as I lift it for him, and the moment I do, he pushes the door closed behind him, sets my glass aside, and lifts me into his arms, carrying me to my bedroom.

When I saw you in that bar the night we met, I didn't know who you were. When I realised, I was in too deep already.

He could have simply walked away today. But he came to me. He knew I needed the truth, and he came to me and told me. He knew I needed comfort—*him*—and he came to me.

And now? I have to forgive him. I have to trust him, believe him. I'm taking everything he wants to give me, because I know I can't do the next twenty-hours alone.

And because I love him.

I love him deeply.

Once he's set me on my feet, he starts stripping himself down to nothing before he starts on me. And I watch. Quiet, so fucking thankful he's here. He pulls my vest up my body, lifting my arms with it, and my hair tumbles around my shoulders as he casts it aside and turns me around so my back's to him. My bra loosens, falling down my arms, and I watch it drop to my feet as Dec slips his fingers into the sides of my knickers and crouches, drawing them slowly down my legs. "Step out," he orders gently. I do as I'm bid and turn back to face him. Naked. Both of us. Bare, exposed, vulnerable.

He takes my hand and pulls me to the bed, throwing the sheet back and helping me in, before he slips in beside me, covers us, and pulls me close to his body.

The heat of him pressed against me feels like sunlight on my skin.

Essential.

I settle into his side, my cheek on his chest, and draw circles across his abdomen. And we lie there in silence, cocooned in each other. Safe. His heart beats steady and strongly under my ear, his lips rest on the back of my head. "Can you breathe?" I ask, my voice husky, my body relaxed.

"I can never breathe easily around you, Camryn," he whispers. "Falling in love with you was easy. Admitting it to myself was the hardest thing I've ever done."

"Why?"

"Because I've never been in love before."

My tracing fingers falter. "Not even with your wife?"

"*Definitely* not with my wife."

"Then why did you marry her?"

My face rises when he breathes in. "Because I was really fucking stupid."

"You never told me what went wrong."

"Everything."

"You're being vague."

"What do you want to know?"

"Anything that will make me feel less shitty about my heartbreaks."

He huffs a little, with laughter I think. "I never want to be a heartbreak to you."

"You might not have a choice," I murmur, staring across his chest. "We don't know what the universe has in store for us. We're at its mercy. Some of us survive the blows, some of us don't."

"You're surviving."

"My heart beats."

Dec moves, and I'm suddenly being pulled up his body until I'm splayed the full length of him, my eyes level with his. My arms frame his head, and his palms hold my arse. "I want you to live again."

I scan his eyes, our noses so close they're almost touching. His pupils are dilated, but not so much I can't see the shards of silver glimmering at me. "For you?" I ask on a whisper.

"For Noah," he whispers back. "Everything, always for him before it's ever for me, Camryn. You can't love someone without one day experiencing grief. And you will never grieve someone without having loved them briefly or infinitely. Infinite love means endless grief. But peace will find its way back into your heart again, baby, and the grief will lighten enough for you to live again."

I'm certain I love him more each time he looks at me, speaks to me, and listens to me. "I'm glad you walked into that bar," I whisper, placing my fingertip on his lip and dragging it from one side to the other as I watch. "I'm glad you followed me out of there and saved me from the bubbles."

His small smile is almost sad. "I'm glad you let me save you." His fingers brush through my hair, and our gazes collide and lock, silence between us falling. But with each wordless second, our breathing becomes more distinct. His eyes sparkle like liquid metal, capturing the dim light with an ethereal gleam. Is he real? Is *this* real? "Tell me," he whispers, his voice hoarse, his breath hot on my face.

"I love you."

He nods mildly and applies a gentle pressure on the back of my head, encouraging my mouth onto his. His soft, moist lips brush lightly over mine, back and forth, slow and measured, in no rush at all. Blood rushes to my head. Life bursts into my tired bones. Dec coaxes my mouth open, plunging his tongue deeply but patiently, and mine soon starts to gently tangle with it. He hums, exploring wide, remaining on his back as I bring my knees up, lifting my hips too, lost in his kiss. I feel his hand come between us, taking himself in his grip, the tip of his arousal skimming me, and I swallow hard, subtly moving my hips, helping him to line up.

And then I slowly sink down onto him, our kiss pausing for a moment while we both exhale with the penetration, my torso hardening as I mould around him. He's buried to the root, so deep I'm struggling with the fullness. I exhale, controlled, and Dec resumes our kiss, deepening that too, but it's still so slow. So controlled. With one hand still cupping my head, the other now cupping my arse, he rolls his hips up carefully, and I rest my forearms either side of his head, my hair a veil around us, my hips falling into the rhythm he's set, and it's perfect. Perfectly quiet, perfectly slow.

Perfectly *us*.

He rolls lazily, and I meet every advance, and he doesn't stop kissing me. My breasts are pressed into his chest, our skin starting to slip as the pressure builds. And yet the pace remains languid and easy, and our mouths remain in perfect control. When his fingers claw into my backside, it's the first sign that he's reaching the cusp of pleasure, and then he moans, his lips stilling on mine, his tongue retreating as he suppresses a hiss, quietly gathering himself. My pants are soft against his open mouth, my skin becoming clammy.

"Okay?" I whisper, and he groans, rolling me onto my back, our connection unbroken, and resumes our kiss. *Still* so controlled and easy, I don't know how he's doing it. This could easily get out of hand, become vehement, but he doesn't want it to be that. Passionate, yes, and it is, but not out of control.

Not fucking.

Dec blindly takes my wrists and places them gently over my head, kissing his way up to my ear. "I'm perfect," he whispers, gently biting down on my lobe before using my arms as a wedge to prop his torso up and look down at me. And he *really* looks at me, grinding, retreating, plunging, rolling. I exhale sharply on every advance, breathe in deep on every retreat. I don't need to tell him I'm reaching the point of no return. I want to bury my face somewhere, clench my eyes closed to deal with the eruption coming, and yet while he's gazing at me as he makes love to me, fracturing the eye contact is impossible.

My lips part, my back arches. Dec's nostrils flare, his jaw twitches, his eyes turn wild. And then he jerks, stills for a moment, and pushes deep and high, holding himself inside me as he shudders, and I go with him on a whimper as an upsurge of pleasure hits me and charges through my body like a tsunami, calm but devastating.

Every muscle starts to ache from me tensing to deal with the onslaught, as Dec shakes above me, a sheen of sweat glistening on his top lip, his hair damp and falling onto his forehead. He collapses to one forearm, his head hanging, his throbbing length swelling against my inner walls. He breathes, laboured, and I reach for his back, dragging my fingers lightly up and down his spine, smiling to myself when he quells a growl at the back of his throat and pulls his shoulder blades in. His body comes down to rest on mine, but he doesn't release his full weight, holding himself with his bent arm, his face going into the crook of my neck. I feel his tongue lick the column of my throat, and I close my eyes, tickling his back, relishing his constant kisses on my neck.

And we stay there, close, sleepy, quiet, for the longest time. Holding each other. Connected. Peaceful. No urge to run out.

Because when you love someone, you do everything in your power to keep them safe. And I love you bone fucking deep, woman. Every broken, beautiful piece of you.

"Thank you," I murmur sleepily.

"Shut up."

I smile to myself and settle into the darkness, not scared of it today, or of my dreams.

December 19th

Low, blinding sunlight blazes though the window, making me squint when I open my eyes. It takes me a few slow moments to register where I am. Who I'm with.

What day it is.

The inevitable twist of my stomach confirms it, and I lift my head off Dec's chest, looking up at him. His eyes twitch behind his lids, his lips are parted, his breathing's light. Peeling my body away, I creep to the edge of the bed and go to the window, looking out onto the winter wonderland that today looks even more wonderful with the sun blazing down on it. The snow sparkles under the rays, a kaleidoscope of colours swirling in the various patches of frost. Looking up at the blue sky, I note the beautiful scene won't be around for long, given the cluster of dense white clouds hovering close by, ready to swallow up the sun and sprinkle more snow, making perfect what wheels and feet have ruined since the last flurry.

December nineteenth.

You're not supposed to be this beautiful.

I reach for the open curtains and slowly pull them closed, shutting out the day. When I turn around, Dec's watching me. He lifts the duvet and moves onto his side, and I pad over, slipping in and crawling into his chest, getting as close as I possibly can, my front pressed tightly to his, my face tucked under his chin. He brings the duvet down over us, covering our heads too, and wraps me in his arms. Protecting me from the world.

I crane my head back to see him in the dim light of our secluded, private space. I just have to see him and look into those eyes and imagine everything will be okay. And he lets me, remaining still and quiet as I study every beautiful bit of his face, reaching for his scruff and stroking my palm across it. I trace his lips, his cheek, his nose, his brow. "You're very handsome," I murmur, but he doesn't smile at the reminder of one of the first things I ever said to him.

"You're very beautiful."

I rub the pad of my thumb across his chin. "Dominic was having an affair." There's no surprise from Dec. Nothing. But he does pull me a little closer. "I'm not mad, I'm not even sad, and I don't know why. But it hurts still. Like someone's reached into my chest and ripped my heart out, and yet by some cruel miracle, I'm still breathing. Like I'm numb but still in fucking agony."

"I want to ease the pain, Camryn."

"You already do," I whisper as he reaches for my hand and guides it over his hip to his back.

"Tickle me," he demands softly. My fingers fall naturally into a sweeping motion, up his back as far as I can reach without stretching, and down again. Repeat. Over and over. Dec hums, brushing my hair back, relaxing into the pillow. "I saw him outside last night." My fingers falter. "Don't stop." His words kick them back into action. "He was worried about you. That's the only reason I didn't lay him out." A gravelly rumble emanates at the back of his throat, and I smile mildly, watching him sustain my tickling fingers. "You can do this all day." He sinks deeper into the mattress, closing his eyes. I gently ease my body away and he rolls onto his front, his head resting on his bent arms as I slip onto his back, having to pull the duvet up to get more material to drape over us now I'm sitting up. I look down at his naked back, marvel at the expanse of toned, smooth skin, my palms swishing across the top of his bum as I watch, the shade of my skin only a tone or two darker than his healthy glow. I don't know how, I haven't seen the sun for any length of time for years.

I place my palms into his flesh and lower my front to his back, dropping a kiss in the centre of his spine as I tickle my fingers up to his shoulders, hearing him hum his happiness. That sound, watching him struggle to deal with my touches, is stunning, could keep me here all day like he suggested. Maybe that's his ploy—a distraction of another kind. I inhale and kiss up to his nape and rub my nose through the soft hair there, sitting back up and tickling my way back down, rubbing firmly into his lower back and going again, lowering, kissing, tickly, massaging, inhaling his manly scent deeply into me. Repeat. I'm sure, sometime later, when his breathing is even and deep, I've tickled him into a coma. I lay my front down on his back and drag light fingertips up to his nape, circling them there, feeling his back muscles roll against my breasts.

"I made you a cake," I whisper in his ear.

I watch his profile, his eyes dragging open, heavy and sleepy. "Go get it," he demands softly.

"Now?"

"Yes, now." He starts turning over, forcing me to lift, and pulls the duvet off us, exposing us to the outside world again. "Go." His stomach muscles tense, and he sits up, planting a kiss on my lips as he helps me off his lap. I wander off, naked, feeling his eyes on me as I go. Looking over my shoulder as I walk out of my bedroom confirms it.

He raises his brows, and I smile lightly.

Pulling the fridge open when I make it to the kitchen, I slide out my masterpiece and set it on the counter, removing the dome lid and placing it to one side. Buttercream is bulging from the centre of the two sponges, with jam dripping down the sides. It really isn't much of a masterpiece, but Mr. Percival said he wins awards for this cake at the Royal British Legion, and I'm taking his word on that. Plus, I've tried his fruit cake. It's insanely good.

Grabbing the pack of candles I bought, I sink one into the centre and scratch through my drawers for a box of matches, exhaling my relief when I find some. I light it, blow out the match, and shield the flame with a cupped hand as I pick up the cake and carry it through to my bedroom.

Dec is lying on his side when I get there, his head propped up on a bent arm, his smile discreet. I nibble my lip shyly as I walk slowly toward him, making sure the candle remains lit, and lower to my knees by the side of the bed, setting the cake down on the mattress. He inspects the pile of sponge, cream, and jam, reaching for the buttercream and dragging the tip of his finger through, taking it to his mouth slowly and just as slowly sucking it off. He hums, while I wait for his verdict, stupidly anxious. "It's good."

"Mr. Percival may have assisted," I admit. "For complete transparency."

He nods, unperturbed, and swipes another bit of buttercream onto the tip of his finger, offering it to me. I gladly take it, my lips popping, my tongue dashing out to sweep up a few remnants on my lips.

"You need to make a wish," I say quietly, picking up the cake and holding it out to him.

His inhale is long and thoughtful as he watches the flame flicker delicately. Then his chest expands, he leans forward, closes his eyes, and blows out the candle. "Are you going to sing Happy Birthday to me?" he asks, his eyebrow raising teasingly.

Oh God. But . . . "I'd do anything for you," I say evenly, meaning it too. Unquestionably anything. So I take a breath of bravery, and I sing to him. "Happy birthday," I start, quiet and plainly awkward, laughing under my breath when Dec's lips stretch into a smile. "To you." I lift my arse off my heels, leaning over the bed to get closer to him. "Happy birthday . . . to you." I put the cake on the bedside table and inch up onto the mattress, and his smile widens more, spreading the entire width of his face. His delight, the rare full beam, injects me with valour and maybe some sass too. "Happy birthday, . . . dear D . . . ec." He chuckles, rolling onto his back, and I crawl onto his front and sink my face into his neck, feeling his arms come over my back and hold me tightly. "Happy birthday"—I kiss my way up his ear, onto his cheek, down the bridge of his nose, and onto his lips—"to you," I whisper, turning my peck into a full-blown kiss, clenching his hair in my fists and losing myself in him for another long while.

"That was beautiful," he mumbles around my mouth, and the odd sound of a giggle bubbles up from the deepest part of me. Such a thing on any normal day would be strange. But today? I break away and hold his face, wanting to see him again.

Wanting to see the reason.

And also wondering what he wished for, but I won't ask. It's bad luck. So instead I kiss him again, reaching back for the duvet and wafting it back over us.

We're two twirls of a tongue and a moan into another mind-blanking kiss when a bang at the front door disturbs us. No need to wonder who it'll be. I sigh and break away from Dec, laughing when he tries to haul me back into bed. The clock on my bedside catches my eye, and I have a mild heart attack. "It's ten o'clock," I say on a gasp, swinging back toward the bed. "We're late for work."

"We're not going to work today," he reminds me, stretching out his long, lovely body, sending me cross-eyed on the spot when every perfect part of him extends. He flips onto his side and plumps the pillow. "I thought I told you to take the day off."

"I was distracted by the news that the man I love is apparently buying the company I work for. So instead of booking a day off, I confronted my boss."

"How did that go?"

"He thinks you were using me."

He huffs. "I made it very clear I wasn't."

I roll my eyes. Of course Thomas wouldn't believe him. "Don't you have a business to swoop in and take over?"

"They'll survive without me for one day." Dec doesn't say it, but I can see in his eyes he's silently asking if I can survive without work for one day. Especially on *this* day. It's already got to ten in the morning, and I hadn't even comprehended the time. Hadn't counted each second, minute, hour, willing them to pass by quicker. Just desperate for the day to be over. Not that the grief goes away with the day. It's just . . . hard. More painful. And though it's still here, heavy in my belly, stirring in my heart, it's sustainable—and it's never been sustainable.

Another knock pulls me back into the room. Into the day. I grab my robe off the hook behind the door and swing it on.

"Is it the mad old man?" Dec asks.

"That mad old man helped make your birthday cake," I remind him. "He's not mad. Maybe eccentric. And he's ninety-nine, so he can be whatever he wants to be." I hurry to the door and swing it open, finding the mad old man. At least, I think it's him. Really, it's only the walking frame that clues me into who's at my door.

"Mr. Percival," I say, trying not to react to the snowsuit—an orange and royal blue affair made of some grotesque shiny manmade fabric that looks wet.

"Are you okay?" he asks.

"I'm fine." I feel at my cheeks, certain they must be flushed.

"You've not gone to work." His eyes widen, and I wonder why for a moment. Until I feel Dec's chest push into my back.

"Good morning, Mr. Percival," he says, unusually cheerful for Dec.

"You stayed the night."

"I did indeed stay the night. Couldn't move after eating all that cake."

"You enjoyed it?"

"Best Victoria sponge I've ever tasted."

"See!" Mr. Percival's chest swells with pride, making the snowsuit expand, almost enough to knock me back a step. "I've won awards for that cake."

"At the Royal British Legion," I add, looking back at Dec on a smile. I won't burst Mr. Percival's bubble and advise him that Dec's only tasted the buttercream.

Dec blows his cheeks out and rubs his belly. Again, very unlike Dec. "Blew me away. Well, as you can see, I'm not holding Camryn against her will, so if there's nothing else?"

The old boy recoils. Then grins wickedly, looking up and down the corridor, prompting me to crane my head and do the same, though who I'm looking for I don't know. "You're skiving," he says. "Both of you. Called in sickies, have we?"

"Actually, I've not called in anything yet."

"And I own the company," Dec says. "So I don't need to call in a thing."

"Oooh, you own the company, huh?"

Dec frowns. "Yeah."

"Impressive." Mr. Percival waggles his brows. "Anyway, kids, gotta dash. I'm late for bingo." He hobbles off, pulling me and Dec into the corridor.

"You really shouldn't be going out in that weather," Dec says.

"How else am I going to get there?"

"A cab?"

"I'm a pensioner. Can't afford one of those."

"I'll pay."

"I ain't no charity."

Dec rolls his eyes, and I chuckle. "Have fun," I call, and then yelp when Dec seizes me and hauls me back inside.

He slams the door, carries me to the kitchen, and sits me down. "So what are we having for breakfast?" he asks, flicking the kettle on and then stilling. He slowly looks over his shoulder. His eyebrows gradually rise, his gaze drifting to the doorway.

"I'll go get the cake," I say, getting up and hurrying through to the bedroom. Plunging my finger into the buttercream on my way back to the kitchen isn't a temptation I can resist. "You make coffee, I'll cut the cake." I falter on my way to the cutlery drawer, distracted by the practically naked man in my kitchen. I sigh, collecting a knife—I must buy some proper knives—and take myself and the cake to the table. Dec finds his own way around my sparse kitchen cupboards, bringing the coffee and plates. I cut a huge wedge of cake for him, then take a smaller slice for myself.

We both sink our teeth into the sponge. "Oh my God," Dec mumbles around his mouthful, closing his eyes and dropping his head back on a hum of approval.

"Good, huh?" I garble in reply, catching a blob of buttercream on the corner of my mouth and sucking it off my finger.

"Fucking orgasmic."

I chuckle around my mouthful. "I'm not sure if his fruit cake is my favourite, or this," I say, swallowing and taking another bite immediately.

Dec's shoulders slump, his exhale loud through his nose. "So today." He smiles as he reaches across and wipes up another blob off my lips, licking his finger clean.

"Today," I parrot, my chews slowing.

"What can I do?" he asks, sliding down his chair slightly and taking his coffee, oh so casual, as if he's here every morning and coffee and cake is part of our everyday routine.

"I don't know," I admit. He's not really done anything so far, and yet so much just by being here. Being close.

"How about we go for a walk?"

"A walk?"

"A walk. You like walking. I like walking with you."

"Okay."

"We can stop for a coffee, avoid the Christmas markets, freeze our tits off."

I smile. "Sounds perfect."

"So are you calling in sick?" he asks, finishing his slice and looking at the cake longingly.

"I am." For the first time in years. I cut him another wedge and plop it on his plate, and he groans as he starts to demolish his second piece, and I wrap my lips around mine, checking the time. Thomas hasn't called to find out where I am. I can't put it down to an assumption on his part that I've bailed the office because of the weather, like ninety percent of his staff have done.

Dec stands, dusting off his hands of crumbs, and comes to me, placing his palms on the arms of the chair and leaning down in my face. "Can I use your shower?" he asks quietly.

"It's . . . smaller than your shower."

"I didn't ask how big it is, I asked if I could use it."

"You can use it."

"Thanks," he whispers, lowering his lips to my cheek, taking my breath with that chaste peck, before he saunters off.

"Dec," I call out, stalling him at the door. He looks back. "Thank you."

"Shut up." And he disappears, leaving me to make the call to Thomas.

Thomas wasn't available, so I left a message with Crystal while I ate another slice of cake. Somehow, I don't think it's of any consequence to Thomas whether I go to work or not, since he's apparently selling TF Shipping.

Dec, in the same clothes he turned up in last night—wool blend grey trousers, a navy, thin-knit quarter-zip over a shirt, and his coat and scarf—stands over Mr. Percival's turkey again, staring at it. "It's definitely dead," I say, pulling my hat and gloves on.

"Ha ha," he drones, taking my hand. "Watch it, there's an icy patch."

"Whoa!" My feet slip from beneath me, and I grab Dec's arm with my spare hand, now clinging to him with both hands.

"What did I just say?"

"Not soon enough," I mutter, steadying myself. "Christ, it's cold." I look up at the sky, no longer blue, but bright white, the clouds packed with snow just waiting to burst out and coat everything beneath in a few more inches.

"Hold on to me," he orders, like he missed me hanging off his body. "It's—" His head snaps to the side when a giant snowball cracks him in the temple, exploding and covering us both with slush.

"Oh my," I breathe, hearing the familiar sounds of cackling kids fading into the distance as they scarper.

His eyes closed, his jaw ticking, his nostrils flaring, Dec gives his head a sharp shake to dislodge the snow in his hair, while I press my lips together, trying my damn hardest not to laugh in his face. "Little buggers," I murmur, reaching for his shoulders and brushing off the snow.

"Yeah, little buggers." His words are tight, sardonic, meaning he has a select few other words he'd prefer. I give him a straight-lipped smile when his eyes open, and he rolls his beautiful greys, scanning the vicinity. "Fuckers."

I lose my battle to hold my laughter back and bury my face in the crook of his neck, if only to hide the sight if I can't the sound. He leaves me there for a time, his arm wrapped around my waist, pressing me into his side. "Come on," he murmurs, nudging me out with his chin. "We're sitting ducks here." Moving his hold to my hand, he walks us onto the street and looks both ways. "The coast is clear." Another chuckle erupts, and Dec smiles across at me as we walk, pleased with himself. "I'd take snowballs like they were being fired out of a machine gun if it means I get to hear that sound all day," he muses, almost to himself.

I hug his arm, resting my head on his bicep, so thankful for this man, especially in this moment. He's skived work for me. Is trying to keep me busy, make me laugh. "Where are we heading?" I ask, our pace slow and easy, not because of the hazardous conditions, but because slow and easy is how we do things.

"We're just walking," he says, gentle and relaxed. "No agenda. Wander, talk, if you feel like it, grab a drink, dip into a few shops if you like."

I smile into his arm. "Okay."

. . .

We walk for an hour straight, hardly a word between us spoken, until we end up on the corner of Hyde Park. Dec spots a small shepherd's hut that's been converted into a mobile coffee cabin. "Hot chocolate?" he asks, pointing to an A-frame sign propped up outside. "It's apparently award-winning."

"Award-winning hot chocolate," I muse, smelling the coffee beans as we approach. "Sure."

"Marshmallows?"

"That's a really fucking dumb thing to ask."

"I'm going to take that as a resounding yes and never ask you that question ever again." He raises his brows to the server, who's casting a smile between us. "Two hot chocolates, one with marshmallows, one without."

"What?" I ask him on a gasp. "No marshmallows?"

He wrinkles his nose. "Camryn, I've eaten enough cake this morning to put Bruce Bogtrotter to shame. I don't know if my cholesterol levels can take much more."

I throw my head back on a laugh. "Oh my God, Matilda is our favourite film. I can't believe a man of your standing knows who Bruce Bogtrotter is."

Dec stares at me, and all amusement drifts from my face when I realise what I've just said. "Yours and Noah's?" he asks softly.

Oddly, I don't fold in on myself. I don't crumble at the realisation that I've talked in present tense about my dead son. "Yeah, mine and Noah's." The lump in my throat though? That's there. And it's okay for it to be there.

"Tell me," he says, handing me a cup piled high with marshmallows and cocking his arm for me to link. "I want to hear about him, if you want to talk about him."

If I want to talk about him. Always. And I feel strong enough to now. "Noah had a teacher called Miss Honey," I say, letting Dec walk us on, watching as the steam breaks through the gaps in the puffs of sugar and dissipates in the frigid air. "He threw a tantrum on his first day when Miss Honey introduced herself as Miss Honey. Stood up from the carpet and declared her a liar."

"Oh God," Dec says around a light, soft laugh.

"Yeah, the first day of pre-school didn't go to plan." I smile to myself, revisiting the moment we had to sit Noah down and explain why his Miss Honey didn't look like *the* Miss Honey. His little four-year-old mind just couldn't get around it. "I bought him the book for his birthday," I go on, dipping and nibbling a bit of marshmallow. "That just made things worse."

"How?"

"None of the characters drawn in the book looked like the characters in the movie."

"Oh, Jesus."

"Yes. It was stomped on and tossed in the recycling bin."

"Poor kid."

"He told all the kids Miss Honey was a fraud."

"The innocence," he muses. "How simple the world is when you're a kid. No adulting to do. No one to keep happy, no bills to pay, feelings to hurt, or grief and heartache to feel."

"Kids are not kids for long enough anymore."

"Here." Dec plucks a marshmallow off the top of my cup and pops it in my mouth so I don't have to release him to do it myself. "Good?"

"Very," I waffle around the lump, making him smile. "Have . . . ou . . . ied . . . ot . . . et?"

"Sorry, what?"

I chew and swallow, licking at my lips. "Have you tried the hot chocolate yet?" I can't get to mine until I've chomped my way through these marshmallows.

Dec dips and blows across the top, making the steam billow away from us, then he tentatively puts the cup to his lips and takes a sip. "Oh wow," he murmurs, his eyes widening at me. "That's insane."

I smile, that statement coming out of Dec's mouth sounding odd. "Good?"

He stops us walking and reaches for my cup, knocking off the marshmallows and sending them tumbling to the ground. "You don't need those. Get to the good stuff."

"It's *that* good?"

"Try it."

So I do, blowing too, before taking a sip, my eyes widening also. "Christ."

"Right?" Dec sups some more, looking up to the sky. "I think it's got a bar of melted Dairy Milk in it."

"Definitely," I agree. "It's so velvety."

"But not too sickly."

"I can't confirm that until I'm finished."

And we stand beside each other, working our way through our drinks, the heat in my belly warming me up a treat. But not as well as Dec's arm around me. I watch him tip his head back to get the very last drop from the bottom of the cup, his stubble-coated throat appearing from beneath his scarf. Unable to resist, and not wanting to, I turn into him and reach up on my tippy-toes, pushing my lips onto his neck, feeling him swallow under my mouth, his cup poised at his lips for a second before he pulls it away and peeks down at me, lowering and angling his head just right to kiss me, our chocolatey tongues swirling softly, our bodies pushing closer.

"Yum," he whispers, sucking my bottom lip into his mouth. When I smile, it pops free, and Dec inhales, taking my cup and tossing it in a nearby bin with his before tucking me under his arm and getting us walking again. "What's your least favourite colour?" he asks.

"Yellow."

"Figures."

"What do you mean?"

"Bet your favourite's black, isn't it?"

"Actually, yes. And I bet yours is grey."

He scrunches his nose and gets me in a headlock, mauling at my ear, and I laugh, easy, light, and . . . happy.

We pass a few pop-up stalls, all loaded with an array of Christmas gifts and decorations, none of which I'm interested in, but something catches my eye and I find myself steering us that way. I home in on a snow globe that's been placed on a raised stand, set apart from the endless other snow globes. This one's different from the colourful Christmas scenes in each and every other glass dome. This one has just a white feather inside it, nestled in snowflakes. "What is it?" Dec asks.

Trapped.

"Nothing." I back away from the stall, forcing a smile when Dec looks at me. He doesn't get a chance to push me. His phone rings, and he roots through his pocket and pulls it out, rejecting the call from *Office*. "Do you need to get that?" I ask.

"They'll text or email if it's urgent."

"Could be about your potential acquisition of TF Shipping," I say casually, watching my feet as I walk.

"I doubt it. Thomas Fryer is hardly prompt when it comes to replying in a timely manner."

I laugh. "I feel your pain. What if he's changed his mind?" I ask. "Off the back of you slashing your offer?"

"Then you get to keep the job you obviously hate."

I nod, breathing in my reality. "Can you believe he was scared to fire me?"

"Yes." Dec laughs, and I nudge him with my shoulder. He quietens down. "You're not the woman you want the world to see, Camryn," he says, hooking his arm around my neck and pulling me closer, pushing his mouth into the top of my head. "And I totally understand why you're like that."

"I don't want to be like that."

"I know that too," he whispers. "And it's one of the reasons why I love you so much."

I smile.

And we walk on. Quiet. Just . . . together.

Hours later, after passing endless Christmas markets, enjoying a few more hot drinks, and having an impromptu mini tour of some of the landmarks hard-core Londoners neglect to appreciate when they're immersed in the grandeur of the city daily, we find ourselves on King's Road. I've talked about Noah non-stop, his funny little traits, his loves, his hates, and I didn't break down once. My throat clogged up, my eyes stung, my heart squeezed, but I never fell apart. Dec listened. He asked me questions. He smiled with me, and he held me close to his side as we walked, squeezing me into him a little harder when I needed it and kissing my hair often. It's been a lovely day—a special day—and I couldn't have done any of it without him.

Dec stops us outside a store window, pulling me round to face it. I'm met by a mannequin in a muted gold mini shift dress, with a chic slash neckline. "You'd look amazing in that dress," he says.

"It's gold." I frown at the beautiful dress.

"Try it on."

"What? No."

He grabs my hand and pulls me into the store. "Yes."

"Dec, it's a gold bloody dress. My favourite colour's black, remember?" Gold is very nearly a shade of yellow, my least favourite colour.

"My girlfriend would like to try on the dress you have in the window."

I freeze, those words knocking all fight out of me. *His girlfriend.* It probably sounds a bit stupid for me to balk at that statement, since declarations of love have been tossed around, but still. It's shaken me. I'm his girlfriend. I'm his girlfriend whom he loves.

"Oh, it would look fantastic on her," the assistant gushes, coming out from behind the counter, all big, bouncy hair and lashes. "Your colouring, your legs."

"You can't see my legs," I murmur, looking down at my jeans.

"I can see your legs," she assures me, pulling one of the dresses off the rail and holding it up. "I'll pop it in the changing room."

She disappears, and I turn into Dec, finding him looking at me fondly. "Why are you looking at me like that?"

"Just imagining you in that dress."

"Do they have it in black?" I ask, semi-scowling.

"No." He takes my hand and pulls me toward the back of the store.

"You haven't asked."

"It doesn't matter. You're trying the gold."

"And where am I going to wear a gold dress, Dec?"

"You're going to wear it for me tonight when I take you out."

I stop, forcing Dec to a stop too, and he turns, his face its familiar impassive beauty that I love so much. "We're going out?"

"Yes," he answers, assertive, leaving no room for protesting. "And we'll keep walking and talking, drinking hot drinks. The only difference is, you'll be wearing a gold dress instead of wellington boots, and I'll have some clean clothes on instead of the clothes I wore yesterday. We might even stop for dinner somewhere. Have a drink. Maybe, who knows? It's all a bit up in the air at the moment, but I hope we'll finish off the day in my bed, for no other reason than I can't bear the thought of not cuddling you all night."

"You hope?" I parrot, my smile stretching across my face.

"More than I've ever hoped for anything."

"You love me. You just referred to me as your girlfriend, so I'd say me being in your bed tonight is a given."

"Go try on the dress," he says quietly, jerking his head toward the changing rooms. "And don't show me."

I slink off and look at the dress hanging on the hook as I strip out of my coat. "I'm buying the dress if I like it," I call.

"Shut up."

The dress was already paid for when I got to the counter, and one look at Dec told me I'd get nowhere if I argued. So I didn't. But I will be paying him back, and I haven't stopped thinking about how since we left the store with my beautiful gold dress. What could I possibly buy him? A man who I'm certain has everything. I'm still pondering this when we turn onto my street. I see a grey Defender parked outside my building, the engine running. Ron. "I'll pick you up in a couple hours, okay?"

"I thought we were walking?" I say with an arched, accusing eyebrow.

"You're going to need heels with that dress, Camryn. No walking for you."

"You tricked me."

He hooks an arm around my waist and hauls me in. "Will you be okay for a few hours on your own?"

Yes, I will. Because for the first time since I lost Noah, I've been able to remember the happy times. I've been able to remember him without feeling annihilated with devastation. "I'll be fine."

He must see the peace in my eyes, as much as I can feel it in my soul. "Okay."

"Thank you for the dress."

He smirks. "Don't be. It's totally for me." Slamming a firm kiss on my lips, he swallows me whole and leaves me breathless as he releases me, making me stand on my own two feet for what's pretty much the first time today. But it's okay. I can get through the next few hours until I'm back with him.

Dec reverses his steps.

"Thank you for today," I blurt urgently, forcing my hands to my sides to stop them reaching for him.

He smiles, and the sight is enough to make me burst into tears. He slips into the passenger seat. "Watch your step," he says, before he closes the door, looking out the window at me as Ron pulls away. I lift a hand, waving, revisiting every wonderful moment of the day. I never imagined today could be anything less than dreadful. And it wasn't. Because of him.

I don't come out of my daze until they disappear around a corner, and I inhale deeply, filling my lungs and expanding my chest. Alive.

I hurry up the pathway as fast as the ice will allow, stalling just shy of the door when I notice something odd. "Huh," I breathe, inspecting the crater in the snow where Mr. Percival's Christmas turkey's been camping out for days. "Well, I hope Maureen didn't munch her way through the tarpaulin," I mutter, hauling the door open and stepping inside. I blow my cheeks out and pull off my hat and gloves, going straight to Mr. Percival's door and knocking. I hear his walking frame bashing the floor when I push my ear up against the door.

"Is that you, Camryn?" he yells.

"Yes, it's me. Is the door open?"

"Yes, it's open."

"Can I come in?"

"Yes, you can bloody come in. Why would I tell you the door's open if I didn't want you to come in? Come in, come in, come in."

He's halfway down the small hallway to the door when I push my way inside, meaning he's practically at the door, given how small the hallway is. "I didn't want to assume. It's mostly wide open when you're home. And actually, Mr. Percival, you shouldn't leave your door open."

He looks me up and down before his gaze lands on the bag in my hand. "Been shopping?"

"Oh, this?" I put the bag behind my back, and I've no idea why. "It's just a dress."

"A party dress?"

"No, not a party dress. Just a dress."

"So you're not wearing it and going to a party?"

"No, I'm wearing it and going for dinner."

"Oooh, with the man?"

"You know his name, Mr. Percival."

"Show me the dress."

"What?"

"The dress. Let me see it." He gives me grabbing hands, and I roll my eyes, relenting to his demand, if only to get him off my back. I pull it out and watch as a grin that could be described as roguish washes over his old, wrinkly face.

"What?" I ask. "Why are you looking like that?"

"That's a party dress."

I stuff it back in the bag. "A party dress is only a party dress if it's worn to a party, and I'm not wearing this dress to a party, so it can't be a party dress. It's a, I don't know . . . a dinner dress."

He chuckles, clutching at his walking frame as he lifts and lowers it constantly, turning around, before heading back into his flat. "Don't tell me I don't know a party dress when I see one," he mutters. "Okay, it's a dinner dress."

I roll my eyes. "I came to check on the turkey."

"What's that, dear?" he yells.

"The turkey," I yell back, following him into the kitchen. "I was checking it's—" The turkey greets me, taking up most of Mr. Percival's table, the gnomes all pushed to the edge to make way for the giant bird, which has its guts in a bowl next to it. Jesus Christ, it looks like a bunch of gnomes have gone all cultish, sacrificed a bird, and are about to drink its blood. "Never mind," I murmur.

"So you're going on a dinner date." Mr. Percival takes a meat hammer and whacks the turkey, and I jump so bloody high I'm sure my head skims the ceiling.

"I suppose so." Is it a date?

Whack!

I jump again.

"You suppose so? Isn't that what it's called when a man takes a lady out for dinner?"

"I suppose so."

Whack!

I see it coming this time, and I still jump out of my skin. "Mr. Percival, why are you beating the shit out of your turkey?"

"Loosening the skin, dear."

"You can do that with your hand, just by slipping it up its—"

"Jacksy?"

I snort as Mr. Percival drops the meat mallet and hobbles over to his stove, where a pot's bubbling. "Try this," he orders, luring me closer when I catch a whiff of whatever's simmering.

"What is it?"

"Mulled wine, dear." He ladles some into a mug and puts it in my hand. "Old Navy recipe."

"That smells really strong."

"Put some hairs on your chest, dear."

"I don't want any hairs on my chest."

"Try it."

Again, I'm pacifying him, not only because I've grown fond of the old boy, but because he's got no one else to be his guinea pig and taste all these weird and wonderful Christmas delights. "Bottoms up," I murmur, taking a bigger swig than I should. And coughing. "Christ." I feel like an atomic bomb just went off in my head. I wince, hiss, my shoulders raising and tensing to get me through the swallow and then the horrific taste. I put a hand over my mouth, worried I'm about to bring it back up again. "What the hell is in that?"

"Brandy."

"That's gone straight to my head." I put the cup down, the aftertaste kicking in, exploding in my mouth and burning my belly.

"You've not finished it."

"I can't finish it, Mr. Percival. I'll be face first on the carpet."

He chuckles, moving over to a chair and pouring himself a straight brandy. "Peckish? I made hog in the bog."

I'm not going to even ask. "I need to get ready."

"Are you looking forward to it?"

"Today's a difficult day," I say, reluctant. "A sad day." I trip over my words, wondering why I'm even telling him this. "I guess I'm wondering if I should even be going."

He hums, nursing his glass as he regards me. "What else will you do? Cry?"

"Probably," I mumble, looking down at the bag in my hand. It was easy to be busy when I had Dec to keep me that way. Only ten minutes away from him, I'm questioning everything. Not him—never him, but . . . I don't know. I just feel like I shouldn't be smiling today.

"My dear Camryn, the cruellest stage of grief is coming to

terms with the fact that you're still alive and life is still happening when a huge part of you has died."

I inhale subtly, taken aback. "How did you know?"

"Loss is a picture painted all over that beautiful face of yours." He sips his drink, looking off somewhere, thoughtful momentarily before shaking himself back into the room. "We have two choices. Move forward or . . . well, the other doesn't bear speaking about."

"I've thought about it," I admit. "On the darkest days, I thought about it a lot."

"And what a tragedy it would be for the world to lose you. You're still here for a reason. You'll figure it out, and I have a feeling the man is helping you."

"Dec." I smile, small and with effort, and nod, as if accepting but not really sure if I can. "Thanks, Mr. Percival." I back out, leaving his door open, and go to my apartment to get myself ready. I stop at the cabinet by the window and pick up the picture of Noah. "Mummy's going out," I tell him, and then I say no more, as if I'm waiting for him to tell me that it's okay. That I can go out. That I can smile. That I can think about something other than the gut-wrenching agony his memory causes me every single day.

I wipe my eyes on a sniff, press my lips to the glass pane over his grinning face, and then put him back in the window to go get myself ready.

I'm not sure who the woman in the mirror is, in a gold dress, her dark hair loosely pinned up with perfect soft waves tumbling imperfectly. Her cheeks glow, her eyes are smoky, her lashes thick and long with mascara. I peek down my bare legs to the dainty cream suede stilettos that I found at the bottom of one of the endless boxes. No tights. Tights ruined the look, but it's sub-zero out there.

I put in some pearl droplet earrings as I go to the cupboard in the hallway and pull out my long cream coat, swinging it on.

And I'm ready.

An hour early.

I tie the belt of my coat and go to the fridge, considering a drink to settle my nerves. Just a little. I pull out the orange wine Mr. Percival gave me and check the label. "Maybe not," I murmur. Thirteen percent? No. I want a clear head for the rest of this day. I close the fridge and sit down at the table. Get back up. Pace through to the lounge.

After a few laps, I snag my phone and call an Uber. I can't sit around waiting; I'll talk myself out of this. I grab my purse, and leave, and as soon as outside comes into view past the glass door, I stop and look down at my cream suede shoes. They'll be ruined before I even make it to the curb. "Damn it." I hurry back to my apartment and get my wellington boots, removing my heels and slipping my feet into them. I catch a full-length reflection of myself in the door when I make it back there—a gold dress and wellington boots. "My God," I mumble, passing through and trudging down the path. Headlights glow at the end of the street, and my ride rounds the corner a second later as I tread the snowy ground to the curb, my toes already icy given the lack of socks.

"Camryn?" the driver asks when I open the back door.

"That's me." I settle in the seat and call Dec, but it rings off and goes to voicemail. I don't leave a message, deciding to wait for him to call me back instead.

I'm only five minutes from his place when he finally does.

"Don't tell me you're calling to cancel," he says before I've had a chance to even say hello. "I'll be devastated."

"I'm not calling to cancel. I was ready early and was hanging around so thought I'd head to your place to save you coming to pick me up."

"Or you missed me and couldn't wait to be back in my arms."

"And that," I admit, unabashed.

"What's your ETA?"

"Four minutes."

"See you in four minutes."

"Okay." Smiling, I hang up and mentally count down those four minutes until the driver pulls up. "Thank you." I hop out and take my time up the steps to Dec's house, then swap my wellies for my heels when I'm at the door, setting my boots to the side and unfasten the belt of my coat before I reach for the doorbell.

My finger doesn't make it to the button. The door swings open, and it's all I can do not to faint on the spot when I see him, his trousers half fastened, his shirt hanging open, his hair still damp from his shower. I drop my gaze down the entire length of his tall body. Bare feet.

"Look at you," he whispers, reaching for my hand and tugging me inside, slamming the door. He pushes my coat off my shoulders and inhales as he drinks in the dress. "Wow." Feeling awkward, I shift on the spot, my gaze dropping. But not for long. He slips a finger under my chin and lifts my face again, finding my eyes. "You're very beautiful," he says gently. "And I'll keep telling you that until you start believing it again." Sweeping one of the many loose strands off my face, he moves in and kisses me gently, and I close my eyes, absorbing his softness, breathing him into me. He doesn't advance the kiss—there's no tongues—but the impact is still so powerful and devastating.

He totally overwhelms me.

"I need to finish getting ready," he murmurs as he pulls away.

"What a travesty."

He grins. "Come." Pulling me along, he leads us into the kitchen and sits me on a stool, pouting down at my dress again. "Totally made for you."

I put both of my feet on the footrest and watch as he goes to the fridge, pulling out a bottle of wine. "Just a small one," I say, making him turn as he grabs two glasses from the glass cabinet that's dedicated solely to glasses of every variety. "I want to remember today." It's a first—for me to want to remember *any* day—and his small, understanding nod settles me more. Dec pours just an inch and brings it to me, perching on the stool next to me. I accept, struggling to keep my eyes to myself when his shirt's open like that, revealing a slither of his lovely chest. But then he takes a small sip, tilting his head back, and my eyes have something else to stare at. He's trimmed his scruff. "You're very handsome," I muse, reaching for his face and feeling. And he lets me, still and quiet while I smooth my palm down his cheek, until it reaches the corner of his mouth and he turns into it, keeping his eyes on me as he kisses my palm.

"I better finish getting ready or we might not make it out." He sets his glass down and stands, leaning into me so I'm forced to bend back on my stool. "Give me a sec," he breathes.

"Okay."

The moment he's gone, I take a breath and face the island, holding on to my glass as I take in his kitchen again. Spotless. Not a crumb littering the work surface, and no dirty glasses or plates in the sink. Even the dishcloth is folded neatly and draped over the huge nickel shower tap.

I hear movement behind me and turn to see Dec's back, his hands full. He puts his shoes and socks on the island, along with a belt, a jacket, and a blue tie that has delicate white polka dots on it. He starts fastening the buttons of his shirt, and I secretly sulk at the loss, pouting harder when he undoes his trousers to tuck it in. I peek up at him and find his eyes shining, hinting to an invisible grin. I scowl a little and take my first small sip as Dec perches on the stool again and pulls on a pair of fancy blue striped socks, lifting his trouser legs, revealing his shin, the dark hair thick. His feet slip into his brown brogues, and he stands and lifts his chin, fastening the top button.

Eyes on me.

I'm coming over all unnecessary, as if he could be undressing, when in fact he's doing the exact opposite. I place my glass down, tilting my head when he flips his collar up and slides his tie around his neck. Long, dexterous fingers fix the knot expertly and with supreme precision. And the whole time he's slowly, carefully dressing, he's watching me. "I know what you're doing," I say, standing and moving into his chest, getting my face close to his as I reach for his collar and pull it down, making Dec's hands retreat. His palms rest on my waist.

"What am I doing?"

"Trying to tempt me."

"Just keeping you busy."

I smile, wriggling the knot of his tie. "And I love you for it."

"Yeah?" He hunkers down, moving his palms to my bum and pulling me in, nuzzling my face with his.

"Yeah," I breathe, impatient for the end of today when I can crawl into his bed and let him hug me into tomorrow. "You'll never know how grateful I am for you."

"We've got a long time for you to show me."

I nod, pushing my face into his neck and taking a much-needed hug right now. "You smell so good." Clean, manly.

"I need some cologne." Turning his face into me, he kisses my neck and gently pries me away. "Be back in a moment." After one more sip of his wine, he leaves the kitchen, and I slowly work my way through the small amount of wine I've allowed myself.

When I'm finished, I take my glass to the sink and rinse it, and just as I'm setting it on the drainer, a sound from the hallway pulls my attention up. The front door closing? "Dec?" someone yells. A woman. "Dec, it's me."

I stand up straight, my stomach doing a small flip, as the sound of heels hit the wood in the hallway, getting louder and louder.

"Dec, are you here?"

Who the hell is that?

A woman breezes into the kitchen, a beautiful woman, a pair of keys jangling in her hand, an oxblood Mulberry in the crook of her arm. She's pristine, in a power suit and a black ankle-length coat, her lips cherry red, her blond bob thick but razor sharp. *Christ.*

She clocks me by the sink and skids to a stop, looking me up and down. I must look like a deer caught in the headlights. "Oh, hi," she murmurs.

"Hi." What the hell should I do? I have no idea, but instinct has me going to her and holding out my hand. "Camryn."

She looks down at my hand briefly, leaving me hanging, before her lips slightly stretch. It throws me. "Who else would you be?" she asks, leaving my hand where it is. "I'm April. Dec's sister."

Oh my God. My body shrinks with the held air leaving me. Relief. I didn't want to think for a moment this woman could be—

Who? Another woman? His estranged wife? I shake my head to myself, and I'm suddenly hauled into April's arms, being hugged tightly. "He doesn't shut up about you," she says, making my eyes widen more.

"He doesn't?"

She releases me and holds me at arm's length. "I'm so fucking excited for you both."

The oddest feeling comes over me. Shyness? I'm struggling to put my finger on it. "Thank you," I say, at a loss. "He's taking me out for dinner."

"Yes, I know. He mentioned it." She frowns. "But he was picking you up."

"I was ready early so thought I'd come here."

She motions down my front. "You look stunning. I love this dress."

Do I tell her Dec bought it? Shifting uncomfortably, finding the compliments all a bit much, I move back to the stool and lower but quickly stand again. "Thank you. Do you want me to get Dec?" What the hell am I saying? "I mean, you probably know your way around here better than I do."

"It's okay." She goes to one of the cupboards on the far side of the kitchen, her back to me, and starts rooting through, proving me right. "I just needed to grab—"

"April?"

Her head whips up when Dec walks in, and I get an immediate hit of his cologne. Dizzying. "Oh, hey," she says, almost sheepish.

Dec checks me by the stool, his face a picture of concern. I shrug. "I see you've met my sister."

I nod, as April gives Dec a guilty look. "I didn't mean to disturb you. I'm sorry, I just . . ." She goes back to the cupboard and pulls something out, slipping it into her bag as she faces the room again. "I forgot something when I was here earlier."

"And now you're leaving, right?" he asks, his voice full of warning.

"Right." She flashes me a toothy smile. "I'm sorry for gate-crashing."

"It's totally fine," I say. "I don't know why he's being so grumpy."

"We must have dinner soon," April says.

"I'd love that."

"Time to go," Dec says, collecting his sister and guiding her out. "You must be busy yourself," he adds.

"Yes, yes, busy, busy, busy." She shrugs him off and gives him a pointed look. "Blaine's in the car. Stop being a grouch." Then she flashes me another one of those wide smiles. "It was so lovely to meet you, Camryn."

The door closes in the distance again, and every set of eyes, including mine, moves to the kitchen doorway as footsteps head this way. "Hello?" a man calls. "April?" A suited man appears, tall and unconventionally handsome.

With a child that's bundled up in a bright blue coat with matching bobble hat and scarf sitting on his forearm. He's four years old. I don't even need to ask. He's almost the exact same size Noah was. As cute too.

My stomach twists.

"Oh, hi," the guy says when he sees me. "You must be . . . Camryn?"

I realise I'm staring at their child and rip my eyes away. I can't fall apart every time I see a child around Noah's age. I quickly go to him, holding out my hand. "Yes, Camryn."

He gives my hand a firm shake. "And what's your name?" I ask the little boy, forcing my smile.

"Albi!" he declares proudly.

Oh my heart. "That's a real cute name."

"My daddy chose it. Like his grandpa and my great grandpa."

"Oh, so cool!" I laugh, smiling and backing off before I grab him and squeeze him half to death with the force of my cuddle. "He's the cutest." I take the glass on the counter, Dec's glass, and drink his wine, feeling a flutter of panic. And judging by Dec's pained face, he knows.

"I'm four!"

"I knew that."

"How?" His little forehead furrows. "I didn't tell you."

"I just knew," I say, feeling Dec's worried gaze set on me.

Albi wriggles in Blaine's hold, obviously trying to get down, but Blaine keeps hold of him, repositioning him higher on his forearm.

Dec looks so uncomfortable, and I feel terrible for that. I shake my head mildly at him, trying to silently tell him it's okay, but his face. It tells me it's not. "Dec never mentioned you have kids," I go on.

April's gaze darts to her brother's. As does Blaine's.

And a horrible icy chill glides down my spine, confirming it.

"They don't," Dec says quietly. "He's—"

"Daddy!" Albi sings, giving Dec grabby hands. "Aunty April forgot my drink bottle!"

I gasp quietly. *Daddy?*

"Mine," Dec murmurs. "He's mine."

For a moment, I'm completely lost. "Yours?" I ask over a little laugh.

"Okay, little fella." Dec goes to Blaine and takes Albi, and then all eyes are on me as I stand before my audience like a fucking clueless idiot, my mind empty.

"He can't be yours." I look at Albi again and realise what I've just said is categorically incorrect. He's the absolute spitting image of Dec. "Oh my God." It's said on a breath as I step back away from them. "You would have told me," I murmur. "If you had a little boy, you would have told me." He's told me he loves me. He's told me I'm his girlfriend.

"I didn't know how," Dec murmurs, not coming closer. Keeping a safe distance.

I look at April and Blaine, as I struggle to breathe. I feel like a freakshow standing here. Being judged. Being pitied.

He has a little boy.

He has a four-year-old little boy.

And I can't stop staring at him.

"Daddy." Albi's little hands land on Dec's cheeks, forcing him to look at him. "Who is that lady?"

Dec smiles, and it's so uncomfortable, as he takes both of Albi's little hands in one of his and pulls them away from his face. "She's a special friend."

"Like Petal's my special friend?"

"Do you love Petal?"

"Yes."

"Then she's like Petal," Dec says, flicking cautious eyes my way. Then he visibly gathers himself and puts Albi on his tiny feet. "Why don't you go find me my cufflinks?"

"But you're already wearing cufflinks, Daddy," Albi says, shoving up the sleeve of Dec's jacket to reveal one.

"Ah, but I put on the wrong ones."

Albi bends, getting up close and personal with the cufflink. "These are your important ones."

"And I meant to put on my *really* important ones. Do you think you could help Daddy out and go fetch them for me?"

"Yes!" He zooms off, excited, and the moment the little bundle of energy has gone, the kitchen is even heavier, all attention on my spaced-out form.

I look between them all, adrenaline making me shake violently under their scrutinizing, sympathetic gazes. "I have to go," I blurt, feeling a full-blown meltdown on the horizon. I absolutely can't control it, and I certainly don't want Dec or his sister and her husband to see it.

"Camryn," Dec breathes urgently as I grab my purse and hurry past them.

"It was nice to meet you," I say to April and Blaine over my shoulder, feeling the walls closing in on me.

"Camryn, wait."

Why didn't he tell me? I swing the door open and rush out in a haze of total fucking confusion. I don't know how I get down the steps without slipping and breaking my neck, but I make it to the street, and I don't recall one step of the way. I start to walk aimlessly. No coat. In my cream heels. The cold hits me like a boulder, and I'm suddenly shaking like a leaf for different reasons—chilled to my bones—my feet sopping wet and like blocks of ice within just a few strides.

"Camryn!"

I turn around, but it's slow and heavy, the temperature hampering me. I can't hold on to my emotions anymore, and the tears pour out of me unstoppably. "You should have told me," I murmur, making Dec skid to an abrupt stop a few paces away. "You should have fucking told me, Dec."

He swallows, his handsome face crestfallen. "Camryn, please."

"Just leave me alone." I turn and walk away, the pain I've managed to handle all day swooping in and making up for it.

Agony.

Misery. My soaked, freezing feet give up at the end of the road, and I flag down a cab, struggling to open the door, my numb fingers failing me. "Shit." I somehow manage to get in and somehow manage to give the driver my address through my chattering teeth.

"Let me crank up the heating for you," the driver says, as we pass Dec standing on the street, his body turning as the cab drives past, following me with his eyes. I can't look at him. My chest constricts. My head pounds. My throat is tight.

My momentary, temporary peace shattered spectacularly.

The drive is long and lonely. I bunch my fists, grit my teeth, and press my palms into my temples. Emotions seesaw inside, up and down, anger, sadness, stupidity.

But out in front?

Pain.

Am I hurting because I feel betrayed? Because I lost my little boy? Because what today is, and now what it's become? All of the above?

How could he hide this from me? How can he declare his love and accept mine when he knows I don't even know who he is?

Because you're broken.

Because he was scared to break you even more.

I hit the leather seat by my thigh as the driver pulls up outside my building, and I jump out and struggle to the door, my hands still numb, every fragment of me stinging from the bite of the chill.

When I get into my apartment, I kick off my sodden heels, unzip my dress, and let it drop to the floor, leaving my clothes in a trail to my kitchen. I open the fridge and pull out the orange wine, wandering through to my bathroom, setting it on the sink and turning the shower on, stepping under the spray, the water burning against my frozen skin.

My legs refuse to keep me upright anymore, and I fold to the tile floor.

My vision blurring and blending between two little boys.

December 20th

I haven't slept. Drifted off a few times here and there, but not for long. I squeeze my eyes closed harder and pull the covers over my head, my body curling into itself more.

Hide.

The duvet feels rough against my naked skin, the pillow like a brick under my head. I can smell him embedded into the fabric, and yesterday starts to replay in my mind, every moment throughout the day until I'm back in Dec's house and realisation hits me.

He's mine.

I swallow down my emotion and throw the duvet back, dragging myself to the edge of the bed and pulling my phone off charge. Five missed calls. Text messages I don't want to read.

Ask yourself why you're angry.

I need a coffee before I even think about visiting that question. I get up on a sigh and go to my kitchen, going through the motions, spooning instant coffee into a mug, stirring as I pour the hot water in. I take myself to the table with my hands wrapped around the hot mug, still feeling like I need to thaw out from last night.

A frown crawls onto my forehead as I look down my seated form. Naked. I feel like I'm in a whole new dimension of dazed.

Stumbling along, unable to control my body or find stability, while also trying to wrap my head around what I'm dealing with and how the fuck it could have happened to me. I want to scream at the injustice, yell angrily at the top of my lungs, hit something, upend things, destroy everything, all with the hope that by unleashing the rage, the unbearable pressure inside might release. And yet I know it won't. And I don't have the energy to lash out.

And now Dec's landed this bombshell on me? Now, in addition to everything, I'm wondering how he could have neglected to tell me something so monumentally important. How could he declare love and not mention Albi? But most maddening, I don't know if it's his silent lie that hurts most, or the fact that this whole time when I didn't think he could possibly know how I feel, he could. Because he has a son. He knows the kind of love I feel.

And his wife has gone. But more significantly, Albi's mother has gone.

You're fucked-up, Camryn. Why ever would he want to share his child with you?

Steam curls up from the surface of my coffee, twisting and turning then disappearing. I lift the cup and blow across the lip, making the vapor's trail flicker chaotically. It's apt. It doesn't know what direction it should be going in.

It settles on disappearing. I've wanted to disappear so many times. Give up, stop fighting, because I still haven't figured out what I'm fighting for if I don't have my boy. I can't remember who I was before I was his mum.

I glance at the clock on the oven. Seven fifteen. I could make it to work on time if I hurry, but I'm not needed there either. I probably won't have a job for long, anyway, because Dec withheld that information as well. What other bombs is he going to drop? And will the next one wreck me like every other silent lie?

"She's a special friend."

"Like Petal's my special friend?"

"Do you love Petal?"

"Yes."

"Then she's like Petal."

The innocence of love in a child. How pure and easy it is. So different from the love between two adults, which can be so complicated and ugly. And yet the same as the love an adult can only feel for their child. Irrevocable.

My love for Dec felt easy. It even felt pure. Now, it just feels like an irreversible mess. I've spent three years avoiding small children, even my niece and nephew. It may have been extreme, it may have been unreasonable, but it was the only way for me. It was too triggering, and I was already running a daily gauntlet of triggers.

Which is why he didn't tell you.

I lift the mug to my mouth with shaky hands and sip my coffee, immune to the scorching hot liquid as I struggle to swallow it down past the golf ball in my throat, my eyes welling.

"Camryn?"

My mug meets the table with a thud, my gaze moving to the doorway. Dec's there, looking like he's just rolled out of bed and thrown on some sweatpants and a hoodie, his hair a dishevelled mess.

And yet he's still the most beautiful example of a man I've ever seen.

My lip wobbles, my heart now yelling at me, refusing to let me shut it down or build an impenetrable wall around it. Begging me to let him in. Telling me there's a way. I shake my head and drop my eyes, my hands going between my thighs, the tears trailing my cheeks before they fall and splash on the table.

Dec's pulling my chair around and kneeling in front of my naked body in a heartbeat, holding my face in his warm palms. But I can't look at him, tears now splashing my naked thighs, my shoulders jerking from the force of my sobs. He curses under his breath and pulls my thighs apart, moving closer and squeezing me into his chest, hushing me quietly. The emotion pours out of my slumped form into the material of his hoodie, unstoppable, hard and never ending, until my body aches, my face is sore, and my eyes are scratchy. A mess. I can't catch my breath, can't breathe, and in utter desperation, I clutch the sleeves of his top, hanging on for dear life.

"Come," he says gently, lifting me out of the chair and carrying me across his arms to my bedroom. I curl into him, willing the tears to stop, as he walks up the bed on his knees, still holding me, and sits up against the headboard, covering us with the duvet. He's cradling me to his body, patient and quiet as I cry it all out, clinging to him.

Scared to let go.

Even more afraid to hold on.

"I love you, Camryn," he whispers, almost with regret. "I'll fight for this. I can't let you go." And that just makes me cry harder because, deep down, I don't want him to let me go. And yet I don't know if I can do this.

I snivel, rubbing my face into his chest, terrified to look at him. He gives me no choice when he tilts my face up to his. "Letting you leave last night was the hardest thing I've ever done. Knowing I was the cause of your sadness killed me. Tell me I've not fucked everything up," he begs. "Tell me you still love me."

The ability to talk is beyond me, as no words can make it past my throat to be heard. So I sink my face into his neck and hold on that little bit tighter. He's wrong. He's not the cause of my sadness. The cause, the root cause, is nothing to do with Dec. I still feel somewhat betrayed, but also not. Dominic and even my brother? They both betrayed me. But Dec? I can't hold him to the same card. Yes, he's hidden things from me, but not for his own benefit. I saw the grief in his sister's eyes. It wasn't pity for me. It was pity for her brother. He hid his son to save me more pain. He's suffering the consequences of my grief.

He's saved my life.

And I walked out on him. I ran. I made him feel like I didn't love him.

I bury myself closer to him, unable to get my emotions under control, and we stay where we are, huddled on my bed for an age, Dec quiet, me waiting for my body to stop shaking with the force of my sobs until I'm able to speak. "I still love you," I eventually murmur, hearing his heart beat harder under my ear. "I can't stop that."

He sighs, in relief, I think, and negotiates me to my back, spreading himself the length of me, now his face in my neck. My hands naturally slip under his hoodie to his naked back and start softly tracing his spine. "I wanted to tell you about Albi," he says, the words hot across the skin of my neck. "Not at first, but as soon as I realised I was growing feelings for you, that maybe I could see a future with you, I wanted to tell you about him. But then you shared your loss, Camryn, and I just couldn't find the words that I knew would send what we have into fucking bedlam. I hated that my son would be the cause for such heartache in the woman I love."

I close my eyes, another wave of wretchedness coming over me. "I hate that too," I whisper. There are so many questions I want to ask, so much I need to know. Not only from Dec, but from myself. Can I handle this? If I try, if I truly want him, can I handle it? "You're a single dad?" I ask.

"She walked out when Albi was four weeks old," he says quietly, pulling out and sitting up, resting his arse on his heels and pulling me up to sit too. He gently wipes my eyes. "We were seeing each other. It was casual. Nothing serious. Then one day she showed up at my office and told me she was pregnant." He flinches, as if remembering that moment. "All I could think about was my father. How absent he was. How promiscuous. Undevoted, undedicated. How he fucked me up. I didn't want to be that man. I didn't want to fuck my own son up by not being around." He clears his throat and brushes some wet hair off my cheek. "So I did what I thought was the right thing."

"Married her."

He hums, his lips pressed together. "I wanted Albi to have a present dad, a stable family unit and, stupidly maybe, I thought that meant marrying her. She didn't do pregnancy well. She did motherhood even worse. When Albi was four weeks old, I got a call from my bank manager saying she was trying to clear out my personal bank account."

I blink at him.

"I told him to let her take it."

"All your money?"

He laughs under his breath. "No, not all of it." He shrugs. "Enough to start someone a new life, though. My sister called me while I was on the phone to my bank manager. April was at my house, and Albi was screaming in his crib."

"She left him all alone?"

"April would stop in most days. I know she was checking up on them, but she spun it differently, played on the doting aunty card. They tolerated each other. Chelsea and April."

"Your sister didn't like her?"

He laughs, and it's not in humour. "That's putting it mildly. The feeling was mutual. April saw a gold-digging, self-important, selfish woman, and Chelsea knew April had figured her out."

"Had you? Figured her out?"

"I had no plans to build a life and a family with her. Not with any woman. She wanted to be kept. Lunches, shopping, going on exotic holidays. Albi got in the way of that. She demanded a nanny, I refused. Then she left."

I stare at him, dumbfounded. I can't believe what I'm hearing. "And you've not heard from her since?"

"Not a peep."

My mind can't compute such heartlessness. How any mother could abandon their child. "And you've done it all yourself since."

He shrugs, like it's nothing. And it's absolutely everything. "I was never supposed to be a father, Camryn. Having kids never crossed my mind. But Albi happened, and here I am. Fucking *loving* being his dad." My heart melts. "April helps out a lot. I have Lynette, who takes care of the house, and Ron who drives us to school and then me to the office each day. I do my best."

Dec suddenly isn't just a beautiful man whom I've fallen deeply in love with. He's a beautiful human. A beautiful *father*. "I think you're amazing," I whisper, reaching for his face, raising to my knees and crawling onto his lap. Cuddling him. Like he's cuddled me when I've needed it. I hate that he's been forced into silence. I hate that I'm the reason.

"And so are you, Camryn. For surviving. For going on, no matter how you dealt with it."

I don't know about that. I became a wretched, cold, hateful bitch.

Until I met Dec.

And, more significantly, the transition happened before I knew about Albi.

"Tell me what I need to do to make this work," he says, grabbing my hair and pulling my head away, looking at me with imploring eyes. "How do I make this okay?"

"No more silent lies," I whisper.

"No more, I promise." He takes my hand and pushes it into his chest, and I swallow, bracing to say the words I need to say but am scared to admit. The words that I'm trying to bury but can't.

"I'm scared I'll fall in love with him, Dec." My voice is broken. "And then it's not just you I lose. What if this, *us*, all falls apart?"

He shakes his head. "It won't."

"You don't—"

"It won't," he reiterates sternly. "I'd never invite a woman into my son's life if I wasn't one hundred percent certain she was going to stay."

"Even me?" I question. "After everything, how can you be so sure?"

"How can you not be, Camryn?" he asks, making me inhale subtly. "Because if you feel even a fraction of the love for me that I feel for you, you must love me a fucking lot."

"I'm a wreck," I whisper, and he smiles.

"You're the most stunning, deep, spirited woman I've ever met. And now it's time for you to stop pretending to be anything other than that."

A broken sob escapes, and Dec takes me down to my back and

kisses it away, reminding me just how he makes everything better. And I trust that he can. Wholeheartedly. "He's so sweet, Dec, and I'm sorry for reacting like I did," I say around his mouth, my hands in a frenzy, feeling him everywhere I can. "I wasn't rejecting him. I was just so shocked. I'm sorry I ran out." *Sorry I couldn't say the words I was feeling.*

"Shut up." He rolls us into the middle of the bed, swirls his tongue a few more times, groans, and rolls us back, crowding me, caging me in, kissing the living daylights out of me. I don't tell them to, but my hands go to the waistband of his sweatpants and start shoving them down his thighs with his boxers, spiking another deep rumble at the back of his throat, as he pushes himself up to his knees and yanks his hoodie over his head, casting it aside and dropping back to his fists, kicking his legs as I wrestle the material down them.

"Are you sure?" he asks quietly, panting down at me, passion and need swirling in his eyes.

Am I sure?

I reach for his neck and pull his mouth onto mine, rolling my hips when he levels up and slides into me easily and slowly, our kiss pausing for a few moments as we both suck in air. He gives it a few moments, the pressure inside me fierce, before he withdraws and starts driving in and out slowly, circling his tongue again.

Eyes open.

It's a beautiful moment full of acceptance and love.

And my body finally thaws.

We both come quietly, both of us shaking wildly as our kiss loses its momentum, and Dec collapses onto me, breathing heavily in my ear. Spent and settled, we lie in a naked tangle of limbs, dozing, our breathing finally back to normal, his fingertips stroking my hipbone. "You said you couldn't have kids," I murmur into his neck.

"I had a vasectomy."

"Extreme," I murmur.

"Maybe. You said you couldn't either."

"I had some women's problems after Noah was born. There was a five percent chance treatment would work and I could go on and have more children." I look up at him. "I work with numbers. I know good odds when I hear them. It wasn't worth the pain."

He shakes his head, trying not to smile at my lame attempt to lighten the situation. "So . . ."

"I had Noah, he was enough, so I had a hysterectomy." I lay my head back down and narrow my eyes. "I often wonder if I'd have another if I could. And I always reach the same conclusion."

"Which is what?"

"No," I whisper. "Because I couldn't bear to lose again."

Dec's stroking fingers falter for a little too long for me not to notice. My words bring us back round to loss. Will that fear ever be gone? "We'll take this slow," he says quietly, and I nod into him.

"What if he doesn't like me?"

"Shut up," he whispers. "Some women in this world don't have a maternal bone in their body. You're not one of them, Camryn."

"I can't be his mother," I whisper. He doesn't expect that, does he? The poor woman who lost a child, grabbing an opportunity to push her instincts onto a kid that isn't her own.

"Camryn?"

"What?"

"I said, shut up."

"Where is he now?"

"April's getting him ready and taking him to school." Dec pushes his lips into my head and starts unravelling our legs. "My phone." He scrambles to the edge, the vibrating phone breaking through the rustle of the sheets. As Dec roots through the pocket of his sweatpants, I think of all the times we weren't together over the past few weeks. The calls he took quietly. The calls he missed. The fact he didn't come to see me later on his birthday. He was taking care of his boy. I can't ask myself how I didn't know, because who would have? There were no signs whatsoever. No kids' stuff around his house, no smears on his expensive suits, no crumbs in his car.

"How did you get into my flat?" I ask, sitting up in the bed, the duvet puddled around my naked body.

He unbends, his phone in one hand, my keys in the other. "You left them in the door." Disapproving eyebrows are raised as he chucks them onto the bed, and I shrink. "April?" he says, wandering over to the window, looking out at the view of the street. I rest back against the headboard and check the time. Eight thirty. I need to call the office. My lips twist in contemplation as I find Dec by the window again. Naked. He works. Is a single dad. Where the hell does he find the time to work out, because that body can't naturally be that firm? "Put him on the phone," he says, wedging a hand into the window frame, making his back muscles undulate. I grab my phone to distract myself, feeling all kinds of wrong admiring his body while he's on the phone to his son. I start texting Thomas to let him know I'm feeling no better.

"Hey, little fella," Dec says, turning and coming back to the bed, sitting on the edge. "We talked about this, remember?" He squints, listening hard. "You loved it yesterday. Lynette spent weeks making it, and you look so cool." He blinks. Frowns. Sighs. "Put Aunty April back on." He drops to his back and stares at the ceiling. "On a scale of one to full-blown meltdown, where are we?" His palm meets his forehead. "Okay, I'm on my way." Hanging up, he drops his head to the side. "I've got to go."

"Is everything okay?"

Getting up, Dec pulls on his sweatpants and feeds his arms through the sleeves of his hoodie, stretching the neck to get it over his head. "It's the nativity play today at school. He's decided he's not going to be in it." He gives me a pained look. "I'm sorry."

"Please, don't apologise." I wave him off, but, unreasonably, feel the loss already.

Dec comes to me, bending over the bed as he pulls his hoodie down his torso. "I'll call you, okay?"

I want to say, *Will you? Please do. Don't forget about me.* But that would be inappropriate. Of course his son comes first. "Okay."

I cup his face with both hands and kiss him square on the lips. "I hope you figure it out."

He blows out his cheeks. "I'm not hopeful. He's got his granddad's stubborn streak, and it's definitely nature not nurture, because he never fucking sees him." I press my lips together, not sure if it's fitting to laugh. "I love you," he says, our eyes level.

"I love you too."

Pushing off the bed, he strides to the door but stops on the threshold. It's a few long seconds before he turns around. "Why don't you come?" he asks and then bites down on his lip.

I still on the bed, thrown. "What?" I murmur, as if I didn't hear him. "Oh, I'm not sure . . ." I fade off. That it's a good idea? "I think —" My eyes drop to the mattress and dart.

"No, fuck, that was a stupid idea." Dec shakes his head. "Forget I said anything." Forcing a smile, he backs out, and I feel so fucking awful, like I've rejected him but, even worse, rejected the most precious thing in his world.

Again.

Dec disappears, and I sigh, wanting to kick my own arse around the bedroom.

Re-reading my message to Thomas, I click send and then falter from throwing my phone aside in frustration with myself when I see Dec's messages from last night. I click them open. And my heart slows with every word I read on all of the five messages.

I'm sorry. I'm so fucking sorry.

I love you. I don't know if it means anything anymore, but I love you.

Please, tell me we can figure this out. I'll do anything you need me to do.

I love you.

I need to come to you, Camryn, but I'm terrified you'll reject me.

I stare at his final message, sent at midnight. He was scared, and yet he came anyway.

I jump out of bed and snatch my robe off the chair, pulling it on as I run to the door, throwing it open. I hurry down the corridor and burst out of the building, my bare feet sinking into the slushy snow. "Fuck," I hiss, quickly stepping back inside. I see Dec up the road getting into the driver's side of a Defender, this one black. "Dec!"

He looks up, the door open, and frowns. "What are you doing?" He slams the door and paces back to the building. "Camryn?"

"Can I come?" I ask, awkward, treading from foot to foot.

A smile slowly stretches across his face. It's fucking stunning, and I made it happen. "Hurry up," he orders softly, coming to me. "I've got a prawn to appease."

"Huh?"

"Just go get dressed." He takes my shoulders and pushes me into the building. "I'll wait in the car."

I rush back to my flat, dry my feet, and throw on my leggings, cropped quarter-zip and trainers, and swing my wool trench coat on as I jog back out, pulling a hairband off my wrist and tying my hair up. Dec's on the phone again when I get in the car, his head in his hands as April talks over the car speakers. "It's fine, I've pushed back my nine thirty," she says.

"I'm sorry." Dec starts the car. "I don't know what's got into him."

"Maybe you," she says gently. Her tone isn't accusing. It's just . . . worried. "He knows you're not right."

I freeze in my seat, mortified. Dec's not right because of me. I'm distracting Albi's dad from being his dad. Kids are like sponges, I know that. Have experienced that. They soak it all up without you even noticing. Until you do. And then, dumb parent, you ask yourself what's wrong with them. Dominic and I always hid our disagreements from Noah, but we couldn't hide our energy. If I wasn't right, he wasn't right.

Dec's gaze is on me, I just know it, and I peek out the corner of my eye confirms it.

"I'm sorry," I mouth, taking the handle of the door I've just closed and opening it. "I should stay here."

Dec reaches across and pulls it closed again. "I'm on my way." He cuts the call and pulls out. "Put your seatbelt on," he orders, focused on the road. I reach back and grab it, seeing a kid's car seat in the back. As I clip my seatbelt in, I look down in the footwell, finding an empty snack bag that once packaged apples. And when I crane my neck around, I see the telltale signs of sticky fingerprints on the leather seats and the windows. "What?" Dec asks.

"Nothing." I return my body forward and rest my eyes on his profile as he drives, my stomach swirling madly. Nerves. I'd never have pinned the title *dad* on Dec, but now it seems to be slapped all over him. "I didn't get to see Noah in the nativity play," I say out of the blue, transported back to that week in the run up to Christmas when my life fell apart. "He was the innkeeper. Or supposed to be."

His hand comes across and lays palm up on my thigh. I put mine in his and watch as his fingers wrap around. "Tell me more," he says, keeping his eyes on the road.

I laugh a little under my breath, closing my eyes and resting my head back. "I tore up a stripy bedsheet and made a cloak out of it. A pillowcase for a floppy hat." I smile, seeing my boy in my mind's eye as I wrapped rope around his head to keep the flimsy scrap of material in place. "My mum sawed over a foot off the bottom of my granddad's old walking stick for him, and we made some sandals out of an old pair of flip-flops and a crappy, old, fake leather belt." I close my eyes and watch Noah stomp across the kitchen, the flip-flops flipping and flopping hard. "Poor kid couldn't walk in them. We glossed over that. He was of an age where they're immune to feeling silly. I was well aware that wouldn't last for much longer." I open my eyes and see Dec nodding mildly. Agreeing. "He had six words to say. *There's no room at the inn.* And four actions. Open the door, step out, say his lines, step back in, close the door. It took six weeks practicing every night."

"That's some dedication," Dec muses quietly.

"It wasn't the lines that were the problem." I let my head drop to the side. "It was stepping out and in again in the homemade sandals." He smiles at the road, pulling a small one from me. "You're not just a mum or a dad when you have a child," I go on. "You're a chef, a therapist, a counsellor, a party entertainer, a teacher, a personal assistant, a taxi driver, a costume designer, a . . . protector."

Dec takes my hand and lifts it to his mouth, kissing my knuckles. "Don't say it," he orders gently.

I swallow down the words, not allowing them to fall out. It doesn't stop them screaming in my head though.

I failed.

"You missed pacifier off your list," he murmurs, keeping our hands in his lap.

"Yeah," I muse, looking out of the window at the white world rolling by.

Slowing to a stop, Dec turns the engine off and the heavy silence remains between us, as it has on most of the drive, both of us quietly contemplating the enormity of what's about to happen. He gets out and is opening my door before my brain's had a chance to filter the instruction to my hand to let myself out. Dec positions me opposite him as he pushes the door closed before laying his palms on my shoulders and hunkering down to catch my gaze.

"We've got this," he whispers, moving one hand to my cheek. I nod, and he nods sharply in return, clasping my hand tightly, telling me to watch my step as we navigate the snow and icy patches.

April swings the door open before we make it there, and I definitely catch a blink of surprise past her stress when she sees me. I want to spill my apologies but hold back. "He's in his den," she says, opening up the way.

Dec takes my hand to his mouth and kisses the back before releasing me and wandering off to the right, opening a door and disappearing inside. A playroom.

"I could do with a coffee," April says. "Join me?" She motions to the kitchen, and I nod, following her, reloading my apologies. She goes to the coffee machine and pushes a button to turn it on while I settle on a stool. She looks as pristine as she did yesterday.

I glimpse down at my bedraggled form, then feel at my hair that was left to dry naturally, meaning it's double the size. "Excuse the state of me," I say, shrugging off my coat and letting it puddle the stool I'm on.

"Oh stop. I was up at five thirty to make sure I was showered and dressed, ready to get Albi up so I could get him to school and me to work on time." She turns a smile my way as she puts two mugs under the double pipe on the built-in coffee machine. "Waste of time that was."

"You stayed here last night?" I ask.

She nods. "I have my own room. Well, *we* have our own room. Blaine and me. We live in Watford, so it's sometimes easier to stay here if I have a meeting in the city or we're looking after Albi. Last night we were going to stay at home with him because Blaine's parents were over for dinner, and it's been a while since they've seen Albi."

But April ended up staying here last night after I met the child I didn't know Dec had and left before I spiralled into a meltdown. Did she stay to make sure Dec was okay? Albi too, because his daddy was distracted? *I need to come to you, Camryn, but I'm terrified you'll reject me.* He didn't come. Not last night, but he did this morning. It took him all night to find the courage. I wince the sharp stab of pain away, just knowing I made him feel like that. Unsure.

"What do you do?" I ask.

"I'm an editor for a women's magazine. Blaine's in trading."

"I remember those days," I say without thinking, prompting

April to look over her shoulder. "Getting up at the crack of dawn to get ready before the whirlwind started."

She seems to deflate before my eyes. "I'm sorry, I just have to hug you." She drops what she's doing and rounds the island to me, pulling me up from my stool and cuddling the shit out of me. I'm at her mercy . . . and totally fine with that. "Camryn, I—"

"Don't, honestly. I'm just so sorry for how I reacted last night."

She pulls out of our hug, her shoulders dropping. "You don't owe anyone an apology." She breathes in deeply and lets it out loudly. "When Dec came to me and said he'd met someone, I was totally thrown. Dec doesn't meet women. He doesn't go anywhere to meet them, so I knew it must have been something. I was thrilled." She breaks away and collects the mugs, bringing one to me, settling on the next stool with hers. "Then he told me about his dilemma." She winces, shaking her head. "Dilemma's the wrong word. I don't even know what the right word is."

"Mess?" I ask lightly, drinking some coffee.

She laughs under her breath. "I told him to tell you last night. Obviously, that was out of the question given the significance of the day." Her cup hits the counter, her exhale hard. "Fucking hell, Camryn, I feel so bad."

"Why?" This isn't on her.

"Well, we made a terrible day even worse by walking in on you here."

"I shouldn't have been here."

"He would have told you. Not last night, but he was totally prepared for it, until I screwed it up."

"It's okay. I could have handled it better."

"And now you're here," she muses, watching me over the rim of her cup as she takes a sip.

"Now I'm here," I murmur.

"And call me presumptuous, but I'm assuming that means—"

"It means I love your brother."

She inhales, her hand moving to her mouth. "That makes me so happy. That he'll have someone other than us and Albi." Naturally, my thoughts immediately go to his wife. But I won't bring her up. Not now.

"It makes me happy too."

"Good." April stands. "I should go check on the boys."

I smile as she leaves and gaze around the kitchen, slowly getting up and going to a cupboard. I open it. Plates and bowls. The next is loaded with mugs. And the next is full of every plastic kitchenware item a child could ever need. I close the door and follow my feet to the right, finding myself in the laundry room. Little trousers hang on a drying rack next to Dec's white shirts. Tiny socks next to Dec's man socks. A picture on the doors of a huge American fridge freezer catches my eye, and I wander over, removing the Mickey Mouse magnet and taking the picture off. It's all I can do not to break down again, faced with a heart-stopping, beautiful picture of Dec and Albi. Dec's sitting on the sand in blue shorts, shades on, Albi standing between his thighs in a matching pair, goggles on. Both of them belly laughing, faces turned up to the sun. Happiness pours out of the image.

So why am I sniffing back tears?

I put the picture back and slip the magnet across, finding a calendar next to the picture. At first, I'm not sure what I'm looking at, but as I move in closer, I see there's a line written for each day in December. I scan the boxes, smiling as I read the words—all memories noted by Dec.

DECEMBER 3RD

I COPED WITH YOUR DIRTY NAPPIES, DOG SHIT ON YOUR SHOES, BUT WHEN YOU'RE THROWING UP, FELLA, I'M THROWING UP WITH YOU

I laugh under my breath, moving to

DECEMBER 8TH

YOU MADE ME A SPACESHIP OUT OF LOO ROLLS TODAY. IT'S BLOODY BEAUTIFUL.

My hand on my heart, I read every memory noted on each square of December until yesterday. It's blank. Dec hasn't written anything there yet, and I wonder what he'll write when he does. Because he spent the day with me. Dec only had maybe an hour with Albi in between our day wandering and me turning up to go out for dinner. My heart aches more, knowing I've stolen that time. Albi would have been at school, but still. Dec didn't take him because he woke up with me.

Backing out of the room, I resist the overwhelming urge to read every moment Dec's noted and see every picture they have capturing moments of their lives together. But there are no pictures on the walls in the kitchen, the snug, or the hallway. It feels like such a waste of wall space, not to be filled with photographs of these two beautiful humans.

Taking a breath, I venture out of the kitchen and follow the sound of Dec's pacifying voice to the playroom. When I get to the doorway, I find April perched on a mini chair and Dec lying on his front outside a teepee. The zip is fastened, and Albi's hiding inside. April smiles at me. It's easy to return it.

"The prawn is the coolest part to play, fella," Dec says softly. "And once your performance is done, you get to play games for the rest of the day. No schoolwork."

"I don't want to be a prawn." His little voice is adamant. I can't see him hidden away in his teepee, but I can see him in my mind's eye. His tiny arms are crossed tightly over his chest and his bottom lip is on the carpet. "Uncle Blaine said prawns are hoovers of the sea," he says, making Dec look back at April with raised brows. She shrugs. "They have poop inside them!" he cries. "I don't have poop inside me, Daddy. I poop it in the toilet and the flushy takes it away."

I press my lips together as Dec drops his forehead to the carpet, rubbing from side to side to the point I begin worrying he'll have carpet burns when he comes up. "Okay, fella, Daddy doesn't know what else to say." He heaves himself up and faces us, shaking his head when he finds me, his palm splattering his face and dragging down his stubble.

"He's a prawn?" I mouth to him, my face surely spelling out my confusion. We're talking about a nativity play, right?

"He's lucky," Dec whispers. "Little Jack Greenshaw is a hairy frogfish."

I recoil. "I don't even know what that is."

"I need a coffee." Dec sighs, looking at April. "What am I gonna do? Coax him into the car and pretend we're not going to school?"

"Definitely not," I say without thinking on a laugh. They both look at me, and I shrink. "Not unless you never want him to trust you again," I add quietly. Reluctantly. Something catches my eye behind Dec, and I crane my head, spotting a cute little face surrounded by pink velvet with two brown antennae bobbing around on top peeking out of the teepee. Albi spots me and quickly disappears back inside.

"I'd better call the school," Dec says, dropping a kiss on my cheek as he pulls his phone out and carries on to the kitchen.

April rises from the tiny chair looking beaten and shakes her head as she passes me. "Thanks, Blaine," she whispers, rolling her eyes.

I turn to follow them but stop when the pink head pokes back out from the teepee. I tilt my head, meeting his curious little eyes.

He shoots back inside, and I smile to myself, going to join Dec and April, putting myself back on the stool as April makes Dec a coffee and he talks on the phone to the school. "I don't know what to say. He was all for it until this morning."

I bite at my lip when Dec reaches for my knee and starts stroking my lower thigh.

"Sure, I'll let you know."

"Tell them I'll drop off the costume," April says over her shoulder. "Albi's understudy will need it."

I snort in laughter, and Dec smiles down the phone, passing the message on, minus the remark about the understudy. He hangs up and drops his phone. "Well, this is a fucking disaster."

"Can we revisit the hairy frogfish?" I ask, making April bark out laughter. "Since when is there a hairy frogfish and a prawn in the school nativity play?"

"Since they've been learning about the oceans and seas."

"Makes perfect sense," I muse. "What's Baby Jesus, a shark?"

Dec turns a tired look my way and April chuckles again. "Ha. Ha." He curls an arm around my neck, hauling me close, forcing me to wedge my palms into his thighs to keep myself on the stool. He scrunches his nose and kisses the tip of mine, but my attention is captured when a darling prawn appears in the doorway, and I have to press my lips together to stop myself cooing at the utter cuteness before me. I tap Dec's leg, and he looks over his shoulder.

"Here he is," Dec murmurs, as Albi checks us both out, his face sullen and moody. I quickly withdraw my hands from Dec and move out of his personal space. Curiosity is painted all over Albi's face. At least, the part of it I can actually see.

"Hey," I say quietly, giving him a small wave.

He doesn't answer, just maintains his scrutinising eyes on me, and I inevitably start to worry again that he might not like me. My stomach drops at the mere thought, my own fears superseded by that fact. It's been Dec and Albi his whole life.

I'm an interloper.

"Where's your pretty dress?" Albi asks flatly.

I flinch, and Dec frowns, both him and April looking at me expectantly, like I might be able to answer him. "I split coffee down it," I blurt like a fool.

"That's okay." He pulls the hood of his costume off, and his dark hair, wafts out, poking up all over the place, static getting it. "You can borrow my costume."

Huh?

He starts to strip out of it, while we all watch on, silent, and once he's down to his little underpants, he brings it all to me and dumps it on my lap. I stare down at it.

"Try it on then," Dec says with a ton of amusement in his tone. I look up at him through my lashes. Oh, how he goads me. But proving I can take being a prawn isn't the objective here. Getting Albi to school in this prawn costume, however, is.

I scoop up the bundle and push it into Dec's chest, and he frowns. "I may as well go," I say, standing and getting my coat on. I don't kiss Dec or even cuddle him goodbye. Baby steps. I saw how Albi looked at me. Suspicion. I also saw the curiosity on his sweet face when he poked his head out of his teepee. I'm depending on the latter, and I won't push the former.

"Are you going home?" Albi asks.

"No, I have some shopping to do."

"Boring!" he sings.

"Well, I was really looking forward to seeing my first ever prawn in a Christmas nativity play. And actually, that stuff Uncle Blaine told you about isn't poop. It's brains. Prawns are the cleverest creatures in the sea. I guess I'll just have to do my boring shopping and be sad." I pout, Albi freezes stock-still, and Dec and April look between us. I'm going to hell.

"That's a real shame," April murmurs.

"Yeah, a real shame." Dec sighs. "My special friend was so excited."

"You want to come and see the play?" Albi asks.

Fuck, what am I doing? "Yes." Christ, I need to shut the hell up before I get myself into a situation I'm nowhere near prepared for. "See you, Albi." I throw him a wave and get on my way, caught somewhere between dread and hope. I want him to take the bait for Dec. I don't want him to take it because there's no way in hell I can put myself in a pre-school full of four-year-olds.

When I make it all the way to the street, I turn and look back at the house. He didn't take the bait. I hate that a small part of me that's relieved. I would have figured it out somehow had he bought into my ploy, maybe declared a horrible sicky bug before we got to the school and made my escape before I had endless triggers thrown at me.

I pull my phone out when it beeps, wondering what the hell I'm going to do now. The message is from Thomas.

> Sounds nasty. Half the office has gone down with some bug! Feel better. Hope you're back soon.

I'm so fucking confused. He told me he wanted to fire me a few days ago, and now he hopes I'm back soon? Spinning the phone in my hand, I look up at Dec's impressive house. Does this mean Thomas has abandoned his plan to sell up? I'd ask Dec, but he's preoccupied with his reluctant prawn. So I quickly text him, wishing him luck and apologising for not being able to help, actually feeling quite defeated. Have I lost my touch? I could persuade Noah to do anything. A little bit of harmless reverse psychology. Make him believe he was the root of all happiness, which was easy because he was. But most of all, I didn't want him to be afraid of anything. I swallow down the rising lump and get moving, but I make it only two steps when Dec's door flies open and Albi appears at the top of the steps.

And he's a prawn again. "I want to be the prawn, I want to be a prawn!" he yells, jumping up and down, the antennae dancing like a pair of over-excitable worms breakdancing on his little head. "I want to be a prawn!"

Dec appears behind him. "He wants to be a prawn," he murmurs, almost hesitant.

My heart soars and sinks at the same time, and Dec's apologetic face tells me he sees that. I blow my cheeks out and make my way back to them, feeling my legs getting heavier as I climb the steps.

"I'm a prawn again!" Albi looks so damn chuffed about that.

"I'm so happy you're a prawn again." I reach for an antenna and smack it, making it spring back.

Albi dashes back off into the house, and we watch him go. "It's a lot," Dec says, keeping me on the doorstep as if he's half expecting me to decline his invitation to go back in. "I don't expect you to come."

I don't know how I'm going to do this, but I must if we're moving forward. "I know you don't, but Albi expects me to come because I said I would, and that's the end of that." I take a breath and step back into the house, hearing him, the little whirlwind, dashing around like a prawn that's had too much Red Bull.

"Well, now you two have everything under control," April says, pulling her coat and fancy handbag off the chaise in the hallway, "I'll be off." She stops before us, half in her coat, and smiles. "I'm not going to get all mushy, but I really love this."

I catch Dec shaking his head mildly, silently telling her to rein it in. It's something else I hate. That he's suppressing his happiness, curbing his enthusiasm because he feels it's insensitive or I might crumple. That's not how this should be.

I hook my arm through Dec's and lean into him, now Albi's out of sight, smiling my appreciation, even if it's slightly strained.

"Take lots of pictures!" April sings, leaving and slamming the door behind her, a breeze swirling around the hallway as she does.

Dec immediately turns into me, holding my shoulders. "When I asked you to come this morning, I didn't anticipate this. I wasn't thinking at all, to be honest. It was stupid and insensitive."

"Shut up," I order gently, and he withdraws, surprised. "It's okay. I'll be okay." I'm not sure how yet, but I'll make sure of it. *You got through yesterday, the hardest day of the year, so you can do this.*

Albi comes racing out the kitchen with his lunchbox and a pack of mini Christmas Fairy cakes, and I quickly move away from Dec. "Come on, Daddy," he shouts, tucking the cakes under his arm to open the door, surely squishing them.

"Like I've been the holdup," Dec murmurs as Albi dashes down the steps to the car. "Ready?" he asks.

I nod.

It's a lie.

. . .

The car ride goes by in a haze of questions from Albi, not all of which I can answer. Or should. "How old are you?" he asks. "My daddy is forty! It was his birthday and Aunty April had a party at her house and we had cake and balloons and Daddy blew out a whole forty candles!"

"Well, that sounds like lots of fun," I say, looking back at the little prawn all bundled up in his car seat. "I'm thirty-seven. And you're four."

"Four and a half. When I'm five, Daddy said I can have an iPad. Just for a little time. Fred at school has an iPad. It's blue with dinosaurs on it. I don't want dinosaurs on my iPad. I want prawns on my iPad because they're brainy and Daddy says I'm a brainbox. Are you clever?"

"I don't think I'm as clever as you." I feel Dec looking at me out the corner of his eye, almost in apology.

"Will you clap after the play?"

"Of course I'll clap."

"Will you sing the songs with us?"

"You bet I will."

"Can you look after my cakes so Herbert Smith doesn't eat them all? He's greedy. One day, he took Ben Cuthbert's Dunkers out of his lunchbox and ate them all *and* his Jam Roly-poly cake. He said he didn't but he had jam all round his mouth."

"I'll look after your cakes," I assure him, smiling to myself as I return forward in my seat.

"Will you stay for the party in our classroom? Father Christmas is coming, and I'm going to tell him what I want him to bring me this year. I've been a good boy, haven't I, Daddy?"

"A very good boy," Dec confirms. "We'll let this morning slide," he adds under his breath, taking a left at the lights. "And I don't think grown-ups are allowed at the party, fella. It's just for children and teachers."

"And Father Christmas."

"And Father Christmas," Dec confirms.

"And Rudolf," Albi adds. "I know all of Father Christmas's reindeers, don't I, Daddy?"

"You sure do."

"Do you know all of Father Christmas's reindeers?"

"I don't." I turn in my seat to face him again, becoming all too addicted to his beaming smiles so full of delight and innocence. "Can you tell me?"

He grins. "Dasher and Dancer and Prancer and Vixen and Comet and Cupid and Donner and Blitzen aannnd . . ."—he claps his hands theatrically—"Rudolph!"

"Wow."

"I'm smart, aren't I, Daddy?"

"The smartest boy I know." Dec scrunches his nose at me, mouthing, "Sorry."

"Stop it," I order. "He's the cutest."

"And a real chatterbox today." He looks at Albi in his rearview mirror, his smile on another level. It's the smile a parent could only give their baby. The contrast in Dec Ellis is incredible. Stoic, serious businessman. Pacifying, playful dad. I fell in love with the former, saw chinks in his armour that made him all the more fascinating. This Dec? I love him the most.

"Do you love my daddy?"

Dec's smile drops, as does mine, despite both of us knowing the answer is quite easy. *Fuck*. "What does love mean?" I ask, cringing as I turn back to face the road.

"It means you want to help him get dressed."

"Oh?"

"And help him have a wash or a bath. And you take him milk when it's bedtime. And you read him a book even when you're supposed to be working. And you cut up his dinner for him. And you give him cuddles and kisses, and you tickle him and play Uno with him. And you let him help you at your office. And you let him eat ice cream at bedtime on Fridays."

Oh my heart.

"Basically, loving someone means you're their skivvy," Dec

murmurs quietly, and I laugh, the sound loud and rich, making Dec smile my way. "Well? Do you love me, Camryn?" he asks, splitting his attention between me and the road, interested.

"If you're Daddy's special friend, you have to love him," Albi declares. "And Daddy loves you because he said you're his special friend."

"Then I guess I love him," I confirm, warmth gushing through me unstoppably. "If that's okay with you, Albi."

"Yes! Daddy, you can come to bed with me, and Camryn will bring our milk now so you don't have to."

My laughter turns up a few more notches, and Dec joins me, as Albi breaks into song in the back of the car. A few years ago, I undoubtedly could have named any song being sung by any four-year-old across the land. Now, I have no idea what's coming out of his mouth. "What are you singing, Albi?" I ask, as Dec's hand rests in my lap, silently demanding I hold it.

"Moana," he tells me, taking a short break to do so, before he's off again, all the way to the school.

Dec drives around the block twice before he finds a space down a side street, and my heart noticeably beats faster as he gets out of the car and lifts his prawn out the back. *Deep breaths.* I step out and close the door, looking down the street to the school gates.

Dec passes me the cakes. Squashed to death. "Okay?" he asks, the car beeping as he joins me, Albi's costume dragging through the melting snow.

I nod and motion down my front. "I would have made myself presentable had I known I'd be debuting at his school."

"Could be worse," he says, taking my hand. "Albi's a prawn."

I chuckle and smack his bicep, and quickly remove my hand from his, looking back at Albi trailing behind us, his lunchbox knocking his lower leg as he walks.

"You've told him you love me, Camryn," Dec says quietly. "I think it's safe to let me hold your hand."

"I heard nothing about hand-holding in the endless acts of services Albi reeled off," I quip, nudging his shoulder and showing him the squashed cakes. "I don't think even Herbert Smith will want them now."

Albi appears between us, and we both watch as he lowers his lunchbox to the ground. Then he takes one of my hands and one of Dec's, joining them between us, before he collects up his lunchbox and ambles on his way, picking his tail up too. "The prawn has spoken," Dec says, smug, as we follow him. I roll my eyes, acutely aware of my chest pulsing. "Camryn?"

"Yes?"

"Breathe," he whispers. "You don't have to do this."

"I really do," I say, continuing to walk toward my worst nightmare. And not just for Albi. I need to do this for me too. And for Dec. "I can't start my relationship off with your son on a false promise."

"Camryn, you told him prawn shit is brains."

I wince. "Sorry."

"Shut up." He stops us, checking Albi's not too far ahead. "I don't want you to do something you're not comfortable doing."

"I have to keep moving forward," I tell him. "No matter how hard, no matter how painful. There has to be some peace for me somewhere on this shitty journey, and I'm really hoping it's standing in front of me." It's come with its minor unexpected plot twist, but . . . fuck. My life has been a plot twist.

"It's standing in front of you," he replies, sincere. Soft. Wholeheartedly.

"I wouldn't dream of doing this without you." I need him to know that. He's taken the edge off the pain—a soothing salve to my devastated soul—making impossibles possible.

Dec brings my hand to his lips and kisses the tops of my fingers. "You're not alone anymore, Camryn. I know I come with baggage but—"

"He's not baggage, Dec." I cast my eyes toward Albi. He's

stopped trudging along, is watching us intently. "He's life." And, scarily, he could be a part of the reason I heal.

Dec nods, as Albi comes barrelling into us. "Daddy, come on!"

"Coming, fella," he says, gently tugging on my hand, so that when I follow him, he knows I'm coming willingly.

I can do this.

We make it to reception, and Dec signs Albi in as a middle-aged woman comes flapping around the corner. "Albi Ellis," she cries. "Where have you been?"

"Sorry, Mrs. Brown," he says sullenly.

"Never mind, never mind, you're here now." She takes his shoulders and starts hurrying him along the corridor. "Take your seats." I don't miss the raised brow she points my way.

"This way," Dec says, dragging me toward a set of double doors. Pushing through, I'm suddenly in a small concert hall with rows and rows of tiny wooden chairs lined up, adults sitting on them. "Here." He finds us two seats on the end of an aisle one row from the back, and I lower, gazing around the hall. Every wall is covered in art and displays, every available hanging space dangling in tinsel and handmade, painted snowflakes of every shape, colour, and size. I swallow, keeping my head still and directed forward, looking around the hall, only moving my eyes.

"Oh my God," I whisper.

"What?" Dec turns a worried look my way. "What is it?"

"You're the hot single dad." Mums at every turn are flicking looks this way, all obviously curious. "They're looking at me."

"They're not looking at you," Dec says tiredly, scoping the place himself . . . seeing everyone looking at me. "Okay, they're looking at you."

I can see it now, all of them vying for his attention, the play date offers, invitations for Albi to every party. One woman is particularly interested, even if she tries to hide it. She's a stunner. And here's me, literally rolled out of bed. "How many have you dated?" Dated doesn't mean sex, as I know that's not been in his life for some years.

He snorts. "None."

"Really?"

"Really, Camryn."

"Okay, how many have fluttered their lashes?"

He shifts on his chair, uncomfortable. "A few."

My eyebrows jump up. "A few?"

"Most of them."

"Hot single dad," I muse.

"Except I'm not single." He leans in and kisses my cheek. "Am I?"

"Keep it PG," I mumble, nudging him back to his own personal space.

"Shut up." He grabs my hand and squeezes as a man in a pair of bottle-green cords and an obscene Christmas jumper walks onto the stage and introduces himself as Mr. Gantree, before reminding parents taking photos is prohibited but they can purchase pictures from the school website when the appointed photographer uploads them.

I take a deep breath and cling to Dec, not quite believing I'm here, that I've put myself in this box of triggers. But then I look at Dec sitting next to me, and I can believe it. He glances at me, concern a constant on his face, some for me, and some for Albi, who's about to make his acting debut. "I'm okay," I assure him, trying not to let my chest inflate as I take a deep breath and return my attention to the stage. "Concentrate." I don't want his worry for me to distract him from such a monumental moment as a parent.

My eyes widen when an octopus wobbles onto the stage and starts to set the scene for the audience, not that we could have missed the big boards with waves and coral reefs painted on them.

"This is Christmas Under the Sea," Octopus declares, as a piano is wheeled on and Mr. Gantree takes the stool, starting to play. And we watch in fascination as Santa's elves that, for the sake of this production, are actually clown fish, all huddle onto the stage and start singing I-don't-know-what. Father Christmas is a merman, and his reindeers are dolphins.

I lean into Dec. "This isn't a nativity play as I know it."

"Me neither," he murmurs. "Where are the three wise men?"

"Are you religious?"

"Not even a little bit." His posture changes, his body sitting up straight, and I look back at the stage when I see Albi waddle on, looking so bloody proud of himself. I don't know who to watch. Albi or Dec.

Albi whips out a scroll and lets it roll out, the paper hitting the floor. "The naughty list," he declares sternly, and all the sea creatures gasp.

"Nailed it," Dec says, resting back in his chair.

I smile, leaning into him. "Which one is Petal?" I ask.

"The jellyfish," he whispers. "She better not sting my boy."

I chuckle and settle, finding Albi on the stage again. His grin is as wide as his face.

And it's magic.

For the rest of the play, I sway constantly from sad to elated. Smiling happily and smiling sadly. I study each and every kid on stage, compare Noah to them all—height, size, hair, speech, cheeks. At one point, when they all burst into an interesting version of Winter Wonderland that involved changing most of the lyrics to fit the production, I thought I might have to step outside, watching them all sing with utter gusto, like their lives depended on it, keen to show their mummies and daddies how well they've done. But, honestly, I didn't want to miss Albi. And I definitely didn't want him to see me get up and walk out.

As soon as the curtains close, everyone stands and a raucous applause breaks out, grown-ups clapping and whooping, so many proud faces in the house. I take it all in. Numb but not. I know what it must feel like, this feeling filling the room, and it's the best in the world. Utter pride and love. Dec's feeling that now, and I am too, to an extent.

The curtains slide open, and I make sure Albi sees us clapping for him. His grin makes him even more edible, so I give him a thumbs up that he tries to return but can't because of the giant pink velvet mitts on his hands. "What are you doing for the rest of the day?" Dec asks as he leans into me, talking just loud enough for me to hear over the continued applause.

"I might have to shower at some point."

He looks down his front, to the sweatpants and hoodie. "We can shower later. Want to come on a date with me and Albi?"

"Now?"

"Yes, now."

"But it's school time."

"It's the last day before Christmas break. What's he going to miss except Herbert Smith monopolising the party food?"

I smile, Dec grins back at me, and then he grabs my hand, pulling me through the crowd toward the stage. The eyes of many women follow us as he leads us round the back, down a corridor, and into a classroom. It's empty. "What—"

My words are stolen along with my breath when he spins me into him and claims my lips with a soft, possessive pressure, tugging my body close with his arm hooked around my waist. And despite where we are, I tumble into the sanctuary of his kiss and succumb to the beautiful effect he has on me, following his pace and pressure for what feels like forever until he hums and slows the swirls of his tongue and sucks my lip gently into his mouth. I open my eyes, dazed. Warm. Madly, deeply in love. "We're in a classroom," I whisper.

He looks around, his wet lips pouting in thought. "Detention for you, Ms. Moore."

"I'm guilty by association. Being led astray. Mixing with the wrong crowd." I push my mouth to his, my arm around his neck to keep him there, feeling his lips stretch into a smile beneath mine. "We better get out of here before we're found and–"

The door swings open, and the woman who took particular interest in us in the hall appears. "Oh, apologies." She pulls her handbag closer into the crook of her bent arm. "I didn't realise the room was occupied. Was I interrupting something?" Her eyes land on me, and it's all I can do not to roll mine. "I'm sorry, we've not met."

"Camryn, Melissa; Melissa, Camryn," Dec says quickly, before starting to haul me out of the classroom. "Have a great Christmas, Melissa," he calls, dragging me along.

"Don't forget my canapés and mulled wine get-together tonight!" she calls. "Seven thirty."

Do I see him shudder? "She's friendly," I muse, smiling when he throws a tired look back at me.

"Shut up," he murmurs, taking us back through to the hall.

"Did you drag me into a classroom just to sneak a kiss?"

"Yes," he answers unapologetically, his neck craning to see over the mass of heads. "Where is he?"

"There," I say, spotting Dec's little prawn standing on the edge of the stage, scanning the crowd.

"Daddy!" he yells when he spots us. Dec drops my hand, but that's okay. He heads for the stage, and when he's a few meters away, Albi launches himself off the edge, landing in Dec's open arms perfectly. Trust. They are quite literally each other's worlds. I've spent little time with both of them together, and yet I see no empty void a mother's left to be filled. I never thought I'd have believed a child could be okay without their mother in their lives. Whether death, selfishness, or force took them away. Albi isn't missing a mother, because Dec's everything he needs.

"That was insane!" Dec exclaims, shifting Albi's little butt onto his forearm. "You're a natural, fella."

"I know," he says, easy, his pink-padded shoulders jumping up casually. "Did you sing?"

"All the words."

"Father Christmas's reindeers aren't really dolphins, Daddy."

"I know, mate."

"And Father Christmas isn't a merman. He's a big fat man with a white beard."

"I know." Dec walks back over to me.

"That was so cool, Albi," I say as Dec lowers him to the ground, kneeling in front of him.

"I'm going to give you two options," he says, holding up two fingers, "and you have to pick one, okay?"

Albi jumps up and claps. "Okay."

"You can stay at school, go to the party and see Father Christmas, or you can come on a date with me and Camryn."

His head springs back, and he peeks up at me. "What's a date?"

"We go for something to eat. Maybe a walk. Maybe stop at the Lego shop."

His excited eyes widen, and he comes closer. "What about school, Daddy?"

Dec puts his fingers to his lips. "Shhh." And Albi copies. "Come on." Dec scoops him up, seizes my hand, and carries Albi through the crowd, pulling me along behind him. "Signing Albi Ellis out," Dec declares when we make it to the reception area, taking the pen on the book and scribbling across the page.

"Oh, is he unwell?" the receptionist asks.

"Terrible. I really didn't want him to come, but he insisted." Dec drops the pen. "He didn't want to let his classmates down."

"Oh, how admirable."

"We're going on a date," Albi declares, putting his finger to his lips. "Shhh."

I snort behind Dec, and Dec laughs nervously. *Guilty*. "To the doctor's, eh, fella? Because you're poorly sick." Dec makes fast work of escaping, and I follow behind, my smile breaking my face.

He puts Albi down and the moment he does, he gasps, his mitt-covered hands splaying his cheeks. "Father Christmas!" he cries. "How will he know what to bring me?"

"Well, I just so happen to know that after he's visited your school, he's going to be at Harrods."

"Harrods?" Albi questions. "Where you buy your work suits?"

"That's right."

"Harrods?" I ask. "You need to be specially invited to see Father Christmas at Harrods."

"Correct," Dec murmurs, taking my hand and Albi's with the other. "Up for it?" He looks at me. Hopeful. Wary.

I nod.

Why get off the rollercoaster now?

Our date is perfect. Father Christmas was magical, and an early dinner at the Rainforest Café was up there too. Albi insisted on wearing his prawn costume all day. I've swayed from heart-stopping happiness watching him soak up the magic of Christmas, to heart-pounding sadness that my boy isn't alive to experience it as well.

And I'm proud of myself too. I've faced so many fears today, done what I thought would be impossible.

And, as I dreaded, I'm falling head over heels for Dec's little boy.

On the drive home, I look back to see he's sparked out in his seat, his head tipped back, his mouth catching flies. Exhausted. "All that chatter's knackered him out," Dec muses.

I watch the lights shining in on the car casting shadows across his face. "Thank you for today."

"Shhh." Dec hushes me quietly, offering his hand, and I accept and weave our fingers together. "Come home with me," he says, keeping his eyes on the road. "We can take that shower we both need."

"And Albi?"

"He's going through until seven, trust me."

"Okay," I agree easily. "If you're comfortable with that."

"I'm not the concern here, Camryn. Neither is Albi." He finally looks at me. "Are *you* comfortable?"

I nod. "I couldn't think of a better way to end today."

After we stop by my place to pick up some things and check in on Mr. Percival, we drive to Dec's in comfortable silence. Lynette opens the door before Dec makes it there, Albi draped over his shoulder, flat out. There's a suitcase in the hallway, and Lynette is wrapped up in a long duffle coat, her gloves in her hand. "I was hoping I'd get to say goodbye," she whispers, pulling the pink fabric away from Albi's face and dropping a light kiss on his cheek. "Will you have him FaceTime me tomorrow?"

"Of course." Dec nods to a gift bag in the corner. "That's for you. From Albi." He dips and kisses her cheek. "Have Ron carry your case."

"Of course."

"Have a great Christmas with your family, Lynette." Dec starts up the stairs, and I can't help my smile following him, Albi's little cheek squished against his shoulder.

"You too." Lynette turns a smile my way as she collects the gift bag. "Look after them while I'm gone," she says, almost reluctantly, as Ron appears on the doorstep and takes her case.

"I will." She doesn't realise that it's them looking after me. "Safe journey."

Ron nods my way as Lynette steps out into the cold and closes the door behind them, leaving me alone in the hallway. I lower my bag and hang my coat on the stand, going to the playroom door and pushing it open. Hovering on the threshold, I take in the colourful space. It's a mess, toys strewn all over the floor, colouring pens scattered across the tiny wooden table in the corner, books stacked chaotically on the mini bookcase under the window.

A perfect mess.

I back out and wander down the hallway, poking my head around the other doors before the kitchen. The study opposite the playroom. The downstairs loo.

A set of closed double doors lure me there, and I push them open to reveal a beautiful formal lounge . . . and a Christmas tree to rival Rockefeller Center. I inhale my surprise, blindly kicking my trainers off before I tread on the lush cream carpet, dazzled by the tree that's drenched in gold glass baubles, satin bows, and thousands of warm twinkling fairy lights. Piles of gifts surround the base, a huge gold-encrusted star perched atop. I wander over and the closer I get, I see there's pictures in the baubles. All of Dec and Albi, ranging from when he was a baby, to now. My heart can't take it, and I press my palm into my chest, looking closely at each and every one of them. All gorgeous. Father and son.

Each other's worlds.

I feel my eyes welling for an entirely different reason. Not for what I've lost . . . but for what Dec *has*. I roughly wipe my face, turning, coming face to face with a large piece of art over the fireplace, a collage of pictures all in black and white. All smiles. All laughter. All them.

Two velvet stockings hang from the oak hearth with their names stitched into the white fluffy edging.

Albi.

Daddy.

Will I fit here? They're so complete. *Whole*.

Feeling a little overwhelmed, I move to one of the giant cream suede couches that frame the fireplace and lower, staring up at the pictures. I had something similar, all pictures of Noah. It's still wrapped up in paper, still hidden away in a cupboard. And the stockings, we did that. Had our names embroidered into our own. Two smaller stockings for Mummy and Daddy flanking Noah's larger one.

My chest constricts, and I stand, leaving the room in a rush and closing the doors behind me. Dec's coming down the stairs, and he stops halfway when he sees me. Or more registers my blotchy face. He sighs and treads down the remaining stairs, pulling me in for a hug.

I never knew how soothing a simple hug could be. "It's a beautiful room," I say into his shoulder.

"It's our favourite." Pulling out, he checks my eyes for tears, running the pad of his thumb beneath each. "Come" He clasps my hand and leads me up the stairs.

The bedroom is basked in a faint apricot glow from the bedside lamps, the curtains drawn. Dec walks us through to his bathroom, turns the shower on, and strips me down, then himself, leaving our clothes in a mixed pile on the floor.

Hot water hits my skin when he walks me in, but it doesn't warm me like Dec can. Taking a sponge, he soaks it under the spray and turns me away from him, dragging it across my back. There's not one inch of my body he doesn't clean. Not one hair on my head he doesn't comb his fingers through, shampooing, rinsing, and brushing conditioner through the lengths. When he's on his knees before me, I look down at him washing my thighs, his concentration intense, his well-honed body glistening under the drops of water coating him, his hair saturated. I know he won't escalate this. Whether he thinks it's inappropriate to or not, I don't know. I sense he just wants to take care of me. I hate that I feel like I need taking care of. I hate that I'm fragile, because I don't want to be a burden. Dec doesn't need someone else to look after.

I drop to my knees to join him, and he lifts his gaze to mine. I hate the sadness I see in his usually glittery eyes. Eyes that are now dull. "Today was the best day and worst all rolled into one," I admit quietly, my voice not broken but definitely cracking. Two emotions —happiness and sadness—swaying like a pendulum. Both catching me off guard when one would creep up and dilute the other. "I think you're brilliant." I cup his face with both hands, holding it firmly, making him see. "I think Albi's brilliant."

"I feel like there's a *but* coming, and I really don't want to hear it."

"But I'm even more scared now because I've fallen in love with him even faster than I fell in love with you."

His lips part, his eyes darting across my face. "You're not replacing Noah," he whispers. "To love another child would never mean that."

"I know. But it doesn't stop the guilt. Or the reminders. Or the heartache."

"I need you, Camryn. Not for Albi. I need you for *me*. You've filled a part of me I didn't know was empty. I went to the bar that night to kill time. April took Albi to the pantomime, and I didn't know what to do with myself. I'm irrevocably his, but I don't want to hold him back. I don't want him to be scared to leave me. I want him to experience life. Travel. Explore the world, become utter greatness. Be successful, fulfilled, a good father. By being what my father isn't, I could hold him back, and I don't want that. But most of all, I don't want him to be afraid of falling in love. I want him to look at me when he's older and know I'm okay. Not lonely. I was so fucking lonely, Camryn. I know it's terrifying, but I want you to stay. I *need* you to stay. *Please* stay. For me."

I take his face in my hands, overwhelmed by the amazing man before me.

"You'll never lose me, I promise you," he whispers.

My lip quivers. "I love you both."

His smile is small but fucking huge, and he stands us up, flipping the shower off before pulling a white towel off the heated rail and drying us. He leads me to the bed and gets us beneath the duvet, pulling me onto his chest, holding me there.

"I love you both too," he whispers.

I fall asleep in his arms, his heart beating strongly under my ear.

And I feel mine pounding in reply.

Life.

December 21st

When my eyes open, I'm curled up on my side, my back to the edge of the bed, the duvet covering my naked body, expecting to see Dec. I don't. I see Albi. Asleep.

He's splayed on his back between us on top of the sheets, legs akimbo, his arms above his head on the pillow. "Oh," I breathe, naturally checking the sheets are covering me. Inevitably, memories stampede through my mind mercilessly, the many mornings I woke up and found Noah had crept into bed with us. My eyes instinctively squeeze shut, trying to push them back. But why? Why am I pushing them back?

Relenting to the power of them, I allow the memories to invade me, inhaling as if I can smell him close to me. My smile is sad, and my chest tight, and yet the visions keep coming.

And I allow them.

I peel my eyes open and lift my head off the pillow a little so I can see Dec. He's in the exact same position as his boy. They both snore softly, both their lips parted. It's a quiet, peaceful moment, despite the heaviness of it. *Precious*. It's something I never appreciated when I had Noah. This simple thing. I don't know how long I stay still and quiet watching them, wondering if Dec realises just how precious this is.

As if he's heard my silent question, his eyes open, his sleepy gaze finding Albi next to him. His frown is adorable as his waking mind slowly brings him up to speed. His eyes jump directly to mine. I smile a little, letting him know I'm okay.

He sighs and rolls gingerly onto his side to face me. "Sorry," he murmurs.

"Don't be."

"Did his snoring wake you?"

I shake my head. "I'm naked."

Dec's eyes widen theatrically, his head craning to see over his sleeping son. His nose wrinkles when he finds me covered, and I chuckle as he edges to the side of the bed and gets out. He wanders across the bedroom. "And so are you," I breathe, admiring him in all his naked glory as he pulls a T-shirt off the chair and brings it to me. "I'll go make coffee." He bends and plants a kiss on my lips. "Be careful. He tends to play football in his sleep."

"He does?" At that exact moment, Albi's foot boots me in the thigh, and he mumbles a few inaudible words as he rolls away from me. Dec winces on my behalf. "Ouch," I whisper, when I actually want to yell at the sharp stab of pain that travels down to my knee. "I think I'll get ready for work." I glance at the clock on the nightstand. Six thirty. "So much for being out for the count until seven." I put my hand out for Dec to pull me up. "Mind if I use your shower?"

"Help yourself." He pulls on some boxers and strides off as I wriggle into the T-shirt and take myself to the bathroom.

After showering, brushing my teeth, and getting dressed, I head downstairs, feeling distinctively different this morning. Lighter. There's . . . a sense of quiet, subdued joy beneath my skin.

Dec's at the island, coffee in one hand, his mobile in the other, talking. "I'll be there at nine." He hangs up. Takes me in. "When do you finish for Christmas?"

"Tomorrow."

"Spend it with us," he says out of the blue, making me pause halfway to setting my bag on the island to get my coat on.

"What?"

He gets up and takes my coat from my hands, holding it up for me to feed my arms through. "I said, spend it with us."

A nativity play, albeit a fraudulent example, is one thing. So is a date to see Father Christmas. Spending Christmas with them? I don't want to cast my shadows over what should be a magical day for Albi. And for Dec. He'll be watching me constantly. Worrying sensitive nerves are being hit. "I—"

"Think about it," he whispers in my ear, his hands on my shoulders. "That's all I ask."

"Okay," I agree for the sake of it, if only to cut this conversation in its tracks. "I have to go."

"Four more sleeps!" Albi comes dashing into the kitchen like a rocket, zooming around the island to the point I'm dizzy. "Four more sleeps, four more sleeps! He's coming in four more sleeps!" He stops, out of breath after his mad dash. "Why'd you sleep in Daddy's bed?"

"Over to you," I breathe, grabbing my bag.

"Right, fella," Dec says, sounding super enthusiastic. "We've got to go to work for a little while."

"Yay!" Albi dashes back out, a total whirlwind. "I'll put on my power suit."

My eyebrows raise. "He has a power suit?"

"A policeman's costume. It's a step up from the prawn." Dec walks me to the door and opens it, and I find Ron on the other side.

"Oh, hi."

"Ron will take you."

"I can get myself to work."

"But you don't need to because Ron can take you and then come back for me and Albi." He motions outside. "Look at it, Camryn." Then he points to my heels.

"Yes, but I have these," I say, dipping and picking up my wellington boots from where I left them.

"They'll look smashing with that dress."

I point a half scowl half smile at him. "Talk later."

"We will," he says, full of authority.

Small talk is the name of the game on the drive with Ron, it seems. Where do I work, how long have I worked there, where did I meet Dec, when did I meet him? I couldn't help but think they were all questions he knew the answers to. "Have you worked for Dec for long?" I ask, if only to relieve him of the pressure to think up any more pointless questions.

"Ten years."

"Wow, that long?"

"It was a stopgap that lasted six years. Then Albi arrived, and I got attached to the little bugger."

I laugh, and the sound is natural. "Not much hope for me then, is there?"

"You're getting attached?" he asks.

"He's adorable."

"He is." He must sense the endless questions I want to ask. The smile he gives me out the corner of his mouth tells me I'm right.

"Are you married, Ron?" I ask, dipping into my bag to find my phone.

"Divorced. She left me for a richer man."

Wincing, I turn a sympathetic smile onto him. "I'm sorry."

"Don't be. He's bankrupt now."

I laugh. "Karma."

"No, Dec Ellis."

"Huh?"

"Dec bankrolled my new business that put him *out* of business."

"Oh my God," I murmur. "Does he get a kick out of avenging people who have wronged him?"

"Dec wasn't wronged."

I shake my head. He's right. "What business are you in?"

"Chauffeur." He smirks. "Dec hired me ten years ago to be his personal driver. Like I said, it was just a stopgap until I got myself back on my feet. Naturally, when one's being driven daily by someone, they slowly get to know them."

"And Dec got to know you, found out your story, and stumped up endless cash to bankroll a new luxury private chauffer business."

"You got it. I bought a fleet of prestigious cars, hired some men, bought some suits, and away I went. We made a deal. He put in half a million for forty percent and if I paid him back within five years, he'd drop to twenty."

"And did you?"

He smiles across to me. "Within three."

I blow my cheeks out. "That's amazing."

"*He's* amazing." Looking at me, Ron studies me silently for a few moments, and I feel wholly scrutinised.

"You're wondering what my intentions are," I say, upfront, asking his question for him as he returns his attention to the road.

"He's an honourable man. In the ten years I've worked for him, I've only every known one woman."

"His wife."

"She's a sore subject."

"Understandably," I say, turning in my seat to face him, prepared to tell him what he wants to hear. Because it's true. "I love him. I loved him before I knew he was wealthy. I loved him before I knew about Albi. He's saving my life one minute at a time, but what I'm struggling with is why he loves *me*." I don't expect Ron to know or even tell me if he knows. "He said he doesn't want to be lonely."

"Being insanely rich is very lonely," he muses. "But's that's not why he's fallen for you."

"Well, that's a relief," I quip, making Ron chuckle. "So why has he fallen for me?"

"I don't know." He shrugs. "Maybe it was your smile."

"Maybe."

"Your beauty?"

"He's not that shallow. But thanks for the compliment."

He laughs again. "No, you're right. He's not that shallow. Your comic genius?"

"Nope. Can you see why I'm baffled?"

"Why do we need to dissect it? Sometimes people fall in love and it's unexplainable but beautiful. Accept it. Roll with it."

"I half expected you to warn me not to hurt them."

"I wouldn't insult you."

"What if he hurts me?"

"There are many things I know about Dec Ellis, and one of them is this. He doesn't spend time on things that he's not passionate about."

"He spent time on his wife."

He shakes his head as he pulls up outside my office. "Wrong. He spent time on Albi."

And what can I say to that? "Well, thank you for the surprisingly insightful ride to work." I smile and get out but stop, dipping to get Ron back in my sights. "If your business is flourishing, then why are you still driving for Dec?"

"Like I said, I'm attached."

I nod my understanding. "Did your wife ever try to come crawling back?"

"She's still trying. Have a great day at work, Camryn."

I laugh a little. "Thanks, Ron." Closing the door, I stand back and watch him drive off to go fetch Dec and Albi.

To take them to work.

In their power suit and policeman costume.

There are many things I know about Dec Ellis. And one of them is this. He doesn't spend time on things that he's not passionate about.

I chew my lip, very aware that I'm restraining my smile.

He spent time on his wife.

No, he spent time on Albi.

He really didn't love her. And that feels like one weight lifted from the various weights on my shoulders.

I tiptoe across the snow and stamp my heels on the mat just inside the doors of my building, noting it's quiet in the foyer. When I make it up to our floor, it's no different. A ghost town. I pass Debbie's empty desk and push my way into my office, dropping my bag on the chair and shrugging off my coat, hanging it on the hook, then I make my way to the kitchen to get a coffee. I don't see one person on my way, and the kitchen is empty too. I scroll through my emails while I wait for the machine to spit out my caffeine, and sip on my way back, flagging and deleting as I work my way through my inbox.

The elevator doors open as I'm passing, and Thomas's son steps off. "Morning, Anthony," I say out of politeness, rolling my eyes when he grunts his reply.

"So what lucky company will have the pleasure of Camryn Moore next?" he asks, stopping me in my tracks.

"I'm not following." I face him. Face his smarmy, smug face.

"We've sold up, Camryn, which means you're out of a job."

What?

"And it isn't your boyfriend who bought us, but well done on your efforts to help him sabotage the deal." He smiles wide. "Merry Christmas, Camryn." Off he goes, an irritating, cocky swagger to his stride as he whistles his way to his office.

"Fuck," I whisper, deflating on the spot. Out of a job. Endless days killing time. Nothing to distract myself.

Feeling like I've got bricks in my heels, I go back to my office and lower to my chair, staring at the screen of my computer, wondering . . . what now?

The door swings open, halting my thoughts in their tracks, and Anthony swans in, a box in his hand. He places it neatly on my desk, still smiling like a psycho. "You're welcome," he singsongs, turning but stopping on a theatrical, "Oh!" He pulls something out from his back pocket—a pile of papers—and slaps them on my desk. "I've highlighted the vacancies that I thought were a good match for your skillset." He leaves, slamming the door so hard it shakes on its hinges. I pull the papers forward and scan the highlighted vacancies. Pot washer. Road Sweeper. Cleaner for the public toilets across various city parks. Chicken plucker.

"Prick," I mutter, shoving the papers away and slumping back in my chair. My phone dings, and I swipe it up, softening the moment I see the message from Dec. It's a picture of Albi in the boardroom in his policeman costume. Head of the table.

How's your day going?

I laugh under my breath. But stop. Does Dec know he's failed to secure the deal with TF Shipping? I contemplate asking, my thumbs hovering over the screen of my phone, but think better of it, dropping it to my desk and blowing out my exasperation. No job. What the hell am I going to do?

Pulling open the drawers on my desk, I start to empty them of my personal things, dropping it all in the box. Deflated. I failed to get TF Shipping ready for the team to come in and prepare it for debut on the market. I shouldn't be so hard on myself. The odds were against me, but I've never failed. It's a smear on my CV I don't need.

A familiar knock sounds on the door. "Come in, Thomas," I say tiredly, surprised once again he's sought me out. "I suppose I should congratulate you on the sale," I say flatly, making his eyebrows jump up. "Anthony wasn't at all creaming his pants when he shared the news."

Thomas rolls his eyes. "I told him I wanted to tell you."

"A lot sure did happen while I was off for two whole days."

"Are you feeling better?"

I toss my paperweight into the box. "Much, thanks." I rest my palms on the edge of my desk and lean on them. "I had no idea who Dec was when I met him." Not that it matters now, since he's failed to buy the company. "And I know he's told you man to man he wasn't fishing."

"He knew what he was doing."

"You think he planned to . . . what? Seduce me?"

"If the boot fits."

"It doesn't." I drop a pile of pens into the box. They're not technically mine, but I have no pens and . . . fuck him. "I want a decent reference."

"I don't think so." Anthony laughs, appearing behind Thomas.

It takes what little energy I have in this moment to stop myself from reacting in a wholly inappropriate manner to his apparent satisfaction. "Look," I breathe, "Dec Ellis drove the price down because he's a smart businessman and he made sure he knew what state your company is in and what he was purchasing. I don't know who's come along and bought TF Shipping, or why they have, given the financial state of it. I can only assume they haven't done their due diligence and you haven't been transparent, but—" But what? What am I going to do? Rat them out? Find out who's bought TF Shipping and call them to make sure they know what they're letting themselves in for? For what purpose? Self-satisfaction? To have the last laugh? Am I about to threaten them to get that good reference?

No. I don't need to. Karma will do all the work. I take a breath and stand taller, reaching for my coat and pulling it on. "I hope you both have a lovely Christmas with your family."

"Oh, we will, won't we, Dad? We're looking at a family holiday to Mauritius, five-star, first class."

"Maybe don't put that on the company card," I quip, smiling sweetly as I claim my box of things. Thomas moves to allow me past, but Anthony does not, meaning I have to shuffle by carefully so there's no contact. He makes my skin crawl.

"Ms. Moore?"

I look up to find the two officers who came to my apartment standing outside the elevator. Jones and Hyde. "Hi," I say, as they both look at the box in my arms. "I just lost my job."

"Oh," Hyde says, "I'm sorry to hear that,"

"Don't be, it was time for me to move on. How can I help you?"

"We wondered if we might show you something?" Jones asks,

approaching. I can feel Thomas and Anthony behind me, interested.

"I'd ask you to come into my office but it's not mine anymore."

"Take it," Thomas says, moving aside and sweeping his arm out.

"No, it's fine, I can talk to them at h—"

"Just take the office, Camryn," Thomas says, almost sternly, motioning back into the room.

"Okay." I reverse my steps, frowning at Thomas as I pass. He looks stressed. "Come in," I say to the officers, and they join me.

As does Anthony. "Since you're on our premises," he says, helping himself to a chair and getting comfortable.

I scowl at the prick. "This is Thomas Fryer, my boss. And his son, Anthony."

"What's this all about, then?" Anthony looks at me with too much interest, no doubt hoping he's about to get some dirt.

"Anthony," Thomas says in warning. "Let's give them some privacy."

He holds his hand up, silently silencing his father, and Thomas throws me a look full of apology.

"Shall we?" Hyde asks, eying Anthony.

"Sure."

Jones approaches me with an iPad and taps at the screen a few times before showing it to me. I withdraw when I see myself on the screen walking through the dark street in the snow. "The footage is very clear," she says.

"I can see," I murmur.

"Thanks to the snow. You mentioned you didn't get a look or even a glimpse of the man in question."

"He was wearing black. And a hood."

"Man in question?" Thomas asks. "What's happened, Camryn?"

Jones glances at me, and I shake my head mildly. "I was attacked."

His eyes fall to my cheek, and I shrink a little. "You told me—"

"I know what I told you, Thomas."

Jones hums, tapping at the screen again and pulling my attention back there. "This is a few minutes before."

"That's outside this building."

"Not so random after all," she says, changing the screen again. "This is a close-up."

"Are you kidding?" I blurt out, getting closer to the screen.

"Do you know him?" Hyde asks.

"Yes, I know him." I look at Thomas. "It's Phillip West."

He balks and joins us, having a peek himself. "Jesus," he breathes. "Camryn fired him."

"For?" Jones asks.

"He filed a false accusation against another staff member," Thomas says, shaking his head, his eyes still on the screen.

"His wife," I add. "He was trying to get her fired. From what I understand, he's met someone else and wants Meredith out of his life in all capacities." I falter, more words waiting to spill out, but I'm not sure I should share, given Meredith told me in confidence. And do I need to? No. "He claimed she got aggressive with him one evening in the office when everyone stayed behind to have drinks. We had evidence that proved it was actually the other way round."

"Right." Hyde looks at Thomas. "I'm going to need a name and an address."

"You're going to arrest a man a few days before Christmas?" Anthony asks, sounding truly flabbergasted. "Based on a few shots from CCTV that put him on a different street a few minutes before Camryn was jumped?"

"The evidence is sufficient," Hyde retorts, clipped, going back to Thomas. "Name and address."

Thomas seems lost in a daze, staring forward.

"Sir?"

He snaps out of it, casting a sorry gaze my way. "I'm sorry, Camryn."

"I fired him, Thomas," I say tiredly.

"Yes, but I should have fired him first, save you doing it, then we wouldn't be in this mess."

"Sir, I'm going to need that address."

"Yes, right, sure. Follow me." Thomas turns and leaves, and the officers follow.

"We'll be in touch. You'll be required to come down to the station to do a formal statement."

I nod, a little struck, having to perch on the edge of my desk, my legs wobbly, as Anthony follows them out. I remain where I am for a while, my mind racing, until I see the officers boarding the elevator with their name and address. Phillip West?

My mobile rings, knocking me out of my daze, and I answer on a murmured, "Hello." unable to muster the strength or effort to sound okay, although I'm quite sure I don't want to tell Dec about Phillip West.

"What's up?" he asks, sounding anxious.

Luckily, I have another bombshell to share, although I'm still wondering if it's new news to Dec. "You didn't get TF Shipping," I say.

He's silent for a few moments. "I hoped to give you the heads-up before your boss. I just found out myself."

"They let me go."

He sighs. "Fuck. Camryn, I'm sorry."

"It's okay." I have a feeling my time here was limited, anyway. This was a double-edged sword for me. I scoop up my box with one arm and head for the elevators. "I'm going to see my mum."

"Call me when you're done, okay? We can do something."

"Sure." I try to smile and fail. It's the week running up to Christmas, a time of year I dread at the best of times. Everyone shuts down for weeks, which means I'm in limbo, unable to actively hunt for a new job until the new year.

Spend it with us.

Think about it. That's all I ask.

Could I do that?

I don't know. I honestly don't know.

Mum's sleeping when I arrive, her room dark and quiet. I dump my box in the corner and do my usual tasks before lowering to the chair and sitting in silence with her. She eventually opens her eyes, and before they even find me, I know they're empty. She turns her head and looks at me. "Hi, Mum," I say quietly, sensing today isn't going to be as good as my last visit. "What did you have for breakfast?"

She squints, as if she's thinking hard about that. "Porridge."

I shift my chair closer. "Sounds yummy."

"With honey. And a banana." She smiles. "That was your favourite when you were a little girl."

My entire being solidifies. She knows. *She knows it's me.* "Yes, it was."

She lifts her head off the pillow a tiny bit. "That nurse was here again last night."

"Which nurse?"

"The one who's been taking my money. She went under my mattress. Ha!" She drops her head back down, and it lands with a soft thud, the effort to keep it up too much. "But I fooled her."

"How?" I ask, animated, as if truly intrigued.

"I hid it all in my pillow." She lifts her head again. "Go on," she whispers. "Get it out and put in in the bank before she finds it."

I bend over her bed and go along with her, slipping my hand into her pillowcase, faltering when I feel a rustle of something. I frown as I grab a handful and pull it out.

"Quick," she whispers, while I stare down at the ripped pages out of a book. "Put it in your handbag. There's more."

"Okay," I whisper back, stuffing the worthless, tatty paper into the side pocket of my bag before reaching in and pulling out more. "I think I've got it all."

"Okay. That's good." Her head plummets to the pillow again and she whips out two pages from my grasp, setting them aside. "This is for Noah. For that football kit he keeps talking about."

I hesitate for a second. Just a second. "Okay, Mum."

Deirdre enters, and she smiles widely at me. "You came for the carols," she sings, thrilled.

Mum flips me a wink as the nurse washes her hands at the basin, and it brings an instant smile to my face. "Oh, that's today?" I ask, zipping up the side pocket on my bag and patting it.

"We're just getting started." Hands on her hips, she takes Mum in. "Now then, Celeste, are we going to get you in a chair?"

"I'll help," I say, getting up as Deirdre pops into the corridor and returns moments later with a huge wheelchair. Or more like an armchair on wheels.

"Where am I going?" Mum asks, looking alarmed.

"It's Christmas carols, Celeste. We got a choir here just for you."

"She's sucking up because she knows I'm onto her," Mum says out the corner of her mouth as I help her to sit up. She lifts with relative ease, surprising me.

"Let's play along," I whisper back. "Can you swing your legs off?"

"I'm not an invalid," she snaps. "It's just the flu, I'll be right as rain soon."

"I wish you would be," I say under my breath as Deirdre moves in to help.

"No, thank you." Mum holds a palm up to stop her coming closer. "This lovely young lady is all the help I need."

And just like that, the wind is taken out of my sails. "It's Camryn, Mum," I say.

"Who?"

"Never mind." I take her weight, which isn't much at all, and get her into the chair. "Ready?" I ask, pulling a blanket off the end of the bed and laying it over her lap.

"Where am I going?"

"To hear some Christmas carols."

"Oh, we used to do that when you were a little girl," she says, happy. "Your favourite was The Twelve Days of Christmas, but you always got the geese and the swans mixed up."

I smile as I wheel her out of her room, down the corridor to the communal room. Yes, I did. Only the geese and swans.

The residents of the home all sit in various chairs in a semicircle around a makeshift stage. "What are we doing in here?" Mum asks.

I grab a chair from the corner, noting the lack of other relatives present, and sit next to her, taking her hand in mine. "Look," I say, as a line of people file onto the stage, men and women of all ages, and children too.

"What are they doing here?" she asks.

"They're going to sing for you, Mum."

"Oh. How lovely."

They start with Silent Night, and it is utterly beautiful. Even better, Mum listens intently, a wistful smile on her face. When one of the nurses appears next to me with a tray, I take two small cups of mulled wine and put one in Mum's hand. And I listen to the truly angelic voices as I watch her sip from her cup and sway her head in time with the music. I don't take my eyes off her. Can't. I just have to watch her. She's so oblivious to the fact I'm losing my sweet mum. She has no clue and therefore doesn't mourn her darling husband who passed away four years ago. She's ignorant to the pain of losing her beloved Noah. Being unaware of the pain of loss is probably the only blessing of her illness.

"This is nice," she says, reaching for my hand and resting it on her lap. I drop my gaze to our entwined fingers, holding on to her tightly. "You look so much . . . lighter, my buttercup. Happy. Shame your new man couldn't be here too."

I shoot her a surprised look, not that she notices. "Yes, a shame," I agree. "I'd love for you to meet him."

"That would be nice."

"He has a little boy, Mum."

She just smiles at the singers. She looks . . . at peace. As if she's needed this. The music. The joy. *Me.*

"I love you, Mum."

"I love you too, buttercup," she says clearly, bringing the back of my hand to her mouth and kissing it. "Love you too."

When Mum's settled back in her bed, she drops off almost instantly, exhausted from her short outing. Deirdre clears away some of the empty cups on her wheely table. "Too many tipples," she quips, chuckling as she drops the plastic cups in the bin.

"She seemed so good today," I say as I watch her sleeping. "Confused still, obviously, but she knew me." And then didn't. Then did again.

Deirdre smiles, checking some of Mum's notes. But she doesn't say anything. Doesn't she agree? I bend and kiss Mum's forehead. "I'll see you tomorrow."

"Did you enjoy the carols, Camryn?"

"They were wonderful." I pull on my coat and swing my bag onto my shoulder. "Do you mind if I leave that here until the snow's cleared?"

Deidre looks across to my box of things in the corner. "What is it?"

"Just a few things from work I don't need. I'll take it when the weather's not so bad and I don't need both hands in case I slip."

"Do you want me to put in the office?"

"There's nothing valuable. It'll be fine there." I frown. "Actually, you can throw it all away."

"Oh?"

"It's just some loose bits of stationery. See you tomorrow."

"See you tomorrow."

I push my way out into the cold, feeling so much better than when I came, and stutter on the steps when I see Dec's black Defender. He gets out and opens the back door, revealing Albi on the back seat, out of his car seat. "Camryn!" he sings, scrambling across to get out.

His face is fucking precious. It could never not bring a smile to mine. "What are you doing here?" I ask, taking the steps down to them.

"We took an early day," Dec says.

"We been busting balls!" Albi declares, practically launching himself at me, forcing me to catch him or let him fall face first into the snow. Of course, I catch him. *Trust.*

He clings to my neck, his face close to mine. I could break down on the spot. "Busting balls, huh?"

"Yeah!"

I look past him to Dec. He looks yummy in his jeans and navy coat, a scarf wrapped around his neck. "You changed out of your power suits?"

"After we busted those balls."

"Poor balls." I plant a kiss on Albi's cheek and lower him to the snow.

"Are you finished work now, Camryn?"

I laugh, looking out the corner of my eye to Dec. "Yep. All finished."

"We are too!" He darts back to the car and scrambles up into his car seat, getting his arms through the straps. "It's ice-skating time."

I recoil. "What?"

Dec looks instantly uncomfortable. "I lost a bet."

"Yeah," Albi sings. "Daddy said I couldn't be quiet for the *whole* of his call, and I was."

"And now I have to take him ice skating."

"Oh, well, have fun."

Dec's face falls, and try as I might, I can't keep mine straight. "You're fucking with me," he breathes quietly.

"You're not coming?" Albi murmurs, forlorn.

"Of course I'm coming." I reach into the car and buckle him

up, and then I still. It's like muscle memory, instinctively doing this. "Will you have a penguin?"

He gasps, utterly gobsmacked. "You know about the penguins?"

"I do indeed."

"How?"

"Because I looked it up, of course." I check his straps and take the door. "Mind your fingers," I say, making sure his hands aren't wandering as I close the door. "Ice skating?" I face Dec. "Of all the things you could have used as leverage, you used ice skating?"

His nose wrinkles and he pulls me into him. "How is your mother today?"

"She was good. We listened to carols and drank mulled wine together." I lean back to get his face in my sights, pondering when might be a good time to tell him about the visit I had from the police and what's transpired. I mentally conclude now. Get it out of the way. "The police came to see me again today."

"Oh?"

"They have CCTV footage of a man they think attacked me."

"Oh?" he says more slowly.

"It's an employee I fired."

"What?" His face transforms instantly from soft and curious to shocked and hard. "Are you fucking joking?"

I shake my head. "The more I think about it, I'm not surprised. He's been physical with his wife, a woman he's apparently loved, so it should be no shock he would get physical with a woman he despises. I'm just telling you this now so we can move on."

"Move on?"

"Yes."

"Right. Move on." I detect a wave of madness in his eyes that I'm quite sure I don't like.

"It's done." I kiss his cheek. "Now tell me about the balls you busted today, because it wasn't Thomas's."

"Ha ha," he drones. "Just some failing tech company." Light thudding interrupts us, and we both look at the window seeing

Albi banging impatiently with his fist. "Ready to go ice skating?" Dec asks.

I look down my front, to my entirely inappropriate attire for the weather, let alone ice skating. "No."

"We'll detour via your place."

Albi's like a jack-in-the-box all the way to my place, so much so, I'm sure he'll knacker himself out and be asleep by the time we get to Hyde Park. "I'll be quick," I say, hopping out and crunching my way up the path to the door. I let myself in and dump my coat on the couch as I pass, unzipping my dress as I go. Five minutes later, I'm wrapped up tight in some jeans and a cosy roll-neck, and on my way back out.

I swing the door open and find Dec and Albi on the other side. "He needs to pee," Dec says, as Albi cups himself with two palms, shuffling on the spot, his little face bunched as he strains to hold it in. "Go, go, go," I say, moving aside to let them past.

"Quick." Dec steers Albi by his shoulders through to my bedroom, and the clatters of the loo seat being flung up ring out loud. "Jesus, fella," Dec says over a laugh. "Get your aim right."

I smile as I pull my hat on.

"We need to wipe the seat," Dec goes on.

"Why?"

"Because you've sprayed all over it."

"I don't wipe the seat at home, Daddy."

"I know, the magic fairies do it at home."

"Do they?"

"Yeah, they're called Daddy and Lynette."

"Huh?"

"Never mind. Wash your hands." The flush sounds, followed by the tap, and they appear a few moments later, Dec looking relieved, Albi no longer clenching his groin area. They look so much alike, except Albi's eyes are on the greener side of grey. "Ready?" Dec asks.

"Ready."

"Who's that?" Albi veers off course to the cabinet under the window and picks up the framed photo of Noah, and my mind quickly empties as he studies the picture. I can feel Dec's worried eyes on me. He's probably blank too.

"Um," I swallow repeatedly trying to moisten my dry mouth, words chasing in circles in my head, but none of them coming together to form a sentence that'll make sense to a four-year-old. "That's my little boy." I didn't mean to say it. I don't know what I meant to say.

Albi's little eyes look at me thoughtfully, his brow creasing as he tries to process that information. "You have a little boy? Like me?"

"Oh God," I breathe, looking at Dec for help. It hasn't even crossed my mind that I might be in this situation, having to explain to Albi who Noah is and why he's no longer here. I don't know where to start, and I don't know if I can get through it without falling apart, which I absolutely mustn't do in front of him. "His name was Noah," I say, feeling hot and bothered, sweating in all of these clothes. "He's gone to heaven."

"Where's heaven?"

"It's where angels go," Dec says, trying to save me the impending panic attack.

"He's an angel?" Albi takes another look at the picture. "Where's his wings?"

His innocence is something of true beauty. So precious. When Noah was alive, I battled with Dominic daily over protecting that innocence. Delaying for as long as possible having to inflict the cold, harsh reality of life on him. When my dad died, I insisted Noah shouldn't be at his funeral. Dominic disagreed, saying we were wrapping him up in cotton wool. Yes, I was. I would have wrapped him up in cotton wool forever if I could. Protected him from all harm and cruelty of life. "That picture was before he got his wings," I say to the little boy I've fallen in love with while he gazes at the love of my life. "He was here for a little while, but then he grew some wings and he had to go to heaven."

"Will I grow some wings?" He looks at me, almost hopeful.

"One day, you will grow some wings too. We all will. But we don't know when."

"I want my wings the same time as Daddy." He sets the picture back on the counter, and I hear Dec inhale lightly. And there's a tragedy that I won't even try to unravel for him. We don't get the blessing of never leaving anyone behind or not being left behind. They're the cruellest parts of leaving life and surviving it.

"Daddy will probably get his wings before you because he's older than you."

"He's not older than me," Albi says, pointing to the picture, so confused.

And this is why explaining death to a child is impossible. Keep them innocent. "You're right." I force a smile. "What do I know?" I look at Dec and shake my head, kicking myself. "I'm sorry," I mouth.

"Camryn?"

"What?"

"Shut up." He comes to me, slips and arm around my shoulder, and takes Albi's hand as he pushes his mouth to my cheek. "Are you okay?"

I reach for my nose and pinch the bridge, wondering how I would have worded it all if I'd had time to think about it. And I still don't know. "I really made a mess of that."

We head out of my apartment, and Dec throws an annoyed look my way. "You didn't make a mess of it. Answer my question."

"I'm okay," I say, my pounding, anxious heart calming as I smile up at Dec meekly. "Kind of."

"Never lie to me about how you feel." He dips and pushes his lips into my hair as we run into Mr. Percival in the hallway.

"Oh, and who have we here, then?" he crones.

"I'm Albi and I'm going ice skating with Daddy and Camryn, and I'm gonna use a penguin because I'm little."

Mr. Percival looks like he could topple over, the bombardment of information bending him backward. "Jeez, kid, chill, I only asked your name."

"Huh?"

Dec chuckles, collecting Albi. "Afternoon, Mr. Percival, how's the turkey?"

"Dead."

"What's that?" Albi asks, zooming past the old man and entering his apartment through his wide-open door. "Oh, wow, cool!" He drops to his knees and swipes up a gnome on a motorbike.

"Careful with that, kid," Mr. Percival says, following him on his walking frame. "The rims are delicate."

Dec snorts, and I cough on nothing, both of us watching as Mr. Percival takes the gnome from Albi and shows him the wheels. "I painted them gold, see?"

"Oh my gosh." Albi registers the hundreds of gnomes in Mr. Percival's apartment, on every surface. "A policeman!"

"Yes, and a fireman, and a doctor and a farmer and a—"

"He has a lot of gnomes," Dec pipes in, dipping to scoop Albi up. He gets shrugged off.

"You have a Father Christmas! *And* his reindeers." Albi bombs across the lounge and drops to his knees again, scooping up the fattest gnome of all. "Daddy, look."

"I can see, fella. Are we going ice skating?"

"Now, that one I got in Lapland," Mr. Percival says, joining Albi and perching on the arm of the chair.

"You've been to Lapland?" Albi asks, his mouth forming an O in astonishment.

"Yeah, I've been, kid. In 1987. A long, *long* time ago. What year was you born, kid?"

Albi looks at Dec. "2021," Dec says.

"Twenty-one," Albi murmurs, shifting onto his butt and crossing his legs in front of Mr. Percival, as if he's in class in front of his teacher.

"So you're four."

"I'm four and a half."

"And have you been good this year?"

"So good." He's gazing up at the old man in complete awe.

I look at Dec. He shrugs. "Want a drink?" I ask.

"Well, it doesn't look like we're going anywhere fast."

"Mind if I get a drink, Mr. Percival?"

"Oh my, how rude of me." He dips. "You wait there, kid, I'll bring back a feast and some eggnog."

"What's eggnog?"

"Magic, kid. Don't move."

"I won't."

"This way." Mr. Percival passes us and leads us into the kitchen.

"What the fuck?" Dec stops on the threshold and gazes around at the chaos. "Are you having a party?"

Food is laid out on every surface, some with ice packs under, some covered with tinfoil, some in Tupperware pots. It's a buffet on steroids. "It's Christmas," Mr. Percival says. "One must be prepared for guests, since you never know when they might show up." He picks up a knife and points it at Dec, making him lean back. "Case in point." He slices one of his scrummy cakes, and I'm first to help myself, humming my happiness. "Sherry?"

"Please," I mumble.

"Sure," Dec breathes.

Then once the old man's seen to our needs, he loads a tray of goodies and rests it on his frame, going back to Albi. "Make yourself at home, kids."

And we do, dropping to the couch and listening while Mr. Percival enchants Albi with tales about gnomes, Christmas, world travels, and the war.

"He's actually talked my son to sleep." Dec props Albi onto his shoulder and takes my hand, walking us up to the front door.

"That was unexpected and quite lovely," I say, reaching for Albi's hat and pulling it down over his ear. "Will he sleep through until seven?"

"He better." Dec disappears up the stairs as I hang up my coat, dropping my bag to the floor and wandering to the kitchen. I stop on the threshold, looking up the stairs. Bite my lip. Reversing my steps, I kick my shoes off and take the steps, following my nose to Albi's room, finding jungle animals decorating every wall. I watch quietly as Dec strips him down and gets his floppy body into some jungle pyjamas before tucking him in, dropping a kiss on his cheek.

The moment he turns around and sees me, I know my face spells out what I want and need in this moment. His arms around me. His lips all over my body. His slow, careful drives as he makes love to me.

He slips his coat off and drops it on a beanbag, then comes at me with purpose and picks me up, carrying me to his bedroom and sitting me on the edge of the bed. His fingers graze my sides as he pulls my jumper up over my head and tosses it aside, then he presses a palm into my chest and pushes me down to my back. I reach for my jeans to undo the fly, but he pushes my hands away, planting one fist into the mattress and looming over me while he takes over with his spare hand, his eyes dancing, moving from mine to his task. His lashes flicker. His lips part. His breath gets louder. Pushing my jeans open, he dips and kisses the flesh just north of my knickers, and I melt into the duvet on a sigh, closing my eyes as I rest my arms over my head, blissed out completely as he trails his mouth up my tummy, past my chest, and onto my throat. His hum vibrates against the hollow, his scruff brushing my skin, my back arching into his chest.

"Take it off," I whisper, reaching for the hem of his sweater and wrestling it up his torso. I need his warm flesh on me, suffocating me, swathing me. He pushes to his knees and rips it up his body, leaving his hair a crumpled mess, and throws it aside before removing his T-shirt as well. Dizziness gets me when his hard chest is bared, his biceps swelling when he yanks his belt open. I shoot up, impatient, and unbutton his fly, shoving his jeans down over his arse and getting my hands there, squeezing.

"Easy," he whispers, standing and kicking his jeans and boxers off. He takes the waist of mine and peels them down my legs with my knickers, and I kick them to free myself, welcoming him back to my body. "Touch me," he murmurs, falling to his forearm and taking my hand, guiding it to his arousal. A sharp inhale pierces the air when I wrap my hand around him, his eyes squeezing shut as I start to stroke him, watching him sustain the pleasure. "Fuck, that feels good." His head becomes heavy, beads of pre-cum dripping onto my stomach as I work him. He opens his eyes and stares down at me, his jaw tight but rolling, his gaze misty and lazy. Nothing is said as we study each other, but endless words are being tossed into the air between our closed mouths. I love him so much. I want to tell him repeatedly with the hope that he may one day comprehend just how deeply. Show him every day.

On that thought, I bite my lip, rubbing the tip of my thumb across the tip of his erection, spreading the wetness, enjoying the continued strain on his handsome face. "Tell me what you want," he whispers huskily, his voice doing unspeakable things to my already raging libido.

"I want you inside me," I tell him, unabashed. "Moving slowing." Connected. "All night."

He groans and rolls his mouth onto mine, kissing me with conviction, the hardest he's ever kissed me, and yet it's still loaded with so much love and reverence. His body lowers onto mine, forcing my hand away from his length, and I grab his shoulders and moan around his lips, widening my legs and wrapping them around his hips, constricting him as our tongues swirl and dance, dip and retreat. The full, hard length of him pulses against my lower belly, yelling for attention again, and my internal walls scream in response. On a gasp and a curse, Dec tears his mouth off mine and pants down at me, looking dazed and shiny with sweat.

"Turn over." He hooks a hand under my waist and rolls me onto my front, encouraging me farther across the bed, away from the edge to give him room to straddle my arse. "I'll be inside you in a minute," he murmurs, dragging a fingertip down my spine, making my shoulder blades pull in. "There's no rush."

My hormones disagree. "Dec," I beg quietly, clawing my hands into the duvet, my cheek squished as I lose myself in darkness. Just feeling him. Sensing him. Smelling him. Tasting him in my mouth.

"Shhh." He swaps his finger for his tongue and licks down my spine slowly, his hardness skimming my bottom, leaving wet trails of his pleasure across my skin.

"Oh my God." My eyes cross behind my lids. I'm burning for him, slowly being driven to distraction. He reaches my backside and sinks his teeth into my flesh, then sucks, licks, and kisses it.

"I've got to taste you," he growls, flipping me onto my back. I don't have a second to brace myself for his mouth's assault. He shoves my thighs apart and buries his face between my legs, sucking my throbbing clit into his mouth. Pleasure shoots up my spine, cracking my body into a violent arch, and I grab a pillow to stifle my scream as his hot, wet tongue laps through me greedily. I'm going to pass out. Overheating, burning inside and out, I toss the pillow aside and gulp down air, panting at the ceiling, the gathering pressure ready to detonate and wipe me out. I look down my body, reaching for his hand on my stomach and moving it to my breast, holding it there as he eats me alive bit by bit. I don't want to come on his mouth.

I reach for his shoulders and disturb him, and he comes up for air, his eyes glazed, his mouth shimmering with wetness. He looks a little disorientated as he crawls up my body and shares my pleasure, kissing me deeply for a few brief, wonderful seconds before he turns me back onto my front and blankets me with his body, nudging my knee out with his to open me up to him. He brushes my hair aside, giving himself access to my ear, and nibbles at my lobe. "Bone deep," he whispers as he rolls his hips and slides into me with ease, dowsing the flames immediately. I go lax from the relief, reaching up to cup his head as he licks my ear, making me shudder as he breathes into it lightly. "Feel good?"

"Hmmm." I push my arse up into him, welcoming him to the deepest part of me until he can advance no more.

"Oh, fuck, Camryn," he rumbles, stilling but kicking like crazy inside me. "You're clenching around me."

I start circling my hips.

"Camryn, stop."

I can't. It feels too good, the pressure back, now with tingles too, and it is out-of-this-world.

"Stop," he breathes, starting to thrust too, his body defying his mind.

"Oh God," I whimper.

"Fuck." He takes a handful of my hair and gently pulls, encouraging my head off the bed and turning it so he can get to my lips. His kiss is manic and fast, his tongue whipping through my mouth as his drives gets harder and faster. I've reached the point of no return, urgency now ruling me, only making our kiss even crazier, our tongues plunging as deeply as his cock. I don't need to tell him I'm close. He doesn't need to tell me. It gets to the point we can no longer kiss—our bodies are banging too hard to sustain it. He curses and stops for a moment, dragging me onto my hands and knees by my hips, and then he let's go completely, smashing into me almost ruthlessly. I strain to look back over my shoulder, suppressing my yells of pleasure, watching him, head tossed back, every muscle straining, as he goes hell for leather. My boobs bounce violently, my fists bunch the sheets, my head hangs as he yanks me back and forth onto him, his fingers clawing painfully into me as he yells his ecstasy.

My climax hits like a firework between my legs, and I cry out at the intensity, as Dec pushes high and deep, freezing, a broken moan filling the bedroom, mixing with my cries as he bursts. His cock expands inside me, and he comes in long, rolling surges. "Jesus Christ," he gasps, his torso collapsing on top of me, pushing me down to the sheets. I can't find air, my body trembling with the force of my release. And I'm sleepy. So sleepy.

Dec pants above me, kissing my shoulder in between his laboured breathing. "That was unexpected."

"You'll never be a man I fuck and forget," I say, breathless, feeling him smile against my skin.

"You didn't fuck me," he whispers. "I fucked you."

He certainly did. And it feels good to feel my heart beating so wildly.

"I love you," he says, nuzzling into my cheek.

I start to turn over, making him lift to give me room. He slips out of me with a wince, and I look down between us when I'm on my back, seeing the aftermath of his orgasm twitching wildly. I reach for his shoulders and pull him down onto me, wrapping my arms and legs around him like a bow, my face in his neck smelling the sweat and sex on his skin. "I want to spend Christmas with you and Albi," I say, feeling him start to move immediately. I tighten my grip, not that it makes an ounce of difference.

He breaks free from my arms, but not my legs, which lock him in a hold. His eyebrows rise as he takes a wrist in each hand and pushes them above my head. "Come and live with us."

My legs immediately go lax around him, along with the rest of my body. "Come live with you?" I parrot like a fool.

"I don't want you to be on your own anymore." Sinking his face into my neck, he kisses his way up my cheek onto my lips, while I stare, struck fucking dumb, at the ceiling. "This is only going one way, Camryn, and that's toward forever." He pulls back and scans my face, his expression somewhere between hope and caution. "Let's not waste time stressing about what's a socially acceptable timeframe for shit like this." Another kiss on my blank face. "I love you." Another kiss. "I want you here." Another kiss. "Say yes."

"Get off."

He stills for a beat then lifts his head to get me in his sights, searching my eyes. "Cam—"

"Get off, Dec." I put resistance against his hands that are

holding my wrists down, and he instantly lets go, pushing to his knees to free me. I get up, my heart bashing madly, and go to the bathroom, closing the door behind me. I feel like a full-blown panic attack is about to cripple me, my breathing shot to bits, my skin clammy. I go to the sink and splash my face with cold water, patting at it as I lower to the edge of the tub, my legs shaking, partly because I'm still recovering after Dec blew my mind and body, but partly because of his soft demand. And it's not even because it's a demand. Honestly, I don't know why I've reacted like this, but I have, and I can't stop it.

I love him. I love Albi. Frighteningly, I want nothing more than to be with them constantly—both of them are a calming salve to my broken heart, slowly healing it minute by minute—and yet something feels so unbearably wrong. Is it the guilt? The emptiness that's slowly being filled by love and hope?

I drop the towel and cover my face with my hands, not crying, but in complete despair. And now I've ran away from him, left him on the bed probably kicking himself, so I can hide in here and chase my thoughts in circles.

A light, nervous tap sounds on the door, and I drop my hands as Dec pushes his way in, his naked body visibly deflated. He takes me in on the edge of the bath, thoughtful, and clearly disappointed. "Forget I said anything," he says with reluctance, dropping the doorknob, his arms hanging heavily by his sides. "It was a stupid idea." He doesn't believe that. Do I? I don't even know. I only just got my head around spending Christmas with them, and now we've leapt into forever.

"He's four, Dec," I say, my words coming without thought. "I met him days ago. His little mind won't understand. It's been him and you all his short life, and I've shown up and—"

"He's smitten with you," he murmurs. "Doesn't shut up about you. At this point, I'm questioning if he'd miss me if I vanished."

"Shut up, he adores you."

Coming to me, Dec kneels and takes my hands. "Erase the past five minutes." He kisses both my hands and stands, helping me to my feet and picking me up, carrying me back to the bed and laying me down on my back where I was before he said what he said.

Coming down on top of me, he resumes his position and hides his face in my neck, picking up where we left off. But something like that can't be unsaid, and as I stare at the ceiling, Dec making love to my neck with his mouth, all I can think about is what lies ahead for us. Because if I can't get my head around starting a new life with him and Albi, what's the point in being here now? It's not fair on Dec. But more, it's not fair on Albi.

December 22nd

The smell of coffee brings me round, mixed with the distinct, lost lingering scent of kids shampoo. I inhale in my darkness, letting that delicate scent sink deeply into me. Naturally, the memories come with it, so I let them take hold for a few moments, enjoy them, before I open my eyes to a new day in a whole new world. I find Albi star-fished in the middle of the bed on his back again, his arms draped over his head, his mouth open. Standard Ellis boys sleeping pose. His crumpled pyjamas have ridden up his arms and legs, revealing his creamy, perfect skin. His hair is a flawless mess. His lashes, like his daddy's, are long and nearly touching his high cheekbones. Lifting my head, I look over his body and see Dec's side of the bed empty. He's making coffee.

I roll onto my side and reach for a stray lock of hair lying across his eye, gently pushing it back, and freeze when he stirs and mumbles nonsensical words. I quickly move back, anticipating what comes next, just as his foot shoots out, missing my hip by a hair's breadth. He tosses himself onto his side and sighs, settling. "Oh, you beautiful little thing," I whisper, shuffling closer to him, unable to stop myself from gently stroking his cheek. Listening to him breathe as he sleeps, watching him, brings back a long-lost sense of peace. I move back, getting more of his strewn little body in my sights, and reach for his hand, brushing across his fingers with the pad of my thumb, staring at the cute dimples where his knuckles are yet to develop. Pure hands that have done no wrong in this world. A mouth that hasn't spoken hurtful or harmful words. A heart that knows only love, whatever kind it might be.

Clarity hits me, and it hits me hard, making my blood warm and my heart beat strongly. This is a life raft. *He* is my life raft. Because I'm scared to think about where I might be now if I wasn't here with them.

Lonely.

Hateful.

Empty.

"I need to go talk to your daddy," I whisper, reaching over and kissing his cheek. I hop out of bed and look down my front, wondering where the T-shirt came from. I lift it. And my knickers too. A vague, sleepy memory comes back to me—of Dec wrestling my uncooperative body to get me covered up. Anticipating the invasion of his bed by Albi.

I smile and head downstairs, pulling my hair up as I go. Dec's standing before the open fridge when I make it to the kitchen, glugging down some orange juice from the carton. In his boxers. I take a brief, quiet moment to appreciate him. His back muscles undulating as he tips the carton, his hand holding the door open making the muscles in his arm solid. But most of all, I appreciate that I'm here with him.

Padding over quietly, I move in behind him and thread my arms through his, hugging his back briefly before kissing my way up to his neck, reaching up on my tippy-toes as he lowers his head and puts the orange juice back. "Morning to you too," he says, spinning around and dipping, getting me onto his shoulder.

"Whoa!" I cry, cocking my head as I watch his butt cheeks tense and swell from his long strides to the island. His palm connects with my arse. "Ouch!" He bends and sits me on the counter, the cold stone sinking into my warm flesh which makes me sit up straight. Shiny orbs of mischief gaze back at me. "Yes," I say before he can speak, sweeping my palms across his shoulders.

"Yes, what?"

"I said, yes."

"What did I ask you?"

"You didn't ask me. You demanded in a roundabout way."

His head tilts. "Go on."

"I want to be with you all the time."

A discreet smirk tilts one corner of his mouth. "Go on."

"You and Albi."

His eyebrows lift, his smile more apparent.

"Here," I add, letting my hands drift down his bare chest as his palms stroke their way onto my thighs. My nose scrunches. He wrinkles his in return.

"I'd ask what's changed your mind," he whispers, slowly bringing his mouth close to mine, making sure that by the time he kisses me, I'm frantic for it, "but I really couldn't give a shit." He takes my neck and holds me in place while he kisses me deep and hard, moving his body between my thighs. Things happen down below that shouldn't be happening when I'm half naked on the island and Albi is within a mile radius, and judging by the deep, guttural rumble that emanates from the back of Dec's throat, it's happening to him too. But I take the moment, enjoying our closeness, no matter how long it lasts. We just have to keep it under control.

"Three more sleeps!"

"Oh my God," I mumble.

"Fuck," Dec hisses.

"Get off!" I shove him away and quickly slip off the counter, hearing the thumps of his little feet getting louder as he races down the stairs. I get myself on a stool and pull my T-shirt down my thighs as much as possible just in time for him to come bombing into the kitchen.

"Three more sleeps!" He runs laps around the island, my eyes following him until I'm dizzy. Blinking repeatedly, I find Dec, who's got his front pushed close up to the counter. He looks in pain. I smile. He scowls.

"Albi, fella, slow down." Dec doesn't move. *Can't* move. Those boxers aren't hiding anything.

"Three more sleeps!" He screeches to a stop, breathless, and looks between us. "I want some Coco Pops."

"You'd *like* some Coco Pops, *please*," Dec says, correcting him. "Father Christmas doesn't visit children who don't have any manners." He frowns to himself, peeking down his front, and I chuckle as Albi climbs up onto a stool next to me.

"Why are you laughing, please?" he asks.

"Daddy's making me laugh."

"Why, please?"

"It doesn't matter." I pat his hand and Dec inches his way along the island, bending and pulling out a bowl before shuffling back and sliding it in front of Albi.

"Thank you, Daddy."

"Welcome. Juice?"

"Yes, please and thank you."

Dec spins and goes to the fridge. "Camryn?"

"I've had some," I murmur, licking my lips, tasting the orange. "But I'll take a coffee."

"Please," Albi adds.

"Please," I say around my smile.

Dec looks over his shoulder, his gaze full of playfulness as he takes a step back and slides the juice onto the counter before going to the coffee machine, keeping his back to us.

Albi hops back down from the stool and goes to the larder cupboard, heaving it open and reaching up on his tippy-toes to get the Coco Pops, tired of waiting for Dec. "Thank you," he says, closing the cupboard and going to the fridge, pulling out the milk and closing the door again by backing into it, his hands full. "Thank you." He comes back to the island, dumps his finds next to his bowl and goes to the drawer to get a spoon. "Thank you," he says to the drawer as he closes it. I watch him, smiling, feeling Dec watching him too as he climbs back up onto the stool and tips his Coco Pops into the bowl. "Thank you." Then he pours the milk, spilling more onto the counter than he gets in the bowl. "Thank you." A big scoop with his spoon loads it, and he shovels it into his mouth. "Thank you," he mumbles around his mouthful.

I chuckle to myself as Dec, finally with the tent he was sporting deflated, brings my coffee over and rests his forearms on the counter. "That good, fella?"

"Yes, thank you." Albi spoons another pile of the chocolatey cereal into his mouth. "Thank you," he says to the spoon.

I can't cope. I snort into my cup as I take a sip, and Dec shakes his head, retrieving his phone off the side and checking it. "What are we doing today?"

"Ice skating!" Albi chants. "Please."

Oh, I thought we'd escaped that. Dec grabs a loaf of bread out of the cupboard and fills the toaster, throwing me a pained face.

"Please can Mr. Percival come?" Albi asks. "Thank you."

"Mr. Percival?" I laugh. "He can hardly walk, Albi."

"I want to visit Mr. Percival again, thank you. Can we go see him after ice skating, thank you? He's ninety-nine, Daddy! Thank you. Nearly a whole hundred! Please. That's a really big number, Daddy. Thank you. I'm only four and a half! Please. Mr. Percival said he flew in a Spitfire." Albi pushes his feet into the footrest on the stool and uses it to stand, leaning over the island to reach for Dec's phone. "Let me show you what a Spitfire looks like Daddy, please. Type Spitfire into Google." He stretches.

Slips.

"Albi!" I dive across and grab his arm before he plummets to the hard floor, and despite saving him, I don't manage to save his breakfast, which goes flying across the island, Coco Pops and chocolate milk spraying everywhere.

"Oopsie Daisy!" Albi sings. "Please."

"Christ, you frightened me." I stand and lift him back onto the stool, kissing the top of his head as I hold it with a palm either side, surely squishing his lips. "Don't move your butt off this stool."

"Good catch," Dec says, shaking his head, his hand resting on his chest to ease his racing heart. "When you're on the stool, your little backside stays on the stool."

"Thank you," Albi murmurs sullenly.

"Albi, you don't have to say please or thank you with *every*thing you say," I tell him, smiling fondly. "Just if someone gives you something, or you ask for something."

"But it's good manners."

I don't know what to say to that. I show the ceiling my palms as Dec rounds the island and comes up behind me, dropping a kiss on my cheek before disappearing into the laundry room, returning a second later with a Vax.

"You didn't say thank you." Albi isn't scowling, but he's close, and I rack my brain for what I needed to say thank you for, coming up blank. "Daddy gave you a kiss, and you didn't say thank you. You said I must say thank you or please if someone gives me something or I ask for something."

Dec laughs as he starts hoovering up the mess, and I'm momentarily distracted by the vision. It really shouldn't be sexy, Dec hoovering. And yet, it is. "Thank you," I murmur, falling into a reverie as Albi tips more Coco Pops into his empty bowl.

A knock on the front door pulls me out of my daze, and Dec looks down his front, to the hoover in his hand.

"I'll go," I shout over the noise, hopping off my stool.

"It's probably April," he calls. "I've not unbolted the door, so her key won't work."

I race up the stairs, grabbing the first thing I can find to cover my bottom half . . . which happens to be a pair of Dec's sweatpants. I have to roll them over at the waist half a dozen times to shorten them so I don't trip over them. Pulling my T-shirt out, I hurry back downstairs and swing the door open.

It's not April.

"Hi," I say, hanging onto the wood, shivering when the chill hits my bare arms and feet, taking in the woman. Well-turned out.

Smart but casual. A blond layered long bob. Piercing blue eyes. *Pretty*.

She looks me up and down. "Is Dec home?"

"Sure, let me just grab him. Can I say who's here?"

Her lips press into a straight line, apparently not forthcoming with an answer.

"I'll go get him," I say, an odd feeling coming over me, something I can't quite put my finger on. But I don't need to fetch him, because when I turn around, he's behind me, hoover in hand, black boxers on full show, along with the rest of his body, his eyes wide and shocked.

I withdraw, getting colder, and it has nothing to do with the sub-zero temperatures.

"Chelsea," he breathes.

It takes a few seconds for my brain to catch up. Chelsea? His ex-wife? Wait, no. They're still married. Chelsea his *wife*. My brain kick-starts, and I suck in air and face her, seeing she visibly stands taller before she steps in without an invite and closes the door behind her, gazing around the hallway. "You've decorated."

I move back, looking between them, my mind running blank. I can hear Albi in the kitchen, his spoon clattering against his bowl, oblivious to who's standing in the hallway. Dec's a statue, just staring. I can't read him. Shock, yes, I can see that, but what's going through his mind right now?

And what should *I* do?

Chelsea's eyes move from Dec to me, and she subtly looks me up and down. I feel so scrutinised and vulnerable standing here in Dec's sweats, my hair pulled up messily, not a scrap of makeup on.

Judged.

Exposed.

And unreasonable or not, I feel stupid, because I have no idea what Dec would need me to do in this situation. I don't know him well enough to make an executive decision. I know he's only ever talked about his wife with contempt. *She's dead to me.* I know that when I asked him what he'd do if she ever showed up, he didn't answer. Not truly. He just said he'd get his divorce quicker. But we didn't touch on Albi because I didn't even know he existed at that point. And since I did find out about him, I haven't asked any of the questions I should have.

Like if he's ever asked about his mum. Like what Dec would do now, except ask for his divorce. Does he still want that divorce? Now she's here and he's looking at the mother of his child, does he want that? He must have felt something toward her. *I wanted Albi to have a stable family. I did what I thought was right.* Does he think it's right now, to give her the opportunity? Assuming she wants it, and it's pure female intuition I'm going on, but Chelsea looks like a very contrite woman. Does he still hate her?

Fuck.

My head pounds, feeling like it could fall off my shoulders with the weight of my thoughts. And the fear inside me? It's so powerful it hurts.

I feel like an impostor.

"What are you doing here?" he finally asks, the words a quiet murmur. It surprises me. Isn't it obvious why she's here? I think I expected him to yell his outrage and throw her out. And he hasn't.

"You look well," she says, lowering her handbag to the wooden floor. Is she about to take her coat off? Hang it on the stand? Go to the kitchen to put the kettle on? Irritation begins to dilute the fear and shock, and that only worsens when her eyes roam the naked planes of Dec's chest. Yes, he looks well. Or *did.* Now? The warm, safe body aside that I love, he looks like he's seen a ghost.

"Thanks," he murmurs, frowning, shaking his head.

"Daddy?"

That one word is all it takes to snap him out of his stunned state, and he swings around, as do I, finding Albi in the kitchen doorway, his face smeared in chocolate milk.

"Oh my goodness," Chelsea breathes, pulling my attention back around. She's staring at him, her hand over her heart. I can't take it. I feel like I'm sitting on the sidelines, helplessly watching all hope slip down the drain. "You've changed so much." She lowers to a knee, and Albi's little eyes narrow as he moves into Dec's side and circles both his arms around his daddy's naked thighs, hugging them.

Dec's arm goes around his boy protectively. "Changed so much?" he breathes in disbelief, his eyes suddenly darkening. Anger. I've seen it on him only a few times, and it's not pretty. "Of course he's changed, Chelsea, he was four weeks old when you left over four *fucking years ago*."

Something in me clicks, and it overrides my fear and uncertainty, *and* Dec's anger and whatever feelings Chelsea's having.

Albi.

I don't even know if it's my place, or if it's what Dec wants, but I don't like the building anger in him, and his language tells me he's not thinking straight. I hurry over to Albi, who's still clinging to his daddy's thighs, and crouch. "Why don't you come show me the Spitfire Mr. Percival was telling you about?"

His scowling face pushes into Dec's thigh some more. He knows. He knows something's not right. *Little sponges.* I smile wide, using every ounce of strength I have to show him I'm not affected. Everything's okay. I wish Dec could do the same.

"Come on," I say, offering my hand. "Daddy needs to talk to the lady."

Dec's suddenly crouched with me, but he doesn't look at me, his full attention on Albi. "I'll be back in a minute, fella."

"Where are you going, Daddy?"

"Nowhere. I'm staying right here. I'll be a few minutes, I promise."

"Come," I say, taking Albi's hand gently and standing, leading him away. He looks back over his shoulder constantly. Suspicious. Chelsea catches my eye. Her straight lips tell me everything I need to know. "Show me this Spitfire," I say, my voice loaded with enthusiasm I'm not feeling as I lead him into the kitchen.

"Who is she?" Chelsea asks as we disappear. "A replacement for me?"

"I can't replace something he never had," Dec snipes. "What do you want, Chelsea?"

I grab Dec's phone but meet a brick wall, the screen locked. "Do you know Daddy's code?"

"My birthday!"

"Which is when?" I don't even know that.

"June!"

"Do you know what day?"

"Fifteen!"

I type in 1506 and breathe my relief when the screen comes to life. Loading Google, I type in "Spitfire" trying not to listen but struggling when there's no attempts to lower their voices. "Oh wow," I say, lifting Albi onto the island and showing him the screen. "Look at that!" He takes the phone and stares down at the plane. "Mr. Percival flew one of these?" I ask.

"Yep. Over Germany!"

"Wow."

"What's Germany?"

"It's a country," I explain. "You'll learn all about it at school one day."

"Mr. Percival said he would teach me."

"I want to come home," I hear Chelsea say.

My body becomes stock-still as Albi chatters, his chubby finger swiping the screen to scroll through the endless pictures. I wait for Dec to speak. To tell her to fuck off. But he doesn't. He says . . . nothing. And then the sound of a door closing reaches the kitchen.

"You sit there a second," I say, lifting him onto a stool. "No stretching, remember?"

"Remember," he confirms, lost in Spitfires.

I creep to the kitchen doorway and peek down the hallway. They're gone, and the double doors to the lounge are closed. My eyes drop and dart to the floor, my heart sinking. I have no right to feel so shattered.

They were never mine to have. They're hers. And she wants to come "home."

To *her* home.

With them.

Where I don't belong.

I turn around, watching Albi slumped over the phone, studying every picture of Spitfires he can find. *He's* not mine.

I lost mine. Not for four years.

But forever.

I cover my face with both hands, squeezing my eyes closed. He didn't tell her to fuck off.

I hear the front door open and drop my hands, seeing April breezing in, all smiles, followed by Blaine. They both falter when they see me, their faces falling. It takes everything in me to try and smile—try being the operative word. I feel completely lost.

"Morning," I say, my voice cracked and broken. I go back to Albi, wrapping my arms around his shoulders and hugging him tightly. "Aunty April's here now," I say, sinking my face into his hair and taking in a strong dose of shampoo and Albi. Then I break away, forcing myself to hold it together as I go back into the hallway. They've got their coats off now. "Albi's in the kitchen," I say, heading for the stairs. "Dec's got a visitor in the lounge."

April frowns as I pass.

"I'm just going to get dressed." I rush up the stairs and change into my jeans and jumper, grabbing all of my things and hurrying back down. I hear the sounds of astonishment coming from the kitchen, Albi no doubt showing his aunty and uncle his new obsession. I don't want to say goodbye to that gorgeous little boy. But if Dec wants to keep his "family" intact and Chelsea comes home, I need to step aside. It fucking kills me, but I have to walk away.

My breaking heart pulls me back toward the kitchen.

My head leads me out of the front door, not looking back.

December 23rd

I don't remember getting home yesterday. I vaguely recall getting a bottle of wine out of the fridge, but I don't remember finishing it. Don't remember having a shower, which I only know happened because my hair was still damp when I woke up. I don't remember unwrapping the collage of pictures of Noah. I don't remember tipping out all the unpacked boxes and hanging Mummy's and Noah's stockings on the wall.

I do remember sobbing for so long my face is stinging and blemished today. And I do know I can't be in this apartment alone a moment longer. I feel numb. Hollow.

Back to square one, except I have an added loss as fresh as the loss of my child to cope with. And more anger, but this anger is all for myself for being so naïve and ridiculous to believe my life could bear any semblance to normal again.

This is on me.

Dec's absolute silence—no message, no call, no visit—screams his answer. He loves me. So much. But the stability he wants for his child outweighs that.

He'll move on. As everyone else seems to do.

I wrap up and step into my boots, pulling a hat on as I search my apartment for my phone, trying to remember the last time I saw it. I can't. And I don't need it, anyway. So I abandon my search and head out, looking up at the white sky when I make it outside. One fat snowflake floats down before me and lands on an icicle that's formed on the bare blossom tree, and something inside the frozen water shines at me, pulling me close.

A white feather is frozen in the spiked ice. Perfectly preserved. As white as snow.

Beautiful but trapped.

Reaching for it, I drag the pad of my gloved finger down the ice, catching a drop of water off the bottom that sinks into the material of my glove. Melting to nothing. Without a purpose. A lot like how I feel too.

December 24th

December 24th

I walked so far yesterday, I had to stop at Boots to pick up some blister plasters. I wake up on a wince when I move, my muscles aching as I get up and walk to the kitchen, my feet throbbing. I get a coffee and sit at the table, staring into space, not allowing my mind to wander. I can hear the wind whistling outside, a snowstorm arriving on time as predicted. I look down into the swirling black liquid, the thoughts I'm fighting to blank out winning the battle to make it through.

I want to come home.

Home.

It's not a place. A building, a house.

It's family.

She's back.

I want Albi to have a stable home.

And I'm far from stable.

God, you're poison.

A forceful bang on my door sounds, startling me out of my

daydream, and I drag my tired, aching body up to answer. Pulling it open, I recoil when I find Anthony on the other side.

"You cunning bitch," he hisses, sending me flying back into my apartment with a brutal shove in my chest.

I cry out, shocked more than hurt, and just catch my footing before I fall to my arse. I don't manage to save my coffee, though, and it spills out of the cup all over my hand, scolding it. "Shit."

"So you think you're smart?" he says, his face twisted in anger. "Swooping in and fucking up *my* plans for your own gain?"

"What the hell are you talking about, Anthony?" I ask, shaking my burning hand, distracted by the pain rather than the raging bull in front of me, looking like he's about to charge at any moment.

"Dec Ellis!" he roars. "The man you're fucking and feeding information to."

I'm so fucking lost. "He didn't buy the company, Anthony," I remind him. "You took great pleasure in sharing that information before you fired me." I go to the kitchen, no longer able to stand the burn, and shove my hand under the cold tap. "Get the hell out of my apartment or I'll call the police." Suddenly, my head is yanked back by my hair, snapping my neck sharply, sending shooting pain up into my skull. "Fuck!" I yelp.

"Call them," he hisses in my face. "I won't be dumb enough to get caught like Phillip did."

I wrench myself out of his hold, surely losing a few tufts of hair as I do. "Get out." I turn around to face him, grabbing a towel and holding it over my hand as he moves in, intimidating and large. "You're nothing but a bully, Anthony. If you're going to hit me, then fucking do it so I can get on with my day."

He raises his hand, but I don't cower or flinch, likely pissing him off some more.

"Anthony!" Thomas appears in my kitchen, throwing me once again. "What the fucking hell are you doing?"

"She's fucked it all up!"

"Thomas, I have no idea what you idiot son is talking about."

"Get out!" Thomas bellows to Anthony, pointing to the door. "Or I'll call the damn police on you myself."

With wide eyes, I watch as Thomas's face reddens, his patience lost. I've never seen him like this.

Anthony snarls and backs off, flinging an arm out, sending an empty bottle of wine and the glass crashing across my kitchen before he stalks out. "Fuck you," he mutters as he goes, and I have no idea whether it's aimed at me or his dad.

I look at Thomas for some answers, flinching when I hear my front door slam. "What the hell is going on, Thomas?"

"I'm so sorry, Camryn."

"For that?" I ask, pointing past him, where Anthony just departed. "Don't be. I've dealt with bigger fears than your son's temper." I get my hand back under the tap. "Tell me what's going on."

"The deal went south," he murmurs, sounding exhausted.

"I'm sorry to hear that." I couldn't give two fucks about that.

"It went south because Dec Ellis intercepted the buyers."

I still where I stand, staring at the blank wall behind the sink. "Intercepted? I'm guessing by that you mean he enlightened the other buyers of the information his forensic accountant found so they pulled the plug."

"You guessed correctly."

Ruthless. "Thomas, you're a smart man." I flip off the tap and face him. "You must have known you'd be found out if you manipulated asset values and accounts."

"It wasn't me," he breathes.

"Anthony."

He nods. "You should know, he met with Phillip West the night you were attacked."

"What?"

"Anthony wanted you out of the way while we saw the deal through. I love my son, Camryn, but he's greedy and unscrupulous, and he needs to answer for his actions."

I wrap the towel around my burning hand. Thomas looks utterly exhausted. "I appreciate you being honest with me."

Another nod, this time reluctant. "I want out, Camryn. I've sold to Dec Ellis."

I laugh under my breath. So Dec won. He busted those balls.

"I'll stay on for a year on a consultancy basis, but then I'm exiting. I want you to stay with me."

Am I hearing him right? He wants me to work for Dec Ellis? "I can't do that, Thomas." I drop the towel on the counter and dip, starting to collect the broken glass. "I'm sorry." I truly am, but only for Thomas. Why didn't Dec tell me about this yesterday? I stall that silent question. A ridiculous question. He's got more important things on his mind, and it isn't me. "If you don't mind, I have somewhere I need to be." I rise.

"Oh, right. Of course. Have a lovely Christmas, Camryn." Thomas comes at me, and his arms open up. Is he moving in for a hug?

"I don't think so, Thomas," I say, backing up, dropping the few pieces of glass I've collected into the sink.

"Come on, no hard feelings." He gives me grabbing hands as I lean back, ignoring my reluctance, and pulls me in for a squishy hug. "I appreciated everything you did, even if my son and wife made it impossible for you."

I succumb to his strength and let him hug it out. "How is Barbara?" I ask, wondering where she sits amid this mess. Were my instincts correct?

"I don't know."

I lean back, breaking free of his arms. "She left you?"

His head tilts. "You knew?"

"I suspected."

"And you didn't say?"

I laugh under my breath. "No, Thomas, I didn't say. They hated me enough, without me getting involved in family affairs."

He huffs out a laugh. "That's fair, I suppose."

Fair? Nothing about any of this is fair. "I'm sorry," I say, feeling bad for the guy. "I hope you work it out."

"Funny," he says, seeming to drift into thought. "I don't." He holds me by the tops of my arms. "If you need that reference, just shout."

"Thanks," I murmur, a little thrown. "Merry Christmas, Thomas."

He laughs under his breath and leaves, closing the door behind him, and I lean against the counter, looking at the mess of glass across the kitchen. Somehow, I muster the energy to clean it up, trying not to let the bombshell of Dec's hostile takeover of TF Shipping take up too much thinking space. I haven't the capacity and, frankly, the loss of my job feels like such a minor blip in my life right now. Because I've lost Dec. I've lost Albi.

I've lost hope.

I look down at my hand as I flex it, wincing at my red skin. I have no first aid supplies. Nothing to cover it. "Fuck," I whisper, reaching for my head and rubbing my sore scalp.

I can't stay here. I grab my keys and head out, hearing Mr. Percival calling me as I go, but I can't face him.

"Camryn!" The sound of his walking frame thumping the ground mixes with his calls, and I stop at the door, squeezing my eyes closed. He'll take a tumble, and I'd never forgive myself. I have enough guilt to handle.

I face him and muster everything I have to smile. "Mr. Percival."

"You in a rush?"

"Last-minute shopping."

"Christ, Camryn, it's Christmas Eve. You should be relaxing and looking forward to the big day."

I haven't got one person to buy for. Sad. And come to think of it, neither has Mr. Percival, not that I know of. He hasn't mentioned anyone. I still don't know who all that food is feeding.

"Will you give this to the little fella?" He holds out a model plane. A Spitfire. "He was so fascinated, and it was a joy to tell my stories to someone who was actually interested."

I swallow and take the small plane. "Sure."

"Everything okay, Camryn?"

I look at the old man, feeling the backs of my eyes stinging. He's been a royal pain in my arse . . . and totally wonderful. I nod, unable to speak past the lump in my throat, and step into him, dropping a kiss on his cheek, hoping he hears my gratitude through that.

"Oh my, did I miss the mistletoe?" He looks up at the ceiling. "You'll make old men blush if you go around knocking kisses on their cheeks like that, dear."

I strain a smile, squeezing his arm, and head out, walking with no direction, slipping the Spitfire into my bag.

My walk leads me to the care home, but when I see my brother in Mum's room, I hold back, not wanting to bump into him or answer his questions. Hear him tell me I look terrible. I get myself a coffee from the vending machine in the reception and go to the family room, sitting down and waiting. It won't be for long. He never stays for long.

As predicted, he passes the room five minutes later, walking with pace. Because he has somewhere to be—a family to get home to for Christmas. Dragging myself up, I go to Mum's room and sit with her in the dim light, curtains drawn, as she sleeps. Two hours pass. She doesn't wake up, even though I wish she would and could be my person to talk to. I wouldn't want to tell her that the happiness she saw in me has gone. I'd just like to hear her voice, even if she's rambling about nurses stealing her money. I'd possibly tell her about Mr. Percival and how many stories he loves to tell to those who'll listen.

But instead, I listen to the wind echoing outside and the various nurses going back and forth between the rooms, checking on their patients. It's never completely silent. Unlike my mum.

After another hour of watching her sleeping, I finally accept that today she's not going to wake up. I drop a kiss on her cheek and stand with effort. "See you tomorrow, Mum."

See you tomorrow, buttercup.

I roughly wipe at my face, desperate to hear those words, today especially, before grabbing my bag and walking out.

I wander until it's dark, or as dark as it can be when everything's coated in white. I find myself outside the The Royal Constantine. I get a fleeting look of surprise as I pass through the lobby. Not because I'm here on Christmas Eve. But because I'm not in my usual office wear.

Julio's standing behind the bar, the cloth he's using freezing mid-swipe when he clocks me. "It's Christmas Eve, Camryn," he says, sighing, abandoning his task and tossing the cloth in the nearby sink. "What are you doing here?"

"What are *you* doing here?" I ask, taking the last stool and shrugging off my coat, letting it drape the backrest.

"I work until nine and then I go home to my family." He leans over the bar. "Where is the man?"

"Dirty martini, please."

He considers me for a moment, eyes narrowed, before he pushes off the bar with a sigh he wants me to hear and gets me my drink. "Have you called him?"

I look up through my lashes. "No." I don't have a phone to call him. I either left it at Dec's in my haste to leave, or I lost it between his place and mine. "Where's my drink?"

He doesn't answer, just shakes his head as he tips the ingredients into the shaker.

It occurs to me as I watch the liquid pour from the bottle that I've not been to the toilet all day, and my bladder is quickly yelling at me to relieve it. "I'll be back." I leave Julio smacking the lid on the shaker and head to the bathroom. I use the toilet, wash my hands, dry them, and I manage to do it all while avoiding the mirrors at every turn. When I get back, my drink is set on the bar.

Something next to it.

I jolt to a stop.

My heart begins to thrum in my chest, quickly working its way up to a full-blown clatter. I don't want to approach, and yet my feet slowly carry me to the bar, the small object set next to my martini becoming clearer.

A snow globe.

A white feather, encased in ice, floating in the center.

I look around the bar, noting I'm alone, until Julio comes through the staff door. "Did you put that there?" I ask, pointing at it with a limp finger. He shakes his head but doesn't look surprised to see it. "Then who—"

"But I did put this here." Julio sets something else on the bar. A small flip calendar, the kind someone would have on their desk, maybe twenty years ago. He fiddles with it for a second, turning month after month.

Until he arrives at December.

He disappears back through the staff door, leaving me alone in the bar with my drink, the snow globe, and the small desk calendar. My chest pumps with the force of my breathing as I blindly lower my arse to the stool, my eyes lasers on the name of the month. This month. The worst month of my life.

I don't want to flip the page to December 1st.

I do want to flip the page.

Visions of the calendar on Dec's fridge invade my mind, all the memories noted of him and Albi, one for each day. To think he's made notes of each day he's known me, too, scares me to death. I clasp my hands together to try and stop them shaking, a conflicting tug of war in my heart repeatedly pulling me from hopeful to cautious. I pick up my drink and take a healthy glug. Then I brave reaching for the calendar and turn the first page, holding my breath as I do.

DECEMBER 1ST

ONLY MY BOY HAS EVER MADE MY HEART TWINGE. TODAY, YOU DID. I'VE NEVER SEEN SUCH A BEAUTIFULLY DULL DIAMOND.

DECEMBER 2ND

I NEARLY WENT BACK TO THE BAR TODAY JUST TO SEE IF YOU WERE THERE. THERE'S SOMETHING ABOUT YOU. I NEED TO KNOW WHAT.

I inhale, the words blurring through my welling eyes. I let them fall, needing to clear them so I can read on.

DECEMBER 3RD

I COULDN'T RESIST GOING TO THE BAR TODAY. YOU WEREN'T THERE.

DECEMBER 4TH

YOU SMELL LIKE MARTINIS AND REGRETS. AND FOR MY SINS, I WANT TO KNOW WHAT THAT TASTES LIKE.

DECEMBER 5TH

ALL I'VE DONE SINCE I LEFT YOU WAS WORRY WHETHER YOU'D GO BACK TO THE BAR AND HOOK UP WITH ANOTHER GUY. I DON'T WANT YOU TO, AND I DON'T THINK YOU WANT TO EITHER. YOU OPENED UP TO ME A LITTLE TODAY. I KNOW I'M RIGHT TO PURSUE THIS. I CAN BE PATIENT.

DECEMBER 6TH

YOU SMILED TODAY, AND I REALISED I'M FALLING FOR YOU.

DECEMBER 7TH

YOU TRIED TO PUSH ME AWAY TONIGHT. AND ALL THE SILENT LIES ARE BUILDING. AS ARE MY FEELINGS.

DECEMBER 8TH

IT WAS EVERYTHING. MORE THAN EVERYTHING. I TASTED YOUR SADNESS, AND I FELT YOUR HOPE. AND YOU LOOKED JUST SO FUCKING BEAUTIFUL.

DECEMBER 9TH

I CAN STILL FEEL YOU ON MY LIPS. TASTE YOU ON MY TONGUE. I HOPE IT LINGERS UNTIL I SEE YOU AGAIN.

I find myself flipping through the days, needing his thoughts more with each one I read. A timeline of our relationship—an insight into Dec's mind. What he felt.

DECEMBER 10TH

IT'S SNOWING. MY LITTLE FELLA IS BESIDE HIMSELF. I HAVE A FEELING YOU WON'T BE. AND NOT BECAUSE YOU HATE SNOW. WHAT'S YOUR STORY, CAMRYN?

DECEMBER 11TH

I MISSED ALBI'S BEDTIME TO SEE YOU. AND YOU BAILED. I JUST DON'T KNOW WHY YOU'D DO THAT. TO ME. TO YOU.

DECEMBER 12TH

TODAY I WALKED OUT OF MY OFFICE AND FOUND YOU FROZEN ON THE PAVEMENT. YOU KISSED ME. I HEARD EVERY WORD YOU SAID WITH THAT KISS. IT DIDN'T SCARE ME. BUT IT'S THE WORDS YOU DIDN'T SAY THAT TERRIFY ME.
BECAUSE I LOVE YOU TOO.

My hands shake as I turn to the next day, my throat thick with emotion.

DECEMBER 13TH

YOU OPENED UP TODAY ABOUT YOUR MUM. BUT THERE'S MORE. I KNOW THERE'S MORE. AND I SO DESPERATELY WANTED TO TELL YOU ABOUT ALBI, BUT SOMETHING STOPPED ME.

DECEMBER 14TH

I WOKE UP AND MY HEART DROPPED.
THEN I READ YOUR MESSAGE. YOU DIDN'T RUN.

DECEMBER 15TH

I DON'T EVEN KNOW WHAT TO WRITE. BUT I KNOW THAT I LOVE YOU. AND I'M PETRIFIED IT'S NOT GOING TO BE ENOUGH.

DECEMBER 16TH

40 TODAY. I WISH I COULD HAVE SPENT IT WITH YOU. I'VE ONLY EVER BEEN THIS SCARED ONCE IN MY LIFE—WHEN I FOUND OUT I WAS GOING TO BE A DAD. I MIGHT BE MORE SCARED NOW BECAUSE I JUST DON'T KNOW HOW TO TELL YOU ABOUT ALBI, AND MORE THAN THAT, HOW YOU'LL TAKE IT.

DECEMBER 17TH

I SPENT THE DAY STILL TRYING TO FIGURE OUT HOW THE FUCK I TELL A WOMAN WHO'S LOST A LITTLE BOY THAT I HAVE WHAT SHE LOST. AND YOU LIED TO ME ABOUT THE CUT ON YOUR FACE. WHY?

December 18th

I FEEL LIKE MY SECRETS ARE ACCIDENTAL. SECRETS THAT WOULDN'T NEED TO BE SECRETS IF YOU WEREN'T THE WOMAN YOU ARE. DOES THAT MAKE ME ANY LESS DECEIVING? WILL YOU FORGIVE ME FOR WITHHOLDING?

December 19th

I JUST WANTED TO MAKE TODAY BETTER. I LOVE YOU SO FUCKING MUCH. I JUST WANT TO TAKE THE PAIN AWAY, AND I FEEL LIKE I'M JUST ADDING TO IT.

December 20th

I COULDN'T STAY AWAY. AND I'M GLAD I DIDN'T. YOU'RE RIGHT. TODAY WAS A CONFLICTING MIX OF AMAZING AND REALLY FUCKING HEARTBREAKING. WHAT YOU DID FOR ME AND ALBI . . . INCREDIBLE.

December 21st

I THINK ALBI'S AS IN LOVE WITH YOU AS I AM. WE WANT FOREVER WITH YOU AND EVERYTHING THAT COMES WITH IT. I JUST HAVE TO ASK AND PRAY YOU SAY YES.

December 22nd

WHY NOW? WHEN I FEEL SO CONTENT, SO COMPLETE, WHY

NOW? YOU RAN. I CAN'T EVEN BE MAD WITH YOU. I JUST FEEL... BROKEN.

December 23rd

I WANTED TO COME TO YOU SO BADLY TODAY. ALBI ISN'T HIMSELF. I'M DEFINITELY NOT MYSELF. I COULDN'T LEAVE HIM—I WAS SCARED TO LEAVE HIM. I JUST NEED TO FIGURE OUT HOW TO FIX THIS.

I retract my hand, bracing myself for today and what it might say, exhaling, as if I've been holding my breath the whole time. I slowly flip the page.

December 24th

IT'S BEEN YOU SINCE DECEMBER 1ST, CAMRYN. IT'LL ONLY EVER BE YOU.

All the air is stolen from my lungs again when I slowly turn and find him sitting in the exact same chair he was when I first saw him.

On December 1st.

"I love you," he murmurs, staying exactly where he is. I want to go to him but can't feel my legs. I want to throw my arms around him but can't stop them shaking. My head is being blitzed by endless questions. What happened? How is Albi? Where is Chelsea?

"You love me," I whisper instinctively, convincing my legs to move. I get off my stool and cross the bar, biting down on my lip to stop it wobbling, and he rises to welcome me, opening his arms for me to walk into. His arms around me are everything.

"It crushes me that you thought for a second I wouldn't choose you," he says into my hair, squeezing me to him. "Never think that again. Ever. Do you hear me?"

I can only nod into his chest, damning my self-doubt and racing mind for diluting what I know about Dec with misplaced possibilities.

"Come home," he orders gently, breaking away and wiping my tears. "And never leave us again." Brushing my hair back, he holds my face. "Leave the room when you need to, go for a walk, remove yourself and take a moment, but never leave us."

I snivel, his face blurring past my tears, and he smiles sadly, kissing each of my cheeks before he settles on my mouth, sharing my salty tears. My lips quiver against his as I fall into the soft, slow pace of his kiss, clinging to his wrists like the lifeline he is.

"Ready?" he murmurs, taking his adoring mouth away from me way too soon.

I nod, burying my face in his chest and letting the last of my sobs leave me as he holds me.

"Come on." He tucks me into his side and walks me to the bar, pulling my coat off the stool and holding it up for me to slip my arms in, before he collects my bag and slips the snow globe and calendar inside. He places a twenty on the bar, just as Julio reappears, nodding his approval. "Merry Christmas, you two."

Dec nods, short and sharp, and I smile as I'm led out of the bar.

To go home.

April opens the door before we make it there, the relief on her face to see me with Dec appreciated more than she'll ever know. "He's still out for the count," she says, as Dec drags my coat off my shoulders and hangs it. A tray of champagne glasses is on the console table, each glass still fizzing, recently poured. April slides it off and offers me one.

"Christ, April," Dec murmurs, and she shrugs.

"Take one," she orders me. "Blaine!"

He appears from the kitchen with a roll of wrapping paper and various bits of sticky tape lining his bare forearm. "You made it," he says, joining us and taking a flute. Dec rolls his eyes as April puts one in his hand, then mine, and takes one for herself.

"To you two," she says, chinking each of our glasses. "We'll leave you alone, but if you're peckish, I've prepared a sharing board. Cheeses, meats, pickles, nothing too fancy." She gives me an excited smile and hauls me in for a fierce hug, forcing me to lift my glass to avoid spilling it.

"April," Dec breathes. "Too much."

"Okay, I'm sorry." She releases me and grabs her husband, dragging him back into the kitchen. "How many left?" she asks.

"Too many," he grumbles. "Can I eat now they're home?"

Dec sighs and takes my glass, setting it on the side table with his. "Sorry. They're staying over. Always do on Christmas Eve."

"That's nice."

"Yeah," he muses, and a weird silence falls between us I'm sure I don't like. Dec eventually rakes a hand through his hair, and it's then I see his blemished knuckles.

"What's that?" I ask, taking his hand and inspecting it.

"Oh, that." He frowns down at is hand. "That's the result of me punching Anthony Fryer."

"What?" I move back.

"You left your mobile here. There were missed calls from him. Naturally, I was curious."

"Naturally," I murmur. "So you didn't put two and two together and come up with the fact he was pissed off because you fucked up his deal and renegotiated with his dad in your favour?"

He shrugs, sheepish.

"I'm not working for you, by the way."

"Thomas told me he went to your apartment and found Anthony there."

"Oh."

"That he suspects Anthony had something to do with the guy who you fired attacking you."

"Oh."

"So, yes, I paid him a visit." He shakes his hand off. "The

police arrested Phillip West yesterday and released him after they'd interviewed him. Obviously, he denied it."

"How do you know that?"

He reaches into his pocket and pulls out my mobile. "They said they'd be in touch to get your statement. I want you to tell them about what happened when Anthony turned up at your apartment yesterday too. Okay?"

"Okay," I agree easily. They're both bullying, misogynistic bastards. I hope they never work again.

"Good." Dec coaxes me into the lounge. "Let's talk. I want you to know what happened after you ran out the other day."

With Chelsea.

Oh God.

Dec sits me down on one of the huge couches and puts himself at the other end. "Why have you put so much space between us?" I ask. "In case I don't like what I hear?"

He frowns and gets back up, coming to my end and dropping to the cushion next to me, taking my hand. "I just want transparency between us. No surprises. She wasn't happy when she didn't get the reaction from me that she wanted, and knowing Chelsea as I *knew* her, and I can't imagine she's changed in the four years since she left, I expect there'll be some backlash."

"Okay," I murmur, buckling myself in.

"She wanted us back." He looks at me for my reaction, but I have no reaction. I figured that out before I overheard her tell him she wanted to come home. "I told her that wasn't an option, which obviously led her on to you."

"Obviously," I whisper, watching him, how uncomfortable he is. This isn't boding well. It feels like he's bracing himself to tell me something damaging.

"She kissed me."

My back automatically pushes back into the couch, putting some space between us that I didn't want a moment ago. "Did you kiss her back?"

"Jesus, no." He looks horrified at the suggestion. "Never. But I know that woman. She will try to spin this and make you believe it was more than me being jumped and pushing her off. April walked in when she heard the commotion, and suffice to say, Chelsea barely made it out alive."

I smile on the inside, mentally cheering April on.

"I'm letting my lawyer take over from here. He's working on a restraining order for the time being to keep her away from us, but it will be in the hands of the family court and I'm well aware they could deem it in Albi's best interests to have contact with his biological mother. She doesn't want Albi. The money she took has obviously run out. My legal team are working on digging up what they can—where she's been, what she's been up to."

"Why are we even talking about her?" I ask.

He withdraws a little. "I thought—"

"You wanted transparency." I smile. "I believe you are a good man, Dec. An amazing father." I take his hand and squeeze.

"Just trying to be a good boyfriend too."

"Have you cleaned your teeth, rinsed with mouthwash, and disinfected anywhere she touched you?" He was half naked.

He smiles mildly. "Scrubbed."

"Then I take you back."

He laughs. "Okay, good."

"Chelsea doesn't matter, Dec. Albi does. What did you say to him?" He must have been a little anxious wreck.

"Blaine took him to his treehouse at the bottom of the garden, so he didn't see or hear anything, thank God." He puts his face in his hands, brushing them down his stubble. "I told him the lady who stopped by was someone who works for me, and now I'm terrified he'll hold it against me when he's older. I never want to lie to him, Camryn."

"You did what you had to do in the moment. You protected him."

He nods, but it's not a convincing nod. He's questioning himself. It's standard when you're a parent. I don't know how many times in Noah's short life I beat myself up over one thing or another, questioned myself, argued with two parts of my mind that were conflicting. We do what we can, and we hope we do it right. I need to move this along. "What time did Albi go to bed?"

"Four."

I laugh. "So, he'll be up with the dawn chorus."

"Possibly before that." Dec shifts on the couch to face me. "He's asked where you were non-stop."

"Don't make me feel guilty."

"It's not intended to make you feel guilty. It's intended to show you how wanted you are. How loved." He takes my hands. "We can never fix what's broken. We can't replace what you've lost, Camryn. But we're here, and all we ask is that you love us as much as we love you."

I soften, hating he needs confirmation of that. "I do."

"Then we'll be okay." He leans in and captures my lips, kissing me down to my back, the cushions getting knocked off the couch. "Tell me we'll be okay."

I nod, fisting his hair at his temples. "We'll be okay."

"I love you." His mouth moves across my cheek to my ear. "Bone deep," he whispers, making me smile and shudder all at once.

"I hate to interrupt." April's voice drifts into the room, and Dec tears his wet lips from mine and scowls.

"No, you don't." He cranes his head to look over the back of the couch. "You said you'd leave us alone." He helps me to sit up as she walks around the couch and places her grazing board on the coffee table, along with the bottle of champagne.

"It's Christmas Eve," she says haughtily. "And what do we do on Christmas Eve?"

Dec narrows an eye on her.

"We watch Love Actually!" she sings, getting the remote control and flicking the TV on.

Dec glances at me, all kinds of awkward, apologising with his eyes. "We don't have to."

"No." I lean forward and pluck a wedge of Brie off the board. "I want to."

"You do?"

I pop it in my mouth and hum, my taste buds tingling happily. "Oh, that's so good." I grab another chunk before I've finished, my stomach suddenly ravenous for food.

"Take it easy," Dec says, alarmed. Then he scowls again. "When was the last time you ate?"

My chewing stops, giving him all the answer he needs. He reaches for the board and hands me another wedge as April loads the movie and Blaine tops everyone up with fizz. "Here we go," she sings, flopping onto the couch.

Dec reaches for the table loaded with food and drink and drags it closer, so the occupants of both couches can reach. Then he retrieves the pillows, plumps them, and lies down, pulling me into his front so he's spooning me. The lights dim, I snuggle down, and Londoners from every walk of life appear on the screen, Hugh Grant commentating over the hustle and bustle of the city I once loved.

And, like life, hope I can love again.

December 25th

The birds sing outside the bedroom window, marking a new day, and I lie on my back staring at the ceiling, feeling the inevitable hollowness growing. And yet, like so many times since December 1st, it's contending with something else.

Contentment.

It's an odd feeling, and I'm still not sure how I should handle it. I can only hope that with time I learn how to grieve and move forward at the same time. How to be sad for my losses but hopeful and happy about my future.

I feel Dec's hand slip into mine where it's by my thigh, as if he's reading my thoughts and wants me to know he's aware. I squeeze in reply. "Happy Christmas," I whisper, smiling as I let my head drop to the side on the pillow so I can see him.

"Happy Christmas, beautiful," he murmurs. "Is there anything I can do?"

"You're doing it."

He nods, looking over me to the clock on the bedside. "I have no idea how he's not awake yet." He moves across the bed slowly, crawling on top of me. My legs spread, giving his body room between them, and the sheets moving sends the glorious scent of Dec wafting around me. He gazes down at me. "You're the best

Christmas present." He kisses me, but I know Dec. He won't push for more, his thoughtfulness not allowing it. And yet I need him as close as I can get him. So I reach down between our bodies and slip my hand into his boxers, and in response, his soft kiss hardens, along with his flesh in my grasp as I stroke him until he's solid. "Are you sure?" he whispers, pushing my T-shirt up my body until it's bunched up around my neck, his mouth moving down my chest to my boobs. I lose my grip of him and sink into the sheets, closing my eyes in utter bliss as he worships my nipples, trailing his tongue around each one in turn before heading south, disappearing under the sheets and inching my knickers aside.

"Oohhh," I breathe, my back bowing as he licks me from back to front, creeping onto my stomach, working his way back up and reappearing from beneath the sheets. He finds my mouth again and kisses me into oblivion, feeling down my body to move my knickers aside again. He pulls himself past the waistband of his boxers and guides himself to my entrance, slipping into me on collective sighs.

"No more sleeps!"

"Fuck." Dec rolls off me, and the shock exit makes me yelp and Dec hiss. "Motherfucker," he breathes, his eyes wide with pain.

"No more sleeps!" The door crashes open, and I prop myself up on my elbows to find him, my discomfort forgotten when I do. He's frozen stock-still in the doorway, a dishevelled mess of a gorgeous little boy. And he gasps. "Father Christmas brought me Camryn!" He comes at me like a rocket, diving on the bed and taking me out, flinging his little arms around my shoulders, smothering me with his fierce hug.

I'm going to cry.

"Thank you!" he yells in my ear, intentionally loud enough so Father Christmas can hear him all the way from the North bloody Pole. My eardrums ring, but I can still hear Dec chuckling beside me. Albi releases me, allowing me to breathe. But I can't breathe. Like his father, he takes my breath away too. "Merry Christmas, Camryn," he chirps, forcing me to blink back the tears.

"Merry Christmas, Albi," I reply, my words rough and broken as I reach for his hair, pushing my fingers through the wild mess.

He dives onto Dec. "Merry Christmas, Daddy."

"Merry Christmas, little fella."

"Aunty April! Uncle Blaine!" He shoots off the bed and runs full pelt back out. "Father Christmas has been, and he's brought Camryn!"

I grab a pillow and pull it over my face, letting my tears soak into the material. Dec soon yanks it off, crowding me again, his face close. "I love you," he says, as if he needs to remind me.

"I love you too," I whisper. "But I love him more."

"And that will *never* not be okay." He gets to his knees and hoofs me up, and I land on his thighs with force, my front crashing into his. "Remember what I said yesterday," he whispers into my neck. "Whenever you need a moment, take it. But you've got to give me a signal so I know."

"What's the signal?"

"Give me your hands," he says, encouraging me out of his chest. He takes the index finger on each hand and pushes the tips together. "Like this."

"Okay."

"Are you ready?"

I nod. "I'm ready."

"Okay." He loops an arm around my lower back and gets us off the bed, setting me on my feet.

"Are you?" I peek down at his boxers laugh when he rearranges himself, his cheeks blowing out.

"Five a.m. is a win," he murmurs, taking my hand and walking us out of the bedroom. We find Albi outside a closed door.

"Aunty April and Uncle Blaine's door's locked," he grumbles, trying the knob again.

"The crafty fuckers," Dec says under his breath as he bends and inspects the knob. "Albi, there's a coin in Daddy's drawer next to his bed. Go fetch it."

He zooms off and returns a few moments later, holding up a

two pence piece. "What 'cha doing, Daddy?" he asks as Dec slips the coin into the dial beneath the knob. "Getting us in."

Albi claps his hands, squealing his delight, bending to mirror his daddy's pose. "What if we wake them?" he whispers.

"That's the point, isn't it?"

"Will they be mad?"

"Do we care?"

"No!"

The lock clicks, and Dec turns a crafty smirk onto his boy. I'm melting bit by bit . . . and pining for Noah at the same time. "Ready?" he asks.

"Ready!"

"Okay." Dec stands, takes Albi's hand, and pulls me to join them with his other.

"Oh God," I whisper, getting the drift. "I'm not sure they'll appreciate me bombing them out of bed too."

Dec kicks the door open, and I don't have a moment to give it another thought. I'm being hauled toward the bed, Albi squealing his excitement. I just catch April and Blaine bolt up, their eyes wide, before we all dive onto the bed.

Grunts and shouts of surprise mix and blend before laughter drowns the room. "Seriously?" April wails, half outraged, half elated.

"Seriously," Dec counters, as I find my way to my feet, embarrassingly out of breath.

Albi's in hysterics as he rolls around in the duvet. "Seriously!" he yells, getting to his feet and bouncing up and down between April and Blaine. "Father Christmas came, Father Christmas came!"

"Come here, you little rascal." Blaine grabs Albi's pyjamas and drags him over, pinning him down and tickling him until he virtually stops breathing, squirming around on his back.

"Get up," Dec demands.

"I'm naked," April declares, her eyebrows high.

"Me too," Blaine adds.

"We're leaving," Dec blurts, pushing me out of the room. Albi overtakes me, and Dec stops, looking back at his sister and brother-in-law. "If I don't get morning sex, neither do you. Get up." Then he slams the door.

"Oh my gosh," Albi breathes, standing on the bottom step looking at the floor in the hallway, where muddy footprints make a trail. He follows them to the lounge and stops. "There's no more footprints," he says, pointing. "Look, Daddy. They stop here." *Just before the insanely expensive cream carpet.* "Father Christmas must know we're not allowed to wear shoes in the lounge."

"Clever Father Christmas," I whisper. "When did you do this?"

"At three a.m."

"I didn't hear you get up."

"Because I'm stealth like Father Christmas."

"They ate the carrots. Oh my gosh, all the presents are here!" Albi starts jumping on the spot. "Look, Daddy. Look, Camryn!" He bombs past us, back to the lounge entrance. "Aunty April, Uncle Blaine," he yells from the doorway. "If Daddy can't have morning sex, neither can you! Get up!"

Dec coughs on nothing, and I throw him a wide-eyed look. "Shit."

"Any suggestions?" he asks.

"Pretend it never happened," I say. "Don't bring more attention to it. And *never* assume he can't hear you."

"Noted."

We both quickly move out of Albi's path when he dashes back past us like a tornado, dropping to his knees in front of the tree, his little face full of astonishment. An unavoidable gut-wrenching feeling comes over me. It's not something I can chase away by having a private, stern word with myself, or by physically shaking myself away from the thoughts and memories coming at me. I look at Dec, seeing he's spotted it, and I push the tips of my index fingers together. He nods mildly as I turn and leave the room, meeting April and Blaine on my way out, both pulling dressing gowns on, both smiling wide when they see me. I try with all my might to return their beams and fail miserably.

"I just need a moment," I say as I pass them, not trying to fool them with excuses that I need the toilet or anything else. This won't be the last time I have to take a break. Today's going to be a bizarre and conflicting mix of joy and sorrow. I just didn't expect to need be take a timeout so soon.

"Of course," April says. "Take as much time as you need."

I make it into the kitchen and brace my hands on the worktop, my rigid arms holding me up. I take some deep breaths, in and out, in and out. Sometimes I wish I could reach into my chest and physically squeeze my heart to stop it thumping so hard. Like now. I can hear it pounding in my ears. I blow out my cheeks and remove my hands from the counter, standing without support. "Coffee," I breathe, going to the machine and staring at the endless knobs and buttons. What do I need to do, talk to it? Abandoning the machine, I find a glass and get some water. Constant squeals of excitement come from the lounge, *oh my goshes* on loop.

I hear Albi.

I *see* Noah.

"Jesus, Camryn," I murmur to myself, glugging down the water, vehemently willing the shortness of breath to piss off. *Breathe*. Long, deep breaths. I rub at my chest and focus on that, breathing, watching the clock on the cooker as the minutes tick by. Five pass before I feel ready to join them again.

Dec appears in the doorway. "Okay?" he asks and then frowns to himself. "Of course you're not." Shaking his head, he pads over and takes the empty glass from my hand before swathing me with his body. He doesn't say anything more, just holds me until I start to feel guilty for tearing him away from Albi.

"I'm good," I say, gently easing out of his hold, despite wanting to stay in it forever. "Has he peed his pants yet?"

"Multiple times." He reaches for a drawer by the sink and pulls out a roll of binbags. "It looks like a bomb's gone off in a wrapping paper factory."

Laughing lightly, I take his offered hand and let him lead me back to the lounge. Blaine is building something—I don't know what—and April's on her hands and knees reaching for various ripped bits of wrapping paper, dragging them into one pile. Albi tears into another gift and holds up a box. "More Lego!"

"Fuck my life," Dec says over a sigh. "April?"

"What?" she asks, totally coy. "He loves Lego."

"You can build it with him then."

"Camryn, look!" Albi leaps over a pile of paper and grabs a bag, thrusting it at me. "I'll be a fireman!"

"So cool," I say, taking the binbags from Dec and ripping one off, starting to fill it. "What else did you get from Father Christmas?"

He grins. "I know he doesn't bring me *all* the presents. Thank you, Daddy!" He throws his arms around Dec's legs before coming at me too. "Thank you, Camryn."

Huh? Oh my. "Oh, baby, I didn't—"

"Welcome, fella," Dec says, eyeballing me. And it's in this moment it occurs to me that I've not got any gifts to give. And I'm fucking horrified, more so when April reaches under the tree and holds out a box to me. *Oh my God.* "April, I—"

"It's nothing, really. And it's for both of you."

"But I—"

"Take it."

I look at Dec, feeling one hundred percent mortified as he takes the box from April, passing it to me. And now they're going to see my embarrassment multiply as they all watch me open it.

"What's Father Christmas brought you?" Albi asks, inspecting the box.

"I don't know. Want to help me open it?" Yes, I'm using the child as a shield, hoping to deflect some attention.

"Yeah!"

I lower to the couch and Albi clambers onto my knee, and I slowly peel the paper away, revealing a black box inscribed with Dec's name. And mine.

There's a date too. I breathe in my surprise and glance at April. She shrugs, nonchalant. I turn my eyes back onto the box.

December 1st

"What's that say?" Albi asks, his fingertip following some scripted gold font.

"That says Daddy's name," I say, pointing at it. "D E C."

"Dec."

"And that says my name."

"Camryn."

"That's right. And that's the date I met your daddy."

"What's inside?"

"I don't know." And I'm intrigued, as is Dec, since he's joined us on the couch to see.

I pull the lid off and find a little gold card on top of a pile of cream envelopes, all with cards in. The gold card read:

A Year of Dates.

"One a week," April says. "You each take it in turns to choose a date each week. Every Friday. Date night. Blaine and I will have Albi."

What? "April," I breathe, "That's—"

"Every Friday night?" Dec asks, interested, taking the box from my hand. "And you'll have Albi? Overnight?"

"I can't come?" Albi asks, sullen. "That's not fair. I want to come on date night with you and Camryn."

"Hush now, fella, I'm striking a deal."

"Are you busting balls, Daddy?"

"You got it. So, overnight?"

I chuckle, hugging Albi close. "We can do date night too."

"Yay!"

"Overnight," April confirms.

Dec looks at me with high, thrilled eyebrows. "I get to choose first."

"Oh? And what are we doing?"

He puts his palms over Albi's ears and brings his mouth close to mine. "We're going to have endless sex without being disturbed," he whispers.

I snort as Albi bats his dad's hands away.

"How long until Friday?" Dec asks.

"It's Christmas Day!" Albi sings, jumping off my lap and wading through the piles of toys, claiming one of the endless boxes of Lego. "Daddy, can we build the police car?"

I smile my thanks to April and Blaine, who both wave off my appreciation as Dec tucks our Year of Dates behind a vase on the mantelpiece. "In the kitchen," he orders Albi gently. "You need some breakfast, and I've got to peel some spuds."

"I've had breakfast," Albi declares, holding up a selection box with three chocolate bars missing from the moulded tray.

"Jesus Christ, you'll be hyper."

"What's hyper?"

"You," Dec says over a laugh, scooping him up from the floor and throwing him over his shoulder. "No more chocolate."

As I watch Dec cart Albi out of the lounge, I remember something. But it's not wrapped. "Mind if I steal this?" I say, grabbing a piece of paper.

"Um, sure."

"Thank you." I jump up and hurry out of the lounge, racing up the stairs to find my bag. I pull out the snow globe first and admire it for a few moments. He saw me looking at it when we were out on the anniversary of Noah's death. He knew it symbolised something.

I place it on the bedside table and dip back into my bag, pulling out the desktop calendar. I could read it again right now. All his thoughts and words over the past few weeks, but I can't. I put it next to the globe and return to my bag, rummaging through and pulling out the Spitfire. Improvisation is my friend right now. Dropping to my knees, I flatten the paper and execute some impressive origami skills that I haven't utilised since—

The memory catches me off guard, but rather than fight it off, I let it take me, breathing through the pictures in my mind, of Noah and me making paper planes and launching them from the patio to see how far down the lawn they flew. His won. Always. I made sure of it. He declared himself a pilot in training that day.

I smile to myself.

What would you have become, my darling boy? A pilot, a doctor, an adventurist?

I ponder that as I wrap the Spitfire without the help of tape, lifting and inspecting my handy work. "I think Mummy did okay," I murmur as I stand and take it downstairs. "I have something for you." I disturb Albi from tipping out the pieces of his Lego onto the counter. "Well, it's actually from Mr. Percival. He gave it to me to give to you."

"What is it?" he asks, as Dec turns away from the fridge, a carton of orange juice tipped at his lips.

"Open it."

Albi tears the paper off and gasps his surprise. "Oh my gosh," he whispers, turning the plane around in his little hands to look at it from all angles. "It's an actual Spitfire from the war!" His Lego is forgotten, and he sets the plane down and gets onto his knees on the stool to inspect it closely. "This is the best Christmas ever!"

"Shall we build that Lego?" Dec asks.

"I want to play with my Spitfire."

He looks to the ceiling in silent gratitude.

"It's very special," I tell him. "And very old. You must look after it, like Mr. Percival has looked after it for many years."

"I will," he says, captivated, gently touching the wing with a fingertip. "Can I fly it?"

Huh?

"You're not fitting in that cockpit, fella." Dec says over a laugh, as he sets out some breakfast things—croissants, jam, and cereals.

"What's a cockpit?"

"Where the pilot sits in a plane to fly it."

"No, silly!" He takes the plane and hops down off the stool, holding it in the air and starting to run around the island. "Like this!"

"Oh, silly Daddy," Dec murmurs, shaking his head.

I'm held in another moment, caught off guard, as Albi races around the island, gliding the plane high and low, swooping it in circles, all the while providing sound effects. I force the vision of Noah away, trying not to imagine him in Albi's place.

"Camryn?"

I blink, coming back into the room on a small jump. "Sorry, I —" I what? I was imaging your son was my son? I was wishing it was? Not that Albi wasn't here but Noah was, just wishing he could be here too? I push the tips off my fingers together, and Dec nods. "I'm just going to get some fresh air," I say, motioning to the sliding doors past the table and chairs.

"Of course." He leans over the counter and hands me a croissant. "Please eat this."

I smile my thanks and accept, taking a small nibble in demonstration before leaving him with a semi-content mild smile, that's more than laced with concern.

"There's a hoodie on the back of the chair and my slippers are by the door."

"Slippers?" I parrot in surprise. "I never had you down as a slippers kinda guy." I never had him down as a daddy kinda guy either, and yet here I am with Dec the Daddy. And what a wonderful daddy he is too.

As I take myself away, I wonder if he's regretting this. Having to keep an eye on me in case I have a wobble. Stealing his time away from Albi to make sure I'm okay.

I set my croissant on the table and pull on his khaki hoodie, which I imagine makes his grey eyes pop beautifully, before shoving my feet into a huge pair of tan suede moccasin slippers and claiming my croissant. "Sexy," I murmur, looking back at Dec. He raises his eyebrows, amused, as Albi continues to tear around the island, swooping his Spitfire.

Shuddering when the icy air hits me, I quickly close the door and take in Dec's garden in the dark again, not that there's much to see, just various levels covered in snow. But I imagine it's beautifully landscaped beneath, and I can't wait to see it in springtime. I take myself to the small, sheltered nook to the right, where a built-in hot tub's been built, and perch on the edge of it. Silence. No breeze, no wind carrying the sound of traffic from the main road. No kids playing nearby, or the sounds of people going about their daily business on the surrounding streets or in neighbouring gardens. Total silence. Everyone's inside their warm homes waking up with smiles and excitement for the day. Kids tearing their way through wrapping paper, cheering his visit.

I fold one arm across my chest and eat the croissant, despite not being even a little bit hungry. I have no idea how I'll get through a whole Christmas dinner. But I will, just like I will get through today.

The branch of a nearby red Japanese Maple tree catches my eye, dusted with snow and hanging lower than the others, encroaching on the covered sheltered area where I'm sitting. I stand and look down at my small feet in Dec's big slippers and hum as I shuffle along in them so to keep them on my feet. My chewing slows when my eyes confirm what they thought they saw.

An icicle that's thick at the top and tapers down almost a whole foot, but it's not complete. It doesn't narrow to a sharp point. It's broken halfway down, and near the top, at the thickest point encased in ice, is a white feather. A perfect white feather.

And resting on the branch above it are two other white feathers. Except those ones aren't frozen in ice. They're free, just sitting there, having floated down from the sky. Three feathers. Two uninhibited, one . . . not.

I swallow, tilting my head, and an overwhelming urge comes over me. Not to break it and free it. It would surely be damaged, the fine feathers ripping. It needs to melt for it to come out of the ice perfectly. This urge is something else, something unexpected. Not that I don't want to see her, but I had planned to visit before lunch. She likely won't even be awake at this godforsaken hour, but I need to see her.

I shuffle back to the doors and heave them open. Dec looks up from pouring milk on Albi's cereal as I kick his slippers off. "Do you mind if I go see my mum?"

Albi immediately stops in his tracks, the plane lowering. "You have a mummy?"

"I do," I say, smiling at his astonishment, but feeling overwhelming sadness for him too.

"Daddy doesn't have a mummy," he declares. "Like me. I don't have a mummy either. I just have a daddy."

How this boy breaks my heart. "And an amazing daddy he is too."

"Yep! Daddy has a daddy, but we don't see him much, do we, Daddy?"

"No, fella, we don't." Dec comes to me. "I'll take you."

"No, no," I reply quickly. I can't pull him away from his boy today. "Please, don't insist or be grumpy about it. I can walk. I'd like to walk." Besides, it's not even six, yet. By the time I'm ready and have walked there, it'll be closer to eight, a more acceptable time to visit.

Doubt creeps onto Dec's face. He's not happy, but he relents, and I'm grateful. "Fine."

"Can your mummy come for Christmas?" Albi asks.

"I'm afraid not, Albi. She's quite old. She can't walk anymore, and she's a little . . . forgetful."

"Mr. Percival is *very* old, and he can walk. He's nearly a hundred!"

"I know, what a champ, eh?" I reach up on my tippy-toes and land a kiss on Dec's cheek before ruffling Albi's mop of hair as I pass him. "I'll be back soon to help prep dinner." I hurry up the stairs, as April comes down them.

"We have to talk or it's bad luck," she blurts, stopping halfway down as I climb the steps.

"Are you superstitious?" I ask, amused.

"Terribly. Blaine walked over three drains on Monday, and my car broke down the next day."

I laugh. "I'm just going to see my mum."

"Is Dec taking you?"

"No, I'm going to walk."

"Walk? But Dec said the care home she's in is near Paddington. Are you mad?"

"It's not that far, honestly."

"Let Blaine take you."

I place my hand on her arm. "I'd like to walk."

Understanding gets her, and she nods, lips straight, and says no more about it. "See you soon."

I take the stairs and flick on the shower, letting it warm up as I brush my teeth seeing as well as feeling how tight my skin is. *All that crying*. I shower, washing my hair too, and when I'm drying off, I walk back into Dec's bedroom and find a hairdryer on the bed. April. I appreciate her so much. Not just for the hairdryer.

I moisturise and blast my hair dry, dress quickly, and grab my phone, hurrying downstairs and pulling my coat off the stand.

"Wait," Dec says, coming down the hallway.

"What?"

He takes my coat from my hands and holds it up for me to get it on, then turns me, ties the belt, and pulls the lapels upright so they're shielding my face. He bunches them with his fists and uses them as leverage to pull me close. "I love you," he says quietly, looking me dead in the eyes. "I'd come with you happily, if you need me there."

And I know he would because he's a good man. I nod and push my mouth onto his. "Thank you. Back soon."

• • •

The streets are empty. It's as good as a phenomenon, as if I'm walking in a world where only I exist. The overnight snow has settled and remains undisturbed by tires or feet, making me feel a little guilty for spoiling the even perfection as I leave boot prints in my wake. It's truly beautiful, the rising sun casting a rainbow of colours across the white canvas. I need this. A walk, some quiet, not to dwell, but to be grateful. I'm so bloody grateful. And yet, that doesn't mean I can't be sad too. I accept that now.

When I'm just half a mile away, my phone rings in my pocket, and it takes me a stupid amount of time to get my glove off and my hand inside to pull it out. My pace slows when I see the care home number on my screen.

And my heart drops.

"Hello?"

"Camryn," Deirdre says, and just by the tone of her voice I know. I just know. "I hate to make this call, especially today."

"Has she gone?" I ask.

"Five minutes ago. I went in to wake her. She looked very peaceful."

A choked sob escapes, my hand covering my mouth. "I'm nearly there." My words are broken. Hardly audible. "I'm on my way to see her." My feet go from a walk to a jog, to a run. "Please, don't let them take her yet," I beg. "I'm ten minutes away." I hang up and run, my legs heavy as I wade through the snow to get there as fast as I can.

The tears falling as fast as I'm running.

Deirdre's waiting in the reception area when I get there. I'm out of breath, and yet I could run for another hundred miles if I needed to. She looks at me with unbearable sympathy and pulls the door open to let me past reception. "They've not taken her yet, have they?" I ask, my panic obvious as I run down the corridor to her room at the end.

"Not yet."

I burst in and find it shrouded in darkness, the blinds all closed. I jar to an abrupt stop and drop my gloves to the chair, creeping toward her bed. It looks like she's simply sleeping. I've sat here in this room countless times and looked at her like this.

I perch on the edge of the bed and reach for her hand, but falter when the cold registers in mine. Freezing. I rub them over my thighs to both warm them up *and* get some feeling back in them, before I take her hand in mine and stroke over the top. I can't take my eyes off her face because, actually, I've *never* seen her look like this since she was brought here.

Peaceful.

No longer a feather in the frost.

Free of that dreadful disease that took my mum away from me long before now. I feel a significant shift in me, a lift in the weight of worry that's lain on my shoulders. I've been grieving her loss for years, and today almost feels like the final stage. At least, for that part of my grief. I don't know how long I have left grieving Noah.

Forever.

She waited.

She waited to go until she knew I was okay. That there was someone to look after me. She waited until she wasn't leaving me alone. "Couldn't you have waited just a few more minutes, Mum?" I ask, my voice cracking. "Just a few more minutes for me to get here?"

My muscles give, and I fold over at the waist, sobbing. I bring her hand to my mouth. Smelling her. Kissing her.

"Camryn," Deirdre says on a sad sigh, resting her hand gently on my jerking shoulder.

"Can I stay with her?" I ask, snivelling. "Can I stay with her until they're here?"

"Of course."

She squeezes my shoulder before she releases me, and a few moments later, I hear the door close. I breathe in, sitting up and wiping my face. "We need some daylight, Mum," I say, setting her hand down gently and making sure she's comfortable. I go to the window and open all the blinds, basking her room in natural light. The sun has finally made it into the sky.

And it's snowing again, thick snowflakes tumbling from the sky.

It's another day that shouldn't be so beautiful.

They leave me alone with her for twenty minutes before the undertakers arrive. The whole time, I just watch her, remembering everything wonderful about her and storing it to memory. I see her hovering behind Dad on Christmas Day with her mop. I see her swat his hand when he tries to dip the pigs in blankets. I see him grab her from behind while she's baking and her giggling like she always giggled when Dad doted on her. I watch as they both kneel in the garden a few metres away from each other, Noah between them. Each of them jangles keys, trying to coax him into walking to them. Both wanting to claim his first steps as theirs. He walked to Dad. Just two steps before he dropped to his nappy-padded arse and Dad cheered and scooped him up, throwing him into the air as he giggled, and Mum yelled the injustice when she found Dad jangling coins rather than keys. "Bribery," she'd cried through her beaming smile as she joined them. I watched from the window, wondering if any kid in the world was as lucky as Noah to have such doting grandparents. Excited for the endless joy he'd bring my parents in their older years.

My heart turns in my chest, my eyes closing, my forehead falling to the bed.

More unstoppable tears. And now they're all gone.

"Camryn?" Deirdre calls softly. I look up and see her with two men in suits, both their heads bowed in respect. "I called your brother."

"I forgot about him," I murmur, wiping my sore face again.

"He's not coming."

"That's okay." I take a breath and stand. "I can't watch them carry her away." I swing on my coat. "Thank you for everything you've done since she's been here."

"It's my job."

"A job you chose. To take care of people." I go over and give her a hug, surprising her. Her arms hang limply by her sides for a second before she lifts them and returns it. "I hope you get to spend some of today with your family."

"My daughter's picking me up at three," she says.

"Merry Christmas."

"Merry Christmas, Camryn." She lets me break away, and I go to Mum and stroke her hair back, placing a kiss on her forehead. And I accept, she did wait. She waited until she knew I was okay. She waited until Dec and Albi found me. "Thank you, Mum." I swallow and tear myself away, not quite believing this is the last time I'll ever see her, taking long, deep breaths as I go.

As soon as I step out into the snow, I call Dec. He answers in one ring, and I just know he's had his phone on his hip. "Camryn?"

"My mum's gone," I say, clear and concise, feeling an odd sense of peace come over me.

"Shit, no, Camryn, I—"

"I'm okay," I say, quick to reassure him. "I'm really okay, Dec. She—" Yes, I'm okay, but I still need to swallow to keep my voice even. "She waited for me to find you and Albi," I say, losing my battle not to let my voice crack. I drop to my arse on the step, immune to the cold radiating immediately through my coat and jeans. "She didn't want to go until she knew I'd be okay."

"I'm on my way," he says, breathless. He's already running to the door. "I'm coming. Don't move, okay?"

I nod and end the call, and sit in the snow, staring at the millions of snowflakes floating calmly from the sky.

Given the weather, despite his Defender technically a farmer's car built for the rough terrain and snow, I didn't expect Dec to get here so fast. He must have broken all speed limits. He half skids half slides to a stop and jumps out, and I smile at the sight of him.

In his sweatpants, a hoodie, and his slippers.

I stand as he jogs over and walk straight into his open arms. The floodgates open again because he's here. I cry into his chest, body-racking, gut-wrenching sobs, as he holds me, rubs my back, hushes me.

Taking care of me.

I let it all come out, a good hard cry, until I'm sure his sweater is drenched. "I'm okay," I murmur, sniffing and pulling away, cheeking his hoodie. Dark patches are dotted here and there, smears of tears and snot. I cringe and try to wipe it away.

"Shut up," he breathes, tipping my head up with a fingertip under my chin.

"I'm okay," I say again, more weight gone, probably from the evacuation of tears. "She was peaceful. They tried to wake her, but she was gone."

"What do you need me to do?"

"Just keep doing you," I say, reaching for his face. "Just keep being wonderfully you."

He nods and reclaims me, keeping me wrapped completely in his arms. "You're cold," I whisper, forcing him back.

"I'm never cold when you're close." He curls an arm around my shoulders, walking me to the car and getting me inside. He buckles me in and drops a chaste kiss on my lips before he closes the door. The moment he's in the driver's seat, he whacks the heat up.

"Can we do something quickly before we go home?" I ask.

"Anything you want."

I bypass my front door and knock on Mr. Percival's, treading the carpet impatiently as Dec joins me. I hear his walking frame coming down the hallway, and the moment he gets the door open, I smile at him. "Look at you," I say, taking in his fine tweed suit, that's probably nearly as old as he is. "Happy Christmas, Mr. Percival."

"What a surprise," he says, hobbling back. "Come in, come in, I have treats in case I have visitors."

In case he has visitors? *Oh, Mr. Percival.* I reach back for Dec's hand and pull him inside. "What are you doing today, Mr. Percival?"

"Well, I'll be eating and drinking for England, as folk tend to do on Christmas Day, I'll watch the King's speech at three, and I'll be taking all the leftovers to the Royal British Legion after I've had a nap."

"There's been a change to your schedule," I say, passing him and going into the kitchen, where there's not a square inch of work surface not taken up with some kind of dish, pan, plate, or bowl.

Or Gnome.

"There has?"

"Yes, you're spending Christmas with us."

"But what about all the food I've prepared? I can't let it go to waste."

"We'll take it," Dec declares. I glance at him, surprised. "I've not even peeled a carrot yet."

Mr. Percival laughs. "You young folk. So underprepared."

"So, are you coming?"

"Camryn, dear, I like to have myself a Brandy or ten. I wouldn't expect any of you not to enjoy an alcoholic beverage so you can bring this old fool home."

"We can get you a taxi."

"Are you mad? It's triple fare on Christmas Day!"

"You can stay," Dec pipes up.

"Stay? At your house?"

"Sure, why not?" He shrugs. "It's Christmas, and Albi's quite fond of you. But not your gnomes. They stay here. And your cat."

I laugh, and Mr. Percival chuckles too. "He loved the Spitfire," I say, smiling wide. "And he'd love to see you too."

His chest puffs out. "Ah, well, if it's the little fella we're aiming to please, then I will graciously accept your offer."

"Good." Dec nods sharply and casts his eye around the kitchen. "Suppose I ought to load the car."

Mr. Percival can't believe his eyes when we pull up outside Dec's house. "Oh, you're one of those posh sorts, aren't you? I should have known."

"What's that supposed to mean?" Dec asks over a laugh as he helps him out of the car.

"Well, the car, the heroics, the fancy clothes."

"I still don't know what it's supposed to mean." Dec looks at me in exasperation, and I grin, looping my arms through Mr. Percival's.

"There's quite a few steps."

"I'll manage."

He does, but it takes a full ten minutes to climb them until we're at the front door. April swings it open. "Oh, well, who is this then?"

"I might ask the same," Mr. Percival says.

"I'm April, Dec's sister. And this is my husband, Blaine."

"Pleasure to meet you, sir."

"Likewise." Mr. Percival hobbles through the door. "Now, this is all very lovely, but we all know I'm not here for you lot." He's a liar. He's totally here for me too. "Where's the alcohol and the kid?"

"Mr. Percival!" Albi dashes toward him, nearly taking the old guy off his feet when he comes in from the side and hugs his thigh. "I've been flying the Spitfire!"

"Oh, now, there's a story for me to tell you," he says, shuffling onward with Albi clinging to the side of his walking frame. "Crash-landed in enemy territory, I did."

"Oh my gosh."

"That's what I said when I come round. Maybe a little more

colourful." They disappear into the lounge together. "But that's not for your ears, kid."

April and Blaine both cock their heads in question at us. "Don't ask," Dec says, putting an arm around me. "But, bonus, we don't need to cook. Blaine, give me a hand getting dinner out the car. And lunch. And supper. And sandwiches for the next month."

I laugh as they head out to unload, and April catches me off guard and hauls me into her body, cuddling me hard. "I'm sorry about your mum."

I welcome her hug, wrapping my arms around her too. "It's okay. She's at peace." I pull out and smile. "I think she waited for me to find Dec."

Her lips press together. It's such a romantic notion, I know that. Idealistic in the most unideal circumstances. And I'm clinging to it with everything I have.

"Do you know where Dec keeps the alcohol?" I ask.

"Yes!" She goes to a tall cabinet and pulls the doors open, revealing a well-equipped bar. "What's his tipple?"

"Brandy."

She hums and scans the bottles, finding it and pouring. "To the top?"

"Why not." I take the glass and deliver it to Mr. Percival. Not that he or Albi notice me.

Mr. Percival looks like he's in his element, and Albi's thoroughly enchanted.

It's the most beautiful sight. A man nearly a century old. And a little boy who's looking at him like he's a hero.

Because he is.

I only need to remove myself from the festivities a couple of times. Once before dinner, which was insanely good. I don't know where Mr. Percival learned to cook, but he does it well. And generously.

And now.

Mr. Percival has Albi on his frail knee, giving him a detailed guided tour of a Spitfire Dec's got up on Google, and all I can see is Noah on my father's lap as Dad taught him how to play dominoes. And Mum sat at the other end of the table sewing a costume for world book day. I smile sadly at Mr. Percival and Albi, and slip my feet into Dec's slippers, stepping outside with my wine. It's stopped snowing, but it'll start again soon if the forecasters are right.

My eyes naturally fall to the red Japanese Maple tree as I step through the snow, but the icicle isn't there anymore. Odd. And neither are the other feathers that were sitting on the branch above. Not so odd, as they could have blown away. I search the snow for any holes where the icicle could have fallen but find nothing. It couldn't have melted; it's still below zero.

I hear the door slide open behind me and turn to find Dec stepping out. I smile when I take in his new slippers. A new pair every Christmas from April and Blaine since Albi arrived. "What are you looking for?" he asks.

"Nothing." I point to my feet. "Does this mean I can keep these ones?"

"Oh yes. I honestly don't know how we're keeping our hands to ourselves while we're both parading around each other in these things. They're not passion killers at all."

I laugh and go to him as he opens his arms, letting me walk straight into them. I nuzzle into his shoulder, holding him with one arm, my wine in the other, and I close my eyes, settling into his body.

"Camryn?" he says softly.

I keep still and quiet.

"You've never asked me what my name is."

My eyes ping open, and I stare forward for a beat before pulling away. His face. I bank it, the look shy and a little awkward, and everything that isn't Dec.

Dec.

"Declan?"

He shakes his head, and I think for a moment.

"That's all I have."

"I'll give you a clue."

"Okay," I say, drawing the word out, my mind going a mile a minute.

"My sister's name is April because she was born in April."

I'm staring again. *What? No, it can't be.* "Your name is December?"

His head tilts, his shoulders jumping up on a shrug. "Mum loved Christmas."

"Oh my God," I breathe.

"I didn't tell you because I know how much you hate December."

"You've just given me another reason not to hate it as much." I pull him in and hug the hell out of him. "But I'm just going to call you Dec."

He laughs. "That's fine by me."

"I love you," I whisper, feeling him hold me slightly tighter.

"It's the slippers, I know."

I smile and open my eyes, blinking when I see something floating down from the sky. *Oh my.*

Three perfect white feathers.

My breath hitches as they all skim my nose softly one by one, and a warmth radiates through me, making my body lift. Dec pulls me in closer in response. "Okay?" he asks, pushing his lips onto my neck. Maybe it's an ideology, maybe I'm going stir-bloody-crazy, but those three feathers?

Noah, Dad, and Mum.

"I'm really okay." She's with them now. Both are looking after my boy. Mum doesn't need to hang on to make sure I'm okay.

Because I will be. *I'm going to be okay.*

December started out so bleak and terrifyingly sad, just like every other month for the last thirty-six. And yet somehow, my heart doesn't hurt so much. It still feels like there are many broken shards within, but the love filling it again is cushioning the stabs of pain those splinters cause me daily. My world was shrouded in screaming silence. I was drowning in my grief. Now? Now, I feel colour creeping back into my life. I feel love like I never thought I'd feel it again. And I feel like it's so okay for me to accept that colour and love, and at the same time still miss him and ache for him with every fibre of my heart and being.

I can still live.

Still love.

Still wish I could have him back. Have them *all* back.

I look up at the white sky and smile through my tears.

It's been you since December 1st, Camryn.

But it's not just Dec who's saved me.

Albi has too.

Dear Santa,

Thank you for bringing us Camryn.
I'll be good forever and ever and ever
and ever and ever and ever.

Lots of love,
Albi Ellis.
Age four ½
P. S My Daddy helped me write this.
Next year, I will do it all by myself.

Epilogue

One Year Later

Christmas Eve

My heel dangling from my foot, I swing it gently, watching as Thomas signs on the dotted line. I don't think so much relieved air has ever left me at the conclusion of a deal. "Done," he says, dropping the pen and blowing his cheeks out. "And I guess I'm retired."

I push my foot into my shoe and stand, going to him, holding my hand out. "It's been a pleasure."

He laughs loudly. "The past year, you mean?"

"Of course."

He chuckles and hauls me in for a hug, and I roll my eyes but accept. "You always said you could make it happen in one year with compliance."

"Yeah, well, I have a new boss to please." I pull away and smile at him fondly. "Good luck, Thomas."

The door bursts open, and Thomas's granddaughter appears. "Grandpa, we'll miss the flight! Mum's waiting in the car."

"I'm coming, Macey," he breathes.

"Thank you, Camryn." Kissing my cheek, he collects his jacket off the chair. "For everything."

I hold up a hand in goodbye and watch as he collects Marcy and leads her out of the building. He's off to Colorado to spend Christmas with his daughter, Gail, and Marcy. I haven't asked about Anthony, as I couldn't care less, and Thomas hasn't brought him up, out of respect, I guess. Barbara, though? She's took Thomas for half of everything and cleared off to France. He doesn't seem too bothered.

I pick up my laptop and empty coffee cup and head back to my office, keen to get out of here and get home to the boys. The building's empty, as everyone's already knocked off for Christmas.

I chuckle when I look at the volume of Christmas decorations. If it's possible, Crystal went even more overboard this year. And I didn't scowl. Well, maybe once . . .

I grab my bag and coat and flick the light off, stopping when I make it to the door and looking back at my desk. I smile, close the door, and leave. I can't say I won't ever be back, because Dec owns the company now.

You always said you could make it happen in one year with compliance.

I achieved what I set out to do. Amazing what a difference compliance makes. I pause a beat as I step on the elevator. Wait. Dec doesn't own the company. The shareholders own the company.

My smile widens, and I pull out my phone and text him.

Signed, sealed, delivered.

The little dots start flickering instantly, the elevator doors open, and I start to step off but gasp when I find Dec immediately outside. "What took you so long?" he asks.

I smile and drop my bag and coat, throwing my arms around his shoulders. "I missed you," I breathe, finding his mouth and kissing him hard.

He hums and lifts me from the floor a few inches, indulging my demand until we hear the doors closing and opening again, over and over. I break away and look over my shoulder, seeing my bag and coat blocking them.

"Oops."

Dec lowers me and collects my coat, helping me into it, before he claims my bag and my hand.

"Where's Albi?"

"In the car with Mr. P."

"Oh, you picked him up already?"

"I think we need to consider some kind of assisted living."

I wince. I can't deny that there have been some heart-stopping frights this year with Mr. Percival. He took a tumble down the steps on the High Street a few months ago, and Dec stopped by only last week and found the bathroom flooded, the bath tap running, Mr. Percival nowhere in sight. "What's happened now?"

"He left a tea towel on the stove." He looks at me with a hitched brow. "The stove was on."

"Oh God. Why was the stove on?"

"He forgot to turn it off after he finished making his seventieth batch of mince pies." God love Mr. P, the man is one hundred, soon-to-be one hundred and one, and still bakes for the masses at Christmas. He was thrilled when he received his one-hundredth birthday greetings from King Charles last January, we all were. He framed the card, which didn't surprise any of us. But these accidents are . . . worrying.

"He refuses to entertain assisted living," I remind Dec.

"Then he comes and lives with us, simple."

"He won't like it," I warn, quite certain I don't want to be the one to have that conversation with him. "I guarantee you'll meet resistance." He's a proud man.

"So will he." Dec smiles across to me. "How do you feel?"

He asks me this often. *Settled*. I feel settled. I'm looking forward to tomorrow, though I know it won't come without its moments, but I'm coping much better when they do catch me. And on the nineteenth—when it was four years since Noah died—it was still incredibly hard. But Dec took the day off, graciously gave me the day off too, and we did what we did the year before. Wandered. Drank silky hot chocolate. He bought me a dress, this one a beautiful emerald-green velvet shift dress, and this time we made it out for our dinner date while April and Blaine watched Albi. It was perfect. And while it had been four years to the day since I lost my boy, I recognised the fact that it had also been one year to the day that I met Albi. *My little lifesaver*. The joy he brings *and* the grief, which will never leave me, still conflict, but I'm at ease feeling both. I understand it.

But Dec wasn't talking about any of that when he asked me how I'm feeling. "I feel like I achieved something today," I admit. "After three long years trying to achieve it." I nudge him. "You weren't so bad to work with." To be fair, I hardly worked with him, because he simply handed me the ropes and let me crack on. And I did.

Dec laughs as we break out into a bleak, grey London. Quite a departure from last year. "Well," he says. "I might have another project for you to spend the next year on."

I stop, pulling him to a stop too. "What did you buy now?" I ask. He looks sheepish. "Tell me you haven't turned your father over again."

"God, no. I'm over that. In fact, he's asked us over for dinner after Christmas."

I recoil. "And how do you feel about that?"

"Indifferent." He shrugs, and I roll my eyes. Indifferent, my arse.

"We're going, you know that?"

Now, *he* rolls his eyes. "Yes, I know that. I also accepted the invitation to Paisley's wedding."

"Oh. My. God," I say, dramatic. *Finally*. It's been sitting in a drawer for weeks. I didn't push it. I could see him silently pondering the idea of us going.

"Shut up."

I laugh as he pulls me on, and I hear the familiar sound of little knuckles wrapping on a window. I drop Dec's hand and pull the door open.

"Are you finished work now?" Albi asks, leaning forward to meet my lips as I pucker up.

"I'm finished."

"Yay!"

"Hi, Mr. Percival," I say, hearing his chirpy reply as I round the car and get in the back with Albi. "What's the plan?"

"Shhh," Albi says, making me frown.

"Why am I shushing?"

"Mr. Percival has a headache."

He does? I lean between the seats, checking him over in the front seat as Dec pulls off. "Are you okay?"

"Yes, yes, dear, perfectly fine." Then he gasps and reaches for his ear, holding it. "Bleeding headache, that's all."

I look at Dec. "We should take him to his doctor." I sit back and fish through my bag for my phone, worried. "How long has it hurt, Mr. Percival?"

"What, dear?"

"Your head," I say, going to my contacts to find his surgery's number. "How long has it hurt?"

"Oh, just for a little while, dear."

"You need to lie down, don't you, Mr. P?" Dec says.

"Yes, yes, a lie down would do the trick."

"No, I think you should see your doctor." I lean forward again. "Maybe the smoke from the tea towel has gone to his head."

"For the love of God," he mutters. "Everyone, stop fussing!"

I rest back and raise my brows, looking at Dec in the rearview mirror, catching that his brows are raised too. *Yeah, good luck telling him that he's getting assistance or moving into our place.* Dec must read me, because when he pulls up at a red light, he turns to Mr. P. "I've been thinking," he says, clearing his throat.

"And watcha been thinking?"

"You're coming to live with us, and I don't want any arguments about it, okay? You're nearly one hundred and one, and—"

"Okay," Mr. Percival says, simple as that. Dec recoils. So do I.

"Oh my gosh," Albi sings. "Mr. Percival, you can sleep in my teepee! We can have milk and cookies together before bedtime, and you can help me build my Lego. Daddy and Camryn decorated my bedroom in Spitfires too! I'll show you. And I have a bunk bed now. I sleep on top. You can sleep on the bottom one."

"Jeez, kid, put a sock in it, will you? I'm supposed to have a headache."

Dec snorts, and I laugh, frowning. "So, again, what's the plan?" I ask. "I need to pop to the store and I have some deliveries to collect."

"I need sticky tape!" Albi declares.

"I need some Scotch," Dec adds.

"I need a nap," Mr. Percival says.

"Okay, let's take Mr. Percival home, I can quickly change, and then we can go to the store."

"Shhh," Albi hisses, his finger at his mouth.

"Sorry," I whisper.

Then he grins. Albi's grins are like sunshine—pure, bright and warming. I hold my hand out to him, and he takes it, squeezing hard. "Love you, fella," I say, my heart swelling.

"Love you back, Camryn," he says, so casually. Like he doesn't understand the weight of those words. And he might not, but I do know that he does, in fact, love me.

"What about me?" Dec asks from up front, casting his eyes to the rear-view mirror to me.

"I love you too," I say, smiling.

"But she loves me more," Albi replies, again casual, looking out of the window while still clinging onto my hand.

He *truly* doesn't understand the weight of those words.

"And that will always be okay," Dec, murmurs, smiling at the road.

Once we're home, Dec walks Mr. Percival up the steps as Albi and I run off in front. "Won't be long," I call, letting us in and throwing my keys on the console table and kicking my shoes off. "Do you need the bathroom before we go back out?" I ask Albi, noticing the telltale sign of him fidgeting as he goes into his playroom and puts a few more pieces on his latest Lego creation. "Albi," I say.

"Yeah?"

"Do you need the bathroom?"

"No."

I huff and go to him, dipping and pulling him to his feet. "Go pee," I order gently. *Always too busy to pee.*

"Okay, okay," he moans, running to the downstairs loo. And always in a mad rush.

On that thought, I dash upstairs and quickly get changed, rushing back down. I grab my boots, hearing Dec in the lounge with Mr. Percival.

April breezes through the door, Blaine in tow, carrying dozens of bags, and freezes when she spots me.

"You're early," I say, checking my phone as I pull a boot on. It's only three o'clock. They're supposed to be here at six.

"Oh, we both got done in the office sooner than we thought so decided we'd make our way over."

"We've got to pop to the shops."

"No problem." Blaine pushes past me, heading to the kitchen. "We'll unpack and get food on for tonight."

"Don't bother with mince pies," Dec says, appearing from the lounge.

"Is he okay?" I ask.

"Is who okay?" April looks between us.

"Mr. Percival," Dec says, going to the table and picking up a letter, starting to open it. "He has a headache."

April grins at me. "Done and dusted?"

"Yes," I breathe, dropping my head back. "Finally. The team moves in January third to start work on floating the company."

"Congratulations!" She hauls me in for one of her much-appreciated, warm hugs, and then joins Blaine in the kitchen. I seriously love having a big sister too. Something I hadn't realised was missing from my life until April filled that space with her unconditional love. It's more than I get from Graham, but at least we're relatively civil now, and it's wonderful to have Mindy and my niece and nephew back in my life. Dominic's baby was born in January. I didn't flinch when Mindy told me. I just felt . . . indifferent, I suppose. And indifference feels like a win.

"W here's my gorgeous nephew?" she yells.

"In the playroom!" Albi shouts back.

"Maureen!" Blaine yells. "Off the worktop!"

I chuckle to myself. Christmas chaos. *Perfect*.

I look at Dec, seeing his forehead crinkled with concentration as he reads the letter in his hand. "What's up?" I ask.

"It's Chelsea."

I stand taller, naturally. She did what Dec expected and told me he'd kissed her. That he still loved her. In fact, she came to my office especially to do so. And I had security remove her. I can't lie, I was shaking like a leaf, but I held my own. We haven't seen her since, but we've heard from her. She wanted half of Dec's assets . . . but not Albi. It's sickening. She was told to jog on by Dec's lawyers, to *try* and stake a claim. But Dec being Dec offered her some money anyway—money for a signature to never come near Albi again. She couldn't sign the paperwork fast enough. I don't know how much money was involved. I didn't ask, and Dec didn't tell.

"Everything okay?"

"I'm divorced," he says, looking up at me. "Officially." He shows me the paper, not that I can see it, because he's shaking.

"You knew it was coming," I say gently.

"I know." He folds the paper slowly and tucks it in the drawer of the cabinet. "I just . . . I don't know. I guess there was always that fear she'd recant on the agreement."

I go to him, taking his hands. "So we're both single, huh?"

He smirks and seizes me, curling his arm around my neck so I'm virtually in a headlock and pulling me closer. "Huh," he murmurs, rolling his mouth onto mine. And it's lush. Relieving.

She's gone. I'm divorced. Dec's divorced.

"We've got to get to the shops before they close," I murmur into his mouth, sliding my hands up his back.

"Hmmm." He agrees but doesn't release me.

And I don't fight him off either.

We're both happy where we are, our tongues swirling languidly, holding each other.

Until we're interrupted.

"Ewwww, gross!" Albi moans, and I laugh.

"Okay, we're done." I release Dec and fight back my fluster, narrowing my eyes when he raises his brows. "Are we ready?"

"Ready!" Albi sings.

"Are you going to say goodbye to Mr. Percival?" Dec asks, grabbing his keys off the side.

"He's not napping yet?"

"No."

"I'll see him when we get back," I say, checking my phone. We're pushing it for time already.

"Just go say bye to him," Dec says, encouraging me toward the lounge. "You know how he is."

How he is? "How is he?" I ask, letting Dec push me on.

"Just say goodbye." He practically shoves me past the doors. "We'll wait in the car." He grabs Albi, and they disappear, and I shake my head in exasperation, finding my email confirmation for my collection as I go to the couch where Mr. Percival's sitting, armed with the remote control.

"Bloody marvellous thing this is, isn't it?"

"What?" I ask, watching as he flicks through the channels.

"Look! Every episode of *Dad's Army*. Bleeding heck, I can watch them all together."

I laugh and dip to kiss his cheek. "Take your nap, we're popping to the shops. Need anything?"

"Got my brandy, dear," he says, tapping the breast pocket of his tweed jacket where his hip flask is tucked in the inside pocket. "Oh dear, you've got your shoes on."

I look down at my boots. Dec's fault. I turn to hurry out. "See you—" I freeze, eyes locked on the wall above the fireplace, where the collage of photos of Albi and Dec hang. "Oh my God," I whisper, trying to take it all in. Not the photos of them, as I see them every day. *Smile* at them every day.

But today there are more. Beautifully framed portraits, all black and white.

Of Noah. Of me and Noah. Of me and my mum. Me and my dad. Noah and my mum and dad. And me with Dec and Albi.

I let out a choked sob, my eyes welling to the point I have to quickly brush them clear so I can see. I approach slowly, rapt. I can hardly breathe through my utter awe. I see them every day. In my mind, in the pictures I have on my bedside cabinet.

But this?

"Do you like it?"

I whirl around, sniffing back my emotion, but I can't stop the flood of tears. "I love it," I choke, pointing back, as if Dec doesn't know it's there. "Look."

"I see, baby," he says, coming to me. "And did you see this?" He puts an arm around me and turns me back to the fireplace.

"Oh God," I whisper. I have a stocking. And so does Noah.

"I found it in the garage," Dec says. "Albi really wanted to put it there."

I can't talk. My throat's too tight. The tears are streaming.

Dec takes me in his arms, hugging the shit out of me. "He's a part of you, Camryn, so he's a part of me and Albi too."

I nod, sniffing. "Thank you."

"Shut up." He pulls me out and wipes my face. "Albi put a gift in Noah's stocking. Will you humour him?"

I laugh a little through my sniff and go to the stocking, smiling at his name as I peek inside. I gasp. "He gave Noah his Spitfire?" I face Dec, shocked deeply. And then I notice something. Mr. Percival's on the couch still, with a front-row seat. He's paused *Dad's Army* and is smiling fondly at us.

"Need a drink?" he asks.

"Not yet," I say, laughing.

"You will do, dear." He winks. I frown. And then Dec rolls his eyes. "I'm meant to give you this." Mr. Percival reaches behind him on the couch and pulls something out. "Here."

It's my desk calendar. The one Dec bought for my home office. Every day, he leaves some words for me, a memory of our lives. Sometimes they're deep and emotional, a declaration of undying love and appreciation. And sometimes they're less emotional, more carnal, like yesterday. When I flipped the day and saw what he'd written, I nearly choked on my coffee.

DECEMBER 23RD

MY COCK CAN'T GET ENOUGH OF YOU. WE'RE DOING THAT AGAIN TONIGHT.

I smile as I take the calendar, but it drops when I see it's still on yesterday. Oh my days, did Mr. Percival see this? I shoot my eyes to Dec.

Mr. Percival chuckles. "Don't look at him, dear."

Oh my God, he's seen it. "Well, I can't look at you."

He laughs harder, and Dec grins. "In my defence, I did warn him not to look."

"That's like telling Albi not to eat the Jelly Babies in the bowls scattered around the house, for Christ's sake," Mr. Percival says over a laugh. "Turn to today."

Mortified, I flip the page to today. And I'm frozen again. It's Albi's handwriting, a beautiful mess of words.

December 24th

We love you, Camryn! More than Spitfires and Lego and Jelly Babies and busting balls!
Will you marry us? Please, please, please say yes!
Thank you. Lots and lots of love, Daddy & Albi xxx

The tears start rolling again, and I'm sure my mascara is streaking my cheeks. And when I look up and see Albi in the doorway, they come harder. He's on his knee, a ring box open being held out to me.

Oh my heart.

"Wait for me, fella," Dec says, hurrying over and joining him, dropping to one knee next to his boy. *Our* boy. "Well?" Dec asks.

"Will you?" Albi chirps. "Please, please, please?"

I have no idea what I did to deserve this beautiful man or his gorgeous little boy. Blessings. Both of them.

I walk across the room and drop to my knees too, pulling them both close to me.

And that's all the answer they need.

I'm never letting them go.

THE END

Also by Jodi Ellen Malpas

The This Man Series

This Man

Beneath This Man

This Man Confessed

All I Am – Drew's Story (A This Man Novella)

With This Man

The One Night Series

One Night - Promised

One Night - Denied

One Night - Unveiled

Standalone Novels

The Protector

The Forbidden

Gentleman Sinner

Perfect Chaos

Leave Me Breathless

For You

Every Silent Lie

The Smoke & Mirrors Duology

The Controversial Princess

His True Queen

The Hunt Legacy Duology

Artful Lies

Wicked Truths

The Unlawful Men Series

The Brit

The Enigma

The Resurrection

The Rising

The American

The Belmore Square Series

One Night with the Duke

A Gentleman Never Tells

This Woman Series

(The This Man Series from Jesse's POV)

This Woman

With This Woman

This Woman Forever

Arlington Hall Series

The Invitation

The Surrender

About Jodi

Jodi Ellen Malpas was born and raised in England, where she lives with her husband, boys and Theo the Doberman. She is a self-professed daydreamer, and has a terrible weak spot for alpha males. Writing powerful love stories with addictive characters has become her passion—a passion she now shares with her devoted readers. She's a proud #1 *New York Times* Bestselling Author, a *Sunday Times* Bestseller, and her work is published in over twenty-five languages across the world. You can learn more about Jodi & her words at: JEM.Website

www.ingramcontent.com/pod-product-compliance
Lightning Source LLC
Chambersburg PA
CBHW011122190726
48289CB00012B/2868

* 9 7 8 1 9 5 7 5 9 7 6 1 4 *